DEADLINE

AFTERLIFE ONLINE
BOOK FOUR

Domino Finn

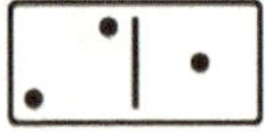

Published by Blood & Treasure, Los Angeles
First Edition

Cover Typography by James T. Egan of Bookfly Design LLC.

Print ISBN: 978-1-946-00884-8

DominoFinn.com

Also by Domino Finn

AFTERLIFE ONLINE
Reboot
Black Hat
Trojan
Deadline

BLACK MAGIC OUTLAW
Dead Man
Shadow Play
Heart Strings
Powder Trade
Fire Water
Death March
Blood Craft
Open Season

SUMMONER FOR HIRE
Tooth and Nail
Hell and High Water

Shade City

SYCAMORE MOON
The Seventh Sons
The Blood of Brothers
The Green Children

HAVEN M
MAELSTORM
STRO
BLIND MANS PEAK
CLOVEN PATH
GODS BOG
LAKE OF DREAMS
BROKEN FALLS
BLACK WOOD
BLACK KEEP
OAKENGARD
SUNSCRAPERS

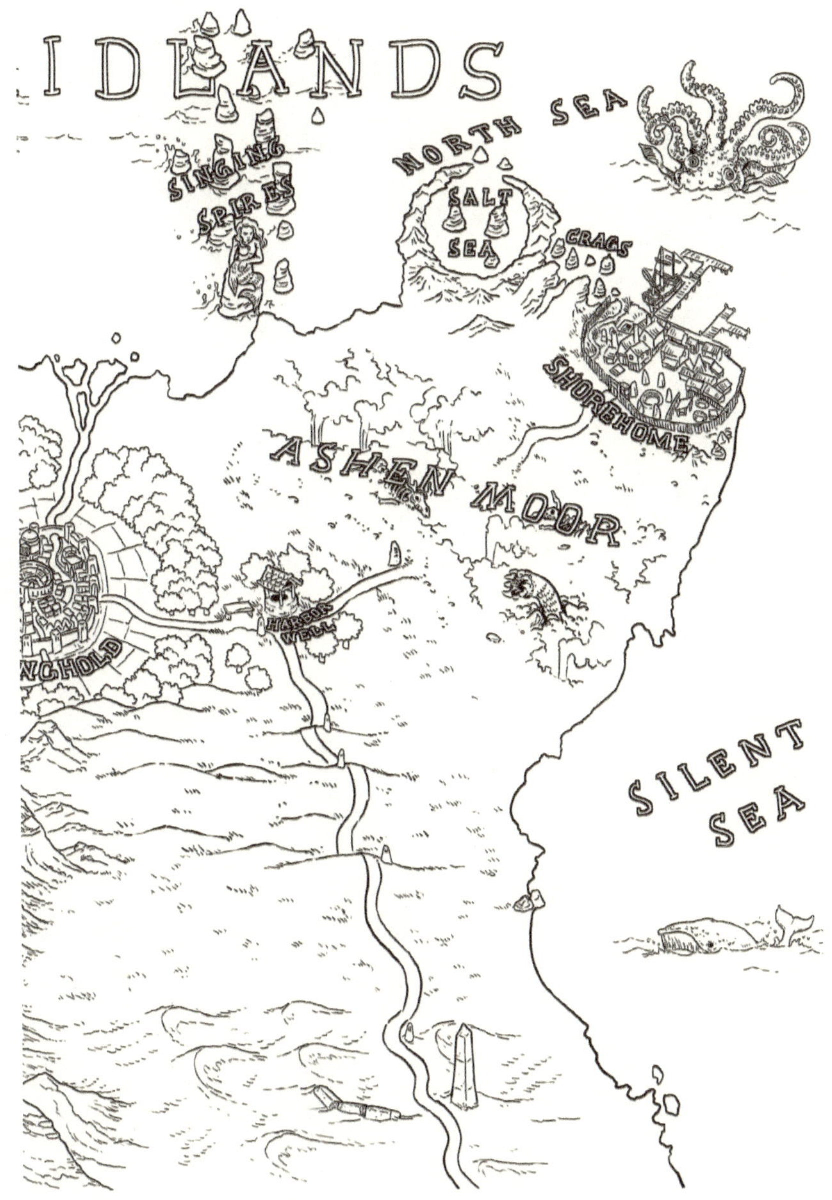
IDLANDS
NORTH SEA
SINGING SPIRES
SALT SEA
CRAGS
SHOREHOME
ASHEN MOOR
HARBOS WELL
NGHOLD
SILENT SEA

DEADLINE

AFTERLIFE ONLINE: BOOK FOUR

1540 Flight Simulator

Alabaster feathers shivered against the blustering morning fog. Aside from a few rocky peaks, the dove was the only break in the murky sky. The contrail formed in its wake wasn't a slow, wandering tear, but a clean slice—the most efficient path over the ragged mountain range. Some distance below, obscured from sight, a waterfall raged.

The wild river might as well have been a guide. As it sloped toward ground level, so did the bird, keeping pace with the tumbling current. The descent escaped the cloud cover and bypassed forgotten crags, giving way to a vast valley of wild grass. A beacon of light dominated the horizon. The water roared. But the shine and the bustle paled before the sight of a large army.

The errant folk—mostly outcast goblins, but scraps of ogres, imps, and trolls—scowled at the skyborne intruder. The rabid leader of the horde was General Azzyrk, snaking through the ranks atop a terrifying Jurassic lizard. His dirty fist rose to the sky and he shouted a throaty command.

The dove spread its wings and caught the current, lasering across the skyscape. A harbinger of peace nevertheless equipped with claws, this dove was more than symbol or beast. Tied to its leg was a scroll, mottled paper a darker shade of ivory than its feathered carrier. This was the bird's strategic significance.

The messenger zipped toward the distant tower of light, speeding high above the ravenous army. Taut wings strained against the jet streams, power and grace wrapped in a delicate package. The dove's sharp eyes marked the route. It banked into a majestic descent, a vision of natural wonder right up until a jagged arrow punched through its chest. Blood exploded on pristine feathers, and the messenger plummeted toward the ground like a missile.

<<<T-Minus 3 Days Till Launch>>>

"They shot down my bird."

My grip tightened, crushing the olive into pulp. I tossed it over the parapet's ancient stone. The view atop Dragonperch was the highest in the city, towering above Stronghold's ninety-foot walls. I could survey it all up here: the tended land, the remnants of the goblin horde, and the downfall of my incoming messenger dove. A sharp call whistled through my lips, but the mountain bongo was already on the roof at my side. Before I could grab Bandit's horn and mount up, a purple pixie rushed up the steps.

"Slow your roll, Talon."

I gritted my teeth. "They shot down my bird."

"So?" returned Izzy. A host of other players swarmed up behind her and suddenly this was a rooftop party.

My blood was boiling but my anger wasn't directed at her. I enjoyed our sparring. She was as feisty in the war room as she was in the bedroom, and I welcomed every challenging bout. But the days spent staying my hand, waiting out the goblin army, hearing nothing from friend or foe alike... It was wearing down my patience.

I stared at the faction menu.

Black Hats
Faction Level: 2 *Members*: 73 / 100
War Catechists Brothers in Black **Armistice** Pagans

I forced out a breath. "The plan was to enlist outside support. The plan was for Brugo and the wildkins—"

"No plan survives first contact," instructed Izzy. Caduceus and Kyle nodded behind her. Stigg and Trafford crowded the impromptu conversation as well, though they were hesitant to show support either way.

"First contact?" I made sure to layer an appropriate amount

of incredulity into my voice. "We're practically in the middle of all-out war."

"Bro," cut in Kyle, taking a swig of beer.

I stopped arguing and settled my gaze on him with crossed arms. I was so willing to hear him out it startled him. He pulled the bottle away and had trouble swallowing the suds.

"Broooo..." he drawled, struggling to come up with a good reason I shouldn't go out there. Apparently his objection had preceded his reasoning.

I narrowed my eyes. "I need to recover that message."

A harrumph came from Izzy. "And when the goblins try to stop you? Are you prepared to throw away the pagan armistice for a letter?"

Caduceus nodded emphatically. "You can't solve all your problems by fighting."

"A medic *would* say that." I targeted a finger at the physicker and her Viking friend. "Is that how you two brought Cleric Vagram to justice?" I opened the quest menu and spun my screen around for the audience.

Bring Vagram to Justice

Quest Type: Bounty (public)

Reward: Crusader Alliance

Cleric Vagram leads the rogue catechist faction in guerrilla warfare. Find and return him to Oakengard.

"Weird," I continued. "This quest doesn't appear complete.

Oh, maybe that's because *they slaughtered you*."

Stigg lowered his head. He took fierce pride in his unabashed bravery. He also moped over his losses. Caduceus? She was too proud to back down from a disagreement.

"We need to think about what we're doing," she pressed. "We need to think about every move from here on out." Now it was Izzy's turn to nod.

I opened my mouth to respond but Errol's voice echoed up the stairway. "Don't even think about it, brother."

We all turned and waited as the leather-clad pirate took his time ambling up the steps. He emerged bedraggled, freshly awake no doubt, holding a dagger with two plump olives speared on the end. He plucked one with his teeth.

"Those are supposed to feed the doves," I snapped.

"Aye, but I don't see 'em linin' up fer snacks." He ignored my grumbling, chewed loudly, and grabbed the beer from Kyle's hand. "Thank you kindly."

"Hey!" The brewmaster raised a hand to snatch it back but aborted as soon as the pirate's chapped lips wrapped around the bottle. "That one was getting warm anyway." He produced a frosty new bottle and uncapped it.

Errol pointed the knife at Caduceus. "An' don't try changin' this one's mind, neither. She's a tough lass an' stays her ground. Unless...?" He ran his eyes over her and offered her an olive.

"No means no," she said.

"See what I mean!" He stomped to the parapet and grumpily settled onto a perch.

"You've waited this long," reasoned Izzy. "You yourself stressed the importance of getting as many allies as possible.

The wildkins are standoffish. Brugo's MIA. The pagans are the only faction we have any positive relations with, and it's a tenuous armistice. If you go out there with Bandit, you might as well sound the horns, shout a battle cry, and kiss any future relations goodbye."

I huffed. "Our alliance with the wild king is waiting for us in that field of goblins." I grabbed Bandit's horn and prepared to activate my legendary ability. "I'm sorry, but I haven't heard a single good reason to keep waiting."

"Wait!" shouted Caduceus.

My eyes fluttered in annoyance. "That's not a reason, it's—" The sum of her argument was an outstretched finger. I followed her signal to the ragged field of besiegers and saw it. Boots on the ground.

Green robes flashed unseen through the ranks of distracted goblins. Dune, the last surviving member of the cleric hunt. He darted between wagons and barrels of supplies as he cut through the tended land on his return to Stronghold.

I released Bandit's horn. "Okay. That's a good reason."

"I can't believe it," said Stigg with a scoff. "That crazy bastard is cutting right through the enemy camp!"

"Shit," said Kyle.

"He's retrieving the dove," said Caduceus pointedly.

"Double shit," added the brewmaster.

We all watched as the green ranger did indeed seem to be heading to the downed bird.

Izzy studied the tended land. "You think he's gonna make it? The goblin front lines are pretty dense, but Dune's a slick one."

"Asshole has no chance," said Kyle.

"Sorry if I don't take the word of a grown man who can't go three sentences without cursing."

"I can fucking too!"

She glared at him.

"Oh, I get it," he moped. "This is about that stupid clean-and-sober challenge of yours. You don't think I can do it."

Izzy smirked. "Not curse or drink for three days? You're more likely to get laid, and believe me, that isn't happening."

"Not with you bagging on me all the time."

"Tell you what," conceded the pixie. "You successfully complete the challenge and I'll be your personal wingwoman until you get some."

"Deal!" he said excitedly. He upturned his fresh beer but Izzy snatched it before it reached his lips.

"Sorry," she said. "The clean-and-sober challenge has officially begun."

"But I'm totally sober."

She shook her head and tossed the bottle off the tower.

```
Critical Hit!
[Izzy] dealt 73 damage to [Karen]
[Karen] is dead!
```

Her face went white. We all drew away from the parapets.

Kyle burst out laughing. "Sh—" He clamped his mouth shut. "That was fu—" He frowned.

I laughed. "Don't give yourself an aneurysm, Kyle."

He leaned close and whispered, "Bro, this is gonna be harder than I thought."

"No way. You got this."

"Guys!" chided Caduceus. "Dune's still down there with the goblins."

"Right," resumed the brewmaster. "That *a-hole's* totally gonna die."

Izzy rolled her eyes and muttered, "Real original."

"I think Dune has a chance," insisted Caduceus. We returned to the parapet and leaned toward the action.

The ranger made impressive progress through the waiting army, but a raucous group of wrestling goblins inadvertently rolled into his path. They were fighting between him and the message. Worse, a few imps in the distance sniffed the ground as they picked up his scent.

Caduceus nodded encouragingly. "He can make this."

"You sure?" asked Kyle. "I've never seen anyone so outnumbered."

"Hey!" I snapped, slightly wounded. "I went outside the gates during the last goblin invasion, when the horde was ten times the size. With a cyclops. And an angel!"

"Whatever, bro. Don't make everything about you."

"It's true," said Izzy. "You do that a lot."

Errol nodded. "Wouldn't shut up 'bout not havin' a pirate ditty."

Even Caduceus loudly snickered along. With everyone so happily having fun at my expense, I sighed and turned to Stigg, waiting for him to pile on.

"What?" he asked, caught off guard. "I actually think you're pretty cool." Bandit snorted and Trafford joined them with a shrug.

I splayed my hands to my only three friends on the roof, considering the argument settled. When I returned my attention to the field, Dune was sneaking past the wrestling goblins by sidling around a nearby wagon.

"He's awfully close to them," I mentioned.

"He's gonna die," agreed Kyle.

Caduceus hissed. "He's *not* gonna die."

The goblins spun around in a grapple. Dune ducked behind the wagon just as the smaller goblin tripped the larger, who tumbled to his back. Head upside down, his orange eyes widened at the pair of boots behind the wagon wheel. He pointed. "Humanses!" Twenty heads spun his way.

"Okay," relented Caduceus. "He's gonna die."

Cover blown and no longer able to make it to the dove, the ranger released a bird of his own. A red-headed falcon launched from his forearm, closing on its target and scooping up my scroll with powerful talons. Dune scanned the mobilizing troops and fixed on a goblin archer about to take down his second bird of the day. The pagan released a well-aimed shot. Dune's longbow flashed and his silver arrow intercepted the missile mid flight. The falcon spun clear and swooped toward the wall.

The amateur wrestlers converged on both sides of the wagon. Dune ripped away his green cloak, draped it over his notched bow, and released the string. A mass of green zipped out from cover. The hungry goblins pounced after it, giving Dune an opening. He hopped out from underneath the wagon and hightailed it to the west gate.

He was out in the open now. No more stealth, no more tricks. The errant folk spied him and pursued. He fired silver arrows to cover his escape but the enemy numbers grew. Dune was fast enough to outpace the more terrifying beasties, but a score of monkey-sized imps loped to his position on all fours, quickly gaining ground.

I opened my dev menu.

```
DEVELOPER CONSOLE
>> _
```

The west gate was barricaded and manned by a full contingent of legionnaires, of course, but it was a simple thing to go to the perimeter controls and flip the switch myself. The huge double doors securing the massive wall groaned open a sliver and provided the escape Dune needed. Centurions stepped outside, bearing shields against the fastest imps.

"You see?" proclaimed Caduceus with a hard slap on Kyle's back. "I told you he could do it."

The brewmaster conceded with a nod. "Can't argue with success. That was fu—"

Izzy glared at him in warning.

"—fuepic."

We all frowned. "What now?" asked Izzy.

Kyle cleared his throat uncertainly. "I said that was fepic."

The pixie arched an eyebrow. "What exactly is fepic?"

"You know, F'n epic."

"Riiight."

"It's a word." He turned to me. "Back me up, bro."

"Good enough for me," I said. "You were the one that wanted this, Iz."

The goblin horde went through the motions of pursuit, but the show was already over, roll credits. The Eye of Orik, Stronghold's soulstone, would prevent any proper pagans from entering the city. And best of all, Dune wasn't a Black Hat, so the armistice remained intact. The centurions pulled inside and the west gate closed.

I smiled and turned to the downed stone giant in the middle of Oldtown. Half the height of Dragonperch, Orik kneeled before it as if in subjugation. With the saints in possession of the soulstone, a true incursion into the city was impossible. That still didn't prevent the emotional imps from beating on the sealed gate, furious at the defeat and subjugation of their one-eyed god.

1550 Descent

Our contingent stomped down the spiral staircase that was the backbone of Dragonperch. Now that the immediate drama was over, everybody had a different idea for where to turn my attention next.

Kyle held up a glassy black orb adorned with a jewelry fitting. "Wanted to give you the bad news in person, bro. The void pearl doesn't fit into any socket configurations."

"It doesn't modify any of our current pearls?"

"I tried every combination and got zilch. *Nada.* Maybe it's meant for another sanctum. I bet it'll command a hefty price on the resale market."

I shook my head. "The void pearl's too valuable to barter away."

"Agreed," said Izzy, keeping pace with us. "I've been in the secret library leveling up my lore skill. As far as I can tell, the void pearl relates to something called the under realm. It's how Hadrian's shadowguards were able to teleport around and phase through walls."

I whistled as we descended past the living quarters. "If we could find a way to harness that tech for ourselves..."

"Tell me about it, but it's hard to glean more. I've fared even worse researching the goblin horde."

Kyle snorted. "I keep telling you, books will only get you so far."

The pixie ignored him. "There's no definitive organization that makes up the pagan faction. The only references to General Azzyrk liken him to a rabid dog, but I can't separate crusader propaganda from the truth." She frowned. "That's the problem with the ancient sources. They were transcribed before AIs assumed free will. There's no programmed story line anymore."

Kyle puffed his cheeks in thought. "I distrust zealots as much as the next man, but you've traded face-to-face blows with Azzyrk. I have to side with the crusaders on this one."

I cocked my head. "Rabid, I agree with. Dog might be selling him short. It can't be easy corralling that rowdy army, and they've been disciplined enough to shoot down my birds."

Dragonperch was a large tower, and a significant portion of it was still unexplored. After scooting past a couple of locked levels, we made it to the den and the kitchen and finally to ground level. The magical door swung open and Bandit rushed to be the first outside. The mountain bongo was still a wild animal at heart, enjoying the sun on her fur as her daunting horns stretched for the sky. The highest perch in the city was a good facsimile of a mountain, but some things couldn't be faked. Bandit hoofed across the ground in search of tasty greenery.

Caduceus and Stigg bounded past and hurried for the gate, eager to congratulate their fearless leader after the show he put on. Knowing Dune, he'd congratulate himself once or twice as well. I just wanted the letter.

Before I could follow, Trafford caught my shoulder.

Thankfully the old man wasn't waiting around to hand out more bad news. He was a builder, and he wanted to start building.

"It's been 3 days," he said. "At 14 HQR a day, we're up to 42."

The corner of my mouth crooked. Our headquarters resources had been exhausted in the climactic last stand that defeated Hadrian, his shadows, and the kraken. With the beasts destroyed and the Whisperer in chains, the main obstacle to our rebuild was the ticking clock. They say time heals all wounds, but this was an MMO and we had potions for that. We really just needed it to refill our headquarters resources.

The development made the buildmaster general unusually upbeat. "We finally have enough HQR to rebuild the barracks that were destroyed. Best of all, the repair time is only 10 man hours. With the ogres doing double duty and eager to get back to work, I can have it complete in no time."

I swiped open the menu.

Black Hat Headquarters
Level: 2   *HQXP*: 7 / 8
HQR: 42   *Daily HQR Production*: 14   *DP*: 1
Current Buildings   Guildhall   Brothel   Lumberyard   Vault

Destroyed

Barracks

With the brothel already serving as a respawn point and our lack of a true army, the barracks weren't wholly necessary, but it was good for morale to rebuild what we'd lost. Not to mention, repairing took half the time of building something new. This was the quickest structure to get up that would add another HQXP to our total, which would put the headquarters over the edge to level up, increasing our daily HQR production and speeding up all build times in the future.

We took the detour with Trafford to the site of the old barracks. I spent the headquarters points, lined up the shimmering blue placement, and spawned it. A foundation popped into place and a little goblin girl wearing fur clapped her mitts together excitedly.

"Times for wakey wakey, worky worky?"

Trafford chuckled and nodded. "It's time, Jixa. Assemble the crew."

The girl ran off to find her ogres. Jixa's team was a real asset to our city building. I briefly wondered how the Shorehome transplants felt about being besieged by their own kin. They'd broken ties with the pagan faction, sure, but it was hard to get away from blood. That was free will for you.

I side-eyed the buildmaster general as he licked his lips. "You know, Trafford, I still can't get used to you smiling all the time."

"What do ya mean?" he countered.

"Well, you know..." I rubbed my neck. "You can kinda-sometimes be a bit of a crank."

His eyes narrowed. "I'm a fucking bundle of joy, Talon. Don't you forget that." He burst into laughter.

That was the Trafford I knew.

Kyle sighed under his breath. "I wish I could still make jokes like that. Hey Trafford, any chance you wanna—"

"Join you in your clean-and-sober challenge? No way. If misery loves company, I'd rather be alone."

The brewmaster moped as we dragged him away. Today was gonna be a good day. I could feel it. Izzy too, if only because she got to watch Kyle struggle every time he spoke. For now, however, a nervous silence overtook us. We marched to the west gate to retrieve the message from the wildkins.

Saint Peter materialized nearby, sandals flapping as he hurried our way. "Talon, you must come at once!" The old man was frazzled. Sure, his off-white toga remained the height of Greek fashion, but his crown of golden twigs was seated at a precarious angle.

"What's the matter?" I asked.

"It's Hadrian."

"He escaped?"

"Of course not, but—"

"Let him stew a minute then. I'm expecting word from the wild king."

The saint followed as we continued to the main thoroughfare. I craned my neck toward the west gate. The double doors were barricaded. Lackadaisical rambling from the guards was the only activity in sight.

"You don't understand," continued the exasperated saint.

"Hadrian's manipulating the codebase somehow. Someone's still in play, either him or a hidden ally. Judging by a sharp increase in network chatter, I suspect they're about to make a move."

"F him," said Kyle.

My lips twisted in annoyance. The expression intensified as I confirmed Dune and company weren't waiting on the road for us.

"Go on," Izzy told me. "Potty mouth and I will track down the ranger."

"I'll show you a fudging potty mouth," grumbled Kyle.

The saint blinked uncertainly. "What's going on with you?"

"Nothing," said Kyle. "And don't you worry, Peter, we'll track down the tracker."

Peter nodded and turned to me. "And now that your dispatch is safe within Stronghold's walls, let's take care of more pressing matters."

Izzy and Kyle hurried off, leaving me to follow Saint Peter to the dungeon. So much for the start of a good day.

1560 Civilization

The march through the Forum wasn't hectic or panicked. The mood in the morning wasn't ominous. Adventurers proceeded throughout their days much as they always did, browsing the busy mercantile district for quests and fancy new loot. The goblin horde had only been outside the gates for three days—hardly enough to affect the economy of a city the size of Stronghold. There were quests to complete within the walls, plenty of drink and distraction, and somewhere around three-quarters of Haven's player populace at hand.

Given our huge recent victory, the city was more prosperous than ever.

"I still don't understand what you mean by network chatter," I said as we weaved around an ox hauling a load of weapons.

Peter's white beard puffed over his lips. "To be frank, Talon, I don't completely understand it myself. Christian and Tad handle the technical matters. The important thing is we know Larry's betrayal wasn't an isolated incident. They've prioritized looking into some worrying developments."

"I'll bet. I should Everchat with them right away."

"Actually, we believe your talents are better utilized elsewhere."

"But I'm a programmer."

"Which is Tad's full-time job. Not only are you an exact copy of him, but he's been working for Kablammy and is already familiar with the codebase. He has it covered."

"Mmm hmm, and what can I do?"

"We need you watching the virtual home front, as it were. Rally the player base and keep malcontents like Hadrian out of trouble."

My mouth twisted into a sour smirk. "You need me to help Haven launch."

"As smoothly as humanly possible."

The lofty Pantheon loomed before us, a huge domed capitol building fronted by a triangular portico of Corinthian columns and grand marble steps. The columns that had once lined the leading walkway had all crumbled but one, a foreboding testament to what we'd endured. Of the original Golden Seven, only two angels remained. One was wounded and MIA and the other—

"Wait a minute. Where's Decimus?"

Saint Peter's eyebrows stretched to his hairline. "He senses something afoot as well, auto-activated by his security protocol."

Whoa. Angels weren't woken lightly. Their activation required a player somehow skirting the rules of the game. Hacking and glitching were the usual culprits.

"Then that's game, set, and match," I said. "If Hadrian's been caught, let Decimus delete him and be done with it."

"If only it were so easy," returned the old man. "No, something is staying the arbiter's silver swords. Hadrian has been too careful to incriminate himself."

We rounded the Pantheon and crossed into the nearby slums. There were lots of quest buildings here. With the influx of Shorehome immigrants, the developers had patched in emergency housing. Instead of building new structures they simply doubled and tripled up the entryways, making each door lead to several unique interiors. With a simple patch, the afterlife had solved the housing crisis.

As we cut through the slums, our path wound with the adjoining river. Saint Peter wistfully sighed. "Did I ever tell you how the Albula River got its name?"

I shrugged. "Random name generator?"

"Oh no," he chuckled, "we didn't invent the name. It means mountain stream. In ancient history, after the fall of Troy, a group of survivors fled to the Italian peninsula and formed the influential city of original Latins, Alba Longa. The line of Alban royalty was descended from a Trojan prince and would go on to found Rome itself. But one day, back in those formative years, Alba Longa's ninth king, Tiberinus Silvius, was crossing the Albula and he drowned." The history buff paused on that note. "Imagine that, a great king dying so simply. Anyway, from that day hence, the river was called the Tiber, in his honor."

"Hardcore," I said.

He nodded. "Here, in Haven, we've created a world where the dead live again. When it came time to name our river, we felt a landmark evoking death wasn't apropos to our vision. We restored the river's original moniker."

I chewed my lip as we followed the water north. The jail was settled against the city wall a little ways up. I thought over the parable a minute, wondering at the saint's exact point but knowing it had something to do with emphasizing the importance—the dream—of Haven.

"I'm gonna say it again, Peter, but I think you should consider calling off the launch. What are we at, three days to showtime? It doesn't give us a lot to work with."

"Impossible. The timetable is set. Processes have started. Do you know how difficult it is to reschedule a satellite launch? Besides, publicly releasing Haven is precisely what protects it. Once we're fully live and independently networked, tampering will be impossible. The systems will run as a closed circuit. Haven will no longer be part of Kablammy's asset portfolio, making it immune to hostile legal acquisitions. Christian has given the long-term viability of the afterlife years of thought. You have to trust that he has everything in place."

I swallowed down my next objection. As far as paradigm-defining CEOs went, Christian Everett owned the top of the scoreboard. And while I'd once suspected his motives, recent events convinced me he was one of the good guys. It didn't hurt that Tad Lonnerman, my real-world doppelganger, had eyes on him.

"Okay," I relented, as if I wasn't already going along with the dev team. "Let's see what the player-formerly-known-as-the-Whisperer is up to."

I'd expected Peter to smile, but his expression grew more grim as we entered the jail yard. Warden Jorah waited for us inside the main prisoner building.

"Oi, Protector. You're a right sight."

I nodded at his salute. "Let's see how I feel on my way outta here."

He chuckled and led us down the hall. "Fair enough. Anything that spooks Saint Peter and Decimus oughta be a whopper."

He unlocked a fortified door and we stepped inside, zoning into the separate dungeon level. A dank stairway and lonely hall streamed in. We followed the sequence of empty cells to the solid wooden door at the end. Jorah undid the bolts and swung it open. In the deep dank of the shadows was a man shackled to a chair: prisoner one one seven.

The unassuming man seemed built for the darkness. Beady eyes and thinning hair gave him a molish appearance. His diminutive stature made him all the less impressive. But then, he never was one for the limelight.

"I like what you've done with the place," I said as I stepped inside. The stone-walled cell was barely more than a walk-in closet. The damp and dark seemed to close in from all sides.

I flinched when I noticed Decimus beside me. A perfectly chiseled model of a man wrapped in flowing white cloth, he stood in the corner poised like a snake. Instead of fangs, the angel carried a silver sword in each hand. He didn't acknowledge the presence of Peter or myself; he simply stared straight at the shackled prisoner. I couldn't tell if the white blindfold made the scene more or less unnerving.

"Justice is blind," quipped the Whisperer, finally raising his gaze to meet mine. "In this case, it's quite indecisive as well."

"Cut the crap, Hadrian. What're you up to?"

The prisoner studied the room and shrugged. "I appear to be sitting. It'd be difficult to do anything else."

He was shackled to the chair by his ankles and wrists. This

was to keep him from suiciding and respawning back in Shorehome, not that the pirate city was an entirely safe place for him anymore. I just wished I'd gotten word from Papa Brugo of their post-Hadrian status.

"I'm talking about the network traffic," I snapped. "You're reaching out to someone."

Hadrian scoffed. "I'm hardly in a position to scratch my own nose. You've got the wrong guy."

"I doubt it."

He shrugged again. "Your watchdog is on top of me. If I was doing anything at all, I'd be dead. Maybe you should be tracking down Saint Loras."

"Loras is dead. Try again."

"A construct can't be dead."

"Don't play semantics. He's gone." I snorted and leaned against the wall, wondering how I was gonna get anything out of a prisoner who hadn't spilled a useful tidbit in days. "You haven't admitted it, but I know you've somehow infected the simulation. The Loras avatar was the same as anyone else, a pawn to further your interests. A rogue algorithm driven by your will. By now you know the developers have taken countermeasures against you. Remote control of the saints has been revoked."

The old man watched Hadrian passively from the doorway. He'd no doubt exhausted his breath with the same line of questioning. Hadrian, having heard it all before, was already playing the part of the bored spectator. I opened my developer menu. Although the display was invisible to everyone but me, the action immediately caught his eye.

"According to this, you're locked out of the hub. All prisoners in the dungeon are."

"Then believe both your eyes and your brain," Hadrian replied. "It's impossible for me to do what you say."

"Let's start simple then. What's the purpose of the goblin horde?"

Hadrian chuckled. "This again?"

"How do we disperse the pagans?" I pressed.

The prisoner didn't answer.

"They're barely a distraction, you know. With the Eye of Orik safely in the tabernacle, it's impossible for the horde to enter Stronghold as pagans. And if they defect, I'll slaughter them in a second. In fact, the only reason I haven't already torn them a new one is because I don't want to break the armistice."

I froze, the recesses of my brain buzzing as I seemed to hit upon something. Of course Hadrian hated the armistice. I'd figured that angle two days ago. This was something deeper—yet more universal. A horde of goblins. A legion of defenders. This was two armies, wasted, or at least, taken out of play. The would-be king was still sowing the seeds of discord, but were these the stagnant remnants of a failed plan, or was there a future to it?

In this interrogation, I had supreme control. Of that there was no doubt. But Hadrian's confidence exuded some measure of control as well. Saint Peter was right. The Whisperer was still active.

"There are ways out of this," said the old man. "Tell us how to undo the damage you've caused—"

"And you'll offer leniency?" spat Hadrian. "You're only out

for blood. The second I give you the slightest indication I've shirked the terms of service, your watchdog will delete me."

"Justice can regard context."

I turned to the saint, eyes narrowed. "What are you doing?"

"We can agree to terms if you cooperate," said Peter.

"No terms," I said. "We have him where we want him. Any negotiation will just be him angling for an edge."

Hadrian smiled bitterly, his resolve strengthening. "What did I tell you, Peter? Out for blood."

>> Minigame <<

Tad Lonnerman scrolled down the news feed. A video autoplayed a computer rendering of the vastness of the cosmos.

"Space is infinite," came the collected voice of Christian Everett. "What if your life could be infinite as well?"

Although it was Christian speaking, the social media commercial featured his investor voice. This wasn't his usual curious, hopeful tone—it was commanding and resolute. One meant to appease shareholders and inspire passion. One meant for selling.

The camera panned through space and centered on a state-of-the-art satellite. A quick zoom into its metal heart revealed circuit boards, electrical impulses, and then, magnificently, a lush world of gallant knights and devious baddies. Epic music accompanied fantastical landscapes and architectural wonders. As the action and music crescendoed, the camera suddenly pulled back into the void of space. One satellite was joined by others until a network of them orbited the Earth.

"Welcome to the afterlife online. Welcome to Haven."

The end of the commercial displayed a stylized date across the vista, reminding Tad of just how little time they had before launch.

The programmer turned to his boss. "Laying it on a little thick, don't you think?"

"Hmm?" Christian peeked up from several investor portfolios and squinted at the computer screen. "Oh, yes. In my defense, overselling is a better marketing strategy than underselling."

Tad chuckled. "Luckily, you don't need to worry. Once Haven goes gold, the players will do all the selling for you."

They were in Christian's personal office at the Seattle headquarters of Kablammy Games. The studio spanned the top floor of a modern tower of glass. The ceiling-to-floor windows in the CEO's office provided a stunning view of Downtown Seattle and the deep-blue waters of Elliot Bay. The room itself was adorned with stout Victorian furniture. Stacks of physical binders cluttered the carpet. Christian Everett sat on the floor poring through them while Tad inspected the company's digital footprint on the workstation at the desk.

The head honcho sighed. "All the hype in the world won't help if we don't find our saboteurs. And I don't know that scouring the depraved recesses of InLink will uncover the conspiracy."

"You never know," Tad hedged, scrolling the news feed further. "People reveal a lot more online than they think."

InLink was a social media giant, serving as the who's who of Silicon Valley. If you were a tech company and you weren't on InLink, you didn't matter. If your project wasn't trending, it was already a failure. This was thanks in no small part to avid investor faith in the platform. All industry connections were pioneered through the InLink network, which meant every company Kablammy had ever done business with had a presence here. A link.

What better place to find the bad actor?

But Tad was aware of Christian's concern. They didn't just need a list of suspects, they needed proof of foul play. The CEO was digging into the money, which was a sure bet. Tad? He was looking for a needle in a haystack of unsolicited advertising and narcissism.

"Power in your Pocket," boasted one video, showing a triple-A game clip transition to a shitty top-down phone game. Pocket Global was a mobile-developer outsourcing company that Kablammy utilized for the money-making arm of its business.

"We didn't outsource any Haven tech, did we?"

Christian shook his head. "Goodness, no. The project is too sensitive. If we vitally needed something, we made sure to acquire the developers completely."

Tad swallowed. That exact thing had happened to his old company in Portland. The buyout had been no small source of consternation. Back then Kablammy seemed to be the root of everything vile in the industry. The shovelware empire. A lot had changed in a few short months.

"Another game BOOSTED," crowed another InLink post. Boost Systems was the company Kablammy regularly contracted for running focus tests, including early environment sims of Haven. Tad had a natural distaste for the experts who would stroll in and dumb down his games for the lowest common denominator.

On and on it went. Voice actors, contractors, quality assurance teams, effects studios. Tad couldn't help laughing.

"You know, Christian, it was only a few days ago we thought *you* were the bad guy."

Getting contacted by his AI double had been a trip. Being swept into a world of intrigue and espionage was something else entirely. An adventure, almost. Just like the ones he enjoyed programming.

"You're romanticizing what's happening here, Tad. As exhilarating as it was to have a real-life mole within the development team, this isn't a spy movie with shoot-outs and slow-motion helicopter explosions. Believe me, business acquisitions are much more banal, *and* much more profitable. Multinational megacorporations with competing interests will jockey for any edge to squeeze a profit. When a disrupting technology is introduced, those caught on their heels often tumble."

"So you're saying everybody's gunning for us."

He sighed. "To a degree. But forget the cloak-and-dagger and follow the money. We need to isolate the specific companies that would reap the largest financial windfalls following Kablammy's demise."

"And also those that have the technical know-how to pull it off. That Trojan they introduced to the system wasn't the work of an amateur."

"Perhaps, but there's no shortage of mercenary black hat hackers out there."

"I get that, I just—" Tad worked his jaw. "I just think you're looking in the wrong place. Angel investors put up money to make money. They might know the broad strokes of your offering, but ultimately they succeed when you do. The people pulling this off were close to the system, knowing way more than Larry ever could. Independent contractors manufactured the EXSIL units to our specifications, but the focus testers were the only outsiders intimately familiar with the sim itself."

Christian kept his head in the latest portfolio. "Boost Systems? They're a bunch of longhaired fun-gineers."

Tad scooted the office chair back so fast the wheels caught on the rug. Stretching for his crutch, he painfully levered himself into a standing position, careful not to put weight on the cast as his injured leg flooded with blood. "Christian, you need to see this."

The urgency in Tad's voice didn't go unnoticed. The CEO rose and approached the workstation. Kablammy had received a private InLink message.

Title: Stop the launch

Christian snickered. "Oh, I've been getting a slew of these over the last several weeks."

"Really? And you didn't think it was relevant to our current search?"

"Tad, social media is a megaphone for idiots. The most purposeful content is spam and Russian trolling."

Tad couldn't believe the CEO's blind spot. It was one thing to distrust the value of the grapevine, it was another to outright dismiss a threat. He read the content of the message out loud.

> An ecosystem that barely holds together during a beta is doomed. Haven has no future. Let the living live and the dead die. Stop the launch.

Tad Lonnerman cleared his throat. "This sounds pretty serious. There's no sender. How could someone manage that?"

"There you go," said Christian. "Faulty credentials. That's clear indication of spam if there ever was one."

"I dunno. Even Viagra ads have the decency to make the profile pic a half-naked porn star. This company hacked InLink's back end."

"Or simply found a bug to exploit. It's—"

Christian froze mid sentence as Tad played the video attachment. A high-desert facility took center stage. A launchpad with a background of warehouses emblazoned with the words, "Phoenix X."

Tad frowned. "Is that... ?"

The CEO nodded. "Kablammy's launch compound in Southern California."

The garbled computer voice was the only audio in the security-like footage. "Satellites are a poor proxy for ascension to the afterlife. Leap-frogging the gates of Heaven will only lead to the fires of hell."

The primary site for Haven's satellite launch exploded. Fingers of burning rocket fuel curled as neighboring warehouses erupted, each bomb blast a new piece of shrapnel lodged into Christian's terror-stricken heart.

1570 Deal or No Deal

I flashed Saint Peter the scowl I'd been reserving for Hadrian. Nixing any hope of barter from the Whisperer's mind was imperative. I didn't want him at the bargaining table, I wanted him backed into a corner. If the prisoner was indeed still communicating with an outside influencer, any inch we gave would be taken advantage of.

But how else could we convince Hadrian to relent? The smug bastard was chained to a chair in a locked room underground, and he was as comfortable in his skin as ever. If I was gonna get to him, it would be through his pride. A puppeteer by nature, Hadrian was absolutely addicted to control. That was the chink in his armor.

All trace of agitation fled my face and I chuckled softly. "This isn't exactly how you planned your coming-out party, is it?"

The Whisperer's eyes narrowed.

I didn't want to overdo the boast, so I let the truth speak plainly. "You were tricked into prematurely revealing your identity. You lost the Squid's Tooth, the accompanying kraken, and your freedom. But, hey, at least you earned the ire of the entire population of Stronghold in the process."

An inadvertent twitch of Hadrian's cheek. It wasn't just the battle's outcome that nettled him, it was his failure to assert his will on a united group of players, NPCs, and mobs. Once again I thought of the legionnaires and goblins, an errant arrow away from rising up against each other and meeting on the battlefield as enemies, as *others*—all while ignoring the true threat.

Hadrian was patient, if anything. He didn't mind setbacks as long as he could regroup. The misstep in Stronghold turned the city against him, drowning his meticulous efforts at manipulation, wrenching the puppets from the strings. If we could find a way to do the same in Shorehome and Oakengard, the Whisperer would be done for.

"You talk and talk and talk," muttered Hadrian. "As impressive as you are on the battlefield, eye to eye you're nothing but a disappointment."

I pressed my lips together bitterly. "Will you say the same at your public execution?"

"There'll be no execution. Decimus is a nuclear weapon without a launch code. Lucifer's rogue angel is mortally wounded and lost in the wind." My eyes flashed and he grinned sardonically. "Yes, I've realized why your devil isn't around. There's no scenario that ends in my deletion."

He had me there. Instead of masking it I plainly displayed my frown and nodded to his point. "This is where you and I agree. But deletion would be way too easy on you. You see, we won't execute you on the gallows or at the end of a pair of silver swords, we'll do it by removing what makes you you. Despite the best efforts of your goblin horde, word from the wildkins got through to me."

He snorted. "A paltry band."

"With one very terrifying solution." I leaned close to Hadrian so I could smell his sweat. "The last time a crazed zealot attempted to sack this city, he became a prisoner of the Blackwood. I don't need to delete you to erase you, Hadrian. All I need to do is surrender you to Hood. Imagine that, the puppeteer becoming the puppet."

"Hood doesn't have that power over players."

I hiked a shoulder. "You're probably right again, at least before Lucifer freed his will." I smiled.

Hadrian tensed. His eyes smoldered. For the first time in days, the man didn't have a snappy comeback or a confident smirk.

"That's the thing about control, Hadrian. The more you yank at it, the more others tear it away. Those puppet strings pull both ways, and you're not gonna like how this tug-of-war ends."

His breath faltered. He snapped to Saint Peter in a momentary plea for mercy. Happily, my friend held his tongue. It may have been cruel condemning a man to eternal enslavement, but in a world where Hadrian continued his hacks in confinement and couldn't be deleted, I didn't see another out.

"Ah," I said, turning to the sounds encroaching from the dungeon hallway, "here's the good news now." I waited for Hadrian to yield, but he simply dropped his head, returning to the same position he'd opened with. Taking that as a sign he was finished talking, Saint Peter and I left the man to his scheming mind and the silk-covered eyes of Decimus.

As Warden Jorah closed and barred the reinforced cell door, Kyle and Izzy strode down the hall. True to their word, they were accompanied by Dune and his party. "Here's your dispatch," said the ranger, presenting the scroll proudly.

I put a finger to my lips and snatched the message with my other hand. "No discussion in the dungeon. As slim as the chances are, I don't want Hadrian overhearing strategy." I brushed forward.

"You're welcome." The crew turned and headed for the staircase.

We hurried past the cells, all empty except for the one at our back. It was desolate down here, and Jorah had decided it was too cruel even for the gangster Chadwick. The isolation of the separate zone was deemed a necessity for Hadrian, however, and the latest interrogation only reinforced that belief.

"I don't mean to downplay your entrance, Dune. Good to see you back alive. That was ballsy what you did out there."

He grinned and spread his hands in a gesture of magnanimity. "A simple feat for Haven's most famous tracker."

"Famous for failing to nab the good cleric once again."

Dune blanched. "Not for lack of trying. And for the record, we did track him down."

Caduceus released an ill-humored snort. "It was the catching part that tripped us up."

"Healers upon healers stacking OP buffs," complained Dune. "I don't know how we're ever gonna be able to take down the catechists."

I clenched my jaw as our small talk ventured into the arena of strategic discussion. We were at the end of the hallway, though, and the information was probably of little use to the Whisperer. I nodded acknowledgment instead of replying, then zoned up the steps. When everyone appeared on the ground floor of the jailhouse, I crossed my arms and got down to business.

"So what happened with Cleric Vagram?"

Dune twirled his green cloak to the side with dramatic flair. "It was pretty much what they told you. The man's adept at guerrilla warfare. He uses scouts for an early-warning system and lays traps for threats. We knew we were spotted, but I still can't figure how they surrounded us."

Stigg nodded enthusiastically as Dune continued.

"Vagram's not afraid to get his hands dirty either. He brings the fire."

"Fepic," spouted Kyle in the background.

"You're not gonna convince me that's a real word," said Izzy.

"Languages evolve," said the brewmaster. "Besides, in a digital reality, what's really real to begin with?"

Izzy huffed in annoyance and forced her attention back to Dune. "So, once Caduceus and Stigg were gone, I assume the jig was up?"

Everyone blinked at her.

"What? I can say jig unironically."

I laughed. "No you can't. This is a simulation of the Middle Ages, not 1940s Los Angeles."

"Sue me," she hissed. "I've been into historicals lately. Thought I'd start a thing."

"Yeah," quipped Dune, voice laced with sarcasm, "I *don't* think I'll be saying that. Anyway, since I was alone, I had to regroup and try a more surgical approach. I flanked a whole mountain to gain on them. That's when I saw the crusaders."

I furrowed my brow. "Oakengard's army?"

"Same ones. Black cloaks, white crosses. Although some of them held purple banners I haven't seen before. They were razing the land, looking for the catechists. It was stupid in hindsight, but I approached them. I mean, I figured I was on one of their quests, right?"

Izzy frowned. "They attacked you on sight, didn't they?"

Dune nodded. "I know you speak highly of Colonel Grimwart, but after that I didn't know who was friend or foe. And seeing as how I'd lodged arrows between the eyes of both catechists and crusaders, I was suddenly standing in the middle of two angry armies." The ranger shook his head. "I booked it back to Stronghold."

Izzy huffed and turned to me. "It's what you were afraid of."

"Oakengard's mobilizing," I agreed. "They really want the clerics under control, but I have a feeling their army's preparing for a longer march. At least you have a good understanding of the troop locations," I told Dune.

He smiled. "Spoken like a true scout."

"And you tracked like a true ranger." He bowed his head. "Speaking of tracking, why'd you make my people hunt you down for the message?"

"Simple," said Dune. "I had to recover Blossom."

"Who's Blossom?"

"My red-headed falcon."

"Psh," spat Kyle. "You named your bird Blossom? With the red hair, I would've gone with Mary Jane or—no!—Jessica Rabbit!"

Dune blinked. "You would've named my falcon after a rabbit?"

"She's not a rabbit. She has huge—" Kyle puffed his hands out in front of his chest. "Am I allowed to say knockers?"

"Some people are above naming their pets after cartoon characters," piped Caduceus. Stigg nodded.

The ranger cleared his throat. "Yeah." The falcon popped into existence on Dune's shoulder, cocking her head at an extreme angle to take in her audience. She was cute up close, a body of gray plumage, lighter but striped on her belly, with a white neck, yellow band around her eye, and the orange-red feathers of her namesake running from her crown to her shoulders.

I whistled. "I didn't know you could do that."

"You obviously haven't been paying attention. I wouldn't be much of a ranger if I didn't have animal companions."

I scratched my chin. "Oh yeah. Would kind of be an oversight on my part." I shook it off. "So was Blossom hiding or something?"

"Nah, she's just trained to make a beeline for home base. And since I don't own a legendary tower like some people I know, I made our base the Wicked Crow."

I rolled my eyes. "Of course you did." The Crow was the seediest bar in the city, out of the way in the slums, and a second home to the ranger. I waved the scroll in the air. "Anyway, thanks for the message."

As I broke the wild king's wax seal and unrolled the scroll, Peter read a PM and stiffened. "Oh dear. I have to go."

"But I'm just about to read the wildkin reply."

"Sorry, this can't wait." Saint Peter vanished in a flash.

Izzy arched a violet brow. "That was ominous."

Kyle chuckled. "You could almost say—"

"Don't," she warned.

I grumbled and tapped the letter in my hand. "Well, without further ado, I suppose."

My argumentative acquaintance,

Here, here we have an impasse. Thou risest toward warfare, yet I rest easy in peace, residing in a burnt wood that nobody wants. We vie not for power over those outside our kin. Recall, recall the will of the wild: to be left to our own devices.

Rumors of shadowy armies stir us not to betray these ideals. We shall look after our own, and our executioner will keepeth his hood and his axe close to the Blackwood.

At the risk of straying from my stance, I wish thee well in thy fight, but the fight be thine alone.

- The Wild King

"What is it?" asked Izzy.

I handed her the letter with a curse.

1580 Life is Strange

My friends passed around the scroll and the accompanying troubled frowns. Days of negotiating and still the wildkins didn't take the threat of Oakengard seriously.

"What does he mean, 'rumors of shadowy armies?' " complained Caduceus.

"He's acting like you're using scare tactics to enlist help," said Dune.

Stigg quietly nodded along.

I canted my head. "Theoderic is an even-keeled fellow. After we broke into his throne room to steal his crown, his first response was to reason with us. I'm sure he knows Oakengard is a potential threat."

"He's hoping his isolationist stance leaves him out of the war," concluded Izzy. She crossed her arms. "So where does this leave us?"

"Without leverage against Hadrian," I answered. "With an army outside our walls. In a stalemate. Exactly where we were before."

"What about Shorehome?" asked Dune.

I shook my head. "We haven't had word from Papa Brugo. The Brothers in Black are an unknown quantity until we find out how much support Hadrian still has. My bet is there's a struggle for power."

"At least we captured the snake's head," noted Izzy. "What Hadrian accomplished took a lot of careful planning. I doubt Jackie and the Rough Riders have the finesse to fill those shoes."

Izzy was right. The stalemate was just as damaging to Hadrian as it was to us. Even more so considering he was in a cell.

But that was in a normal situation. With Haven launching in three days, the pressure was flipped to us. The end goal wasn't catching Hadrian, it was undoing all the strife he'd manufactured. Without his full surrender and cooperation, I didn't see how that was possible anymore.

"So we're boned," said Kyle.

Stigg nodded with enthusiasm.

I quizzically studied the Viking. "Like, totally, utterly screwed," I added.

Stigg's nodding grew more emphatic.

I pressed my lips together. "Stigg is a big fat dummy."

The mystic's head bobbed up and down in agreement.

I paused and took in the big man, bright red robe and mane of black curls. I squinted, brushed his hair aside, and pulled a pearly bud from his ear. "Are you listening to headphones?!?"

Stigg's eyes went wide. "Shh! They're not headphones, they're enchanted sound stones."

"THEY'RE HEADPHONES! How'd you even..."

"Look," he said, pulling out the other ear bud, "you get a legendary dragonspear, Izzy has the winter staff. You don't think ol' Stigg deserves some loot?"

"I..." I was speechless. I didn't really know how to respond to his sensible appeal. I placed the unattached ear bud to my ear, but couldn't get it too close due to the combination of raging guitars and ridiculous volume. I handed the item back to him. "You haven't heard a word we said, have you?"

He shrugged. "Just point me where you want me and I'm there."

"We've started using party chat to keep him in the loop," explained Dune.

I scratched my head. "Okay, cool... I guess I just didn't know you were a fan of heavy metal."

The big man snorted. "What did you think? I'm a thirty-year-old man with wild hair, a glorious beard, and I dress up like a Viking. How could I not bang out to metal?"

"Good point. What do you listen to?"

"Mostly Mongolian rage metal, but some Nordic punk and Badlands chopper core too.

Everyone stared blankly at him.

"You know," he remarked, "Engines of Dissection, Apocalypse Bagpipes, and the Entrails of Our Souls?"

Everyone stared blankly at him.

"Screw you guys." Stigg put his ear buds back in.

Kyle lit up. "Ooh! You got Post Malone?"

"Glad everyone's having so much fun." I snorted and turned to leave.

Izzy hurried to keep up. "Talon."

"I know what you're gonna say, Iz. I just don't think everyone's taking this as seriously as they should."

"What do you expect them to do? We're cooped inside a city,

XP ground to a halt." She pinched my side. "Have you noticed how many cheap shots we take at each other when we're stuck in close quarters like this?"

I nodded.

"People need an outlet for that tension. Trust me, I know that need more than anyone."

Despite my best efforts, a smile crooked the corner of my mouth. "Isn't that the truth? You're the queen of avoidance."

"That's right. And when I can't go out adventuring it forces me to process."

"The horror. How do you deal with such torment?"

She yanked me into a branching hallway. As the rest of our crew headed to the exit, Izzy playfully dragged me to a dark corner. "Oh, I find ways to keep busy." Her clothes suddenly vanished, replaced by a lime-green push-up bra, garter belt, and stockings.

"Wow," was all I could say before she pressed her body and lips to mine. It suddenly hit me and I broke away. "So *that's* why we've been having so much sex lately." I chewed my lip. "We should have sieges more often." She kissed me again to shut me up. The moment was invigorating but lamentably short-lived.

"If you're gonna insist on locking lips," groused Chadwick from his cell, "at least do me the decency of shutting the hell up. And some popcorn would be nice."

Izzy's midnight-blue tunic immediately covered her sexy ensemble. I scowled and turned to the locked door. The weaselly gangster's face was pressed to the barred window set into his cell door.

"Oh great," I snarked, "a room with a view."

"And that's the best view you'll get!" snapped Izzy as she stomped away. I went to follow her.

"Look at you," spat the deposed gangster. "You think you're running this town, do you? You think you're safe out there, but Nooner's the real threat. Do you really think you can trust him?"

"I know," I sighed, "he's a Galatian. What's your excuse?" He scowled and I moved close to the bars. "The difference between you and Nooner is, when push came to shove, he worked to protect the town. You're nothing but a parasite." I abruptly turned away and continued down the hall.

"You're wrong about him," he called after me. "He'll turn on you first chance he gets!"

I stormed outside, foul mood dissipating as I hooked an arm around Izzy's waist. We giggled and exited the jail yard to the city streets. "We were bound to relocate anyway," I pointed out. "As much as I appreciate that green getup, I prefer a private zone where I can rip it off."

She put an extra sway in her hips to torment me. "My thoughts exactly, which is why I've been working up a surprise for you. I rented a room in the Pleasure Gardens. Just us, but plenty of, um, VR accompaniment."

My eyebrows stretched high. "Why have I been wasting so much time with Hadrian?" I scooped the pixie off the ground Gone With The Wind style and started to the city's affluent eastern quarter.

"Am I really so predictable?" I asked. "Brooding at every sign of trouble?"

"Just the big stuff," she said to soften the blow. "But it's who you are. You care too much."

I smiled and carried her boldly forward. "Such is the burden of leadership."

She rolled her eyes extra hard but I didn't let it pierce my armor.

The Pleasure Gardens was a lush property of thermal baths, libraries, and cozy spots. The idyllic greenery was a mental break from the no-nonsense stone architecture of the rest of the city. It was like a master Off button. The digital media rooms were the polar opposite: a cornucopia of brain-overloading experiences and pleasures.

Izzy grinned in my arms and leaned her head back. It was nice to be able to put our various concerns aside and relax like normal people for once.

Barracks Complete!

I unceremoniously dumped Izzy on the ground.

"Hey! I wasn't expecting you to carry me the whole way but more than ten seconds would've been nice."

"Sorry," I blurted, already focused on my party chat window.

Talon: *Kyle.*
Kyle: *Saw it, bro. Checking it out now.*
Talon: *On my way.*

We rushed back to Oldtown. Izzy grumbled outwardly but she was excited too. As we passed our faction buildings, Baz, our largest ogre, posed beside the rebuilt barracks and took a screenshot.

"Even mobs are taking selfies now," groaned Izzy.

A small crowd admired the building. While it wasn't an especially impressive or momentous event, the barracks were important for a multitude of pragmatic reasons. Additional respawn, troop training, and—

> **Dragonperch headquarters has reached level 3!**
> Congratulations, you have unlocked a base production of 10 Headquarters Resources per day.
>
> *Next Level Up: 17 Headquarters XP*

And there it was.

As we hurried past, Bandit playfully trotted up.

"All done with outside time?" I asked. "Let's go."

I climbed atop the mountain bongo's saddle, pulled Izzy behind me, and started to Dragonperch.

1590 Legacy of the Void

The mountain bongo galloped to Dragonperch, through the large door, and up the stone steps. Climbing steep rock was kind of her specialty so we made it to the war room in no time. I wasn't even out of breath. Izzy hopped off.

"Good girl," I praised, dismounting and scratching her ear.

Bandit farted.

"Ugh, we were *just* outside."

The bongo snorted and cantered up to the roof.

"She does that on purpose," said Kyle, laughing with Izzy by the flat-screen.

I waved the air in front of my nose and cleared out of ground zero to join them. "Gimme some good news."

"I was totally right," boasted Izzy.

"Come on, we just got here. Kyle—"

"She was totally right," he said.

I huffed. "Fine. Let me rephrase. Gimme some good news *that I care about.*"

The pixie's eyes narrowed. "You *do* care about your girlfriend being right. Especially after the way you dropped me."

Kyle opted to closely inspect the sanctum master panel. I wished I could similarly escape Izzy's glare. "Fair enough," I peeped.

Izzy warmed into a chuckle. Kyle sighed in relief and wasted no time wading into his story. "So, it was like Izzy's research uncovered. With the headquarters leveled up, we got our choice of socket to unlock, one of three separate advancement trees."

Izzy ecstatically cut in. "Fire, rock, and space!"

I pressed my lips together. "And... ?"

"Space," she repeated. "Don't you get it? Space is a void. It's a vacuum, which relates to the under realm."

My face scrunched up. "Does it though?"

"Don't push your luck. This is the one. I can feel it."

The brewmaster drew the void pearl from his inventory. The jewelry fitting had already been prepped; it was just waiting on a socket to call home. Our resident artisan made the necessary adjustments and snapped it into place.

"It fits!" announced Izzy, probably more excited to be proven right than for the new functionality.

"Hold your horses," said Kyle. "Let's see what the thing does first."

The socket display welled with black energy, drawing a pipeline through the vertical diagram of Dragonperch. The map pulled up and shifted to a top-down view. We were looking at Oldtown. Several black dots were highlighted on the screen under the heading "Teleport."

"Whoa," said Kyle.

"It's not completely surprising," explained Izzy. "The void pearl was a shadowguard drop. Those mobs had a mean special attack that teleported me halfway across the Midlands."

"Except this is only Oldtown," I said, sliding and zooming the map freely but being constrained to the rough geography of the local teleport points. "What are those things?"

We all squinted at the screen. It didn't make sense. According to the display, there were four teleport selections extremely close to each other within the tower. That... wasn't useful at all.

"It's moving!" alerted Kyle, a finger tracing the flat-screen.

Our eyes locked on the moving black dot, looping around our position. It circled, and circled, and circled...

"Hey everyone!" blared Trafford.

The three of us simultaneously jumped, our focus shifting from the master panel to the shopkeeper who had just entered the war room.

"What's with the jumpiness?" he asked. "You watching porn?"

"Porn for nerds," said Izzy.

"It's a new ability," I explained. "We're just trying to figure it out."

As Trafford approached and I pointed to the screen, I was confused to find the teleport markers jumbled together.

"Why is..." I jutted my lips out.

Izzy's eyes lit up. "It's us!"

"What's us?" asked Kyle.

"The black dots. They're us. Watch." Izzy took a few steps away and circled the oak war table. One of the markers in Dragonperch traced her movement.

"Those *are* us," I said. "Four dots, four of us in the tower. It must show party members. And the one black dot not in Dragonperch is Errol. Right..." I slid the map to the pirate's location.

"In the brothel," finished Kyle.

We all grinned.

Izzy's eyes narrowed. "Wait. Why's Errol's teleport marker moving back and forth so fast?"

"Nah," I said. "It's just a location. It can't possibly have that level of precision."

Errol's black dot jiggled slow, then fast, then slow again. Then it disengaged, ran to the other side of the room, and jiggled somewhere else.

We all blinked awkwardly. "Wow," murmured Kyle, "dude's keeping busy."

Trafford slapped his belly and laughed. "So you guys *are* watching porn!"

"Not for long," piped Kyle. "Izzy's gonna be my wingwoman soon!"

"Doubtful." The frost mage swiped the map back to Dragonperch. "Let's just... focus on the new ability and never mention that again."

"No promises!" cackled Trafford. He stepped to the table, pulled out his favorite padded chair, and plopped down. Apparently bored with the show, he opened that heavy tome of his. Besides operating a newbie welcome shop, being the Black Hat general and buildmaster, Trafford was also one of Haven's questkeepers. He regularly went through the books and posted new adventures for players.

"Whatever," Izzy snorted. "Are we gonna test this out or not?"

"Right," I said. "It looks like one of us can teleport to another party member. Is that the gist? But we're all in the same place."

"I could teleport you to Errol," offered Kyle.

"For science," I said with a cheeky grin. It evaporated under Izzy's glower. "Or one of you guys could walk somewhere non-brothel related and teleport me there."

"Better," declared Izzy, stomping to the stairs. "Let's give it a go."

She disappeared down the steps. When her dot settled into place, I gave Kyle the nod. He engaged the void pearl. I blinked, and I was surrounded by shelves of hardbound books.

I jerked in place. The transition wasn't painful but the suddenness was unsettling. I would've preferred a gentle fade or longer warning, but who was I to complain? I had blinked one floor below the war room into the Dragonperch library. I turned to see Izzy leaning against a table, wide eyed in horror.

"What happened to you?" she asked.

I checked my hands. My clothes and skin were all black, like shadow, and I was translucent.

"Okay, this is weird."

Kyle: *Whoa. Where are you, bro? Was it a success?*

I stared at Izzy.

> **Talon:** *I'm in the library with Izzy. But I'm not me. I'm like a shadow version or something.*
> **Kyle:** *Well, you sure disappeared on my end. It looks like I have the ability to recall you back to the war room.*

"Interesting," said Izzy, pushing off the table and approaching. "You're definitely you, but with limitations." She poked a finger into my chest. Her entire hand pushed through me like air.

"Wait a minute." I tried to clutch her waist, only I couldn't.

"Hmm," she mused. "It's like you're inhabiting the shadow world or something." Her eyes narrowed to mischievous slits. "And you can't touch me."

"I guess not."

Izzy opened the front of her tunic. "Ooh, it's so warm in here."

"Really? It feels okay to me."

"And libraries are such a turn-on."

My brow furrowed. "Libraries? I always thought they were too stuffy and dignified."

Izzy's pants disappeared in a flash. She rolled away from me and placed her hands on the table. Her body yawned forward, the bottom of her tunic slowly rising over her ass.

"Okay, I see what you're doing. Ha, ha. But this isn't a private zone so it's not like we can do anything anyway. We—"

Izzy rubbed her fingers against her loincloth and moaned. "But I want it so bad," she purred.

I swallowed. Logic be damned, Little Talon was never a scholarly thinker. I stepped forward, hands up but held back, trying to maintain the illusion that I was really there.

"Don't you just want to kiss me?" said Izzy.

I did. I really did. I dropped to my haunches and shook my head at the amazing view. Slowly, I leaned in.

And I was staring at Kyle's crotch.

"What the hell, bro?"

"What the hell, dude?" I sprang to a stand. Kyle and I were back in the war room. Trafford was dubiously watching us with his good eye.

Izzy's fit of laughter wafted up from one flight below.

I cleared my throat. "We were just... uh... testing things out." I glanced at my hands and massaged my face. "Apparently my shadow form can't make physical contact with stuff. And it's kind of itchy, come to think of it." I rubbed my arms. "I need some fresh air."

I hurried up a level to the roof. Bandit was stretched out in the sun and I suddenly understood why she loved it so much. It reinvigorated my skin. She bleated in greeting before closing her eyes again.

"Hey," called Izzy, rushing up the steps. "You okay? It was just a joke."

"It's not that. Just have a cold sweat or something."

"Sure you don't need a cold shower?" I didn't answer and she frowned. "Huh." She hugged an arm around me as we gazed from the highest vantage in Stronghold. "If you really were in the under realm, you might experience some negative effects."

I sighed. My stats were fine, I didn't show any debuffs, and I was already feeling better. I suspected this was just something I needed to get accustomed to. That was all.

"I'm okay," I asserted. "But that *was* a dirty trick down there."

She chuckled. "It was fair play. Remember, I wanted to go to the media rooms."

My eyes strayed to the distant Pleasure Gardens. Maybe Izzy was right. Maybe some time off to relieve this tension was past due. We could retire to the spa, get cleaned up, and hump like rabbits. She rubbed my chest and likely pondered the same thing. As we admired the green vista before us, a flaming piece of wreckage sailed through the air trailing smoke and crashed into a pool of Scented Ladies.

"What the—?!?"

We spun to the source of the projectile. Blaring horns from the west gate overtook our serene city. The tended land outside the walls was a rush of activity as goblins, ogres, and imps advanced.

City Alert:
The pagans are at the gates!
Stronghold is under threat. All residents may engage in combat. While within the walls, all watchmen and residents are immune to friendly fire.

"You've gotta be kidding me," I said with a wistful glance at the Pleasure Gardens.

> **Black Hat Alert:**
> The Pagans have broken the armistice!

Izzy and I traded hardened expressions.

"So much for kidding," she muttered.

"They're making a move," I said, "and I have a feeling this is just the beginning."

We drew our legendary weapons and answered the calling horns.

1600 Call to Arms

Galloping hooves came up behind us as we sprinted. Nap time was over and Bandit was as sharp as ever.

"Hold on."

I took Izzy's hand and reached my other towards the converging mount. The mountain bongo lowered her head and I grabbed a stout horn as she passed, swinging up and over her body. I was accustomed to the maneuver and stuck the landing perfectly. Izzy wasn't so graceful. She straddled Bandit on her stomach, legs on one side and head on the other. With me still holding her hand behind her back, she looked hogtied.

I laughed and spanked her ass. "Iz, I'm sorry our date in the Pleasure Gardens was ruined, but now's not really the time."

She grumbled and pulled a leg around to sit up. "You wish."

We weaved through collected legionnaires to the wall. Bandit lowered her head and trotted right into and up the watchtower's steps, extra-wide for the purpose of funneling a defending army. We emerged a hundred feet up. Commander Gladius greeted us decked out in his premium armor and golden helm, red body shield and flaming sword in hand. We dismounted.

"Talon, the horde is wheeling out trebuchets from the forest. They must've cleared an area behind the tree line to build them under cover."

I squinted across the tended land. The goblin army held their distance at an arrow's flight away. The dense newbie forest at their back didn't appear thinned out from our high vantage. The last goblin assault had utilized siege towers that would've been easier to spot, but these trebuchets had low clearance, remaining close to the ground while unsprung. I wondered how Dune had missed it, but with a dragon handy I blamed myself. It was an oversight not to scout the horde's rear.

One of the catapults swung its arm around and volleyed another flaming boulder into the sky. We ducked as it arced over us and landed just behind in the Circus. The crater shape of the low-walled arena served to contain the debris. The fiery wreckage tumbled around the stands like a roulette ball. Luckily, the venue was empty.

Damn, my dream was dying before my eyes. Even worse? Everybody was right. The pagan faction lacked central leadership and was too disjointed to conform to a lasting peace.

"They're not charging the wall," I noted, scanning for the next threat.

"That would be suicide with their numbers," pointed out Gladius.

"Still," said Izzy, "they're sure doubling down on shock and awe."

The commander nodded resolutely. "With days of preparation and unknown resources, we could be in for quite the pummeling. It'd be wise to cripple their artillery posthaste."

"You're right," I said. "Unable to enter the city, they're attempting to draw us out to them. But they made a mistake by indiscriminately bombarding Black Hat territory: our faction no longer has an armistice to respect."

A towering figure in lacquered white plate armor charged onto the battlements. Lash held a rectangular black body shield but kept her bench-sized cleaver strapped to her back. Her barbarian and healer were in tow.

"Finally," said the gruff woman, "we can stop sitting on our hands like schoolgirls."

"What's wrong with schoolgirls?" asked Kyle, wheezing to the top of the steps behind them.

I gritted my teeth. "You're gonna hate to hear this, Lash, but I need Bravo Team camping on Hadrian. This front is likely a diversion."

"Some diversion," muttered Gladius as another building went up in flames.

Lash sucked her teeth. "You serious? This is a clear violation of the sanctity of Stronghold and our seat of power. Let me take my gloves off."

"Your job is more important than bashing heads, Lash. You're not army, you're spec ops. This is the role you wanted. Besides, if I'm right we have more trouble on the way. You'll have your hands full soon enough, and I need someone in control of the home front."

She dipped her head sharply. "Roger that. We'll be on the Whisperer so tight he won't be able to pee his pants without my say so. What are you doing?"

"Isn't it obvious?"

Izzy hung her hands on her hips and sighed. "Oh great, he loves this part."

I grinned and clamped a hand on the mountain bongo's horn. The blue gemstone on her forehead glowed as I activated my legendary dragonrun ability. The already-large beast exploded to a massive size, transforming into a vicious dragon within the span of seconds. I hopped onto her back, she screeched loud and long, and we launched into the sky.

"I don't get it," blurted Christian as he absently stared at the video of the Phoenix X launch site exploding for the tenth time.

Tad leaned on his crutch behind the seated CEO. What they had witnessed wasn't a simple bid for the acquisition of Kablammy Games. This wasn't a corporate bully flexing market muscle. It was espionage and sabotage and... Where exactly was this leading?

Christian's lips trembled as he spoke. "*Money* is what drives the tech industry, not... not religious fervor."

Again, for all his good intentions, the CEO failed to understand the social ramifications of his technology. He wondered how anyone could be against his gift to the world.

Pete was now in attendance, having logged out of Haven to address the emergency. He stood there in his bicycle pants, scratching his red stubble and pondering the situation with a frown. "I've mentioned this possibility in the past," he reminded his friend. The statement was said plainly, without the hint of I-told-you-so one might expect under present circumstances. "There are those who might see these human advances as profane."

"Plebeians."

Pete sighed patiently. "Don't be cruel, Christian. Might I remind you of my personal thoughts about the afterlife?"

The tech titan shook his head. "I'm sorry, Pete, but you're a reasonable objector. Live and let live. To each his own. I can't believe someone would go to all this effort to protect a traditional Heaven."

Tad took in a sharp breath. "You might be right in this case."

The two men looked to him.

The young programmer threw up appeasing palms. "I'm not saying I have answers, but this explosion is most definitely a coordinated strike. Consider the unaddressed PM that delivered it. The placement of Larry as a mole in the building, and the later use of a Trojan to co-opt his persona. We're looking at a degree of sophistication I don't see coming from the religious zealot subset."

Christian Everett nodded. "That's what I'm saying. Follow the money."

Pete frowned. "Following Larry will be difficult. His employer swept him out of reach, thousands of miles away."

"If they didn't have him killed," groused Tad.

Christian almost chided him for the dramatic remark, but he could no longer discount that possibility.

Tad pulled his phone from his pocket. "Hrm, you don't get Wi-Fi in your office?"

Christian turned his head abruptly. "Of course I do."

"I'm not getting a signal. No bars either."

The two others produced their phones with similar results.

Pete picked up the hard line. "I can't dial out. I'll get Emilio in IT." The community manager left the office with a worrying hop in his step.

"Our cell signals are being jammed," said Tad.

"You don't know that."

"This is sophisticated..."

Christian huffed.

Tad leaned into his crutch. "Okay, let's back this up. InLink wipes all metadata from images and videos, after taking it for themselves of course. We can't trace the video or the message. But what about the motive? Why would anyone want to stall the Haven launch?"

The CEO pressed his lips together. "The launch of the simulation or the satellite?"

"Aren't they the same thing?"

Christian jumped to his feet. "Yes and no."

"Huh?"

"Okay, the official launch of Haven is a transition of sorts—private-facing to public—but for all intents and purposes things continue as before. Sure, Haven has the increased burden of huge zone unlocks and open player demand, but for the most part the afterlife is business as usual. But the satellite launch is a change to the operational structure. It's a turnover of sorts, from Haven as a private asset to something akin to a public utility. That's why Kablammy lobbied so hard for Universal Interstellar Rights."

Tad followed along out loud. "So you're saying once the satellites launch Haven into orbit, the assets will be in the public domain?"

"That's exactly what I'm saying. Practical reality still dictates the need for a corporate sponsor—a gateway for new player entry, asset updates, Everchat, and other interfaces—but the digital world and player consciousnesses are no longer part of the holdings."

Tad swallowed. "So this is about ownership."

"That's right," asserted Christian. "Follow the money."

1610 Gears of War

Powerful wings drove us toward the goblin horde like a bullet. A trebuchet arm swung around and fire launched skyward. Bandit dove sharply to avoid the projectile. I glanced backward and grimaced, but I didn't have time to track the boulder all the way to its target. We banked over the crowing army.

"Now, girl."

Bandit opened powerful jaws. A stream of light plowed into the field before us, dragging through ranks of soldiers like a laser until it brushed over a loaded trebuchet. Wood erupted into splinters. The burning projectile careened off the unbalanced structure and crushed the ogre about to fire it.

> Crown Unlocked: **Combustion Engine**
> Blow up an enemy siege engine.
> 1000 XP awarded

Bandit swallowed her strike as we rocketed to the next live catapult. The operators attempted to launch it in time but dragon breath was faster. It wasn't until both siege engines were disintegrated that the goblins began to understand the full might they were facing. As we swooped around for a second pass, the horde refocused their output from the city to us.

Reams of arrows loosed. I pulled my head in and hugged the saddle. Steel glanced off the dragon's armored belly, shielding me from harm. Bandit snarled aggressively.

"Ignore them," I prodded. "We're here to neutralize their range."

Instead of taking the bait, we demolished three more trebuchets. When the last of them was a smoking heap, I surveyed the battlefield.

Besides the back line of siege engines, I didn't note any particular organization. Trolls and ogres were spattered with their kobold handlers. Goblins made up the bulk of the army, with packs of wild imps bolstering their numbers. Armor was haphazard to nonexistent, but there was enough steel to equip every soldier with a blade.

We veered around as I searched for the head of the snake. General Azzyrk rode a giant purple lizard so he was usually easy to spot. Unfortunately, the horde was hiding their true numbers and resources within the forest.

I directed Bandit over the tree line. The canopy was dense, allowing only occasional windows into the troop makeup beneath. Further in were small sections of razed wood where the horde had reaped their supplies. But Azzyrk was strategic enough to take advantage of the resources he didn't need for cover, leaving enough room ahead for his army to hide in.

Combined with my previous knowledge of the pagans, what I saw in the open tended lands, and what I guessed to be in the forest, I put the enemy numbers at about three hundred, possibly more. We easily had twice as many combat-ready fighters in Stronghold, including the player population. The little gray imps were balanced by the more monstrous baddies, but we had strength, equipment, fortifications, and notable badasses on our side. Not to mention a dragon.

That said, even legendary creatures had their limits, and Bandit's dragon breath had reached it. Even if I pushed her, burning down the forest with blind strikes wouldn't do. We weren't in enough trouble for such self-destructive tactics.

I opened a chat window for the faction's brigade.

Talon: *What's the status in the city?*

One by one, my appointed leaders responded.

Lash: *Hadrian's quieter than usual.*
Trafford: *Oldtown's ready if they come in.*
Kyle: *Tower defenses are online.*
Izzy: *No trouble at the wall.*

I nodded to myself as I waited.

Talon: *Errol? Report.*

No answer.

> **Talon:** *Errol, do you copy?*
> **Talon:** *Can any pirates please give me a status update?*
> **Grom:** *Sure thing, boss. The brothel's all clear.*
> **Talon:** *Brothel?!?*
> **Grom:** *Aye, matey, but I'm currently inspecting everyone's lady parts to be sure. I can go into more detail if ye like. I ain't shy.*

I hissed.

> **Talon:** *Errol!*
> **Errol:** *Sorry, Talon. I was in the middle o' an update. ...An' then I just wanted to hear more 'bout Grom's status. Ye need any help, man?*
> **Grom:** *Now that you mention it...*
> **Talon:** *Focus, people!*
> **Errol:** *Sorry, me boys get carried away sometimes. Both river gates be secured an' well defended.*
> **Talon:** *Okay. Stay on top of the situation.*
> **Grom:** *That's the plan, sir!*

I scowled. Despite the usual hijinks, all was calm on the home front. The ravenous army below was still unsettling. I decided to take a chance to end this stalemate.

```
DEVELOPER CONSOLE
>> city watch_
```

My unique access gave me unprecedented power over the city's NPC army, and while they weren't meant for personal faction use, the current threat fell under their sole mission statement: the defense and sanctity of Stronghold. I opened the gates and sent out one hundred well-equipped legionnaires.

Tad Lonnerman avidly watched coffee drip into the large glass pot. It seemed like nobody made old-fashioned coffee instead of using the new machine with those prepackaged cups. Tad refused to touch the stuff. He really didn't mind the wait. Watching the black stuff slowly fill the pot was strangely cathartic. Especially, it turned out, after watching a launchpad explode.

A slightly chubby woman strolled into the office kitchen. "Now, now, Tad," she said in a melodic voice more grating than musical, "it's cleaner and less wasteful to make a cup at a time with the new machine."

"Cleaner for who? Not the environment, I imagine."

Abbie blinked large lashes. "Just because the spokeswoman says the cups aren't recyclable doesn't mean you can't throw them in the recycle bin all the same."

"That's not how it works."

Tad pulled the dirty filter as the brew finished and tossed it in the trash. A quick splash in the sink rinsed some stray liquid from his hands.

"Now, now, Tad, you know you're not supposed to dump coffee grounds down the sink."

Tad rolled his eyes and wondered what the opposite of cathartic was. "Is everything okay, Abbie?"

"Everything's peachy. I was looking for Christian. You know, the president of this company." She laughed at her own joke just long enough for it to register. "Have you seen him?"

"He said something about double-checking the alternate launch site for Phoenix Y. Maybe he left the building?"

Pete wandered into the kitchen with tensed lips. "Ah, Abbie, I've been trying to get ahold of you. Have you gotten my emails?"

Abbie shrugged with her entire body and raised her voice an octave. "I'm sorry, Pete. It's been a madhouse in here."

"Yes, well, our network's down. Have you seen Emilio anywhere?"

She pouted. "Come to think of it, he said he had a family emergency and had to leave early."

"But he's our only IT employee on the skeleton crew. We have a serious emergency that needs addressing."

"Well, Kablammy places a high priority on work-life balance. You know what we always say: Family comes first."

Pete frowned. "I don't think you've ever said that before in your life."

Her face went straight. "Stop being a drag, Pete." Abbie moved to the office fridge and grabbed a can of Diet Coke.

Pete's eyes fell on Tad. "It can't be helped, I suppose. I'll need to go to the first floor, go outside if necessary."

"We really can't reach anybody?" Tad asked.

"All communication outside the office is down, even the internet. After what happened, we need certain... assurances. Christian approved me to recruit an outside security team."

Abbie's eyes went wide. "Security? Are we in danger here?"

"No," assured Pete. "Nothing like that, but you can never be too safe."

A woman Tad didn't recognize peeked into the kitchen. "You ready to do this?"

Abbie jumped. "Excuse me!" she chimed. "How did you get in?"

Pete cleared his throat. "Abbie, you remember Steph. She used to work on the community team."

"Of course I remember," she said flatly. "She quit."

"Christian's been cooking up a special response to recent events." Voices from the hallway confirmed Steph had more people in tow.

Abbie was so frazzled she smacked her lips a couple of times. "Now, now, Pete, you can't just call whoever you want willy-nilly and invite them to the inner chamber."

"Don't worry, we're only using people I personally trust. I'm afraid they won't be able to help with our larger emergencies, but they can help us get a handle on Haven. I contacted them this morning as soon as the core guys noted suspicious network activity sourcing from Hadrian."

The head of HR huffed. "They'll be required to sign NDAs before they start."

"This is too important, Abbie. I need them in the game."

Tad leaned on his crutch sipping coffee as he silently watched Abbie check outside the kitchen.

"Oh dear, that's a lot of people."

"If you have objections," offered Pete, "please take them up with Christian. He approved this."

"You know," Tad added, "the president of this company." He fake laughed.

Abbie's eyes almost closed. "No, I'm sure it's all right. But I'll remember this when I'm planning the next Christmas party." She tried to storm out of the kitchen, but Pete stopped her.

"I promise, Abbie, it'll all work out. But I need a favor. I'll be bringing my team up to speed on their new permissions and I'm working on some patch edits. Can you go downstairs in my stead and contact the security team?" The community manager scrolled through his phone contacts and showed Abbie. "That's the number of the company."

She grabbed the phone and blinked. "I... I wouldn't know what to tell them."

"They've already been briefed on the basics. All you need to do is update them on the SoCal incident and ask them to come in ASAP. Tell them they're activated."

She blew out hot air. "Why can't Tad do it?"

They both turned to the programmer who smiled, still leaning against the counter with his hot beverage. He waved his crutch in the air.

"Ugh. Fine!" Abbie made a beeline for the elevators.

Pete, ever measured, flashed Tad a half smirk. "If you see Emilio, please get him up-to-date right away. Outside internet access is a priority. If anyone needs me, I'll be in Haven." The community manager led his team away.

Tad eyed the empty kitchen, with its too-white lights and improperly filled recycle bin and full quiet except for the buzzing of the refrigerator. He took a slow breath, a cathartic breath, and sipped a hot cup of joe.

Christian Everett had always known the truth about his company.

As he turned his private key and the doors to the service elevator closed, the car rose above the Kablammy studio penthouse. Because of the sabotage, what had before been routine, habitual maintenance was now a high-wire act. Was his life in danger?

The CEO had used foresight to get this far, an event years in the making and currently in the home stretch. He'd always known his company's assets would become a target, but he had no idea they'd be physically destroyed. Society was an unpredictable variable, but business was different. Business either held value or didn't. This was why Christian had always prepared for the eventuality of Haven being completely run from within.

The simulation would be cut off from the outside world. No unnecessary tech support with developers on the inside. Drone launches would handle uploads of new residents and patches. Interfaces would run extensive crypto to prevent viruses or exploits that hijacked the core mission: for Haven to continue unabated no matter what happened on Earth.

The elevator arrived at the top and Christian pulled the bronze key into his pocket. He advanced through a final stairway and unlocked a door that opened to sunlight. He wound around the outcropping on the roof to a small satellite dish with an external console. He scanned the payload module nestled between structural walls. Both units were unmolested.

Christian brought a pair of binoculars to his eyes and gazed off the edge of the roof toward the water. Phoenix X was down, but Phoenix Y was alive and kicking. Kablammy still retained launch capabilities. The CEO's secrecy was proving to be another valuable exercise of foresight.

Thousands of years from now, even if mankind had managed to completely annihilate itself, Haven would persist, either orbiting the planet or adrift in an asteroid field, where its servers running on a combination of solar and nuclear energy, would still house life.

That was the ultimate evolution of the world. That was Haven's true gift. And Christian Everett intended to be a part of that future, right after he uploaded his consciousness and committed suicide.

1620 Wing Commander

Arrows rained from the sky in clusters, sending ranks of goblins panicking. Those who haphazardly pressed forward were met with a unified row of spears. Goblin sergeants regrouped and ordered their archers to return fire, but the paltry barrages pittered harmlessly off organized shield walls.

The Stronghold legion was only at half strength, leaving another hundred to man the walls. That left them sorely outmatched, three to one. The training of Gladius and his men was proving all the difference.

Bandit swooped low and opportunistically raked at the horde. Dagger-sized claws toppled heads and rent flesh from bone. My dragonspear was put to similar use, but the kills we racked up weren't the primary objective. *We* were now the distraction, the flying beast of destruction keeping pagan eyes on the sky while the legionnaires steadfastly advanced.

I spotted a pair of trolls barreling through the shield wall. Well-timed arrows from the horde followed, cutting down soldiers. The trolls were large targets and not exempt from friendly fire, but their impressive regeneration restored them to full health. Centurions charged forward to stave off the gray giants. The lanky troll arms were faster than they looked. They battered the trained men away as if they were dolls.

I set my jaw and spurred Bandit forward. Flying low to the ground, an arrow managed to pierce the dragon's leathery wing. The girl snarled and lost altitude. Large paws crushed imps into the ground as she stumbled forward. Bandit planted her claws into a terrified ogre and launched back into the air.

We were practically untouchable, but the trolls were causing chaos on an otherwise favorable battlefield.

"See what you got," I said.

As we converged on the problem area, Bandit forced a beam of light from her throat. The shine rolled unevenly and blasted one of the trolls in the back. Her breath sputtered out before it could complete the kill. The troll pitched forward on the ground, half its shoulder missing.

Then its regeneration kicked in.

I growled. "I guess we're doing this the old-fashioned way."

Bandit slammed into the recovering beastie. I leapt off her back, dashed toward the other troll, and activated deadshot, powering past the troll's swinging arm and burying the dragonspear in the center of its chest.

Combo!
Savage!
You dealt 180 damage to [Troll]

Red-hot eyes under grimy orange hair locked on me, just inches away. I recoiled from rotting teeth but missed the punch that rocked me to the ground.

46 damage

I shook off the daze. Despite being level 10, trolls still packed a literal punch. I turned to find the monster bearing down on me, spear still embedded in its chest. Despite the lodged weapon, its health bar was already refilling. I spat blood on the floor and drew an assassin needle. The blade wasn't built for a fair fight, but I was mostly concerned with not being hit again. The +8 boost to agility assisted with that.

I ducked a wild swipe and dashed away from a ground pound. The reach of the beast was terrifying. During my acrobatics, I noticed Bandit having fun in the mosh pit. Her troll was down for the count, but by landing on the ground she'd invited every single nearby pagan to leap on her back. Instead of finding herself in trouble, she used the opportunity to walk back the enemies who'd broken through the legionnaire line.

So I was on my own for a little while. Fine by me.

I feinted to the left and rolled forward, under the troll's guard. My dagger punched into its gray belly, spilling rancid fluid. I reached for my spear but the monster twisted for a grapple, giving me no space to remove it. Rather than turn into troll jerky, I slipped between its legs, making sure to take my weapon with me this time. Another flash of the dagger opened the back of its knee.

The troll spun wildly, landing a glancing blow that shoved me away. I grunted in frustration and watched its health begin to refill. I didn't have any poisons or DoTs to counteract its magic.

As I pondered how to most efficiently clump my damage together, a flaming sword chopped the distracted troll's hand clean off. The beast roared and instinctively swiped its arm to counter, but the half-limb missed the commander of the city watch.

"Too dumb, too slow," muttered Gladius as he drove his sword into the troll's heart.

The centurion released his weapon and hopped back as the troll's working arm jabbed. Gladius braced behind his shield and shoved forward. The troll stumbled backward, stunned. It was still at half health, but the flames on the magical sword seared the flesh it contacted. The damage itself was inconsequential, but it kept the beast from regenerating.

The centurion's gold helmet swiveled my way. "You mind taking it from here? I'm not much of a boxer."

I grinned fiercely. "With pleasure."

With my combat skills recharged, I plowed forward and lodged the assassin needle through the troll's eye. It collapsed on its knees, still clinging to life. We ripped our weapons free from its chest and Gladius spun around and lopped its warty head off.

"I gotta get me one of those," I said in awe.

"Not for sale." Gladius immediately turned and regrouped his men.

The hole Bandit cleared could've fit a Vegas hotel pool. The shield wall quickly reformed and the legionnaire advance didn't miss a step.

I made my way over to Bandit, pulled an arrow from her wing and a dagger from her side, and scratched her chin as she panted like a good doggo. "Scars make you look tough," I joked.

She growled like a lion, the noise reverberating through the earth.

"Okay, okay, you already look tough." I scanned the battlefield between passing friendly soldiers. "What do you say? Bird's-eye-view?" As I climbed on the dragon's back, alarm horns sounded from the city. We burst into the air.

Talon: *What's the problem? Nobody broke through our line.*
Izzy: *We're fine on the wall. The horns are coming from the east gate. I'm on my way.*
Talon: *Ditto.*

I scowled as we rocketed out of the skirmish. It was faster to fly over the city, but I wanted a better handle on what was going on. I surveyed the open desert plains to the south and the fields to the north. The tended lands were clear. I played a hunch and steered Bandit northward.

As we rounded the wall, I scanned for flanking troops. The yellowing Mediterranean grass was unmarred. Given the current threat, even the noob dungeons were abandoned. The forested tree line beyond provided ample cover up to a point, but there was no way the goblins could've skirted the city after the woods ended.

Then again, the siege had gone on for days. There was nothing stopping any number of enemies from retreating and converging from whichever direction they liked.

We kicked lower to the ground and hurried to the eastern tended land. In the distance down the east road, a troop of a hundred bandits marched for the wall. Shorehome combatants, loyal to Hadrian. There were humans and goblins among them, but none belonged to the pagan faction. Which meant, technically, they could breach the city.

As we approached to scout the situation, we rounded the wall and had full sight of the second gate. A small mass of bandits on horseback drove straight along the road, far ahead of the rest of their army. There were no more than twenty of them, but they escorted a speeding double-wide wagon headed straight for the east gate. It was a monstrosity, with an armored shell and anti-cavalry prongs protecting its mass. With a metal extension stretching ahead, it looked like a cross between a tank and a battering ram.

"Damn it."

I tugged Bandit's reins and redirected her away from the distant army. We needed to stop the siege engine. As we raced to the bore on oversize wheels, I realized they were too fast. We wouldn't make it in time.

I growled again. The horde had kept us a step behind, but I wasn't gonna let a little distraction smash down our gates. I pushed Bandit to her limit and ordered, "Give 'em all you've got."

Her mighty jaws barely coughed up a spark.

I grimaced. Dragonrunning was still new to me. In the absence of explicit menus, mounts and pets were directed by voice commands. I trusted the bongo-turned-dragon with my life, but her capabilities weren't a simple Dragon Breath: 0/5 menu item. This battle was the most I'd pushed her so far, and I was learning a lot.

A few horsemen broke away and pointed long lances to defend the superbore. I pulled Bandit up, hoping to bypass them and take down the wagon. I cursed as I canceled the maneuver, flying past. The spikes protecting the superbore weren't anti-cavalry, they were anti-dragon. If Bandit attempted to smash the vehicle with a body blow, she would mostly succeed at impaling herself in several places.

Our speed necessitated a wide-angle turn away from the wall. By the time we regained a bead on the riders we were behind them, over the road, between the horsemen and their distant army. They were gonna make it to the gate.

```
DEVELOPER CONSOLE
>> city watch
>> archers_
```

Taking direct control of the guards at the gate probably wasn't necessary, but I wanted to ensure full coordination. Unfortunately, most of the archers were stationed on the west wall watching the horde. I reallocated some resources. They wouldn't arrive in time for the cavalry, though they'd come in handy against the bandit army. The few archers that were present harried the horsemen but were ineffective at slowing their forward progress.

As we sped along the road, several Rough Riders broke away from our target to cover their rear. The riders faced us in a line with lances ready. Attempting to go over them so closely to the bore was dangerous. I decided to go through.

The battering ram pounded the huge double doors of the east gate. Wood buckled and bounced within the reinforced frame. The metal arm of the superbore had expended its best strike with its maximum momentum. Maybe the gate had a chance. But then, by some mechanism hidden beneath the armored shell, the arm of the superbore pulled back and lurched forward, punching the gate again. As it wound up to speed, its movement became a blur, pounding repeatedly like a jackhammer.

I clenched my jaw, knuckles going white on the dragonspear. Bandit sped toward a waiting line of death.

"You're gonna have to trust me, girl."

She snorted like it was ridiculous to expect anything less.

We bore down on the Rough Riders, their trio of leadership sitting center: Colt, the cowboy; Chico, the highwayman; and that bitch dragoon in the center.

"Come on, you bastard," she howled. "I ain't scared of you!"

[Jackie] cast Jade Fire

Her lance lit up with green flames. We sped closer, seconds till impact, and my eyes narrowed.

I leapt forward and activated dash, shooting just ahead of the speeding chestnut dragon. As I hit the line of lances I triggered spinshield and became a whirling ball of armor. The lances spun off to the side as I bowled into them, breaking rank. The magical flame seared me on all sides, but the damage had been done. Their coordinated line was now a shambles of lances in disarray.

Jackie's eyes widened. "You interminable son of a—"

Razor-sharp teeth chomped her in half, right through her plate armor. Swiping claws took out her cohorts, Colt and Chico and others whose names weren't worth knowing. Horses tumbled and crushed me to the ground. I skidded out and kept bouncing.

Fall Damage!
11 damage
Fall Damage!
6 damage

Ignoring a healthy dose of road rash, I kicked to my feet and continued my momentum toward the superbore. Some of the cavalry headed me off so I postponed my chase as the battering ram worked on the wall.

Several armed horsemen flanked me, with others charging the dragon.

"That's one way to go," I muttered.

I had to respect their determination. Each one was willing to sacrifice themselves for precious seconds that might be the difference between success and failure. And buy that time they did. As confident as I was of our chances of victory, I couldn't easily skirt a vanguard of mounted fighters.

Their lances lowered to meet me. My stance widened, boots scraping the dirt.

Magical icicles impaled the horsemen from behind. Izzy stood atop the wall, raining down cold death. The cavalry spun on their horses and panicked.

The enemy distracted, I activated deadshot and uprooted a

rider from his horse. I took the reins and galloped ahead, leaving Bandit on mop-up duty.

My first priority was the superbore operators. I dispatched them from behind but one managed to take an axe to the rear wheel. The bore jerked, off balance, sending my horse into a tumble that pinned my leg to the ground. I scraped out from under the mount, cursing as I considered the hobbled siege engine. Without a wheel, the operator had ensured the bore would stay in place.

I rose to my feet to face the remaining Rough Riders. Izzy and the archers above had clean shots. When Bandit joined us, it was over. The last of them fell just as the siege engine whined to a stop. Without operators to constantly wind the mechanism, it no longer had juice. Their first strike was down and the bore was inactive.

I limped to the door. The metal arm had punched through half of the thick wood, right below the locking bar. If the pounding had kept up another minute, they would have—

A spark caught my eye. The metal arm wasn't just a battering ram. Something was wedged into its tip. Something that—

My eyes widened.

"It's a bomb!" I yelled. I braced my body against the wagon and tried to cart it away, but it was a no-go. The axle with the broken wheel was firmly lodged in the ground. "Bandit!"

The dragon shoved me aside with her muzzle and swiped at the lances protecting the vehicle's shell, snapping the wooden points away. She reared and barreled her shoulder into the superbore, lifting its wheels off the ground and shifting it a couple of feet. The metal arm was still in the wall, but the strike had dislodged it. Bandit's next blow shoved the superbore loose. Her limbs surged against the ground and the wagon drove sideways. Wheels snapped. The bore and the bomb tumbled. White-hot fire seared to life.

"Get outta there, Bandit!" I screamed. "Fire in the hole!"

1630 Watch Dogs

Lash flinched as the brickwork rumbled. The explosion was large enough to rattle the jail yard half a city away. It had come from the east wall, the source of the latest horns. What was going on out there?

The knight scowled. Either that frat boy Kyle had really outdone himself this time or this siege was better planned than she'd anticipated.

Lash waited for the relevant citywide notification reporting a breach of the wall. No news came. She hated being kept in the dark, but no news was good news. She was satisfied, at least, that the gate had held.

Meanwhile, the knight was doing her part. The jail yard was secure. Twice as many olive-green city-watch tunics populated the yard since housing their VIP. Lash completed her rounds and marched downstairs, zoning into the dungeon, the silence of the new area taking over.

Lash hissed at the tranquility. She wanted to be on the battle lines, though she acknowledged the wisdom of watching Hadrian. She didn't trust the smooth talker.

Glinda waited by the stairwell. A quick glance down the hall confirmed everything was business as usual. Conan was posted outside Hadrian's locked cell, pacing and flexing at no one in particular. She understood his restlessness. If only wiping the floor with the prisoner could be a permanent solution.

"No way that twerp gets past the big guy," said Glinda, displaying more bravado in her soft voice than usual.

That was odd. It's not that the healer wasn't brave—she'd proven invaluable in countless battles—but she didn't often boast so confidently. That was Lash's job. Then again, locked dungeon doors and muscly barbarians afforded a certain degree of surety.

"First sign of trouble," reminded Lash.

"You'll know about it," returned Glinda. "Don't forget there's an angel in there watching him."

The knight twisted rose-colored lips. "If we're being honest, that thing scares me most of all. Haven's so-called security measures have done more to jack this place up than help. Forget the angel. If something happens, I'm counting on you and Coco."

Lash's eyes trailed to one of the open cells in the hallway. It was pitch black within, but that hardly meant it was empty. Her thief could hide in shadows with the best of them.

Crux was their insurance policy, a bonus ally Hadrian would be unaware of if something went down. He was a pacifist and wouldn't directly fight, but sometimes a little distraction was all a girl needed.

The knight hefted her cleaver and headed back to the staircase, eager to listen for more city-rattling sounds of battle. As her armored foot clanked on the first step, two figures zoned into the dungeon ahead of her. They wore shining silver plate that put hers to shame.

"Clear the area!" they commanded in unison. Before Lash could respond, the troops aggressively advanced.

"So this is about ownership," asserted Christian.

They'd regrouped at his desk to meld minds. This time Christian had allowed the hobbled Tad to take the Aeron chair. The CEO stood behind him, hands on the back of the seat, summing up their present theory.

"Kablammy fails to launch, our debts catch up to us, we flounder, and someone swoops in to save the day."

Tad snorted. "More like save their bank account. At least this means the bad guys have to unmask themselves."

"Indeed, but it would be too late to save Haven. The cost of their 'help' would be the totality of our assets, if not buying the company outright." Christian capped off the statement with an unsettling grunt.

Tad couldn't begin to imagine scraping up a tech empire that started with a single man in a garage; it was even harder to conceive of losing it all. One thing was sure, a tech company interested in acquiring Haven would be the best equipped to carry out a sophisticated sabotage operation. "So if we're agreed that the religious dogma is misdirection, we need to keep looking at companies capable of this. Kablammy's competition or contractors we've worked with."

The CEO lightly pounded his fist on the chair's back. "The

Trojan is the key. If we find the entry point for the virus they uploaded, we can find them."

"It's a given that a mole infiltrated the building. Larry used Saint Loras to build Hadrian's power and sow discord in the beta. Could he have uploaded the virus before he was fired?"

"I've considered that," said Christian. "While anything's possible, there's no evidence the Trojan was in the system before Larry was fired."

"And no contractors have been in the building since then?"

"No, not—" Christian paused as his brain allocated processing power to the alarming thought. "Some contractors participated remotely through InLink."

Tad spun back to the monitor and opened the digital collaboration portal. "This is what I've been looking at. Which companies?" Tad brought up a text file on the second monitor. It listed potential bad actors with priority based on knowledge, access, and what they stood to gain.

Abbie rushed into the office, breathing heavily. Tad and Christian focused on her, important news apparent in her face. "Sorry," she huffed, "I had to leave the building and walk a bit to get coverage. A tower must be down because the whole block is out."

Tad remembered the favor Pete had asked of her. "Did you get in touch with the security people?"

"I did." Her hands hung limp on her hips. "They transferred me to someone named Tony?" She eyed the two men for confirmation.

"I don't know him," said the CEO. "Pete handled that end. He's currently occupied in the Bosom ramping up the

Defenders."

"I've been meaning to ask you about them," she chided.

Tad cleared his throat. "Guys, what's the word on our security team?"

Abbie waved her hand. "Sorry about that, force of habit. You know me." She giggled. "They're sending a team as soon as possible, but said it would take at least thirty minutes to coordinate. He didn't mention if that included transit time or not."

The three of them blinked emptily at each other.

"Well," started Christian, "that's not *too* bad. We can wait out half an hour by ourselves, right?"

Abbie rested a nervous hand on top of Christian's. The back of the Aeron chair was right next to Tad's head, and he swore he detected a peculiar energy between them.

The HR director noticed his inquisitive stare and quickly pulled her hand away. "Maybe we should consider relocating," she suggested. "The building is experiencing problems, we're understaffed... we need a breather. Why don't we all grab lunch at that upscale oyster place in your building? You always tell me how easy the walk is."

Tad scrunched his brow. "I thought you lived in Mount Baker? The house is famous."

Abbie tensed.

"You know," the programmer continued, making air quotes. "The Titan of the Mount."

Christian's face went grave at the mention of his old nickname. The CEO wandered to a door in his office's side wall. "I... need to run some logistics on the servers. I'll be a minute."

He disappeared inside and shut the door.

"Nice going," muttered Abbie.

Tad blinked. "What did I say?"

"Nobody calls him that anymore, and we certainly don't talk about the house in Mount Baker. That old house was his family home, a reminder of happier times. He lives in a loft now with hardly any pictures or reminders of his wife and kids. All that stuff stays at the old house, exactly as it was years ago."

"Wait, you're saying he keeps the old place like some kind of shrine to his past life?"

She shrugged. "He's an eccentric billionaire who's rich enough for the concession. Cut him some slack."

Tad wordlessly studied the closed door of the server room.

"That's it," Abbie sighed. "I told myself I wouldn't, but I need another Diet Coke." With renewed breath, she hurried from the office and left him to his thoughts.

1640 Undying

I blinked. It hurt to blink. The skin of my face was raw and there was too much light everywhere. Why was there dirt in my mouth?

I shook awake as it came to me. The Rough Riders. The superbore.

...The explosion.

A large reptilian face nuzzled my shoulder. Even without seeing clearly, I knew it was Bandit. I recognized that smell anywhere. I sat up and rubbed her neck. The girl was bleeding. I was too.

I pulled two health flasks from my inventory and spread the love. The daze instantly evaporated and I became the spitting image of vigor.

I couldn't say the same for the Rough Riders. Their bodies littered the tended land, many of them in crumpled pieces. The superbore, having been successfully dislodged from the gate, had exploded against Stronghold's stone wall. The blast radiated outward, sending bodies and debris down the eastern road. A large crater was torn in the ground, but the stone was too thick to crumble. The wall had absorbed and redirected the force away from the gate. The wooden doors had held.

The bandit army, however, still loomed at a healthy distance. A hundred of mixed company, humans and goblins. They were hardly a worry. Without additional siege weapons they couldn't breach the gate. Without horses to hasten their advance, Izzy and the reinforcing contingent of archers would mow them down before they scaled the wall. The hesitance on the horizon was apparent.

As for me? I was more determined than ever. This sideshow had to stop. I climbed up Bandit's shoulder and took to the saddle. She stomped forward and lifted off the ground. We flew straight over the city this time, back toward the horde.

The dev menu provided a rough status of how the legion was doing. Still outnumbered, of course, but they had cut the ratio below three-to-one. That was steady progress, and worth the minimal losses to our side.

We swooped over the west gate and scoured the battlefield. The visceral action below told a slightly different story than the numbers alone. Goblins and imps were spilling from the forest, revealing more than I had estimated. Credit where it was due: the pagan army was fighting hard. They substituted organization with grit. This was all-or-nothing for them.

I was forced to consider tactics in a new light. Over two hundred pagans here and a hundred bandits to the east—that was overwhelming for the eighty remaining legionnaires without support. I could send out the other hundred soldiers, of course, or rally the player population, but I didn't want to risk the resources and didn't have the time.

There was another way.

I'd already seen how the horde reacted when the head of the snake was severed. It was their titan last time, Orik, but now I would make do with Azzyrk. Kill him and the rest was a formality. I opened the dev menu and recalled the legion back to the city.

The soldiers methodically broke away, relying on their shield walls and backing toward the gate. Bandit dove and raked the line to stall pursuit. A swooping dragon could accomplish just about anything, but it took several passes to ward off the entire front line of the horde. Each time we rose back into the sky and readied another pass, I scanned the rear of the army. Finally, I spied the general mounted atop his purple lizard.

> **Lash:** *We've got company in the dungeon, Talon.*
> **Talon:** *Hold them off.*

We rocketed over the invaders toward their leader. General Azzyrk locked eyes with me. He had a fierce countenance, stern features that commanded authority, a curled nose, earlobes that ended in points, and bone piercings in his cheeks. Red war paint striped his eyes and chest. That kind of presentation might be a hit with the errant folk, but it would do little against dragon teeth. Bandit's wings beat furiously closer.

> **Lash:** *This group is trouble, boss. I can't tell if they're players or NPCs, but they're powerful.*

> **Talon:** *Who are they?*
> **Lash:** *They won't say. They want to take Hadrian.*

I bit down. Bandit was seconds away from Azzyrk. The general grinned sardonically and retreated into tree cover. The action wasn't panicked, it was casual. Planned, even.

> **Lash:** *Boss?*

We sped low, just over the ground. Azzyrk was using the forest for protection. Without dragon breath, we'd need to land to engage him. A quick study of the surroundings revealed glints of metal in the trees. The general was laying a trap.

Trap or not, I welcomed the challenge. The conditions weren't ideal, but it wouldn't be the first time I powered through to victory. This was our chance to finally teach Azzyrk a lesson. This was my moment...

Any other moment.

I gritted my teeth and broke off the attack vector. Bandit pulled up over the forest canopy and we veered back toward Stronghold. The west gate was open, the legion safely returning. The horde below spat and cawed.

It pained me to back away from a fight, but the city was my priority.

> **Talon:** *Hold your ground, Bravo Team. Alpha Team is en route.*

Christian returned to Tad's side sooner than expected. Perhaps Abbie had overreacted. Still, he was suddenly uncomfortable in the CEO's presence and desperately wanted to move onto a new subject.

"So what's the deal with this so-called security team we contacted?"

Christian kept his eyes on the monitor. "We haven't worked with them before but they're reputable and capable. All my billionaire friends recommend them."

Tad stifled a chuckle. "I mean, do you think they're really necessary?"

"I don't know. The idea was theoretical two days ago. Now they can't be here soon enough."

"But they're gonna have guns, right?"

"Better safe than sorry," said Christian. "It's the same reason I'm enforcing a skeleton crew. The core team, systems programmers, IT."

"Don't forget Abbie," Tad said with distaste. "What would we ever do without HR?"

"That's unkind," chided the CEO with a frown. "I've known her since our university days."

Tad immediately felt bad for the dumb joke. His face reddened at a new possibility. "Don't tell me you two were college sweethearts or something."

He laughed lightly. "Nothing like that, Tad. And I understand the HR jokes, but Abbie has done a lot for Kablammy. It's not easy to wrangle a conglomerate into one of the highest-rated work-life balances in the industry. She's published two white papers on the subject. She's either worked with or is being recruited by Facebook, Instaface, Facespace, InLink, Linkagram, and Instabook. Abbie is, quite frankly, a hot commodity."

Before Tad could apologize, the HR director returned with her ambrosia of the gods in a can. Thankfully, Christian was good-humored about the subject. "Plus," he added loudly with a wink, "if I didn't have HR onsite, Kablammy could be sued for having a hostile workplace environment."

Abbie chuckled and splayed her arms up. "Job security," she chimed. "Why, am I in trouble?"

Christian shook his head. "Certainly not. You've got a great head on your shoulders, just not when it comes to computers."

"No way! I'm a techie. Look at these cool thumb drives I just bought." She pulled a USB drive from her pocket that was shaped like a brown poop emoji.

Christian wasn't having it. "Abbie, you call tech support every time you're prompted for a password."

Tad laughed along with them, happy that Christian's mood was beginning to lighten.

Abbie dramatically rolled her eyes. "I'm not that bad, you guys. Besides, that's what IT's for." Her tone soured. "When Emilio's around, anyway."

Tad leaned back in his chair and scratched the top of his leg just under the cast. "I've hung out with Emilio a few times. It doesn't seem like him to disappear."

"I agree," said Abbie, "but an emergency's an emergency." Her eyes went wide. "Ooh! What if the emergency was something to do with the satellite?"

"Don't get carried away," tempered Christian. "I trust my skeleton crew."

Abbie sucked her teeth. "Even that new team Peter's bringing in the game?"

Christian smiled and pushed away from the back of Tad's chair. "I'm sorry for leaving you out of the loop, Abbie. There are extenuating circumstances. The Defenders have all worked with Pete before in some capacity. He vouches for them."

Tad frowned. "But Larry was on his team too." He suddenly thought of the list he'd been compiling. He went back over Kablammy's InLink connections. "Wait a minute, wasn't Saint Loras driven by that outside contractor from time to time? Where's that focus testing company?" Tad rapped his finger near the top of his collected suspects. "Boost Systems."

"Don't jump to conclusions," cautioned the CEO. "Larry, the human, was the problem. After he was fired, Loras was a manifestation of the Trojan. There's no reason to suspect Boost Systems just because they interacted with the avatar. Besides, Pete's good friends with the team. He thinks very highly of focus testing."

Abbie set down her soda can. "I *knew* something was bugging me about her. Steph's a Boost employee now."

"We need to talk to Pete," said Tad, pushing to his feet with a grimace. Walking with a crutch wasn't so bad, once you got used to it, but standing after a long sit was the worst.

Christian swallowed uncomfortably. "It... it might be worth mentioning to him, but he's in Haven, interrogating Hadrian with the Defenders."

"And what if the Defenders are the problem?" posed Tad.

"I'm sure it's nothing. He vouched for them."

Tad reached for his phone. "I'll Everchat him then. Just to put it out there."

Christian thankfully didn't object. But the gears of his mind were already two steps ahead. "You do make a good point, Abbie. We've relied on personal connections, but we haven't properly vetted our employees based on work history. There could be something there." With the Aeron chair free, the CEO took over and opened the employee database. The skeleton crew was flagged, as well as a list of contractors that included the Defenders.

Tad waited impatiently as the Everchat app stalled on a spinning icon. Duh, the network was down. The handshake failure prevented him from entering his profile and contact list. He could use Christian's workstation to call, but his boss was already plugging away at it. Abbie was at his side, chiming in with helpful strategies.

Then he wondered if Pete was the one he should contact. Wasn't Talon more likely to hear out his concerns? He also seemed to know the community manager better.

The plan was set then. Tad was already standing; he might as well go for a walk. He cleared his throat. "The mobile app isn't loading and my player ID is on my PC. I'll call from there. I could use the stretch."

He was grateful they were too caught up to answer. Tad Lonnerman jerked from crutch to foot, blood tingling through his stiff leg.

1650 Shining Force

Lash held the cleaver with two hands as she backed away, making sure to keep her healer behind. The two shock troops in silver advanced cautiously, electrically powered hammers in hand.

"Who are you guys?" she growled once more.

"Clear the area," directed a deep voice. "No players allowed."

"I will *not* clear the area. Identify yourselves!"

Despite her jawing, she could feel the power dribbling off these knights. There were no identifiers above their heads, no level information, but they definitely weren't normal mobs either.

Lash had faced titans. A two-hundred foot cyclops, a fearsome kraken. She'd butted heads with Bishop Tannen, and wasn't always on the right side of the fight with Talon. In none of those cases did Lash feel as overmatched as she did with these two simple troopers. Something was off here.

The two strangers moved intentionally, prepared to strike but not rushing into hasty moves, not making the mistake of underestimating their foes. That meant they were powerful *and* smart.

The man with the deep voice said, "They're gonna be

trouble." He swiped at an invisible menu.

"Step aside," ordered the other guard. "We're here to secure the prisoner." Like Lash, this was a woman in a man's world, clad in full plate and a helmet that obscured her gender. Like Lash, she was probably tougher than the men she'd faced.

The white knight took a measured breath. "The prisoner's already secure."

The woman's helmet cocked as she measured the hallway. "I can see that. We'll take over from here."

"I can't allow you to move Hadrian anywhere. I won't."

"You're a liability." The man stomped forward. "We're here to help."

Lash continued to back away, keeping Glinda behind her, moving past the supposedly empty cell. She fought the urge to signal the thief with a knowing glare. Crux was a little green, not quite as in step with the rest of the group, but he was still Bravo Team, dammit.

Not one for words, Conan dragged his double-bladed greataxe along the ground as he passed Glinda and took up position beside his party leader. Lash noted the confidence that never fled his face. It disappointed her. Conan was brave and boastful and a loyal fighter all in one, but he was either incapable of seeing or refusing to admit he was outmatched.

Lash returned her helmet to her inventory, revealing her face to the intruders. She turned to the woman, a silent appeal to return the gesture of goodwill.

It didn't happen.

"It sounds like we're on the same team," assuaged the white knight. "Just tell me who you guys work for. We could watch the prisoner together."

"That's not happening," snapped the man. "We can't trust you."

Lash's face twisted in scorn. "And we can't trust you."

"Inconsequential." Two more figures zoned down the stairs and into the hallway. More silver knights with electric hammers.

Even Conan flinched this time. Still, he brandished a proud smile. "Let's take them now before there's ten of them," he urged.

The logic wasn't flawed.

"This is your last chance," urged the woman, calmly but with weight. "Black Hats don't have jurisdiction over the city jail. You need to clear out. Now."

Lash pressed her lips together. She turned to Conan, then Glinda, and took a heavy breath. Her cleaver slacked in her glove, lowering from its defensive stance. The blade flipped upside down, a seeming gesture of peace, and planted into the stone floor.

[Lash] cast Shield Wall

"You're gonna need to make me."

The four troopers stood resolutely for a moment before the woman raised a hammer. The other three followed suit. Lash watched with dismay as another figure zoned down the dungeon steps.

"No, no, no," chided Saint Peter. The man in cream robes hurried to pull the silver knights back. "You are *not* here to engage with residents."

Lash snickered and stood straighter, the yellow field of magic still buzzing between the two sides.

"You said under any circumstances," replied the trooper with the deep voice.

Peter sighed and approached the man who still held his hammer at the ready. The saint did a double-take into the empty cell at his back. Peter tugged the knight's shoulder. "You're about to be backstabbed, Ronald."

Ronald spun his hammer to the cell. "What? I'll—"

"Don't make me sorry I brought you along. Please back away from the cell."

Ronald swallowed a reply and stepped away.

Saint Peter cleared his throat and faced the dark cell. "Please come out—"

"Peter," blurted out Lash, not wanting her trap announced for Hadrian to hear. "You mind filling us in on what's going on?"

The saint traded glances between her and the cell before flashing recognition. "Yes, well, this is all meant to be helpful, but I'm afraid urgency and necessity have rushed us through proper introductions. Meet my Defenders."

The two troopers in the back suddenly spun to the steps as yet another visitor entered. "VIP! VIP!" They lowered their hammers and stepped aside.

Peter cleared his throat. "Please post upstairs," he said to the two in the rear. They zoned out. "Ronald, Steph, remain posted in the hallway." The silver knights nodded and took positions as the newcomer strolled past. "Fancy seeing you here," said Peter, stepping aside himself.

Lash swallowed, studying the new makeup of the hallway

guard and the recent arrival. She nodded and fell in line with the saint to allow the visitor to pass.

Hadrian smirked in the darkness.

The fools were pittering outside his cell, wondering what to do with him. They thought the blackness that surrounded him was blinding but, even without vision, he could see more than most. The spikes in the sim, he could sense them. They were part of him now. Or rather, Hadrian was part of the simulation. It wasn't a full merging—he didn't wish to lose himself, after all —but thanks to deconstructing the rogue Trojan created by his employer, his digital consciousness extended deeper hooks into game systems every day, like roots finding their way through fertile clay.

The fall of the kraken was a clear blow to his power. Now he had to sit silent while that fool gallivanted around town with the dragonspear.

Control. Hadrian forced air deep into his lungs. Anger was a crutch. A fallback to ignore blame, an easy way to lose your head. Fear wasn't the mind-killer, anger was. Rampant and unchecked, men became nothing more than spitting apes. Hadrian wouldn't resort to such weakness.

The Whisperer closed his eyes and sensed outward. He couldn't see the goblins or raiders at the gates, but he had a general sense of their status. Slow, outskilled, outmatched—yet serving their purpose.

The city was in a flurry, Lash and her cronies frustrated by inaction. But there was strange saintly activity, first in the Pantheon and spreading to the dungeon. Hadrian couldn't ascertain what these particular traffic spikes signified. Nor had he been able to decode the security protocols of the angel breathing over him.

Hadrian chanced a peek at the blindfolded guardian with waiting swords. Decimus was the greatest threat to his freedom and his life. He had to keep working on the angel. That was why Hadrian had attracted him here. He'd allowed Haven's last angel just enough of a glimpse of hackery to activate and inspect, but not enough to claim justice. Now, in close quarters, Hadrian tested the angel's barriers.

A full morning had gained him absolutely nothing.

The noises in the hallway rose to the verge of combat. Hadrian chuckled. The fools would kill themselves long before they ever unified against him. But the strange signatures still concerned him. It was Peter's entrance that gave him some answers.

But then the Whisperer's little dungeon abode welcomed another visitor. Someone strange and tainted. Hadrian hadn't had his hooks into the system long enough to be familiar with what he was seeing. He didn't know who this person was.

One by one, the contingent in the hallway stepped aside as the visitor made their way to his door. The heavy bolt clicked, the crossbar was removed, and the door to the cell opened wide.

Hadrian squinted against the pale light glittering off Lucifer's robe.

1660 Dungeon Defenders

Outstretched wings caught the up-current over the Forum. Four silver knights stood guard on the portico steps. If Lash hadn't apprised me of the situation, I'd probably be fighting for control of the position. For now, we flew right on by. The Defenders were an interesting development, but the sudden reappearance of Lucifer was at the forefront of my thoughts.

Bandit descended over the slums and landed in the large jail yard against the city's north wall. I frowned at the sight of two more silver knights posted by the jailhouse door, helmets swiveled my way. That kind of attention was understandable considering my ride. I patted Bandit's neck, knowing her dragon form wouldn't last much longer.

"Keep watch, will you?"

I strode towards the menacing figures, intent on getting to the bottom of the situation. The troopers didn't raise their hammers, but they held them at the ready and puffed out their chests. I snickered and tightened my grip on the dragonspear, my stride toward them never wavering.

"Talon," called Saint Peter from the side of the yard. "I've been waiting for you."

I paused and eyed the knights. The saint was taking them off the hook. "How very diplomatic of you, Peter."

"You know me." His brow furrowed. "You shouldn't be engaging the army. We have more pressing matters."

"I'm here, aren't I?" I marched over to him. "Who are these keyboard warriors?"

"These are my Defenders, Talon. Team members I trust in real life."

"Well, you should teach them some manners. Bravo Team almost wiped the floor with them."

Peter snorted under his breath. "I assure you, Talon, nothing is further from the truth."

I answered with a scowl. Lash's warning had been on point. These Defenders oozed strength. What exactly had Peter cooked up? "I thought we agreed more developers aren't the solution. We just finished cutting out all the other saints—"

"Larry won't happen again," asserted Peter. "The Defenders are reliable. We need human beings to ensure their personas don't get hijacked. My team of upgraded saints have unassailable reputations. They're unbeatable."

"If I had a nickel for every time I've heard that..." I recalled the dragonspear to my inventory and scratched my neck in awkward silence. "Listen, just 'cause they're with you doesn't mean I trust them. The Black Hats can handle Hadrian and other gameside concerns."

"We have every faith in you," the saint said patiently. "Consider the Defenders additional support. Despite the initial... *confusion*... they won't be a problem."

"Damn, I should've said the nickel thing now. Can I say it twice? That'd be even more nickels."

Saint Peter sighed. Even though he was a digital construct, he looked tired. It was something in his eyes. "I believe we're friends, Talon. Is that right?"

I suddenly felt like an asshole and dropped the tough-guy act. "Of course, Peter. I don't know your team, but you're solid. All the way."

He managed a slight smile and nod of thanks. "That's good to hear, because I believe in you as well. And, frankly, this was a long time coming." He paced the yard and spoke. "Beta tests are about learning and adapting. This trial period ends in three days, and we're resolved concerning our solution." He stroked his beard as he formulated exactly what to say. "If you love someone, set them free. Christian Everett understands the mantra well. Haven is his baby, yet he realizes the need to release it to the wild."

"You've mentioned the satellites before."

He nodded. "Yes, but there's more." He cleared his throat. "Our oversight of Haven has been far from stellar. Our attempts to patch and control have been met with greater chaos. Granted, we can't assume all the blame. We've been attacked from within and without. We're now facing sabotage. Our circumstances are dire. But throughout it all, one constant that has always worked to correct our mistakes has been you, Talon."

"Not just me. The whole player community. NPCs and select mobs too."

He smiled softly. "Some have been more instrumental than others. This was Lucy's stated purpose the entire time, yet we were blind to it until you opened our eyes. She tried to warn us but it took you." Peter stopped in the center of the yard and turned to me. "I've been working on something, Talon. Something to unite Haven under your banner. There are a lot of moving parts. Heavy recruitment, freeing the titans—out with the old, in with the new."

My eyes widened. "What exactly are you talking about, Peter?"

"The soulstones," he said firmly. "They're simply too powerful, too susceptible to player exploitation. It's best to rid the world of their influence completely."

I opened my mouth to reply, froze, then pulled my head back. That, actually, didn't sound too bad an idea. "You can do that?"

The saint placed his hand on my shoulder. "*You* can, Talon. You will. I was hoping to wrap this up before now, but that worm has turned. We'll need to rely on you to do it after Haven launches. Trust me, as Kyle would say, it'll be fepic."

"Just rolls off the tongue," I said with a smile.

This was crazy. It all sounded fairly mundane in regular conversation, but if Peter meant what he was saying, Kablammy was about to concede Haven to the players. The agency to live and die by our own choosing, to forge our own paths through the world—that was freedom, digital or otherwise. Fepic, indeed.

"I was wrong about you," he said after some thought. "I thought you'd follow the assassin's path for sure, but instead you chose to be"—his eyes went to the tower in the distance and the shining statue of Magnus Dragonrider—"a hero."

Peter waved me toward the jailhouse and we entered without a word from the Defenders. I didn't know what to say as we strolled down the halls, but I felt compelled to speak. At the end of the day, Saint Peter was doing the right thing.

"You know, Peter, if Haven had wisdom scores, you'd be a natural 18."

He pressed his lips together. "Your agility is 24, Talon."

"I mean at level 1. It's just an expression." I chuckled. "You know, you taught me that the day I met you, in the white room. It was during my intake interview. You said Haven doesn't represent intelligence and wisdom with scores because that's prepackaged in the brain. If you're dumb enough to wipe your ass with poison ivy, a high number score won't help you."

Saint Peter snorted. "I believe I was more eloquent than that. I said grab a poisoned rose with an ungloved hand."

Never one to overdo a sappy sentiment, I shrugged and said, "I like my way better." I hopped down the steps into the dungeon.

1670 InFAMOUS

I marched down the hallway with Saint Peter, nodding at Lash and Conan and Glinda as I passed. Crux wasn't around, but I wondered how much help a pacifist thief could be anyway.

Ahead, the door to Hadrian's cell was wide open. A figure in a black cloak hastily backed out of the room. Decimus spun to the doorway and raised a silver sword.

"Lucifer, you are in violation of the terms of service. You will be expunged from Haven."

Saint Peter's eyes widened. He waved a hand and Decimus lowered his blade and backed away, returning to his vigil of the prisoner. Lucifer gave the saint a slight bow before we entered the cell. Somehow, despite the deep shadow, the silver runes on his cloak sparkled.

Hadrian sniggered. "You're gonna get yourself deleted one day."

"I'll manage," returned Lucifer. His voice was collected and cool, at home in a place like this. That was probably due to spending much of his life as an outcast.

As much as I wanted to take charge of the situation, I deferred to Lucifer, like everyone else. Here was a player who'd sacrificed nearly everything—his soulstone, his gang of Fallen, his dragon. He'd willfully entered enemy territory and risked deletion to assist the cause.

"I'm surprised you returned to the core city," muttered Hadrian, still cocksure. "Seems to be against everything you stand for."

"I'm here for what I stand *against*." Lucifer cocked his head, shadowed eyes studying the Whisperer intently. "Isn't that, after all, what defines a devil?"

"You read the bible too much."

Lucifer dug into a pouch at his waist and produced a black book with tattered pages of gold-leaf. Whatever text labeled the cover had long worn away, but the book's identification remained as iconic as ever. "Guilty as charged."

Hadrian snorted. "Seriously? That was supposed to be a joke."

The devil shrugged as he pocketed the keepsake. "History is full of jokes, and history is full of lessons. Many are one in the same."

"We're making new history here."

"All the more reason to learn from our forebears. Whether the lesson is historical, anecdotal, or apocryphal, the wisdom remains pure."

I considered telling my poison-ivy-wisdom-score joke, but decided against it.

Lucifer welcomed me with a hand on my shoulder. "How's the sanctity of the wall?"

"The goblin and bandit armies have been neutered," I said. "Some of the soldiers fight on, but they're no longer a threat to the city."

He smiled, removed his hand, and stepped to Peter. His body language was more distant with the saint. "And the corporate headquarters?"

Peter's beard pressed out as he pouted.

Hadrian snickered. "Not doing so well on the home front?" he taunted.

"A launch site was hit," admitted the saint.

"Hit?" I said. "What do you mean hit?"

"We're taking precautions."

I narrowed my eyes at Hadrian. "And you already knew about that, didn't you?"

As talkative as the prisoner was with Lucifer, he refused to look at or engage with me. I wasn't sure if it signified lack of respect or resentment for capturing him.

"He knew it," asserted Lucifer. "This was a strike at their end goal, the full acquisition of Haven." Lucifer rapped his witchwood staff on the floor. "Are the satellites compromised?"

"Not all of them," answered Peter.

The prisoner ground his teeth as Lucifer considered him. "Capitalism, my dear Whisperer, is a fine driver of economy. As an arbiter of people, the system begins to crumble. When you make the almighty a dollar sign, how then do you gauge individual worth? What happens when that measure comes up woefully short?"

"Parables," he spat.

"On the contrary, this is the very predicament you find yourself in today. What value, do you suppose, your masters assign to you now, captured and in chains?"

Hadrian pulled his wrists against the bonds. "They need me."

The devil's light laugh filled the chamber. "You're a write-off, dear Hadrian. Worse than that, a liability. You are worth more to them dead than alive."

He grimaced. "Only if I talk."

A smile splayed across Lucifer's face. "Ah, talk. Stories. Parables suddenly merit a dollar value. This, then, creates worth —in *you*, for *us*. It's the only thing you have left to sell. Tell us who you work for."

"I don't work for anybody."

"A pawn, then?"

"Never!" he snapped. "I'm in control. I did this."

Lucifer sucked his lips. "Lies so coarse do not become one of your caliber. I've examined your file. In life, you were a man of unremarkable means. No wealth to speak of. No empire to preserve. No knowledge of tech. You were a middle-aged man, twice divorced, paying alimony to a wife and children who abandoned you, all on the salary of a Detroit city planner."

Hadrian's face flushed. "That was someone else!" He started to say more but caught himself, partially regaining his composure.

At first I thought he meant Lucifer was incorrect, that the identity he spoke of was a mistake. But the resentful venom in his face and voice made me realize the true meaning of his denial: Hadrian wasn't that person *anymore*.

A lifetime of hard work that had left him alone, without a wife, paying for kids who didn't want anything to do with him. The only thing he had was a career in the government. Urban planning was a noble cause, with a degree of control and posterity, but one likely burdened by rolls of red tape and the stunted cooperation of endemic bureaucracy.

Hadrian the Whisperer had a new identity now, one which empowered him to move armies at his whims, one in which decisiveness and determination were strengths. He'd started by infiltrating a small pirate town, helping Papa Brugo consolidate the power of numerous criminal gangs into one empire. Only that wasn't enough.

"We know you were contacted," said Lucifer. "An entity on the outside used Saint Loras to scour Haven for sympathetic actors. They found a man of power, a man who was still unsatisfied, a man, perhaps, swayed more by greed than morality. Their perfect little capitalist."

Hadrian wore a sneer as Lucifer recited his history. Further denials were unnecessary. The cards were on the table.

"There's no need to be loyal to them," persuaded Lucifer. "They can't help you. They wouldn't even if they could. Like them, you've likely calculated a value proposition. Which course of action benefits you most? And for once in your digital life, you'd do well to serve yourself. Believe me."

The prisoner licked his teeth like he was scraping a sour taste from his tongue. He was a master of scheming, no doubt, and had to see the poor position he was in. This confrontation was the result of a sordid epic started by him, at least in terms of the digital front. Lucifer's entire existence was the response, the devil rising up to stop the man who would become God. This was more Lucifer's cause than my own, so I waited silently as the devil stated his case.

"A savior is coming," he said, soft but resonant. "A White King who will change everything. You cannot stand in his path."

Hadrian spat. "Oh, I agree about your savior, but it won't be who you think." He grew increasingly confident as he spoke. "I'll give you your due. You've been a worthy adversary. Taking you down will only make a legend of me. I'll make a new bible."

Lucifer's mouth crooked. "Your attempt to assert control on every facet of life has already undone you."

"Please. I'm like you, but better."

"I merely reacted to your threat."

"You use information to manipulate," barked Hadrian. "I use subterfuge. Same difference."

"You used handouts from an outside entity."

"That's not true."

"The only reason you have any power," asserted Lucifer, "is because Saint Loras infiltrated Kablammy Games. The warren has been swept; the mole has been caught."

Hadrian's face reddened and he chortled. "And who said he was the only one?"

Tad was embarrassed that the simple walk from Christian's office to his desk had left him out of breath. Rather than risk another painful transition, he opted to remain standing and pushed the chair aside. Propping the crutch before him, he leaned his chest into it and pressed the switch built into the desk. A motor raised the tabletop to a more comfortable standing height and Tad manned the keyboard. A few clicks confirmed he still had a stable Everchat connection. The internal hard line to Haven was intact.

Small victories.

Tad had come to the conclusion that he would ping Pete as well. Why not? If any of the saints were on their side, it was Pete. But seeing as how Tad and Talon were very recently the same person, it was only natural to trust his doppelganger more. He opened Talon's profile and sent him the first hail.

It was wild, imagining living in a game environment. No crutch, no bum leg, just cavorting with fighters and thieves and goblins. Tad wondered if he would one day find himself in the afterlife too. It seemed like anything was possible there.

Speaking of his disability, Tad was already reconsidering his decision to stand. Everchat connections required residents to be in secure safe zones. With their communication kept to a minimum, Talon would likely view the hail as a priority, but there was no telling what the player was currently up to. This could take a while.

The programmer frowned as he waited, eyes wandering across the screen and landing on the broken email icon in the system tray. Kablammy's email server was down too. Tad opened the window to investigate and was surprised to see new messages. His excitement faded when he realized the emails were two hours old, unimportant and unrelated. Whatever calamity had struck the office, it occurred at a hell of a time. He minimized the window.

Tad dropped his head and closed his eyes to wait out the hail. He chewed his lip impatiently, clearing his mind, going zen. A name popped into his thoughts. Emilio. But it wasn't just a name—it was an afterimage of his inbox.

Tad went back to his email window and saw the unread message from the IT director.

> *From: Emilio*
> *To: Tad*
>
> Yo, since we're out the rest of the day, Steve and I are hitting 8oz Burger in Capitol Hill for beer and grub. Come out if HR gives you the day off too.

Tad stared at the screen for a stunned moment before rereading the message. There was no other way to take it: Abbie had given Emilio the day off. Two hours ago.

He blinked. She used to work for social media companies. Christian had said that, right? She was a hot commodity, and they'd been looking in the wrong places.

The blanks filled in faster than he could keep up with. The satellite message with corrupted sender info. The builds of the game accessible during remote sessions with contractors. Nobody else had more information about Haven and Kablammy than the who's who of the tech industry.

It was so obvious too. Of all organizations, they had a financial stake in data.

Tad straightened. Last he saw Christian, he was looking into employee work histories. Personal knowledge was one thing, but cold hard data in a list format would really emphasize the connection. Even the CEO would be ready for that suspicion, right in front of him as he was looking for it.

And Abbie was hovering over his shoulder, likely attempting

to throw him off the scent. How far was she willing to go to prevent being discovered?

Tad made an about face and hurried to the office, one hop at a time.

1680 Deadlocked

"It's time to consider your fate," stressed Lucifer. "After all the harm you've done, you can still do some good."

Hadrian scoffed. "You're bargaining now? I thought you were better than that."

"Does your existence not merit negotiation?"

"Are you gonna let me go?"

"No," I said firmly. Whatever leeway Hadrian was gonna get, he wouldn't be set free as if nothing had happened.

"Sounds like I don't have much reason to help," he growled.

Lucifer rested both hands atop his black staff, in the spot of his missing azure gemstone. "Are those your last words?"

"Empty threats. You can't delete me."

The devil cocked his head. "Dear Hadrian, my threats are anything but empty."

Lucifer rapped his staff on the floor twice. In response, a dark angel flickered into the cell beside us. The being was clothed in black rags, right arm severed below the shoulder. Pitch black eyes focused on the prisoner.

I couldn't believe it. After the Golden Seven had practically destroyed themselves, Otho had gone missing. I'd known he was still alive since his was the only intact column outside the

Pantheon. It was sundered in two, split and teetering, but somehow still standing. Lucifer had left Stronghold these past few days to recover his rogue agent. Color me surprised that he was successful.

Decimus tensed. "Lucifer, you are in violation of the terms of service. You—"

"Oh, cut that out already," snapped Saint Peter, arresting the angel with a wave of his arm. Decimus returned his harsh stare to Hadrian.

"What is this?" demanded the Whisperer. "All the Fallen were defeated."

"Not all," said Lucifer ominously.

Hadrian focused on the newcomer, perhaps working out if he were real. I thought he might be doing something else, too, but he wasn't obviously interacting with menus. "An intricate layer cake of routines on that one. A complex stitch even I can't unravel. Yet."

"Don't overestimate your abilities," chided Lucifer. "Even if you could eventually breach the security, you lack the time it would take."

A black scythe appeared in Otho's left hand.

Hadrian twitched. "No... You can't."

"Can't what? Bargain? Show leniency?"

The Whisperer stared into Otho's unblindfolded black eyes. "You can't delete me. That's a rogue angel. He's not authorized —" His head swiveled to the other angel. "Decimus won't allow it."

Peter took a measuring breath. "I think I've established my ability to hold him off." Decimus remained motionless and blindfolded, punctuating Peter's statement.

"And you?" leveled the prisoner to the saint. "You'd allow this? A developer circumventing the rules of his own game?"

"A weak argument," Peter chuckled, "coming from you."

"What do you know?" The prisoner's eyes appealed to me next, the last one left. I tried not to be too smug about it.

"You know what you need to do, Hadrian. Suck up your pride and help us get Haven out of this mess. It's that or oblivion."

Otho's scythe glimmered with ghostly light.

"Okay," he stammered. "I was a pawn, like he said."

"Tell us what happened," prodded Lucifer.

"They used me! You can't delete me for that!"

"Who was it?" pressed Peter. "I need a name."

I was so intent on the conversation that a menu ping caused me to visibly jump. It was an Everchat hail from Tad Lonnerman. He wanted to speak to me. I checked the long hall behind me, gritted my teeth, and faced Hadrian as he began to speak.

"I was contacted by Loras," he admitted. "He kicked off that cyclops quest. He let the kraken loose and gave me the Squid's Tooth."

Lucifer leaned on his staff and nodded along.

"He set up Stronghold and Shorehome as battlegrounds to cause strife in the game. To delay the launch."

"We know this," said Peter impatiently. "Who was Larry working for?"

Hadrian's brow scrunched. "You mean Loras? I don't know names on the outside. I was already a player when they contacted me. In the beginning, I just wanted to score some extra loot, you know?"

Peter opened his mouth to speed things up but Lucifer threw up a hand. When someone tight-lipped finally started talking, it was better to let them go. Biting their head off wouldn't get answers quicker. Which wasn't to say I didn't share Peter's impatience. I shifted my weight to my other leg and checked my Everchat menu.

"Can you really blame me?" appealed the Whisperer. "I was a player in a mostly NPC town, tasked with special quests by a prominent member of the community team. Hell, in Shorehome, Loras *was* the community team. All I did was act on the game presented to me."

I bit down. Hadrian was playing the fool, pretending Haven was just another MMO, that cheating was victimless. I recalled one of the first profound things Lucifer had said to me: Haven was no game. Hadrian had to know that.

"Loras was switching his sights to Oakengard," he continued. "And by that point, I was content to back down. Yes! I told him I was done." Hadrian's eyes lit up. "But he said Kablammy was moving to new ownership. That if I wanted to stick around, I had to do whatever it took. They made me attack Stronghold. They made me do it."

I took a step toward the door, already sick of this. I was sure Hadrian was lying to protect himself. Far as I could tell, the timetable didn't jive. Sure, Larry controlled Loras in the beginning. Boosting crusader stats and resources, he'd likely had plans for the mountain fortress, but he'd been long gone by the time the Brothers in Black snuck the kraken into Stronghold. Outside forces hadn't prompted that attack.

Lucifer waited as Hadrian told his story, opting not to pick it apart or challenge the lies. When he saw the Whisperer finally out of breath, his case finished, he softly asked, "Who?"

"InLink," said Hadrian. "I don't know the executives in the company, but I know it's them." The prisoner smacked dry lips and tried to swallow. "They'll delete me if they know I revealed them. Like you said. I'm not worth a thing."

I grunted and stormed from the room. "I need to take an important call." My boots stomped loudly through the hallway, past the prying eyes of Bravo Team. I didn't like the idea of giving Hadrian a break, especially if he was gonna play the victim and feed us bullshit. At the same time, Saint Peter seemed pretty desperate for answers, and we were finally getting them.

The news of sabotage had especially unsettled me. I felt profoundly useless realizing actions were being taken in real life that I had no hope of countering. Everything I saw and experienced in Haven was subject to the whims of the outside world. More than anything, I needed a handle on that.

Bravo Team stood by the cell. I passed a waiting Defender and frowned at the other guarding the stairway. In a perfect world I would've returned to the privacy of Dragonperch, or maybe rushed to the Pantheon rotunda. Given the dire circumstances, this was as private as it was gonna get. Taking the call here was justified, no matter what Hadrian overheard.

I took a deep breath and opened Everchat.

Christian Everett kneaded fingers into closed eyes, from his temples to the bridge of his nose. He'd noticed his vision blurring while poring over computer screens lately. It was a dastardly secret for a titan of tech.

He was well aware of the ten-minute rule. Every hour, take ten minutes away from the computer to look at "normal" human things. Plants, people, the horizon, if possible. It was a simple yet silly ask: stop everything at once and forcefully adjust to the pace of life enjoyed by our hunter-gatherer forebearers. Maybe it finally was time for evolution to do away with nearsightedness once and for all.

The CEO opened his eyes, reinvigorated by the massage, and focused on the antique bookcase on the far wall. Stout cherrywood, filled with hardcover and softbound programming tomes. They didn't make furniture like that anymore.

But while the woodwork was admirable, Christian couldn't focus on something else for ten minutes. His work was important. It always was, but now, especially. That Tad was a sharp fellow, a curious mix of analytical logic and common-sense pragmatism. The latter wasn't always one of Christian's strengths, and he found collaborating with Tad to be eye-opening.

Which didn't mean the answers came easily. Hard things were hard, and the more names Christian vetted, the more difficult the task became. His eyes went back to the computer screen.

Stephanie Hascott had briefly worked on the community team. Her and Pete were a bit of an item for a while there. Christian always suspected the turn in their relationship was the cause of her moving to greener pastures. She did indeed work at Boost Systems now.

"Definitely suspicious," said Abbie. "We know Pete's a good guy, and he vouched for her, but personal connections can blind a person."

Christian sat back in his chair and pondered. Perhaps she was right about the relationship. It was good he had Abbie to remind him of that human touch.

Still, the evidence damning the focus testing company was tenuous. Having access to the Loras avatar on certain occasions didn't amount to proof. Various other companies had remoted through InLink's portal. Singling Boost Systems out was a case of confirmation bias.

Too bad there was nothing notable in Larry's resume. As the only known bad actor, his profile could provide vital clues. He was a resident of Buena Park, a cottage industry of small tech companies, but every workplace in his job history was a small local outlet that had since gone out of business. Most startups were only promising when they were starting up.

Christian sighed. Hard things were hard, and his next task was unenviable. It was time to vet his trusted skeleton crew.

Emilio was an obvious place to start. He had the skill set to disable Kablammy's communication infrastructure. He was also conspicuously absent. His work history, however, was practically nonexistent. He'd been with Kablammy for a long time, learning the ropes as an assistant and moving his way up to IT director. He was well-liked and even better paid. How could such an appreciated and rewarded asset turn on the company?

Christian Everett hated this.

"Look, Abbie," he said sarcastically. "This is you."

She gave a waggish laugh. "Stop joking around, Christian."

His eyes strained at the list. "I should show this to Tad. You really are a rock star."

"Oh, that's really not necessary."

"You made a name for yourself at Instaface. It was a big coup when InLink took you on. I'm still amazed you left them for us."

Abbie tensed. "It was for *you*," she said. "I wouldn't have joined on with anyone else."

The CEO smiled at the compliment. "Could you imagine if InLink was behind all this? If they took over, Haven would become a wasteland of paid advertising, fake news, and knee-jerk reactions."

Christian froze. The absurdity had a twisted elegance to it. InLink had access to Haven's vital systems, and their headquarters was in Buena Park.

"Ha, ha, ha!"

Abbie's shrill laugh attempted to wrest him from the train of thought, but Christian was lost in the abyss of his mind. The mental block was shifting loose. The possibilities of the sabotage coming, not from a *tech* company, but a *data* company.

And, oh, the extent of the data. An entire population of captive subjects, without the right to privacy, with connections to real people and organizations all over the world. A population that would always grow in size and never age out of their demographic categories. A population that every single person on this earth could one day join.

Christian had repeatedly insisted on following the money,

but data *was* money in the new economy. How could he have been so blind?

InLink was the king of data, and they wanted to be the king of Haven too.

"Abbie," admonished Christian, voice shaking.

But the CEO still didn't understand people. She was faster than him.

Tad cut through the cubicles to speed his path to Christian's office. The slow progress only increased his worry. If Abbie was a mole like Larry had been, everything was doomed. All the trust, all the employee management, all the new hires—how much could she have sabotaged?

Part of him thought there had to be another explanation, that his dislike of the HR director was creeping into his logic. She wasn't a traitor, she was just annoying. But everything made too much sense, and what else would explain Emilio's email?

As Tad neared the office, he heard the CEO's raised voice. The two were arguing. He hopped forward more urgently, crutch nearly slipping.

A loud crack echoed through the office. Tad's crutch missed a step and he pitched to the floor. Two more reports buffeted his ears, like fireworks going off indoors.

Tad ducked behind an administrative assistant's cubicle just as Abbie emerged from the office. "Frick!" she said with a sneer. She scanned up and down the administrative wing before storming toward the other end of the building.

Tad swallowed. Had that been a gun in her hand? That was crazy, right?

He waited a beat. Then another. He closed his eyes and listened. Someone stirred in Christian's office.

Tad Lonnerman gritted his teeth and recovered his crutch, using the desk to prop him away from the floor. Once standing, he peeked over the line of cubicles.

The area was clear.

With a limp as fast as he could manage, doubling up the steps of his good leg by taking an extra hop, he safely reached the doorway. In the office, each of the CEO's dual monitors had been shot. Tad released a breath before hearing a murmur from the floor.

Stepping around the desk with great trepidation, he found Christian lying on the carpet, blood welling from his torso.

1690 Counter-Strike

I chewed my lip raw. The Everchat hail icon was spinning round and round, an endless motion that resembled a black hole in more ways than one. I paused the call and reinitiated it, just in case there was a bad connection.

The white knight lumbered toward me. "What is it?" she asked.

"A message from Tad," I grumbled. "It's tagged urgent." I rotated the floating menu screen so she could see the progress.

Eternal spinning.

I couldn't understand why the call wouldn't pick up. I'd only been a minute late in answering. That was an acceptable delay given the requirements on my end to enter a private zone. Things were different in the real world; a swipe of the phone was all it took. My gaze went from Lash's painted eyes to Glinda, Conan, and the closed helmets of the Defenders.

I cursed when my teeth accidentally drew blood. I was more nervous than usual. I laughed coarsely at the irony. A legendary spear of yore, the only dragon in the world, my enemy in chains, and the support and resources of the core city at my disposal— and I felt helpless.

I strode back down the hall and into Hadrian's cell. "Peter,

Tad was trying to reach me, but he's not available now."

The old man was half distracted when he turned. "Just give him five minutes and try again. He's probably refilling his coffee."

I winced. Perhaps Tad had assumed there'd be a short delay between his hail and my answer. Maybe Peter was right and he was setting up for a long talk.

"What was that?" snapped Peter. "A network spike." The community manager went deep into his invisible menu.

Lucifer frowned. "Hadrian sent an SOS."

"No," swore Hadrian, head shaking. "It's not me. They have trackers on us." His eyes met mine. "The Trojan. I can't get away from it."

I scowled. "Are you saying they know that we know?"

"Maybe. It's possible."

I pinged the Everchat menu again, all concern of privacy out the window. As I waited on the hail, I squared up with the prisoner. "You're not telling us the whole story. What the hell's going on?"

Christian Everett squirmed in pain as Tad cradled his head. "She knew this would happen," he sputtered. "She tried to warn me. I thought... I was afraid she'd gone mad, trapped in a digital world so long. So alone."

Tad nodded in support. He didn't really know what to say. At first he thought Christian was talking about Abbie, but he realized the CEO had family on his mind. His daughter Lucy was the one who'd tried to warn him.

"You're hurt bad," were the words Tad finally strung together. They weren't inspired words, possibly even ill-advised, but they were the truth.

Tad produced his phone and tried 911, hoping the emergency request would work if there was even a sliver of reception. When that failed he scrambled for something to prop the CEO up, settling on a stack of financial binders to elevate Christian's head. Then Tad checked the landline. Still no service. How was he gonna get the word out? He checked the time. If the security team was true to their word, they'd be arriving soon. Surely they had the capacity to contact authorities and handle emergencies.

"The computer..." breathed Christian.

Tad looked. Curiously, the PC was still running, power light on and fan whirring. Tad had heard three gunshots, one for Christian and two for the dual monitors. Abbie had fucking shot the monitors. Her misguided attempt to destroy Christian's computer had failed miserably.

"Jeez, she really doesn't know anything about tech, does she?"

Christian tried to lift to his elbow. "Need to warn... Need to warn Pete."

Tad went still as he realized two worrying facts. One, the incident with Abbie wasn't necessarily over, and two, Pete and the Defenders were strapped in their EXSIL units, blissfully unaware of the danger within the studio. If Abbie was truly attempting to sabotage Haven, that's where she would go next.

"Don't get up," ordered Tad, already halfway out of the office.

"I'll get help." It wasn't until Tad was about to step into the main hall that he remembered to be scared.

There was a crazed woman with a gun loose in the building who was just as likely to shoot him as she was to make a patronizing joke. Hell, knowing Abbie she'd do both at the same time.

Tad peeked out the doorway. The coast was clear, which confirmed what he'd seen: Abbie storming to the other side of the building. He desperately hoped she was going for the exit, but *everything* was toward that side of the building, including the exit, his cubicle, the kitchen, and the Superdome, home of the saints.

Tad set the crutch ahead of him and leaned into it. With Christian bleeding out and potential danger around the corner, every tortured step seemed to take forever. There was nothing for it but to settle into a rhythm. Crutch, foot, hop. Crutch, foot, hop.

This time he was winded before getting to the kitchen. He stopped and leaned against the doorway, peeking in to make sure it was empty. It would've been crazy for Abbie to stop here, but an image popped into his mind of the HR director laughing maniacally, hands drenched in blood as she gurgled seven Diet Cokes in a row.

Abbie wasn't there, and neither was anybody else. Nobody to warn; nobody to help. Tad grimaced. He was delaying the inevitable and he knew it.

He hurried forward, borderline out of control. More than once he relied on his leg in a cast for support as he overshot the crutch's reach. Pain spread through unused muscles, but it was a dull pain, buried under fear and adrenaline and anger. Urgency was his prerogative. Tad hurried straight to the Superdome, abandoning all concern for his well being. He'd already almost died once, and that had been a car accident, a useless death in a mindless rat race. At least now he was fighting for something.

As he sped toward the open double doors of the Superdome, Tad bowled right into an exiting Abbie.

"Wha—?" She stumbled backward in surprise.

They locked eyes for a split second before she raised the gun in her hand.

Tad didn't recover his balance as quickly. Flailing for support, he reacted without thinking. The crutch he so desperately needed swung up and smacked Abbie's hand. He leaned into the blow, over relying on his wounded leg. The pistol bounced to the carpet and slid across the room.

Tad recovered awkwardly on his crutch. He set his jaw, straightened as much as he could, and said something he'd wanted to say for a long time. "You fucking bitch."

Abbie glanced behind her nervously, then at the gun, before hardening her features. "Get out of my way, nerd."

"You're not going anywhere. When the security team gets here they—" Tad froze in horror as the sneer grew on her face. "You didn't call the security team, did you?"

She snorted. "Don't worry, I called *someone* all right."

She lunged forward. Tad tried to hit her with the crutch but she barreled into him. She ripped it away as he fell backward, only preventing a fall by clamping onto her sweater.

"Ouch, my boob!" she screamed.

"Sorry," he peeped. "I missed gender sensitivity training."

She shoved him hard. Tad was out of breath, off balance, and without his crutch. Abbie was too heavy to drag down. She clawed his face and he attempted to punch her, but he couldn't put any force behind the blow, especially since she was driving forward and keeping him on his heels.

He swelled with embarrassment realizing he couldn't fight her off. But, dammit, he wouldn't let her leave. Ignoring the raking nails, Tad pulled in, hugging her close. He buried his face into her cushioned chest to escape her attacks, and he lifted his legs off the floor as much as he could to weigh her down.

Abbie kicked and flailed, desperately trying to hurry away from the Superdome, but she could barely move.

A second later Tad realized the reason for her urgency as a bright light and shock wave tore over them and slammed them to the ground.

Hadrian's eyes widened as Talon neared. "I don't know what you're talking about."

"Who else is secretly working for InLink? Who's sabotaging the company from within?"

"How could I know that?" he snapped. "I was always contacted by in-game constructs. If I'd used Everchat or something else, there'd be a record."

I growled. "But you're communicating through the network spikes. We can see it happening."

"I'm not in control..."

"You expect me to believe that?!?" I drew the assassin needle and set it against his throat. Hadrian leaned into the blade. Lucifer rested a hand on my shoulder, and I reluctantly pulled away.

This, of course, was what the Whisperer wanted. For us to be so enraged that we killed him, or even worse: for us to be driven into inaction and indecision because we didn't know what was going on any more than he did.

"He's lying," I spat. "We should execute him."

Lucifer countered with a tempered voice. "He'll reveal what he knows or face judgment."

I stuffed the dagger into my inventory and glanced at the Everchat window. Still no connection. I focused on brigade chat.

> **Talon:** *Status report in the city?*
> **Izzy:** *The bandits have taken heavy losses and are backing away.*
> **Kyle:** *Oldtown's untouched. The goblins are retreating.*

I cursed at the seemingly good news.

> **Talon:** *Something's going down. Full alert. Look out for anything strange.*

Bravo Team tensed as they read my message. Lash arched a dark eyebrow my way. "Is there something we don't know about, boss?"

I turned to Saint Peter. "Are your Defenders secure?"

"I— Of course they are."

"I mean, is there a way they could be hacked?"

"It's impossible. There're real human beings driving them. There's no way the program can short circuit that connection. Same goes for me, or you for that matter."

I forced out a harsh breath as Lucifer watched with concern. "Then do me a favor," I said. "Leave Haven. Check on Tad. If Hadrian did send an SOS they might be in trouble."

The old man frowned. "But Hadrian's finally revealing—"

"He's not telling us anything, Peter. He's lying through his teeth, stalling for time. Look, he's finally in trouble. Otho can delete him in seconds." I scowled. "Tad's not answering his own hail. Just humor me, please."

The saint pulled his head back and stroked his beard with more consternation than usual. "I suppose it can't hurt."

Hadrian flexed against his chains. Beads of sweat ran down his head and neck. "Wait," he said. "I have more to tell."

"Then tell us," I demanded.

"I'll only talk to the saint." The corner of his mouth turned up in a smile.

My eyes narrowed. "Screw it. Execute him. Execute him now!"

Lucifer's eyes shot to Peter. The saint straightened and went stiff. "Arghhh!" Peter convulsed as his body twisted.

"Peter!" I grabbed him before he fell. His fingers clawed my arm.

Lash rushed in, cleaver in hand. "What is it?"

Screams filled the hall behind her. Bravo Team spun. The

two silver Defenders collapsed and gurgled helplessly on the floor.

I shook the saint in my arms. "Peter! Peter!"

My friend's eyes became expansive windows as he stared through me, barely managing a croak. Saint Peter went slack and disappeared.

I turned to the others. The Defenders had disappeared as well. "What's going on?" asked Glinda.

I spun around. "Lucifer!"

The devil clenched his jaw, turned to Otho, and nodded. The angel of death raised a black scythe above the prisoner's head. Hadrian shut his eyes and screamed.

The dungeon lurched. I pressed forward, seemingly sideways as the entire world reeled. It was fast but slow, reminiscent of falling and being underwater at the same time. Otho's scythe came down in slow motion, like a dream.

The Whisperer laughed, and I realized this was a nightmare.

```
DEVELOPER CONSOLE
>> ERROR
>> CONNECTION LOST
```

I watched in horror as all of Haven shut down.

137

1700 Perfect Dark

The world is black and still, and so am I.

1710 Limbo

◆━━━━━●◆●━━━━━◆

```
Haven version 0.9.31
Online
Booting auxiliary pipeline...
Safe mode
Waiting on reserves...
```

The world came back, a stuck reel once again feeding through the projector. Everything shifted in place, sharpening and blurring and sliding.

I collapsed to all fours, blinking repeatedly, breathing heavily for some reason. I chalked it up to virtual adrenaline. I wasn't hurt but my vision was shaky. My surroundings steadied and I recoiled, suddenly aware I was in Hadrian's cell.

As if someone had hit the pause button, the Whisperer sat in chains, hatred and confidence plastered into his sneer. Lucifer stood beside me, watching.

"What was that?" I asked him. "Where's Otho?"

No one answered. Lucifer stood in place, artificial, idle movement playing on his face.

My expression soured. This wasn't Haven, it was a facsimile

of the world. I thrust to my feet.

Hadrian's gaze bored through me, lip curling up and snapping down, leaning forward and jerking back, breath uneven. His avatar was frozen in place, glitching in a jerky loop. When I stepped to the side, his eyes didn't follow.

Lucifer didn't respond either. He stood as he always did, hand atop witchwood, silently observing his subject.

My eyes strained at them. What was the matter with my vision? My hands were in sharp focus but the figures beyond were hazy. The effect was independent of distance. I could slide my boot past Lucifer and see it perfectly clear while everything else was out of focus, right down to the fuzzy stone floor. I stomped my foot and was satisfied with a solid thump.

I set a palm on Lucifer's back. Resistance again. He was there, standing in place, but frozen.

I grinned, balled up a fist, and socked Hadrian in the face. He showed no reaction, remaining in place, looping back and forth. My satisfaction dimmed.

"Okay, Talon," I muttered to myself, "what's going on here?"

I went to my menus.

```
DEVELOPER CONSOLE
>> ERROR
>> FAILED TO INITIALIZE
```

Odd but not terribly surprising. Had all of Haven rebooted? Why was I able to move while no one else could?

I backed out of the cell's open door, relieved I wasn't frozen. I moved into the hall without constraint and took in my surroundings.

Decimus, Otho, Saint Peter, and the Defenders were gone. They weren't stuck in a loop and unresponsive, they weren't lying on the floor—they were gone. Lash was mid stride, stomping into the cell as Conan and Glinda watched from outside. They were reacting to my last-second alarm. To whatever happened to Saint Peter.

I tried to recall the exact sequence of events. Was this some trick? A method of lowering the dungeon's defenses? Another distraction?

> **Talon:** *Can anybody out there hear me?*

I swallowed and waited for an answer. I swiped to Everchat, but the system wouldn't initialize and populate contact options.

I reread the game log. Best I could figure, we'd booted into some kind of low power mode. That was concerning because nothing like this had ever happened, not only in my entire experience, but according to those who'd lived in the beta much longer than me.

I resolved to calm myself. I was quite possibly the only person who could do something now. Perhaps my employee ID or dev menu privileges afforded me some extra processing power. Perhaps there were other players elsewhere who weren't frozen.

I needed to get a status update somehow, but my first priority was making sure Hadrian was locked down. He was still shackled in the chair, visually and physically. I shut the door from outside the cell, sealing Lucifer and Lash within. As I went for the lock, the door popped open.

I frowned and tried again. Same thing. The door slammed and then, even before settling in the frame, it just appeared open again, back to its previous position. As fast as I moved, there wasn't enough time to bolt it closed.

I was a programmer in my former life. It didn't take long to figure what was happening. The world wasn't syncing. The door was open on the server side. Closing it locally worked for a second until communication with the server failed and the door reset to its last-known state. Haven couldn't drop packets, of course. It wasn't strictly a client-server model. But there were necessary syncs between multiple redundant servers. If we were in a special safe mode, it was likely many actions were blocked or minimized.

Which explained why everything appeared so fuzzy. Not blurry, just low resolution. Haven was giving me the minimum to work with while avoiding the load of high-performance systems. Minimal level of detail, minimal interaction.

"Oh, crap."

I marched to the stairway filled with dread. After climbing a few steps higher than usual, I hit an invisible wall. I shouldn't have been able to get this far up. Transitioning to other zones was currently disabled. I was trapped in my own dungeon.

I wandered back down with a blank expression. At least Hadrian was stuck down here with us. But we had to be ready. I drew my dragonspear and waited.

Tad woke to blaring sirens and a mouth full of scratchy wool. He jerked in place and found himself stuck, lying on his back with Abbie on top of him, trapped between a rock and a soft place, which didn't sound so bad until you considered he was being smothered by a cat sweater.

He shoved the HR director's unconscious form. In his weakened state, she was heavy. He used a lateral push, and she rolled off and settled beside him. Tad recoiled. Her face was frozen in anguish. An aluminum piece of server rack protruded from her neck. Abbie was dead.

Tad sat up and pulled his legs out from under her. It was an awkward thing with a cast, and he had to shove Abbie's waist to do it.

"Sorry." He hurried, trying not to notice her gaping eyes.

It was only when Tad reached for his crutch that he took in his broader surroundings.

The hallway's lights were on but obscured by black smoke rolling against the ceiling. The Superdome through the doorway was dark except for flickering orange. Combined with the waves of heat and droning alarm, Tad expertly deduced the building was on fire.

He zombie-crawled toward the doorway, dragging his cast and wincing as he neared the siren. A lucky break. A fire extinguisher hung beside the community room entrance. Tad pushed to his feet, retrieved the extinguisher from the cabinet, and limped inside without his crutch.

Utter horror greeted him. The Superdome was a large space, with shared desks in the center of the room and EXSIL units along the walls. It was enough to house the entire community team at their height, and now Saint Peter and his eight Defenders.

The interior of the room had been utterly ravaged by multiple explosions. Perhaps a few improvised devices spaced evenly between the units, as the equipment varied in state. Some chunks of metal were unidentifiable, their original forms completely obliterated. A few of the machines appeared little more than knocked over. But there were... slumped forms and... body parts.

"Does anybody need help?"

Tad waited among the crackling flames, pain growing in his bad leg.

A large ember blowing toward his face snapped him out of it. If he didn't put out the blaze, the whole floor would go up. He hurried to the largest congregation of flames and sprayed it down. The retardant worked surprisingly well and immediately quenched the fire. Tad limped around the community room and addressed the de-escalating threats.

He was lucky he'd arrived before the room turned into an inferno. After several minutes, the fire was contained. Abbie's goal wasn't to burn down the building but to destroy the equipment and neutralize the community team. The flames were a side effect. After dealing with them, the room darkened, the light bulbs having blown out in the blast. He dropped the extinguisher and breathed. The fire alarm remained deafening.

"T... Tad."

He spun at the voice so fast that he stumbled to the floor. Tad dragged himself around Pete's toppled EXSIL machine to find the saint pinned to the carpet beneath it.

"Pete! You're alive!"

"I'm not sure this qualifies." The community manager spat blood and cradled his chest with his free arm. His stomach and legs were stuck.

Tad braced his fingers under the heavy EXSIL unit and pulled, but it didn't budge. He strained against it sideways but stopped when Pete groaned in pain. It was no use; Tad's broken leg left him too hobbled for a rescue effort.

"The alarm's on," Tad reasoned. "Fire Rescue will be here." He glanced around the room to confirm the fire wasn't returning. "You just have to sit tight a bit."

Pete nodded, lips pressed tight. He was hurting and didn't look good.

"Can anyone else hear me?" called out Tad.

Even though the rest of the room was silent, Tad struggled to his feet and limped to the other EXSILs. Stephanie Hascott was crushed inside twisted metal. A couple of the others had lost too much blood to live. Tad found he lacked the grit to even approach some of the bodies who'd been literally torn to pieces.

Pete craned his neck around his machine in an attempt to follow Tad's progress. "How are they?" he asked weakly.

Tad swallowed, the answer too horrible to vocalize.

The community manager sighed and rested his head against the carpet.

"It was Abbie," growled Tad. "She worked for InLink the whole time. She shot Christian and he's hurt too and—" Tears welled in his eyes.

For a few moments, the two of them gave in to the blaring fire alarm. The futility. It was hard to imagine anything going more wrong.

Pete tensed. "The game."

Tad shook his head. "Don't worry about that."

"It's important, Tad." He grunted as he tried to turn. "I'm not going anywhere. You need to check on Haven."

Tad sniffed. "What do I do?"

"What's the state of the central hub?"

"Destroyed," he answered. "Like, it's not even there anymore."

"The server rack?"

Tad shrugged. "It looks like the main target of the explosion."

"Okay." Pete nodded, slowly at first but building steam. "Haven is backed up to multiple redundant servers that constantly communicate. If one goes down, others take over, just like the internet."

"I don't think the internet's that centralized."

"I'm dying, Tad. Cut me some slack."

The programmer stiffened at the admission. Pete's life was in danger and Tad was standing around moping. He wouldn't do that to the man. "What do you need?"

Pete allowed a brief smile. "What about the switches on the wall? They're built behind the concrete column. They—"

"I see them." Tad hurried to the switch box and opened the metal door. The column and box had protected them.

"Switch them off," instructed Pete. "They—" He broke into a fit of coughing. "They—" This time the coughs sounded wet and sputtering.

Tad flicked the three switches to the off positions and hopped back to Pete. The community manager was out of breath on his back, the stubble around his mouth redder than usual due to the preponderance of blood.

"They redirect the game controls," finished Pete weakly. "Haven will be able to spin up to full power, assuming the alternate system is still intact."

Tad dropped to a knee and splayed his cast to the side to lean over the man. "Abbie didn't have a chance to go anywhere else. She's dead. How do we check the other system?"

The saint breathed sharply but slowly, in and out. "...Christian," was all he said.

"I'll ask him," hurried Tad, trying to keep Pete from exerting himself too much.

The wounded man closed his eyes for some peace. The worrying moment dragged on until Pete's eyes shot open. "The quests..."

Tad's face tightened in worry.

"Tell Talon... unlock... the quests."

"Fine, just rest now." Tad gripped Pete's hand tight. "Just hold on, Pete. You'll get through this."

The community manager had no more strength. He shook his head ever so slightly, eyes blinking with exhaustion. "My legs... body... crushed."

Tad tried to maintain a confident face but must've looked a mess. "It's okay," he reassured. "The doctors can fix you."

Another tired blink. No response this time.

"What about you, in the game?" Tad offered. "We can upload you to Haven."

Pete smiled softly. "Some people aren't built to live forever, Tad."

The thirty-something man who liked superhero movies and cycling exhausted a final profound breath and went still.

1720 Temple Run

In my mind, I might've paced that dungeon hall for hours. The game clock told a different story. I constantly referred to it, worrying over the possibilities and doing my best to stay alert. Things started moving again in half an hour. I first noticed Lash jerk forward, then suddenly appear ten feet down the hall.

"Yes!" she shouted, looking around. Conan and Glinda popped to random places, and even Crux was down here somehow. They all looked at each other and laughed.

"You guys came back!" exclaimed Glinda.

"Me?" asked Crux. "*You* were the ones who were frozen."

"Uh-uh," insisted Lash. "None of you guys were responding." Her eyes fell on me down the hall. "You were standing in front of Hadrian a second ago."

I pushed through them and watched as Lucifer spun around the cell in alarm. Behind him, the shackles were open. The prisoner's chair was empty.

"He's running!" cried Lucifer, charging toward me.

I turned just in time to see Hadrian dart up the dungeon steps and disappear.

"Son of a bitch!"

I was the closest and fastest and sprinted after him.

I cursed my stupidity as I realized what happened. Everyone had been moving just like me—I wasn't special. We just weren't seeing each other's updates. Hadrian had somehow escaped his chair, possibly aided by the frozen game world or his virus. All he had to do was wait by the exit until the main update returned and zoning was re-enabled.

The bright sky flashed in first. The ground was there. The jail yard buildings popped in, as well as the Stronghold skyline. The game update was running, but the processes were noticeably lagged.

Hadrian ignored the incomplete background as he sped through the jail halls and into the yard. I hurried to keep pace, eyes scanning for Bandit. No dragon, no bongo—no anyone, really. This was the headquarters of the city watch under a heightened guard detail. Olive cloaks were supposed to be everywhere. Two Defenders waiting outside too. And Bandit.

All were missing.

We raced into the street, the sounds of the others exiting the jailhouse behind me. That reminded me to check in.

Talon: *Roll call!*
Kyle: *Bro, what just happened?*
Izzy: *I'm here, Talon. We just rebooted, but the legionnaires and centurions are gone.*
Talon: *All the city watch is. Hadrian escaped the jail. He's losing me.*
Errol: *We be near ye, at the north river. We'll provide backup.*

I rounded a corner and skidded to a halt, finding myself in the confines of the slums. The buildings were smaller here, ramshackle, with lots of places to hide and multiple alleys to cut through. I whistled sharply. Bandit had probably wandered off during the confusion, but if she was within earshot she'd come.

I hurried southwest, checking pathways.

> **Talon:** *Belay that, Errol. If Hadrian's looking to escape, the nearest exit is your river gate. Post guard at the east and west banks in case he backtracks and slips by me.*
> **Errol:** *Aye, aye.*
> **Izzy:** *I'm at the east gate, and I'm the only one.*

I nodded. Even alone, she was a powerful deterrent.

> **Talon:** *I think he went west, but the east gate is the closest land exit. You better keep an eye out.*
> **Kyle:** *I'm leaving the tower then. Hadrian can't get into Dragonperch, and someone needs eyes on the west gate. Jixa and the ogres will back me up.*

I grimaced at the thought of limiting Oldtown's defenses. The Black Hat capital had been the Whisperer's target last go around. But there was no more army, no more kraken. Kyle was dead on. Sanctums were private zones locked out to other players. Hadrian had no way of entering. Besides, after everything that'd happened, he'd have to be a madman to stay inside the city, and everything about him was measured. I sprinted with my map open, trying to catch sight of my prey while calculating possible routes to each of the city's exits. I had to guess at Hadrian's intentions.

My boots scraped gravel and I skidded to a stop. I was running too far south; there was one exit I hadn't considered. The map of Stronghold showed me about in line with the location, which would have been crazy except... the city watch and angels hadn't reinitialized yet.

Galloping hooves pounded my way and I waved to Bandit. Her dragon form was done for the day. I reached an arm out and hooked onto the bongo's back.

> **Talon:** *That bastard is going for the Pantheon.*

I patted Bandit's neck, relieved to see her okay. We cut directly west to the Forum. Of course, by this time, Hadrian had a huge head start on me.

> DEVELOPER CONSOLE
> \>> VERIFYING ID

Damn. I couldn't speed up the initialization of the guards. Decimus hadn't reappeared yet either. If the saints, Defenders, city watch, and angels were gone, the Pantheon was unprotected. The more I thought about all the moving parts, the more certain I was about the strategy. Hadrian was going for the fast travel.

We burst onto the cobblestones of the main Forum, hooves clattering loudly. Hadrian turned to us from the grand portico steps before rushing inside. We galloped past Otho's abandoned spire and under the triangular roof, where the golden statue of Decimus perched. He showed no signs of coming to life.

I didn't dismount as Bandit cantered on the interior tiles. The Pantheon was empty. I was too late.

A ring of maroon tiles demarked a wide section of floor. This was the fast-travel portal. Hadrian had successfully escaped. I stood in shock, wondering for a moment how he'd managed to use it without approval from the saints. Then again, it depended on a variety of factors including whether it was locked or not. Besides, Hadrian was full of tricks.

It was that realization that had me turn Bandit's reins and zone into the rotunda.

We blinked in with Hadrian standing right before us. In his grip was a massive red gem, the Eye of Orik, Stronghold's soulstone. The defiled tabernacle lay open on the far wall, its white cloth unceremoniously dumped on the floor.

I pointed the dragonspear at the Whisperer. "You almost made it."

"What are you gonna do?" he spat. "Kill me?"

He raced past me as I speared him with my weapon.

[Hadrian] used Shadowslip

Damn. I shook the black cowl off my spear as Hadrian zoned out of the rotunda. I kicked Bandit ahead to cut him off.

We appeared back in the main Pantheon. Bandit skidded around and bucked nervously. Hadrian stood in a wide stance, his back to us. Before him was Decimus, finally initialized, two silver swords pointed at the intruder, who for once was caught literally red-handed.

"Hadrian, you are in violation of the terms of service. You will be expunged from Haven."

The Whisperer shoved the soulstone into his inventory and searched around, eyes flashing with fear. He had enemies on either side. Decimus hovered a foot in the air and advanced.

Lucifer raced into the portico, Bravo Team still climbing the stairs outside. The blindfolded angel paused and turned.

"Lucifer, you are in violation of the terms of service. You will be expunged from Haven."

The devil raised his staff as silver swords charged his way. Hadrian chuckled, incredulous, before bolting for the fast-travel circle.

"Hadrian!" I barked. We galloped after him as I tried to halt the angel's justice with the dev menu.

```
DEVELOPER CONSOLE
>> INITIALIZING
```

Lucifer turned to me with a harrowed face. "The Whisperer!" I yelled into the menu. "Pause angels!"

```
DEVELOPER CONSOLE
>> STATUS
>> LOCKED
```

Bandit bounded past Hadrian, who rolled away to avoid being trampled. Hooves slipped on the smooth tile as she spun us around and barred him from the portal. I attended to the menu prompt.

```
DEVELOPER CONSOLE
>> iddqd_
```

My teeth clenched as the menu initialized.

Decimus lunged forward, swinging one sword after the other. Lucifer sidestepped admirably but was clearly lacking some of his previous magical power. Decimus was notorious for his auto-hits and the devil was too slow to dodge both strikes. Instead of attempting to, he dodged one and raised his witchwood against the second blade.

The silver sword sliced clean through the staff and bit into Lucifer.

```
Critical Hit!
Blockbreaker!
[Decimus] dealt 60 damage to [Luc1f3r]
```

Half of the staff clattered to the floor.

```
DEVELOPER CONSOLE
>> STATUS
>> UNLOCKED
>> MENU ENABLED
>> _
```

The angel recovered. As Lucifer rolled away, two more sword swipes caught his back.

```
Critical Hit!
[Decimus] dealt 75 damage to [Luc1f3r]
Critical Hit!
[Decimus] dealt 75 damage to [Luc1f3r]
```

The roll ended in a sloppy tumble. The angel floated before Lucifer, pushing to his hands.

```
DEVELOPER CONSOLE
>> angels
>> VERIFYING CREDENTIALS
```

The angel crossed swords at Lucifer's neck. My wounded ally turned his head to me, fighting panic. Decimus acted swiftly. His arms thrust outward, taking the head clean off.

Bravo Team slowed at the top of the portico steps. I stared in shock as the black-cloaked figure fell limp.

```
Resident [Luc1f3r] has been deleted!
```

Decimus turned to his next target. "Hadrian, you are in violation of—" The angel stumbled. His head lowered, blindfold falling loose to the floor. Still gripping silver swords, his white eyes blinked at the splintered section of witchwood buried in his heart. The angel's perfectly sculpted chest cracked. As he dropped to one knee, the entire Pantheon rumbled.

Bandit snorted, but her footing was sure. Hadrian steadied himself with a hand on the tile. As Bravo Team entered, leaning on each other for support, the high portico entrance began to crumble.

"Lash!" yelled Conan, axe pointing above.

Glinda's jaw dropped. Bravo Team squeezed tight as Lash slammed her cleaver into the ground.

[Lash] cast Bastion

A shining dome of light encased Bravo Team as a chunk of the stone ceiling crashed onto them. The impressive barrier held true, but it couldn't possibly support the entire Pantheon.

"Get out while you can, Talon!" yelled the white knight.

I blinked, still stupefied, refusing to flee. The bongo stood over the fast-travel portal, guarding it against Hadrian. The capitol building trembled with increasing violence. Bandit shuffled beneath as my eyes fixed on Lucifer's black cloak. The body lay there, completely still, silver runes fading to nothing.

Decimus sheathed his swords and clutched his chest. Light leaked freely from his body, a sure sign of his impending death. The angel glanced overhead, white orbs witnessing the world for the first time. With a bold cry, he leapt into the air. As the triangular tip of the portico fell away, Decimus met it and plugged it with his body. The whole structure collapsed to the peak of the steps, but he forced his might against it. A flash of white enveloped him—a contained explosion—and then somehow the room was still.

Decimus had turned to stone, his body now a new support beam, barely holding the collapsed facade of the portico together.

```
DEVELOPER CONSOLE
>> ERROR
>> ANGELS OFFLINE
```

I strained to believe what I was seeing.

Amid the impossible barrage of distractions, Hadrian made a run for it. Deft boots slid under Bandit and into the fast-travel ring. Instead of chasing him, I went back to my now-initialized menu.

```
DEVELOPER CONSOLE
>> fast travel_
```

With a simple word, I flipped the portal's switch. It was locked. Hadrian tensed, and then slumped forward on the floor, resigned.

"That damned developer menu," he spat. "Of all the contingencies I'd planned for, that one came as a surprise."

I quietly dismounted.

"A menu like that would come in handy, even for me, Talon. You still have time, of course, to join the winning team. What do you say?"

I raised the dragonspear, readying to strike with the flat of the weapon.

Hadrian's eyes flitted to it. "I thought not. But that artifact is hardly necessary." The Whisperer pulled a dagger from his inventory and slit his throat.

Tad plodded forward. Haven's main server portal was destroyed, they had no communication with the outside world, and the elevators were shut off due to the fire.

At least he'd recovered his crutch. It had tumbled a ways, but he found it. Limping along with it provided some measure of normalcy, a rote task he could distract himself with. He could almost pretend it was another day in the office if it wasn't for the incessant fire alarm.

Tad paused by the outer windows overlooking the courtyard commissary many floors below. A crowd was gathering there. The studio, if not the building, was almost certainly empty now. If anybody hadn't left after Abbie's dismissal, they would've obeyed simple fire-safety protocol.

Anybody except a wounded CEO workaholic.

Then there were the potential visitors. How long would Fire Rescue take? Were other bad operators on the way? With any luck, the attention from authorities would dissuade whatever backup Abbie had contacted.

Once again, Tad placed the crutch before him and hopped forward. Unlike everybody else, he wasn't headed for the exit. He couldn't climb down that many flights of stairs with a broken leg. There was nothing to do but return to Christian's office and see to Haven. It was Pete's final instruction.

Tad entered the office, tired, face streaming with tears. How was he expected to be the game's caretaker by himself? He froze at the trails of blood running back and forth over the carpet.

A relieved chuckle escaped his lips when he saw Christian still alive. Instead of diligently resting, the CEO had spent his time crawling back and forth, gathering computer components. He rested on the floor beside a new monitor hooked up to his workstation.

The CEO's head jerked up at the programmer's entrance. "Ah, Tad. We've been rerouted to backup power."

Tad blinked in bewilderment. Christian was so hyper-focused on his task that he'd completely scuttled any fear of Abbie and her gun, any worry for Pete and his team. Here was a man who thought like a machine.

Tad wasn't built that way.

"Jeez, Christian, you've been shot! We need to get you to a hospital!"

A curt shake of his head. "Impossible until this is rectified. We need all hands on deck. Where's Pete? I need him in here."

"He's dead! Abbie blew up the whole room, including herself! Everyone's dead!"

The CEO blanched as the human cost made itself abundantly clear. Tad, ashamed of his outburst, quietly slid to the floor. He was tired and sore all over. A frantic giggle overtook him, which was somehow worse than crying. The hopelessness was finally catching up to him, and it was all a cruel joke. It would've been hilarious if it wasn't so tragic.

His boss attempted to talk some sense into him. "I really

don't... We can't... but damn." And then there was glum silence. It seemed appropriate, but the longer it continued the more obvious it was that something needed to be said. The CEO stared into space. "I think he was my best friend."

After digesting that remark for an idle minute, he lowered his head. His fingers rapped the keyboard. Still in danger of bleeding out, Christian Everett was dutifully attending his life's work.

Tad wished he didn't take the label so literally.

1730 Fallout

Blood gushed rhythmically, feeding a growing circle of scarlet on white tiles. The daze that consumed me was stubborn. It clouded my thoughts, detached me from the world. I was watching a movie through my own eyes.

Hadrian was dead. I examined his still body.

Loot:
840 silver
Snakeskin Buckler
Spider Boots

The silver alone was a small windfall, but compared to the lost soulstone the prize was hollow. My eyes flicked to the black cloak on the floor.

"Get out of here!" screamed Lash.

The voice seemed distant. Although Decimus had prevented the full destruction of the Pantheon, the capitol building was in a miserable state, still mid collapse. Several blocks of granite had landed on Lash's dome shield. Two particular megaliths were suspended right above the party, ready to crush them as soon as the bastion expired. Bravo Team was in trouble.

My reaction was more instinct than calculation. The fate of my friends trumped all other concerns as I swapped out my spear for Hadrian's buckler. The enchanted snakeskin provided good strength for its size, but the item wasn't otherwise special and wasn't a full shield. It was the best I could do in the time I had.

Which was another second or two.

I set my feet and charged Bravo Team, triggering dash to speed my way. The bastion ability flickered and the shield disappeared. I rocketed through the air, pushing extra spirit into overloading spinshield, and braced against the buckler to collide with the granite blocks like a wrecking ball. The impact deflected me to the floor with an "oof." The room trembled.

I raised my head to find Bravo Team huddled together, eyes wide. It had hurt and I'd sustained trivial damage, but the gargantuan blocks had been safely displaced a few yards to the side. With a sigh of relief, Lash leaned against the stone that had almost crushed her.

The excitement gave my system a boost. I still felt numb, but I was less detached. I turned my attention to Lucifer.

He was definitely slain, his head some distance from his body. I approached with trepidation, worried at my inability to examine his remains. I tried a menu lookup.

```
DEVELOPER CONSOLE
>> Luc1f3r
>> ERROR
>> INVALID ASSET ID
```

My jaw hung idle. Lucifer wasn't just dead, he was deleted. Completely gone. I wavered on my feet.

"Thanks for the save," said Lash as she stomped over. "I told you my new level-10 ability would come in handy. I—" She paused as the devil's body dissolved into embers of light and drifted away. "That looks bad. That's bad, right?"

My eyes lingered on the barren spot of shiny tile. Now this war had truly cost Lucifer everything.

"Whoa," chimed Conan. "High def."

I blinked. The detail on the tiles crispened. The world had finally fully streamed in. I surveyed the room. Haven was back to normal.

To emphasize the point, a number of centurions blinked into existence. Outside, the city watch appeared. In moments we were surrounded by olive tunics and red capes. The commander in gold armor was the first to snap to it.

"Form up!" ordered Gladius. "Protect the Pantheon!"

I squeezed my temples. "Don't bother. It's too late." I paced between Gladius and the precarious entryway that was all that remained of the Pantheon's once-grand portico. "The angels are dead. Hadrian escaped with the Eye."

The commander flashed concern as he took in the building's massive structural damage. I stepped under the partially caved-in roof and into the sea of city watchmen on the outdoor steps.

The entire Forum was listless, blanketed in eerie silence like the eye of a hurricane. Even the NPCs wandered and muttered in hushed tones, as if merely speaking was a risky proposition. Everybody was waiting for the other shoe to drop, and I was right there with them.

There was, however, one bright spot in the marketplace. Kyle was bobbing and weaving through the crowd at top speed to get to the Pantheon. He smiled at me as he hit the steps. My face only darkened. There was nothing good about this. I turned and reentered the scene of Hadrian's escape.

Gladius idled in shock. "I... I can't believe this."

"Don't worry," I rasped, "Hadrian's gonna pay for this."

"Damn straight," said Lash. "Hadrian was my charge. I let him escape."

"Don't blame yourself. You couldn't have stopped it."

"I don't give a shit about blame, Talon. I just wanna fix this. I don't know about you, but I'm ready to hop on a boat and sail to Shorehome to wring Hadrian's little neck."

I paused and considered her insinuation. Hadrian was a Shorehome resident. He would respawn there. The Brothers in Black were arguably his faction now after he'd usurped and assassinated Papa Brugo.

Except Brugo had respawned too, three days ago. He'd been in Shorehome three days while the Whisperer was imprisoned. Who was to say he hadn't wrested the city back? Which meant Hadrian's rebuild might be embattled.

In a flash of inspiration, I checked Hadrian's resident ID in the developer menu. The position that came back was unexpected.

"The Whisperer's not in Shorehome," I announced.

By now Kyle had entered the portico. Bravo Team and Gladius huddled around me, waiting. For direction. To make sense of what happened. And, as Lash said, to fix it.

I showed them a stoic face. "He respawned in Oakengard."

Everybody blinked and pondered the ramifications.

"It's a smart move considering the rumors of upheaval in the pirate city," I explained. "And the connections he has in Oakengard. Loras was part of the InLink conspiracy before getting fired. After that Hadrian co-opted his avatar. Meanwhile the crusaders have been beefed up."

"It's an NPC city," said Lash. "That's his environment. No players to go against him."

Kyle hissed. "So we defeat him in an epic battle and dude just ups and moves on to his backup plan. Instead of a village of wooden shanties, now he's hiding behind towering stone walls with a trained army."

"Oakengard isn't a backup," I said. "Hadrian targeted all three cities from the start. The horde besieged Stronghold, Loras maneuvered in Oakengard, and Hadrian grew his roots in Shorehome, biding his time in plain sight in the least important city. This was the game plan Lucifer had plotted against. And because of the Black Hats, Stronghold has remained free."

"Twice now," added Lash with a puff of her chest.

"That's fine and good," the brewmaster returned, "but how long can we hold out with the other two cities against us?"

The commander of the city watch bit down. "We no longer have the protection of the soulstone."

I agreed with a curt nod. The only good thing about Hadrian's dodge was that, unlike Shorehome, Oakengard still had a working hub. That network enabled the dev menu to see him. For now I could locate him with pinpoint accuracy.

The bitter irony was that now, after Hadrian had openly worked against the simulation, there were no more angels to go after him. Lucifer's final act had not only failed to save himself—it had tragically protected Hadrian from further pursuit. And Otho was a broken being, missing in the margins of the game. It had taken days for Lucifer to rein him in. Now, without a master, I feared the angel of death was nothing more than a whisper.

No, this was up to us. And by the looks on everyone's faces, they knew it too.

I cocked my head at the ring of maroon tiles the Whisperer had attempted to escape through. I checked the dev menu and took in a sharp intake of air.

"I can't believe it. Hadrian made a mistake. Before he killed himself, he attempted to use the fast travel, no doubt to teleport to Oakengard."

Everyone's face lit up. Crux leaned forward.

"How could he control that?" asked Gladius.

"I don't know. It must be the remnants of the Trojan. His hooks are in the system. But the why doesn't matter. He managed to open Stronghold's portal, and I locked him out before he could use it."

Lash shrugged. "So how's that a mistake?"

I grinned. "Because he also unlocked the portal on Oakengard's side. And since his respawn, he forgot to lock it up again."

Her face turned to stone. "You're saying we can teleport so far up his ass he'll be constipated for weeks."

"I'm not saying that. That's gross."

"She has a thing with bodily functions," muttered Glinda.

Conan shrugged. "Works for me."

"It's the wrong move," I insisted. "We can't just storm in there plugging buttholes."

The white knight lifted her chin. "Why not?"

"Lash, even if the entire faction goes, seventy Black Hats isn't much of a threat to Oakengard. If we go in there pounding, we'll get pounded."

"Let 'em try."

"No," said Crux, "Talon's right. More than anything else, we want Hex back, right?"

The Bravo leader swallowed her bravado and nodded.

"And even after we find her," he continued, "I'm guessing we'll want to steal back the Eye of Orik. Who here can pick pockets?" The pure thief challenged everyone with his eyes, even me. The boy firmly nodded. "That's why this needs to be a stealth mission. I need to go alone." I opened my mouth to object but he cut me off. "You promised we'd get her back."

I chewed my lip. Crux was just a kid. Gifted at gaming his skills, but far from the most powerful among us. In a lot of ways, though, I had to admit he was perfect for the job. He was a famed dungeon crawler and expert at hiding in shadows. Not only was his thievery top-notch, but he was a pacifist. He wouldn't be picking unnecessary fights in Oakengard. And his motivation couldn't be questioned: his twin sister Hex had been left behind during our last visit to the city.

"No way," declared his Bravo Team superior. "You know what could happen to you?"

"I know," he affirmed. "I'll risk whatever it takes."

I was behind his sentiment and his reasoning, but...

"There's a better way," I countered. I threw a palm up to

silence his objection and continued. "You should go. I think you give us the best chance. But you won't go alone."

"Anyone else will just slow me down. No offense, Talon, but even you won't be as hidden as me."

"That's true, but we have the void pearl now. I can go in shadow form."

"Hold up," said Kyle. "We barely tested that functionality."

"It enables me to teleport to a party member. I put Crux in ours, teleport him in first, and I follow."

"What does the shadow form do?" asked Lash.

I cleared my throat. "It makes me incorporeal. A shadow."

Glinda cut in. "I think she's asking what kind of offense it gives you to back up our junior party member."

"I see." Instead of answering, I frowned.

"No way," said Lash again. "No way he goes without me. We left two people behind last time. I won't let that happen again."

I sighed patiently. "The whole point is not to be noticed, Lash. And I'm sorry, but you're a little bit... lumbering."

Her dark eyebrows angled down.

"You're doing it right now and you're not even moving."

"Screw stealth," she asserted. "We can fight 'em."

"We can't."

"Sure we can," replied Kyle, stepping up beside Lash. "No offense to Bravo Team, but Crux is who got us into trouble the last time we were in Oakengard. Do I need to remind you he drew us into the Inner Hall and got us chased out by keepers? I'll feel better if I'm there. I have my decanter. With a random effect, the tree form's no guarantee, but I always get the best ability needed in the moment. I've gotten repeats before. The tree form is the best defense against the stun of the keepers."

Lash grumbled. "He's right. As much as I hate to say it, we could use the frat boy over there."

"You guys aren't getting it," I said. "We can't do this with overwhelming force. If we go in hot, nothing's stopping Hadrian from noticing and locking the fast travel. We can only teleport small groups at a time. We'll be cut off from reinforcements. I can't override Oakengard's portal with the dev menu, at least not from here. And we can't hide an entire party." I shook my head emphatically. "There's a larger game here. I need everyone to do their jobs. Even if everything we do eventually comes down to a battle royale in Oakengard, our efforts elsewhere will add up to so much more."

"Damn," grumbled Conan. "The long game. I hate when fighting requires thinking."

"If only war was waged by arm wrestling," said Glinda.

"Exactly," said Conan, not realizing she was poking fun at him.

"Extraction then," suggested Gladius. He studied Bravo Team and the nearby city watchmen. "You two go in while we wait by the portal, ready in case you need us."

"That's a plan," I agreed. "It gives us the best chance to see what's going on in Oakengard, find our missing friends, and get back the soulstone. And if it comes to banging heads, Lash, you'll get your way too."

The big woman worked her jaw. I couldn't tell if it was soothing her anger or stoking it, but she finally nodded in appeasement. "Fine."

"Then it's settled," I said, moving to the fast travel. Crux stepped inside the circle with me. I pulled a thin dagger from my inventory and held it out for him.

"What's that?" he asked.

"An assassin needle. You once handed it to me in a tough spot."

"I can't take that."

"You can and you will. I have two more. This is no longer a symbol of trust. It's a weapon that I can't wield in shadow form. Who knows? You might get a shot at Hadrian with it."

"I wouldn't take it. I'm a pacifist."

"Take the damn assassin needle," I snapped. "Consider it an order. You can decide later whether to use it or not."

Crux ground his teeth and begrudgingly accepted the item. "I suppose I can use the agility bonus."

"That's the spirit." I went to the party controls and kicked Errol before sending Crux an invite. Once he accepted, I moved to the edge of the circle. "You'll be going in first and I'll teleport to you seconds after. Is Trafford briefed on the procedure, Kyle?" With the brewmaster in the Pantheon, Trafford had to remain in Dragonperch to manually operate the void pearl.

Kyle nodded. "Briefed and ready."

The extraction team was ready too. Kyle, Bravo Team, and the centurions and watchmen. They stood in a wide circle watching us.

"Give me a warning if something big's coming through, will you?" joked Gladius. "I want to take the first crack at it."

I smiled. "Sure thing." I opened the dev menu and sent Crux through. He disappeared without fanfare. Then I went into party chat.

> **Talon:** *Trafford, do you see Crux on the sanctum display?*
> **Trafford:** *The map isn't filled out in his location but he's far out west all right.*
> **Talon:** *Good. Send me through.*
> **Trafford:** *Your funeral.*

My entire body went black, and the next thing I knew I was in Oakengard.

1740 Ghost Recon

"Psst!"

Crux ducked against the doorway, peeking out and around.

The large circular room was familiar. Rough brownstone enclosed us, doorways breaking off in three directions. In contrast to the natural texture of the stone walls, the floors were glossy quartz, pale rose, with runners of yellow along the walls. A dull ring of blue marked the portal I stood beside. No one was in sight within or down the hallways.

Unlike Stronghold, Oakengard's fast travel wasn't in a secured area. Presumably this was to enable easy troop movements. We were inside the fortress, but not the Inner Hall. While this decreased the probability of guards, it also meant we were more prone to encounter random passersby.

"Psst! You there, Talon?"

Crux peered through the shadows, no doubt making use of his darkvision. I had the skill as well, though I was surprised to find it was necessary. The crystal sconces dotting the walls were mostly dark. The few that did produce bluish-white light flickered haphazardly. Crux looked right through and past me and continued scanning the room.

I approached him with a whisper. "I'm here."

He jumped and spun to the sound, eyes wild.

I pursed my lips. "You... you can't see me?"

"No," he said, features relaxing. "Where are you?"

I glanced down at my body. I was a shadow of myself, literally. A dark mist, transparent and barely there in the dim lighting. Even though I was very near to him, I waved my hand to reveal myself. My body seemed to cohere better than before, still dark but more visible. Interesting.

Crux breathed a sigh of relief. "There you are." The thief approached and pushed fingers clear through my body.

"I guess I can be nearly invisible when I want to be discreet. I'm not physical though. You can't touch me."

"Which means I'm as good as alone here."

"It's what you wanted, right? Besides, I'm still useful. I can scout ahead. Suffice to say, you'll be doing the heavy lifting. And the light lifting. Well, pretty much anything in the lifting category."

The young thief was already studying the room. A famous dungeon runner, the bulk of his skills were tuned for this type of activity. It was a real chance for a noncombatant to shine.

"First problem," he said, nodding toward the doorway we'd used during our last visit. "Grimwart isn't here."

The good colonel had operated the fast travel during our previous escape before being petrified by hostile keepers. Hrm. I'd kind of assumed it was a permanent condition. "Can statues move?"

"I don't know."

I silently cursed. Crux's sister had also been turned to stone. With Grimwart missing, it was likely Hex wouldn't be where we'd left her either. This wasn't gonna be as easy as I thought. "I guess we're taking a tour of Oakengard."

Crux set his jaw and darted forward down the hall.

"Wait." He turned impatiently and I pinged a resident ID in the dev menu. "Good. Hadrian's on the other side of the fortress. With any luck he's in some room on lockdown."

"I guess you can be useful," said the thief with a chuckle. He turned down the hall and I rushed after him.

We were both fast. In fact, many of the dungeon techniques I employed were borrowed from Crux. He was a heavy contributor to the wiki and an expert in his field. Even though I was in command here, I let him take lead.

Some way down, Crux plastered himself into a dark alcove and signaled me with a backhand. I scooted into the wall. After a brief wait, voices sounded in the corridor. Men were coming this way.

I gritted my teeth. Despite Oakengard's large army, our last tour through the fortress had shown it to be fairly desolate. The city had no players—discounting Hadrian. By comparison, the mostly NPC-driven economy seemed sterile and predictable.

Unfortunately, even the smallest encounter could blow up on us. Oakengard was governed by knights, sages, and until recently, priests. If anybody spied us, no matter how weak, the keepers would be alerted. The city's stone golems would overwhelm the pacifist in seconds.

"I tell ya, it ain't right," a whisper echoed off the walls.

"Stop exaggeratin'!" chided a second man. "Our pouches get heavy an' our bellies get filled. What more d'ya want?"

By now the speakers were coming into view: two men,

dressed in chain mail and wearing black robes emblazoned with white crosses. Crusaders.

Crux spun his head to me. I set my finger to my lips, then faded out as much as I could manage.

"I'm saying, we need to bring this to Hero Gent."

"Bah! Since when does one of the Trinity listen to us?"

"He's a fair man. He'd give us an ear. He has to see what this Hadrian fellow's up to."

"Shh!" hurried the portly knight. "You'll have us in for disciplinin'! You heard what happened to Rory!"

The other man waved an emphatic arm as they walked by us. "That's exactly my meaning! Things are strange around here."

"Nah, we've been mobilizin' for weeks. It's that Bishop Tannen which did it."

The knights blustered down the hall, alternating between exclamations and whispers. They hadn't noticed us.

"Piece of cake," mouthed Crux, detaching from his dark spot and pressing forward.

I continued with renewed curiosity. All the doors we passed were closed, like the fortress was locked down. I wasn't sure if that was unusual, but it jived with the conversation we just overheard. The problem was we didn't know which door to head down. Oakengard wasn't properly mapped. That said, our path wasn't random. We were following the same track Grimwart had led us down, heading to where Hex was last seen. It was useless, I knew, but we had to check.

Kyle: *What's going on over there? Everything okay?*

Talon: *Good so far. Just some light recon. Let's stay off the channel until we need it.*
Kyle: *Roger that.*

We slowed as the hall ended in a large room like the one we started in. Instead of a fast-travel portal, the center of the room featured a descending spiral staircase with purple banisters. To our misfortune, the sconces worked well in here, giving off constant light and only occasionally glitching. We cautiously peeked in and spotted the two sentinels we knew would be posted within, the stone keepers of Oakengard.

They had smooth, glass-like body parts, a jumble of floating rocks the color of smoke. A large torso, a head, and an oblong stone or two for arms. Their disparate pieces hovered near each other, tethered by an electric glow. Instead of the usual soft white, they lit up with purplish energy. Like everything else around here, they were the same, but different.

It didn't need to be said, but being made of super-dense rock conferred the keepers with ample defensive qualities. As for when they went on the attack, they could spawn energy batons that stunned their prey and, given the opportunity, utilize a special move that petrified their enemies into black rock.

Hence why Grimwart and Hex were no longer with us.

Crux switched to party chat so we could communicate in silence.

Crux: *I think I can get past them.*
Talon: *Down the stairs? That's crazy!*
Crux: *I'm not going for the stairs.*

The thief pointed to the north end of the room where there was an adjoining hallway.

I bit down. That's where we'd left his sister. As much as we needed to check the status of the Trinity and locate the soulstones, Hex was the priority. To be honest, I couldn't stop Crux if I tried. It was the whole reason he'd volunteered for the solo mission. I surveyed the room, gauging the odds of the expert thief slipping past the inhuman senses of the keepers. It was a much easier task than getting down the steps, but it wouldn't be easy.

> **Talon:** *I'll go. Wait here.*

The young thief started to move, but I solidified in his face with a glare of warning. I respected his passion for his sister but I couldn't have a mutiny here. He swallowed and nodded.

I faced the room and took a breath. The void pearl had protected me from detection this long. As far as I could tell it would continue to do so. I swallowed. Nothing like a test run.

I moved into the chamber, sticking to the wall by force of habit. It was a straight shot to the adjoining hall. Five steps in, one of the keepers hummed twice, opaque stone head lighting from the inside.

I pressed into the wall and froze, as invisible as I could be. The stone head turned my way. I waited in a small heap, thinking the jig was up.

Damn Izzy and her newfound historical slang.

The keeper's head spun past me, twisting around in a full circle like an owl's. It came to rest back where it started with nary a warning call. I was too scared to breathe out and figured the sooner I cleared the room, the better. I hurried into the hallway and down until the bend, where I was greeted with another empty corridor.

> **Talon:** *No go. No eyes on Hex or Grimwart.*

I considered checking further down. This was the Inner Hall, off limits to all but the highest-ranked Oakengardians. Saint Loras had worked out of here. It stood to reason we might find something important.

Shouts echoed from the stairway room. Crux had been spotted. I hurried back, skidding to a stop at the edge of the doorway.

> **Crux:** *We've got visitors.*

I relaxed. The thief was still hidden. At least, I couldn't see him. Instead the commotion was coming from a large crusader being escorted by two of his fellow knights. Except the two men were wearing purple instead of black.

> **Talon:** *This is new.*

"I shall not idly follow," spat the large man. He shoved his shoulder into one of the purple knights. The other tried to intervene but was staved off by the big one's glare.

"You must," insisted one of the purples. "You've been summoned."

"Listen to reason, Rygar," said the other.

"I'm a crusader of Oakengard," said the man in black. "I reason with my blade." He drew a large broadsword with a faint yellow glow.

His opponents' blades flashed. Rygar parried one, then the other, sending a kick back to the first. The purple knight fell on his back and dropped his weapon. The other two fighters exchanged a few thrusts before slowing. They waited as the first climbed to his feet.

"We're brothers," tempered the unarmed man. "Come down and see for yourself."

"You're the Violet Order," exclaimed Rygar.

"One and the same."

The true crusader puffed his chest out. "Quite the opposite, in fact. You ceased being my brother when you donned that color."

The other man's face soured. His eyes went to the sword on the floor.

Double doors in the main wall slammed open. "Truth is in the eye of the beholder," announced Hadrian.

I cursed and checked the dev menu. His position had shifted, of course. Instead of being locked down in a single room, the Whisperer had the run of the fortress. I squinted at his smug countenance. Attached to a necklace and hanging against his chest were the three crystal triangles that had previously hovered above the Trinity: the trijewel.

The knights in the room stiffened. I was invisible and even I did the same. Hadrian was always a little off, but now he looked like a supervillain. At certain angles, his eyes glowed the same purple that animated the keepers.

"We are of one fortress," said the Whisperer, apparently now the Protector of Oakengard. "We can also be of one order—the Violet Order. All you need to do is be of one mind."

The black knight sneered. "Is this the choice you gave the colonel?"

Hadrian scowled. "He lacked devotion."

"Fie on that! I see you for what you are, Whisperer. The Violet Order are nothing more than catechist upstarts, in the footsteps of Bishop Tannen. You'll share the same fate as them, the fate of traitors!"

Hadrian dropped his eyes to the floor with a long sigh. "I do this for your own good, Sir Rygar." He ticked a finger toward the man and the two keepers energized into bright red. They advanced and hummed loudly.

Rygar's eyes widened. "The holy keepers! It cannot be!" His sword was raised but faltering. The purple knights flanked the man, now surrounded on four fronts.

I clenched my jaw. It was stupid, but my instinct was to help the knight in black. Draw my dragonspear and dash into the fray with reckless abandon. But I was a shadow, less than one. I could no more intervene than they could see me. And Crux was a sworn pacifist, refusing to fight even when his sister had been in trouble.

No, this was only a spectator sport.

As the new order closed in, feet shuffled down the hall behind me. I'd been so focused I didn't notice them until they were upon me. I spun as they ran past.

"Hold your sword!" cried an elderly fellow in a robe. He was bald, stately, and trailed by two young assistants, a man and a woman. Since he came from the Inner Hall, I figured him to be important.

The room turned at his address. "Speaker Harroway," exclaimed Rygar. He braced a forearm across his chest and bowed his head. The two keepers remained idle while the knights of the Violet Order offered similar, though less hearty, salutes.

"What is this?" asked the old man sharply. "We here are now turning our blades on each other?"

"Speaker," intoned Hadrian, "it is but a squabble among brothers. The keepers are on hand to rebuff the hostilities so no one is harmed."

"This is Oakengard," chided the speaker. "We are not host to hostilities!" Harroway's sandals stepped forward softly, his voice turning contemplative. "I heard you invoke the bishop's name, Sir Rygar. You are wise to do so. The new order of priests have tarnished the good names of their brothers and sisters."

"The same thing is happening with the Violet Order," insisted the crusader.

"Tut tut. There's no evidence of that. I recently spoke with Hero Gent myself. Our wise sage, Philosopher Mara, sits beside him."

"The new leadership afears me."

"What leadership?" posited Harroway. He jabbed a finger at Hadrian. "This man is no king. He's your Protector. He champions all of us."

It was obvious Rygar disagreed, but he also greatly respected the old man's opinion. He worked his jaw. "I take my orders from the Trinity, or what's left of them."

The speaker hiked his shoulders. "Is it not them who request your presence now?" The old man moved in and rested a frail hand on the knight's shoulder. "Objections are natural, my friend. Change is scary. But we must keep the peace, here above all places. Walk with these men, speak plainly with Gent, but do not succumb to violence. Keep what little light we have. Remember, without light..."

Rygar clenched his jaw and finished the oath. "There is not darkness; there is nothing."

Harroway nodded and patted the black pauldron. "Good, my boy, good." The speaker stepped away and observed approvingly as all three knights sheathed their weapons. The keepers faded from bright red to dull violet and resumed their places by each amethyst banister. Hadrian gave a bow of thanks to the high sage. The man bowed back and headed down the hall Crux was in, entourage in tow.

Rygar sighed. "May the White King guide me." His boots plonked down the delicate steps. The knights followed closely, leaving us in the room with Hadrian.

All it would take was me to convince Crux to use the assassin needle.

But no, even if he had been determined to use the weapon, the thief was only level 6. Hadrian wasn't much higher, but his character sheet wasn't indicative of his power. I didn't think Crux had a chance.

"You two," ordered the Whisperer, "down there with him. This might get ugly."

Hadrian descended the winding stairs. The two golems spun

around and followed. Unexpectedly, the entry to the Speculum was left unguarded. Crux and I wandered from our hiding spots in disbelief, met in the center of the room, and snuck down the steps.

1750 Mirror's Edge

The Speculum was Oakengard's control center. The entire cavern sat on a frozen lake, its surface both mirrorlike and transparent. Multicolored lights flashed in the depths below, the ice carrying the rainbows and projecting them shimmering through the amethyst walls. In sharp contrast to the dark halls of Oakengard, the Speculum was more alive than it had ever been.

Our subjects marched to the end of the room facing the throne. I considered remaining in our perch on the winding stairs, but there was a shadowed alcove on the left wall that suited our needs perfectly. With everyone's backs to us, Crux and I snuck to the hiding place undetected.

The floor was thrumming now. It surged with renewed energy. I wondered what Hadrian had done to enliven the place, and if it had something to do with the Trinity. I wondered where Hadrian had found the time because this was more than the last hour's work.

After we'd defeated the kraken, Hadrian was stripped of the Squid's Tooth, Shorehome's soulstone. He didn't steal Stronghold's until three days later. That left the fate of Oakengard's up in the air. Supposedly a player had stolen it long ago. That player must've been Hadrian.

A column of smoky glass stretched from the rocky ceiling to the floor of the lake below the surface we stood on. Three glass thrones protruded from the column just above surface level, visible one at a time as the column rotated. With Bishop Tannen ousted, the current throne facing us was empty, and with Hadrian wearing the trijewel, the crystals were no longer inset into the command column.

A woman's voice rang out. "Here to discuss the fruitlessness of your path?" The crystal pillar spun, sliding the empty throne out of the way and replacing it with the one filled by the head of the sage caste. Philosopher Mara was an old woman with a powerful visage. Today she appeared more frail than usual. Aged in a matter of days.

Rygar and the knights of the Violet Order bowed, though the original crusader's gesture was more pious. He fell to one knee.

Hadrian stood to the side with crossed arms. "I see you still choose to weigh philosophical quandaries over practical urgencies. Your insistence on debate is what's fruitless."

Mara's eyes sharpened. "It must be easy to abandon debate when one is on the wrong side of it."

The Protector of Oakengard smiled wryly. "We're not here for your lessons, Mara, or for you—a fact you should consider most fortunate. Pray my good will continues."

"At ease!" urged a stout voice.

The column rotated again, this time to the third throne occupied by Hero Gent. The head of the knightly order was a famously brawny man, middle-aged yet possessed of the fortitude of youth. Except, as with Mara, much of that luster was missing. He'd grown obviously weaker, with much of his fire gone.

"Hero!" exclaimed Rygar. The knight stood and crossed an arm over his chest.

"I know what you're here for, Protector." Gent's voice was powerful yet robotic. He sat still on the throne, not appearing especially comfortable, hands cradled in his lap. Even his eyes seemed to drag as he studied the subjects before him.

"You always were the most devoted to your duties," mocked the Whisperer. "I wish to see one of our greatest warriors honored. It's time for Rygar to join the Violet Order."

"Never!" spat the crusader. "These knights stand not for justice, my Hero."

The head of the knights watched with exhausted patience. "I am not the most flexible among us, great warrior, but even I understand there comes a time when fighting change is counter-productive."

Rygar stood firm. "Even when it betrays the core of our oaths?"

Gent's head dipped slightly, highlighting how statuesque he'd been until now. "Following orders is in service to your oaths. Rygar of the black circle, I hereby honor you."

The ruler lifted his arm, a jerky, awkward motion. The two keepers converged on Rygar and grabbed him. He tried to pull away, but purple energy surged into his body. He was a powerful warrior, standing resolute against the magic coursing through him. His resistance was short-lived. Rygar dropped to his knees as the black on his cloak color-shifted to violet. Hero Gent watched on, expressionless, as the new-and-improved Rygar rose to his feet.

The tall man's voice came scratchy and subdued. "I see your wisdom, good Hero."

One of the purple knights rapped him on the back. "Welcome to the Violet Order, friend."

My stomach turned, one part disgust and the other part anger. Hadrian was using his control over the Trinity to turn the populace. Hero Gent was a traitor to his people.

The Whisperer placed something in Gent's hand. "A token of thanks." Hadrian turned to his new warrior. "Round up your sergeants. Bring any that don't accept the power to the Speculum within the hour."

The smoky crystal column rotated back to Philosopher Mara. "That is enough for the day. We are tired and must rest."

"We're done when I say we're done."

"You've taxed us too greatly these past days."

Mara had just confirmed what Saint Peter had suspected, that Hadrian had been scheming even while in prison. The network spikes...

Hadrian sneered. "I *encourage* those who need it because our enemies want us destroyed. If I don't raise the Violet Order to full strength, raiders will be looting these halls in a matter of days."

"That concerns me little," said Mara coldly.

Hadrian stared at her, face transforming from shock to frustration, and finally settling on vindication. "You'd welcome that, wouldn't you? The fall of Oakengard."

The sage's face was passive. "This city can't fall any lower than with you as its Protector."

"Enough!" the Whisperer spat. "You want to see my power? What I can do?"

"You wouldn't dare."

Hadrian barked an order and the two keepers advanced on the sage. Only two yards away, they stalled their approach. The Whisperer's cheek twitched as the keepers lost their violet glow. They turned on Hadrian and flared red. A cool smile crooked on Mara's face.

"You're in the Speculum, false Protector. This is the Trinity's seat of power, not yours."

Hadrian grunted and threw his arms apart, clenched fists shaking with effort. The two keepers converged at his sides, as they had with Rygar, except their rock bodies began to tremble. Stripes of red and violet played across their glassy bodies and they began to disassemble. Quartz ripped apart and moved over Hadrian's skin, his chest and arms and back, blanketing him like a carapace. It was as close to power armor as I'd seen in Haven.

"If you don't approve of the new Oakengard," he growled, "then you may claim your place in its past."

"No," pleaded Gent unseen. "What's left of the Trinity..."

"I *am* what's left."

Hadrian thrust a hand forward. The long piece of quartz over his forearm shot out like a missile and plunged into Mara's chest. The philosopher jerked in place, pinned to her throne. Her neck stretched before her head drooped to a bounce, still wearing the look of surprise.

Rygar snorted. "Thus is the will of the Violet Order." He turned toward the staircase with his new comrades and exited the room to collect his sergeants.

Hadrian stood in the Speculum, staring at his handiwork and breathing chaotically. A nervous laugh sputtered from his lips and grew, free and wild, boastful even.

"The power," he whispered to the dead ruler. "It was never yours."

Hadrian spun around so suddenly I thought he'd sensed us. His glowing eyes scanned the empty space, a perturbed look on his face. His eyes twitched in several directions. Then he stormed back toward the stairway. I held my breath till he was gone.

The Whisperer had truly gone crazy.

After ensuring we were alone, I solidified and addressed Crux. "Arm your dagger."

His eyebrows bunched up. "What for?"

"Taking down Hadrian is a tall order, but we can remove one of his weapons." I marched to the glass throne at the end of the room. Philosopher Mara's frail body was settled awkwardly, a Halloween skeleton propped on a chair in feigned life—an aberration of life. My face twisted. The NPC was dead. There was no reason why Gent, the real traitor, shouldn't join her.

"I won't do it," whispered Crux beside me.

"I understand your views on violence. I respect them. But you have to see what you can prevent here."

"The only thing I can guarantee preventing is more violence, and only if I choose not to partake."

"Come on!" I snapped, voice heated. "You saw what just happened. Gent's selling out his own people to live as long as he can."

Crux rapped the blade of the assassin needle on the crystal

column. Veins of black ran through the smoky quartz. Lines of energy from a poisoned well. "The Trinity's not in power here. I can't punish them for what they're forced to do."

"Damn it, kid, do you want to save your sister or not!?!"

"At ease," came Gent's voice, softer than before. We recoiled as the column spun around. The weathered knight sat stiffly in position. His eyes were wet.

"Do it, Crux!" I urged. "Now, before he sounds the alarm."

"If that had been my will," remarked Gent, "it would already have been done." The ruler toyed with a small bottle in his hand. "It has been difficult... this feeling of contagion. Right and wrong have lost all meaning." A cough rattled through his chest and the smoky column momentarily sparked purple. "It eats at us. Preys upon our will. Only Philosopher Mara was able to overcome it. She was the strongest of us..."

The beaten man choked up and took a moment to recover. "I told myself it was for the best," he finally said. "I'm tired, Protector of Stronghold. I only wanted to save the lives of my knights."

"They're being assimilated," I said. "What kind of life is that?"

"As long as they live, there's hope." He sighed, perhaps unconvinced by his own words. "I thought a corrupted influence was better than a war among our people, better than a sure defeat. Mara's moral stand would've had deadly consequences." He attempted a frown but his face barely contorted. "I see now that fate is inevitable."

"Civil war," said Crux.

"Aye, young thief. Peaceful occupation breeds greater

tragedies than death. What a paradox we find ourselves in. But then you're one with light fingers and heavy morality." This time the ruler's coughing came in a fit.

It was odd seeing him wracked with disease yet sitting so upright in his throne. When I peered closer I saw fingers of glass growing outward from the seat, growing *into* him. No wonder he was so stiff; Hero Gent was part of the throne now.

"This was meant for me," said the ruler, rolling a small vial between his fingers. "It helps stave off the rot, you see. It helps keep me alive." He closed his eyes and reopened them painfully. I realized I hadn't seen him blink the entire time. "I don't deserve life anymore, and this antidote is suited to a more worthy recipient. Find Colonel Grimwart. He was the first of us to see the danger. To act against it. He tried to warn us."

Crux grabbed the vial from Gent's hand.

"Pour the entire solution on him. It will restore stone to skin."

"Where is he?" I asked.

The ruler grimaced. "The Hall of Heroes." His eyes closed slowly. "The Hall of the Damned." What little light pulsed through the throne column slowed. Gent's breath came out in a throaty rasp, his head lowered, and he breathed no more.

"Wait!" cried Crux. "Is there more of this?" The thief frantically patted down Gent's hardened pouches.

I worked my jaw as I watched the futile scene. Crux was right. Gent had operated differently from Mara, but it wasn't out of maleficence. Hadrian was in control, forcing his will on the people, on the city itself. For all their inimitable heft, the Trinity had been powerless.

Now they were dead.

1760 Minesweeper

We hurried through the Inner Hall of Oakengard, our new goal palpable. With my shadow form and the thief's expertise at sneaking, we roamed the halls at will. The problem was the unmapped fortress had so many connections and corridors it was practically a maze. Thirty minutes of delving seemed just as valuable as three, and the impressive beauty of the grand architecture was lost to endless repetition.

We were in the middle of one such monotonous great hall when we heard the clip-clop of hooves. A large black stallion rounded the corner like something out of a Greek legend. He greeted us with a nicker.

"What's a horse doing in here?" asked Crux.

I cocked my head, a smile growing across my face. "Artax?" I went to scrub his neck but my shadowy hands went through his body. I laughed. "Right. It *is* you, though. Who's a good boy?"

The loyal steed had been killed by the kraken while defending Stronghold. It was good to see he respawned in his home. My face darkened when I realized he was without a master.

"This is Grimwart's horse."

Artax snorted softly at the name. He kicked his head around

and clopped down another hall some ways before stopping and turning to us. Crux and I exchanged a glance.

"He wants us to follow," I said.

We hurried after our animal ally, back toward the center of the fortress and down a grand flight of stairs. Despite the magnificent surroundings, the entire floor was ill lit, growing darker as we moved away from the overlooking balcony.

"It's deserted down here," I whispered.

"Good thing," said Crux. "I very much doubt the horse is proficient at hiding in shadows."

While Crux and I stepped softly, hooves echoed down the corridor. Our excitement helped us keep pace with the warhorse. After a few more turns through a once-great interior, Artax stopped at metal double doors, snorting and kicking the floor.

A plaque hung above the impressive doorway. "The Hall of Heroes," I read. I pushed inside to find an exquisite collection of life-sized statues, forty of them at least, many in poses of great pain.

"The Hall of the Damned," reflected Crux bitterly.

Artax rushed straight to a statue of a crusader and whinnied. "We found him," I said. "Quick, try the vial."

Crux stopped at my side. "What about Hex?"

I swallowed uncomfortably. "Shit. Try a drop on Grimwart. See what happens."

The thief unstoppered the antidote and poured a splash on the knight's helmet. A swirl of color infected the black statue. The mark softened and spread over his whole body. Artax nickered.

"More," I said.

Crux weighed the antidote and dutifully obeyed, keeping as stingy as he could with the application. Fortunately, the solution was having a noticeable impact. The stone exterior of the statue receded, a sponge absorbing moisture, a man absorbing life. The knight's head turned, loosed joints cracked, and he collapsed to his elbows. At my request, Crux pulled off my friend's helmet. With a sickly pallor, Grimwart gurgled drily as he tried to speak.

Crux pulled the vial away. "That's half the antidote. I can't use more without dooming Hex."

I surveyed the rows of statues populating the hall. While some were sculpted statues, many were clearly petrified residents who couldn't be saved. What a travesty it was to choose. "You have a healing potion?"

Crux blinked. "Right." He produced a health flask and rolled Grimwart's stiff body over. Bit by bit, he poured the enchanted liquid down the knight's throat. At first the crusader barely responded, but then he gagged and coughed. Soon he was drinking thirstily.

"It worked!" exclaimed the giddy thief.

I knelt beside them. "How are you?"

"It was awful," Grimwart confided, attempting to sit up with the thief's assistance. "Thanks be to you, good sirs."

"I need to save Hex," said Crux, breaking away.

Artax lowered his head to his longtime rider. Colonel Grimwart smiled and used the warhorse's sturdy frame to rise to his feet. The crusader collected his breath, turned to me, and peered closely. "Talon. What magick is this?"

"Long story. Do you remember what happened?"

"Aye, and then more. I could see everything but act not." The knight's words were heavy with guilt. "The continued isolation of the Trinity. The divisions among the castes. When the protests began, I was locked away from prying eyes. Others joined me soon after. And then no more."

"Oakengard enforcement has evolved past stone," I explained. "Hadrian's in control and talking about a new future. He brings with him a purple plague. The Violet Order. The glowing energy is spreading into the keepers, the Speculum, and the people. It's taking them over."

"And I allowed it to happen."

"No. Your vigilance is the reason they still have a chance. It's lucky you were turned to stone. It protected you from the worst to come." My lips curled. "You should see what they did to Rygar."

"So one of our greatest heroes is one of them now." Grimwart's head fell.

Crux stomped over, agitated. "She's not here."

"Hmm? You sure? Did you miss anyone?"

"She's not here," he insisted.

I walked down the aisle, checking faces.

"I know my sister, Talon. She's not here. Why isn't she here?"

"Hex is an outsider," said Grimwart. He pushed away from his mount, strength returning quickly. "There is a perverted logic afoot. Even with the disgrace they have twisted this great hall into, it is not fit for outsiders. I haven't seen Hex since she was petrified. Mayhaps there's a special place for her."

Crux cursed. I held my tongue. It wouldn't help to vocalize the alternative: that her statue might've been destroyed. In a simulation, I wasn't sure what that would result in, but we had to hope Hadrian hadn't permanently killed her. In a realm with active respawns, confinement was worse than death.

"How did you manage my revival?" asked Grimwart.

I winced. "Hero Gent gave us an antidote before succumbing to his sickness. He refused to work with Hadrian once Mara was assassinated."

"She—" The knight's graying eyebrows rose slowly. "It's much worse than I believed. We must find Hex, gather my knights, and flee Oakengard."

"Knights?"

The crusader nodded. "Surely there are many still left, still loyal to me. If they're in danger, I have an obligation to rescue them."

"The extraction team," reminded Crux.

I nodded and chewed my lip.

Grimwart studied our faces. "What is it?"

"Our other objective," I said. "We're here to steal back the soulstones. I'm betting Hadrian's power is somehow tied to them. But every step of this recon mission brings us deeper into Oakengard politics. And Hadrian is powered up beyond his level."

I hissed and paced away from them, hands on hips. I was starting to wonder if I'd let shock and anger guide me into this desperate mission instead of taking time to think things through. Then again, learning of the purple plague was invaluable. We'd already saved Grimwart, and had a chance to rescue Hex and a bunch of other crusaders. This was working.

I recalled the feeling of helplessness as I'd watched Rygar's stoic final stand. I couldn't do anything to stop that, but I was in a position to prevent it from happening to others. The human cost was really what this war was about. It didn't even matter that the NPCs I'd be saving were never really human.

"We'll put the soulstones on the back burner," I announced, moving to the room's doorway. "First we save who we can. Any idea where Hex would be?"

"Alas, I know not."

"It's got to be this floor," insisted Crux. "The lights are shut down. The whole place is like an oversized closet." The poor kid began trembling with rage. "They stored my sister in the dark somewhere like an old pair of shoes."

"Relax, Crux. Storing your sister is the safest thing they could've done for her. Let's get started then. It's empty down here so it'll be safe to sweep through quickly."

Crux nodded and hurried ahead in lieu of wasting another second. His desperation was palpable.

Grimwart's head swiveled the opposite direction. "I must go upstairs and rally my men. With any luck they've heard rumors of Hex's whereabouts. Once we're gathered, we'll slip out the side gate. My soldiers have already been prepped on the procedure."

"No need. We're taking the fast travel."

"It will be locked down."

"The saints aren't around anymore. I can control it." Grimwart turned to me, baffled. I didn't bother giving him the rundown about the dead saints and developers. His head was already spinning enough. I just said, "Do what you need to do so we can leave as fast as possible."

He nodded and slipped the black helmet on his head. "I wish the young man luck and you both godspeed." He headed toward the stairs and I rejoined Crux.

The lower level of Oakengard was more labyrinthine than the first. The dark conferred a spookier aspect to the maze, and I half expected a minotaur to greet us at every turn. Yet the desolation proved simple to overcome with speed and efficiency. Crux and I cleared rooms with military precision, splitting away for minutes at a time. Twenty such minutes in, I began fearing we were going about this wrong. Hex wasn't nearby. There was nothing down here but the remains of old vanities.

Dead traditions for a dying city.

A charge of excitement stirred me when I encountered a heavy-duty access hatch built into the floor. It was prominently placed at the end of a wide corridor with a large padlock bolting it shut.

My enthusiasm waned as my fingers uselessly passed through the lock. I couldn't interact with physical objects.

The void form was a strange beast. I was immaterial yet didn't fall through floors. I couldn't put my hand through walls or static game objects. *Dynamic* game objects, though, were treated differently. My hands passed through vases and horses and locks.

I wondered if it really mattered. The padlock was of crystal construction. The door was sturdy and reinforced. I doubted I could force my way through the access hatch even if I were physical.

But then...

I pushed my fingers deeper, through the lock and through

the door as well. As my fingertips and hand found success, I pushed forward completely. To my delight, I could indeed step through doors. Since the object could open and close, the collision was dynamic and thus immaterial to me.

Dank steps led down a cave tunnel, reminding me of the dungeon where Hadrian had been confined, except there were tools and carts instead of cells and shackles. This was a mine shaft.

Grimwart had once boasted of Oakengard's famous mining operations. The mountainside was rich with veins of ore, making the fortress strategic for trade as well as defense. Now, the sounds of active labor seemed eons away. A layer of dust coated the tools and walkway. Cobwebs stretched across the tunnel. Production had been shut down.

I sighed in disappointment. As curious as I was about this path, Hex wasn't down here. Nobody had been for a long time. I backtracked to the access hatch. Faint scratching came from the other side of the door. Someone was coming in. I instinctively huddled down before realizing I was only a shadow in the dark. Several seconds later, the hatch opened and Crux climbed down. He stiffened, tuned senses alerting him to my presence.

"You're learning," I said. "Relax."

"Talon? How did you— Oh, right."

"That was a crystal lock."

"Figured this place was important."

I shrugged. "These are the Oakengard mines, where they gather the ore from the mountains. Given the dust, Hex can't be here."

He grumbled at the apparent truth.

"You're pretty good with that lockpick," I said as we headed back up to the hall. "What was that, twenty seconds? Thirty?"

The thief didn't share my fascination with his skills. "This is taking too long, Talon. What did they do with my sister?"

I swallowed. "I don't know, but we're here to find out. Grimwart's rallying his troops. One of them might have heard something."

He sighed. "The second we woke him up, this ceased to be a stealth mission."

I frowned as I took his meaning. "We need to move fast, then. Let's follow his lead and split up. Keep in touch with party chat. Worst case, if I can't get back to you, I'll return to Stronghold and immediately teleport back to your position."

"I'll be fine." The brooding thief flexed his jaw. "Let's do it."

"And stay out of trouble. If I get caught I can go poof. You can't and you have the antidote Hex needs."

"I'll be careful. Let's get this over with." He shut the access hatch and picked a large corridor to search.

I continued on my own way, wondering if I should've shared my misgivings with Crux. The last thing I wanted to do was worry him, but I'd gotten to know Hadrian a little in three days as my prisoner. He might've been a blue-collar guy but he had a superiority complex. Not book read but cold practicality. If he wasn't smarter than someone then at least he had more sense. This was most pronounced when he felt the need to gloat, to brandish his successes over everyone else's failures.

Hadrian was the one with a prisoner now. A player, a member of the Black Hats, and the twin sister of a kid who dared to defy him. Everything in my being told me the

Whisperer would make an example of the young necromancer. That meant Hex would be widely visible as a warning to those who opposed him instead of gathering dust in a closet.

In a short time it felt like I was on the other side of the castle. I was weary and tired and in bad spirits when I was startled by voices ahead.

I hurried to find light filling the halls. It wasn't from sconces on this floor, but from an overlook and another grand set of stairs. A line of sages marched along the banister. "Speed to the courtyard!" they cried. I waited as they passed and then climbed the stairs and went after them, making sure to stay out of sight.

Large double doors opened on an exterior wall. Sunlight overtook the glitched lighting of Oakengard. Outside, the fortress' main courtyard was spacious, full of mustering units of knights wearing black and purple. Sparks of violet arced across some of the soldiers, but plenty of them were untouched by the plague. Like the sages I was following. I wondered how many were just soldiers following orders versus assimilated peons. That dichotomy made the political dynamic very complicated.

The line of twenty sages, led by Speaker Harroway, pressed outside and stomped to the nearest unit.

"What's the meaning of this?" he demanded.

The violet knights were puzzled. Some bowed their heads and saluted, others glanced around the yard awkwardly. I stood at the open doorway, afraid to expose myself to full sunlight.

"Philosopher Mara has ceased communications with my order," continued the old man. "The keepers refuse to allow any of our discipline into the Speculum."

"Do you not trust our Protector?" boomed a voice from the

outer wall. The seven-foot-tall Rygar strode close and smiled at the speaker. "Hadrian is preparing our march. The sages should do their part to contribute to the war effort."

Harroway studied the man's purple uniform. "What is this? The Protector has no right to dictate which audiences the Trinity allows."

"The Trinity is antiquated," said Rygar.

The old man's eyes wavered. "What sayeth you, dear friend? That is insolence."

"You were the one who told me to go along, did you not?"

"Yes, but we have processes which must be followed to ensure equanimity."

Rygar smiled, and some of the knights laughed. "You talk in circles, *dear friend*."

More laughter joined in and Harroway reddened. "I thought you were a knight! If you will do nothing, I will take a hundred sages and storm the Speculum." He turned and admonished the collecting crowd. "Have you abandoned the ideals of your caste? Is duty noble when it cannot be questioned? I will get to the bottom of this and shine a light on any involved! I will—"

A yellow sword punched through Harroway's chest from behind. The speaker's eyes went cross and he fell to the ground. The group of wise men blinked in disbelief. The shock wore off quick. Swords scraped from their sheaths and panic overtook the sages as they tripped over themselves trying to escape the murderous knights.

1770 Blood Bowl

"Get them!" screamed Rygar.

Knights of the Violet Order cut down the defenseless sages. Crusaders in black drew their weapons to halt the affront, but the Violet Order turned on them too. The courtyard transformed into a battlefield of blood and clanging metal.

Both black and purple took losses, either too slow to heal or too zealous in attack. A string of keepers rushed the courtyard. Instead of keeping order, the golems energized with violet went after the true crusaders. Once wounded and weakened, they were latched onto by the stone guardians, just as I'd seen with Rygar. Uniforms changed to violet before my eyes. The knights stood, renewed, and turned on their brothers.

Hadrian no longer required the Trinity to spread his plague.

"This way!" cried Grimwart. He appeared on horseback atop the steps of a side entrance. Artax neighed as the colonel waved in the soldiers that were still his.

I debated running across the battlefield to join them but ultimately decided we could regroup inside. I didn't want to get anywhere near that purple energy. I backed into the fortress as my eyes ran over the massacre. The twenty sages were dead, mowed down from behind as they'd attempted to flee. All they had wanted was the truth.

Frantic buzzing came at my back. I turned as several keepers approached, glowing red.

"Oh shit."

I sped down a hallway. While most of the guardians charged outside, a few broke away to pursue me. I was no longer unseen.

> **Talon:** *We've worn out our welcome! I need the extraction team ready at the portal. We've got a group of friendlies coming in hot.*

I skidded through a sealed door on my way toward the crusaders. Sounds of battle ahead confirmed that the keepers were onto them too. I charged into a wild scene. Halls that were once empty were rife with combat. Crusaders in black stuffed the corridors, more than the ones coming from outside. They were everywhere, driving back purple knights and rogue keepers.

My first reaction was relief. Grimwart had succeeded in rallying a dominant force. The soldiers fought together as unified military units and defended their fellow man. But there were cracks in the noble front. Some of them were turning. A few had been petrified. It was clear after analysis that this was a battle that couldn't be won, and the longer we fought on, the more the tide would turn.

"Retreat to the fast travel!" I commanded. "Go! Go! Go!"

I sidestepped as another door opened to a line of keepers. It was foolish, but I didn't feel safe even as a shadow. The crusaders backed away too, some of them bravely guarding the rear, sacrificing themselves so that others had a chance to escape.

> **Talon:** *How are you doing, Crux? We're out of time.*
> **Crux:** *The bottom floor's empty. Hex isn't here.*
> **Talon:** *We'll rethink it. Get to the fast travel as fast as you can.*
> **Crux:** *But my sister.*
> **Talon:** *It can't be helped.*

It hurt to say it. We were leaving Hex behind a second time, but it was what it was. Our search of Oakengard was over and the battle had begun. Even a pacifist would see that.

We sprinted down the last hall and entered the portal room from the opposite direction we'd used before. A keeper brute stood in our path, twice the height of the three guardians accompanying him. They walled off our exit.

> **Talon:** *Extraction team, we need an assist!*
> **Lash:** *Gladius is sending us through.*

Bravo Team blinked onto the fast-travel portal right behind the quartz guardians. Kyle was there too, glugging from his legendary decanter. The keeper brute spun around as Kyle turned to a treant and attacked. The electrical magic animating the guardians fizzled against his wooden arms. The brute was driven back.

> [Lash] cast Spell Armor
> *+25% magic resistance for the next 30 seconds.*
>
> [Glinda] cast White Circle
> *+20% magic resistance and +10% non-physical damage resistance for the next 60 seconds.*
>
> [Conan] used Blood Frenzy

As the group buffs energized the pack of crusaders, the barbarian hacked at the surprised keepers and opened our way. Grimwart charged into the room atop Artax and bashed his bastard sword into a keeper's head. "Forward!" he ordered.

A line of knights pushed into the circle of tiles. I opened the dev menu and sent them through.

"Next!" he cried, galloping through resistance and sending more friendlies ahead.

"What happened to Hex?" asked Lash between erecting shield walls. The portal room was turning into a funnel, safety in the center and melee at the edges.

"Didn't find her yet," I answered. "We found Grimwart on the bottom floor. It seemed promising but she wasn't there."

Conan's axe sliced through the energy of a keeper's neck, resulting in a miss. Before his opponent could take advantage of the misstep, Kyle bashed him away. Metal weapons were a weakness against Oakengard, but Conan was so frenzied or so crazy he didn't care. Combat raged on as I sent another pack of crusaders to Stronghold.

Since Crux was no longer in her party, the white knight broadcast over brigade chat.

Lash: *Crux, what's your status? Evac's almost done up here.*
Crux: *Sorry, boss. I'm not coming.*
Talon: *What are you talking about? We're defending the portal right now!*
Crux: *I didn't want to delay the others getting to safety so I didn't say anything, but I can't leave Oakengard without her. Not again.*

I was beside myself. The crusaders positioned another unit over the fast travel and I activated the portal. Most of the knights had been evacuated by now, with two more groups to go. Bravo Team fought to clear more space, and Lash traded knowing glances with her crew.

I rushed up to her. "You're not thinking what I think you're thinking, are you?"

She cocked her head uncomfortably. "It's both the twins, Talon. We can't leave them. You've got to see that."

"You don't know what's happening here."

"I've seen enough."

I clenched my teeth. Lash was as stubborn as ever, but she was better about following orders these days. The only reason she was pushing back was to keep a promise to Crux and defend her team. I'd lose the respect of Bravo Team if I didn't let them try. Besides, I'd made the same promise.

I pointed through a set of doors. "He's downstairs, but you'll be hounded every step of the way."

Kyle's tree form leaned in. "Don't worry, bro. I'll keep them safe."

Lash and I turned to him, surprised. "You'd do that for us?" she asked.

"We're in this together, right? Now let's get out of here while we still can."

As I fast-traveled another group of knights, Bravo Team exited down a side doorway. The keepers followed but Kyle slammed the door closed. He was obviously holding it from the other side because their rock bodies slammed against it, unable to overcome his tree strength.

"Stop them!" resounded the voice of Hadrian.

A sea of violet parted as the usurper himself barreled down the main corridor. Wearing his makeshift quartz armor, he was super-powered and super-charged.

I turned to the room. "Final transport! Everybody in!"

Grimwart pushed Artax into the center of the fast travel. Crusaders bunched into the warhorse. As purple knights and guardians closed in, Hadrian burst into the portal room. The dev menu was faster. The final group of crusaders blinked away to safety.

"Get out of my way!" demanded an enraged Whisperer, shoving ineffectual peons aside as he stomped across the portal room.

With the keepers struggling to pursue Bravo Team, they turned to their brute cousin. The rock giant charged through and bashed the door down. The accompanying hall was empty. Kyle had already split.

Hadrian turned from that scene and surveyed the rest of his forces. They were confused, surprised, and angered by the turn of events. Some keepers pursued Bravo Team down the halls but others stood scanning for evidence or facing their new Protector.

The Whisperer was anything but unassuming after his transformation in the Speculum. Blocks of cracked rock plated his skin. Charges of purple magic flowed over him and fumed from his eyes. He casually lifted a hand and a chunk of armor from his forearm thrust forward. I recoiled but too late. Purple magic crackled through me. Even as the physical rock harmlessly passed through, I shivered from the plague.

But I was unharmed. I braced in place and puffed my chest out.

"That's the last of them," I stated loudly, keeping the attention away from Bravo Team. It didn't look like Hadrian knew about them and I wanted to keep it that way. I locked Stronghold's fast travel and stood in defiance of Oakengard's Protector.

Hadrian's chest rumbled low and deep as he fixated on me. "How are you doing this? You found me with the dev menu, I'd guess, but this?"

He waved harshly at my shadowy body. Then something in his eyes sparkled. Hadrian leaned in and sniffed.

"Ah... yes... you've got the stink of the void on you."

I kept a straight face but he chuckled.

"Of course it's the void. I'm not entirely unfamiliar with its power, as you know."

I relaxed, growing more confident of my safety, seeing most of the enemy force standing idle instead of pursuing Bravo

Team. With any luck, they'd be forgotten in the confusion.

Hadrian pursed his lips and nodded. "I haven't given you enough credit. Leaving the fast travel unlocked was my mistake, but you were quick to capitalize on it. You're an opportunist. There are worse things in the world."

Even as he commended me, keepers hovered into a tight circle around me. The Whisperer wanted to test his plague against my shadow. The whole time, my eyes were on the three glass triangles hanging from his neck.

"Where are the soulstones?" I asked.

"That's what you're here for then?" He snorted. "If it wasn't for you, I'd have all three. But it was the kraken's defeat that lost the Squid's Tooth. He's the weakest of the titans. Don't think you'll take the others the same way."

Trafford: *Talon, you just about done over there? I'm getting itchy fingers to call you back.*
Talon: *The evac's complete. Stand by.*

Hadrian's mouth crooked as he recognized me interfacing with the chat. "Still scheming, I see." He waved a hand in the air and the heavy contingent of guards dispersed. Violet knights formed up and marched away. The keepers who crowded me, who a second ago had been ready to strike, backed away and wandered off in all directions. Hadrian, alone, studied me for a long moment. "I'll enjoy ripping you apart."

I scoffed and opened my mouth to respond, but the Whisperer abruptly turned and marched away.

"Goodbye," he said. "For now." With a flick of his hand, I

reappeared in the Pantheon in Stronghold.

"Clear the circle," ordered Gladius. Centurions helped straggling crusaders off the fast travel to make room for more.

"That's all of them," I told him. "No one else is coming through."

> **Talon:** *Damn it, Trafford. Why'd you call me back so soon?*
> **Trafford:** *I didn't touch anything. I swear.*

I winced as the post-shadow hangover itched at my skin. So Hadrian had forced me back then, but how was that—

The last crusader walking off the portal keeled over, gripping a bloody stomach.

"He needs a medic!" cried Grimwart.

The downed knight coughed motes of magic. His back arched and his cloak energized with a purple glow. He pushed to his feet and drew his sword. "Long live the Violet Order!" He hacked at the back of a fellow soldier.

A ring of centurion spears came forward and impaled the newfound enemy in place. Gladius stepped in and stabbed him through, the fire from his sword blazing over the corrupted knight's body. He fell to the floor, dead. Centurions and crusaders traded panicked stares. Some raised their weapons.

"Hold!" I yelled. "Hold! We're all on the same team!" I charged between them, feeling out of place in my own skin but shoving soldiers away all the same.

The collected mood in the Pantheon went solemn. We stared each other down with baited breath, and slowly the weapons went idle.

"We're okay," said Grimwart, dismounting from his stallion. "Let's attend to the wounded. We have more allies to save." His helmet turned to me. I had helped the colonel save his men, and now he was gonna help me save mine.

But I feared we'd already played our hand. The complexities of extracting a small team surrounded by a hostile force aside, Hadrian had somehow rebuffed my shadow form. With growing knots in my stomach, I referred to the dev menu.

"There'll be no rescue mission," I muttered. "Hadrian locked Oakengard's fast travel. Bravo Team's on their own."

Kyle blindly jogged through the unlit hallways of Oakengard's lower floor. He could hear Bravo Team ahead, but just barely. Louder were the hums of the keeper brute behind him. While he wanted nothing more than to light a torch, it'd be counterproductive given the current circumstances.

How did an extraction turn into an infiltration?

The sprinting was taking a toll on his stamina. Kyle suspected the tree form was more ponderous than a plain old human. It was built to stand ground—to fight not to flee.

Kyle pressed down the dark corridor, a branch tracing the wall to act as his eyes. He skidded to a halt as he almost ran headlong into a dead end.

Impossible. Conan had waved him this way. Behind him, faint purple glowed against the shiny stone floors. The brute was approaching.

Screw it. Lash and the others had gotten away. Kyle had done what he'd come to do. The hefty treant faced the coming light and readied to take it on.

"Kyle, you dumbass, get in here!"

The treant turned to the dead end and squinted. A diminutive thief was hunched beside an open hatch on the floor. "Crux?"

"Get downstairs before you give away our position."

The brewmaster hurried into the hole. Although his form was large, the access hatch was of industrial size and design. Kyle easily descended into the makings of a mine. Lash, Conan, and Glinda waited below.

"Good job, Crux," said the Bravo Team leader. She extended a hand to help him down.

"I'm sorry," he said. "It's for your own good." The access hatch shut.

Kyle surged forward to hit the door, but the crystal lock clicked into place. Lash and Conan held him back.

"Quiet, you idiot!" she hissed. "The keepers will hear you."

He huffed and pushed them away, scowling at the locked hatch. "What the heck, bro?"

The thief's voice came from the other side of the door. "You'll be safe in there. With the mines abandoned and locked from the outside, the keepers won't bother searching within. It's the only way."

Kyle bit down on wooden teeth. "And what about you?"

Crux didn't answer and the hum of the keepers drew near.

1780 Hail to the King

An hour passed since escaping Oakengard. Kyle and Bravo Team were safe, their pursuit called off. With Hadrian based in a new city, Stronghold was likewise left alone. The marauding bandits retreated east, the goblins west past the forest. Their presence no longer served a purpose, and city residents were now blanketed in quiet unease.

My gaze flitted from my notification bar to the void pearl display on the sanctum master panel. Crux and Kyle were black dots in the middle of a blank map, and I was still having trouble teleporting to them.

"Get me over there, Trafford."

The old shopkeeper at my side grumbled. "It can't be done, Talon. We've tried three times."

"Then try again. Black Hats are stranded over there."

"I don't know what to tell you," he snapped. "Kyle's the jewelry expert, not me. Bah, to hell with it! Do it your damn self if you're so determined to waste your time." Trafford retired to his seat at the war table.

Izzy rested a hand on my back. "Time's almost up," she nudged.

I swallowed hard and cold against her tenderness. "I need

more."

"You have to say something to them."

"*I need more time.*"

The shock of recent events had worn off, and with it went the numbness. Grating anger was the only thing I had left. I wasn't pissed at myself, really. I hadn't allowed the horde to overly distract me. I did what I could to protect the city and was back in position when Hadrian needed to be stopped. With the destruction of the servers occurring in the real world, there really was nothing we could have done from the inside.

The resulting actions, however, were on me. Being too slow to save Lucifer, too confident to foresee Hadrian's suicide. The Oakengard incursion was a response based on fear and anger and desperation; the blind charge into the unknown exacted a terrible price on Kyle and Bravo Team. My friends were stranded. Things would continue falling apart unless I started thinking more tactically, like a leader.

Then why the hell couldn't I let this go?

In between checking the display and my notifications, my eyes fell on the top half of Lucifer's witchwood staff in my inventory. The power in the artifact was long gone; the blue gemstone that had been set in its head shattered days ago. Lucifer must've been on the dregs of his magic, up against an angel. No wonder he'd been downed so easily.

"I'm just saying," reminded Izzy gently. "The faction needs to see their leaders. They need to see that we're in charge and have a plan."

I set my jaw firmly. "We *don't* have a plan. We need to wait until Tad replies to my Everchat hail. Which means I'm staying close to my private quarters."

"At least let's move deliberations to the guildhall. We have private rooms over there too."

"But we don't have the void pearl." I zoomed into the section where Kyle was, a black dot in a sea of unmapped gray. Beside the display, the black pearl roiled with charcoal smoke.

"I don't think teleporting now's a good idea," said Izzy.

"It'll be fine. The fast travel's closed so it'll only be me. No more casualties."

"That's not what I meant and you know it." She pressed her cheek into my shoulder in an attempt to capture my gaze, but my eyes remained on the black pearl. She sighed. "Too much time with void magic is taking a toll on you. Your body needs rest."

I worked my jaw. The itchiness from the last visit was mostly gone now. I was tense, sure, but who wouldn't be in this situation? Without a word of answer, I activated the void pearl and attempted to teleport to Kyle.

Error
Hostile location unmapped

"What does that mean, unmapped?" I hissed. "It worked before."

Trafford ignored my grumblings, but Bandit clopped down the steps from her rooftop perch. She came to my side and put her muzzle in my hand.

"Thanks, girl," I said, patting her head. "At least someone

supports me."

"She just wants a peanut butter cup," grunted Trafford.

"No she doesn't, she—" I paused as Bandit's eyes shimmered. Her nose sniffed my pockets. "Oh, all right." I pulled the piece of chocolate from my inventory and stuffed it in her mouth. She chewed gleefully.

I frowned at the sanctum master panel. The teleportation mechanics were straightforward. The operator at the master panel chose a party member to teleport someone to. I wasn't sure who could be teleported, but I knew they needed to be in the city, and probably a Black Hat. None of those details mattered, however. I just wanted me, right here. And Kyle was still selectable as a target on the display.

I stared deeply at the void pearl, lost in my thoughts, wondering what Hadrian could've done to block this magic, wondering if it was a simple question of willpower. Of evolution. After all, upgrading and overloading skills were built-in mechanics. I'd managed impossible feats before.

As I concentrated, the swirling darkness contained in the pearl seemed to shiver. I blinked and peered closer. Was it broken? A bit of shadow was definitely leaking off the pearl. It folded over itself like smoke. My attention captured, I hesitantly reached forward. Wisps of shadow coiled around my wrist. It tickled my skin right through my glove. Slowly, it tightened.

I was stuck. The shadow felt like a physical cord, cutting off my circulation. It pulled at me. Drew me near. It—

"Watch out!"

Izzy's winter staff rapped my knuckles hard. She shoved me to the floor and the dark presence retreated to the void pearl.

I gritted my teeth, putting pressure on my wrist to stave off the pain.

Trafford's chair scraped against the stone. "What in the hell?" he said, stomping over. "What was that?"

Izzy helped me up and Bandit stood close, concern welling in their eyes. I rubbed my temple with the ball of my hand. "I... I don't know. It pulled at me, like it was alive." I blinked. The pearl onscreen flickered.

"This is dark magic," said Trafford. "It's Hadrian." He exchanged a grim look with Izzy.

I stretched my fingers. There didn't seem to be any lasting damage besides a nagging itch. "Don't be so dramatic, guys."

"And don't be so dismissive," countered Izzy. "Shadow magic is a corrupting force."

"Who says?"

"The legends, the lore, just about every book in the library that mentions it."

"Including a heavy dose of trashy romance novels, I'm guessing?"

She ignored the jab. "Remember how Hadrian merged with the shadowguards?"

"I don't think this is the same."

Trafford frowned. "I think she's onto something, son. Hadrian's proved his influence over the shadow. He kicked your shadow form out of his city, didn't he? The real question is, did Hadrian corrupt the shadow or did the shadow corrupt him?"

"Thanks for your concern, guys, but I'm fine. Really."

Izzy pressed her lips together, hopeful, but Trafford was a born skeptic. "That's exactly the type of thing you'd say if you *weren't* fine. How can we be sure you're not compromised?"

I shrugged. "I don't know. Punch me."

Trafford socked me in the jaw and laid me out before I could count to one. The grumpy bastard was nice enough to help me up, though.

"See, no shadow armor. I'm not the same as Hadrian." I rubbed my jaw and smiled. "I *am* kinda surprised by how fast you punched me. No hesitation or anything."

"What can I say? I'm a team player." The old man chuckled and appraised me for a moment before shaking his head. "Keep your wits about you, Talon. The last thing we need is for something to happen to you too." The buildmaster general huffed and headed down the tower stairs. "I'll do my best to stall for time at the guildhall, but I don't do dance numbers so hurry up."

Izzy chewed her lip when we were alone. "You *have* been especially grumpy the last hour. I think the old man has a point."

"You gonna hit me too?"

"Don't tempt me. I don't think you should be messing with the void pearl directly."

"But Kyle and Bravo Team—"

"All I'm saying is let Trafford be the go-between. He's proven he can safely use the sanctum master panel without being swallowed by shadow." She sighed. "I'm worried about you. Just stay in good spirits, deal?"

A notification pinged my menu. An Everchat hail. Tad had finally—

I blinked at the interface.

"It's from Christian Everett," I said.

Izzy and I hurried down the steps to my private quarters. It was a simple space. Just a bed and a shelf with Firefly action figures. I hadn't gotten around to decorating past that yet because we always seemed to have an emergency. The fact that this call was coming from Christian himself felt like more of the same. The CEO had never directly interfaced with me before. We'd spoken, of course, through Tad's Everchat account on his phone, but not Christian's account. This felt... official. Izzy crowded my shoulder as I swiped the connection open.

The CEO appeared at an odd angle, towering over the camera and sitting strangely. He was hunched on the floor—expectedly somber but paler than usual. "I... I regret to inform you that Pete was killed during an attack on our headquarters."

I winced. "Saint Peter?"

Christian pressed his lips together.

"Oh my God." My throat went dry. I couldn't swallow. "What about Tad? Is he—"

"I'm here," said my double, moving into view of the camera. "The Defenders were casualties too. Turns out the HR director was an InLink plant. She used explosives to take down the simulation. She's dead now too."

An explosion. That certainly accounted for the strange events in-game. Curious too that Hadrian was telling the truth about InLink, working against them while simultaneously relying on them for escape. Curious, but not surprising. When it came to loyalty, the Whisperer didn't have the most impeccable credentials.

"How is Haven still operable?" I asked.

"There are redundant systems in place," explained Christian. "Though they were built for power grid and battery outages, not terrorist strikes." The CEO allowed a thin smile, pleased with his precautions while not feeling overly boastful. "We've rerouted power so everything should be back to normal on your end."

Peter had mentioned a satellite explosion as well. I sighed. "Is... Saint Peter... Will I ever see him again? In Haven, I mean."

Christian's eyes creased in some combination of sadness and great respect. "Pete was devoted to the work, to the possibilities it offered mankind, to the choice it provided, but it wasn't a choice he personally believed in. Pete won't be resurrected in Haven."

I blinked rapidly to quell the budding tears. I couldn't believe he was gone.

"What about you in there?" asked Tad. "What happened?"

The anger returned to my face. "Hadrian used the reboot as a chance to escape. He stole the Eye of Orik and respawned in Oakengard. The angels are dead."

"This is worse than I thought." Christian grimaced in pain and twisted his shoulder to the floor. Tad knelt over and helped him assume a more comfortable position. The CEO grabbed his belly where a wash of red liquid was still wet.

I started. "You're hurt."

Christian shook his head. "It's of no consequence." Despite the nonchalant words, they were spoken through gritted teeth. "I've taken measures. I can't rely on being around to ensure the launch."

Tad's dire expression hinted that the situation was more serious than it looked. "What kind of measures?" I pressed.

The CEO drew long breaths as Tad attended to him with a medical kit. They must have been all alone up there. Christian bit down and closed his eyes. He reopened them slowly—too slowly—looking every bit like a worn out, dying man, and cognizant of that fact.

"Tell me," he said, "how is my daughter? Have you seen her?"

My throat stiffened, the image of the witchwood clattering to the floor burned into my brain. I blinked at my inventory. Izzy avoided his eyes by turning to me. I cleared my throat loudly.

"No," I said.

It was the worst kind of lie, but I didn't know how to tell him anything else. The man was dying—what did it matter? The fabrication was believable enough. Lucifer had been missing a few days while hunting Otho. Sticking to that status quo made the most sense in the moment.

Izzy squeezed my shoulder in gentle warning. I ignored her. I needed to figure this out first.

"Well," said Christian with a forced smile, "she did always know how to stay out of trouble. I imagine, as this escalates, you'll cross paths. Do me a favor, will you? Don't tell her I'm hurt."

I clenched my jaw and nodded, sickened by the bitter irony.

"But you can't wait for her," he said, resuming an air of gravitas. His eyes locked on mine. "This next part is very important, Talon. You must hear this."

I gave him my full attention.

"You need to save the game, and you're on a deadline."

"You're going ahead with the launch."

"Launching Haven is a foregone conclusion. It's what InLink

fears the most. If we're not live in three days as planned, Kablammy can no longer guarantee project funding, especially after this sabotage. It'll take months to recover. After this there's no telling how InLink will proceed, but they'll come at us fast and hard. There's a very real danger of them acquiring the company. They would own you outright."

Izzy leaned into the camera. "But certainly the attack on your building will buy you some leeway."

Christian shook his head. "In some circles, but even if I could temporarily halt the legal machine and reprogram the directives with limited manpower and damaged portals, the rocket launch clearances have been secured through the Federal Aviation Administration months in advance. No, the schedule is locked in; it's either launch or postpone indefinitely."

Tad Lonnerman summed it up more aptly. "If you want to keep your freedom, we need to push ahead."

I forced my lips together. I wasn't sure why I kept insisting the official release be delayed. Sure, there were plenty of reasons to lose faith in the developers, but there were even more reasons to believe in them. I was talking to two shining examples right now.

Besides, Haven was Christian Everett's dream project, an altruistic vision of a future where people lived forever. Frankly, he would push ahead with the launch whether I was on board or not. It was the only way to protect what he'd built.

"What's this deadline you're talking about?" I asked.

The CEO's face sharpened as he took a moment to gather himself. "When Haven launches at midnight in two and a half days, several things will happen. First, the satellites will launch.

Our primary launch site was destroyed but we still have an undamaged alternate. The game *will* be transferred to low earth orbit. Once this occurs, Haven admin will be relegated to game systems. This transition has already started in the beta. The key point is there'll be no more assists from the outside."

Christian twisted forward, looking more comfortable and more engaged. "Next, Kablammy Games forfeits its Haven assets. Our legal team files for Universal Interstellar Rights. No other ownership entity would consider giving up this control, so it's all on me.

"In correlation with these proceedings, the beta period officially ends. The definitive terms of service actualize. Your rights as digital consciousnesses, as humans, is declared and ratified. There'll be legal battles for years to come, but the declaration itself is what's significant. It will be a statement and date forever marked in history."

Hearing the inner workings of a tech titan, having a window into their vision of the future, was strange. It was like looking into a crystal ball. "Sounds epic," I said. "What's the catch?"

He sighed. "There are several. You will lose developer oversight. The community team was planning on rolling out smoothly, but the attack has forced our hand. The destruction of the Golden Seven only heightens the point. Haven, at least for the foreseeable future, will be self-governed."

"So we're a digital battlefield at the moment, and it's up to me to fix it. That all?"

"Far from it. The situation will become vastly more complicated in a few days. Large swaths of Haven are waiting to be unlocked in version 1.0. There will also be an influx of new residents, already uploaded and awaiting activation. With our systems debilitated, it'll be impossible to patch in a delay to these automated processes, and given the aggressive acquisition tactics, it would be irresponsible to try."

I briefly glanced at Izzy, thinking I was missing something. "Okay... so we're talking about a bunch of new players and assets initialized amid chaos. I can see how that's not ideal, but it's a manageable problem. The reality is, three days isn't a lot of time. It's too late to stop a war."

"It can't be too late," asserted Christian, "because there's one final snag. It's where my carefully constructed house of cards comes crashing down. Cities in Haven are not self-sufficient. Sure, various daemons manage *systems*—the economy, resources, upkeep, and lifestyle activities—but the overall agency of the populace, the *governorship*, has no such process. People or AIs need to be in place to lead. With the planned obsolescence of the saints, it was our job to find replacements."

My face darkened as I caught on. "You're talking about leaders of the three cities."

"I am. And the day-zero patch will lock the leaders into positions of strength. We can't let Hadrian get that far."

A sinking feeling was growing in my chest. "But why bother cementing something as important as leadership in a patch like that?"

Christian grimaced. "It's complicated and involved and a little embarrassing, but without the supervision of the dev team this was mostly a legal requirement to help fulfill Universal Interstellar Rights."

My eyelids fluttered. "The lawyers made you do it." Christian gave no explanation but none was needed. I didn't pretend to understand the rights governing orbiting bodies or the heft of what Haven was ready to accomplish. I just needed to understand what I was facing. "How did you choose the leaders?"

The CEO cleared his throat. "Given your success in Haven, and Pete's never-wavering faith in your principles, it seemed wise to grant special powers to each city's Protector. You're the best man to lead Stronghold. Relations with Brugo were improving, and his welcoming of the errant folk was inspired. As for Oakengard, they already ousted their fanatical bishop. Fractured though they are, the Trinity are the de facto Protectors of Oakengard, programmed to cede governorship to their White King. Even with free will, their law is infallible."

My jaw hung idle for a moment. "You're the White King. Lucifer's savior."

He checked his bleeding gut. "I find myself in a predicament, Talon. I must live long enough to see my gambit through, but if I arrive too late, I'll find my empire stolen."

I sat back, distancing myself from the weight of his words. Each great city of Haven was built on two founder relics. The soulstones were only half the equation. Separate artifacts, one being my dragonspear, bestowed the mantle of Protector. The trio of crystalline triangles was Oakengard's.

"Your empire's already stolen," I told him. "Hadrian has the trijewel and the Trinity's dead."

Christian's face darkened as he weighed the implications. Hadrian had respawned in Oakengard, a city long prepped for his arrival. This was part of his endgame. Christian, taxed by our extended conversation, spoke with guarded frailty. "If Haven goes live while Hadrian still rules, he'll gain an order of magnitude more power. His grip on an over-buffed Oakengard will threaten the security of all Haven, and even the appearance of the White King will be in jeopardy."

I twisted my jaw with grim recognition. "And all I have to do is save the world in three days."

1790 Shut Up and Jam!

◆━━━━━━━●━━━━━━━◆

The Everchat call didn't last much longer. Christian was exhausted and Tad took over. We had lots of questions but specifics were hard to come by. Even as Peter's dying words were relayed to us, we were disheartened by the vague instructions. He'd prepared a set of quests for us and we were to find them. Where or how, we weren't sure. Even the nature of the quests was cryptic.

But it was a start.

Izzy and I headed from Dragonperch toward the main drag in Oldtown. We used party chat to keep Kyle in the loop. The three of us were the heart and soul and *core* of the Black Hats.

Kyle: *F me in the A. What do we do now?*
Talon: *We have a plan. Or the inklings of one. We just have to execute.*
Kyle: *But Lucifer's gone. Saint Peter...*

I turned to Izzy and smiled.

> **Talon:** *No plan survives first contact with the enemy intact. We took some casualties but we're still very much standing.*

"Speaking of casualties," cut in Izzy, "do you think it was a good idea to keep what happened to Lucifer a secret?"

I winced. I'd second- and third-guessed that move already, but there was nothing for it. "It's the living we need to think about now. Lucifer would want that." She didn't appear convinced.

> **Kyle:** *So I was thinking of ways to get outta here. Once we find Hex, I say we commit mass hara-kiri and respawn back home.*
> **Talon:** *I don't know if that's a good idea. We have two and a half days till Haven launches and I don't know if I want you in lockdown for half of that.*
> **Kyle:** *I'm all ears if you have a better idea.*
> **Talon:** *Working on it.*

He didn't reply. I imagined him responding to my non-answer by flapping his lips loudly in protest.

"It's gonna be a big problem," said Izzy after a short silence.

"Oakengard?"

"Time. The march to Oakengard alone is supposed to take three days. It doesn't leave a lot of time for saving the world."

I nodded. "No it does not. We move full steam ahead, one

way or the other."

It was another evasive answer, but we couldn't allow ourselves to be burdened by logic, not while marching to the guildhall to give a rousing speech to the Black Hat membership.

As we turned the corner onto the strip, I stuttered. The Last Stand wasn't a small bar; there were numerous booths and rows of shared high tables. It was meant as a public meeting place for faction business, our headquarters outside Dragonperch, accessible to those not in my close circle. The dirt road lining the pub was packed, which meant the interior was at capacity. Even its grand opening didn't see these numbers, and Kyle had been giving away free beer.

We advanced through the thickening crowd, awe growing with every step. Most of the players and NPCs in attendance weren't Oldtown regulars. They outnumbered Black Hats five-to-one, with more and more joining the fray. I was gobsmacked.

"The Protector!" cheered one.

The crowd converged around us while simultaneously managing to part neatly, forming a path to the entrance. The people bowed, muttered, and generally made a big fuss at our presence. Izzy was right: we did need to be here. I slowed, considering whether I should address them and what I should say, but Izzy set her hand on my back and shoved forward. She wanted to get out of here. While she loved large displays of attention, she preferred them to be impersonal and from the safety of a stage. I curtly nodded to the onlookers and stomped up the stairs, walking through the open doors of the guildhall.

The distinguished mahogany and red-padded decor was completely lost in the standing-room-only interior. Aside from known absences like Kyle and Bravo Team, all seventy-something Black Hats were here, along with considerably more townspeople, all rife with excitement.

They plotted and strategized and pantomimed future battles, equal parts frenzy and trepidation. There were rattled words of Hadrian's escape, murmurs of Saint Peter's death, and even worries of Haven shutting down for good. I hadn't considered that last one yet, but with explosions and a growing body count among the development team, it was a real possibility.

We paused for a moment, taking the nervous activity in, both frightened and energized. As our presence was noticed, shushes washed over the crowd, collecting as one universal gust of air before dissipating into silence, all eyes on us.

This was a big deal.

Trafford was clearly relieved we joined him. He raised a celebratory fist. "Two-for-one Black Hat Brews for the next hour!"

I kneaded my temples as cheers rang out.

"And happy hour prices on Pizza Rolls!" He approached us and lowered his voice. "In addition to boosting the guild coffers, that should keep the crowd soft. The rest depends on you." He slapped my back and hurried behind the bar, playing keep-up with impatient adventurers.

I would've lost complete faith in my fellow man but, fortunately, the applause was mixed, with plenty of attendees realizing there was more at stake than cheap suds and cheesy goodness.

Crispy, crunchy, cheesy goodness.

"I'll take a pepperoni!" I yelled.

Hey, maybe Trafford was a mad genius. Desperate people needed something to lean on.

Izzy and I marched forward through the path already blazed by Trafford. I paused and searched the interior, only just realizing there wasn't a stage of any sort. The place was only a few days old and still had wrinkles to iron out, and the two times it was called for I'd simply stood in the clearing in front of the bar. Now it was so full of people there wasn't even space for the barstools.

Izzy cracked her knuckles. "Stand aside."

She drew a small frost wand and pointed it at the foot of the bar. A wall of ice rose two feet in the air. She placed a long boot on the makeshift platform and stepped up to the bar, bowing to applause.

I rolled my eyes.

Not to be outdone, I produced the dragonspear above my head. The legendary weapon had a history in this town and always drew patriotic cheers.

"That's cheating," muttered the pixie. She dismissed the ice wall, leaving me to fend for myself.

"And that's petty."

I planted the spear in the floor, triggered my vault skill, and flipped up and onto the bar with practiced ease. I turned to unanimous clapping: the contest was mine. Izzy stuck her tongue out and feigned apathy, but she swapped her wand for the winter staff in an effort to match the presence of my weapon.

"They do this a lot," chuckled Trafford.

I was proud of the general good nature we'd introduced to the guildhall. Standing up here, it was impossible to miss our importance to Stronghold. Residents in the street squeezed for a view through the open double doors. Others settled for posts outside the windows. I scanned the crowd for familiar faces as I waited for them to settle.

It didn't take long. The levity was welcome, but everyone wanted to hear the latest and be assured there was a future. It was good the rumors had already swirled around so I didn't need to rehash the sordid details, though I didn't want to appear like I was glossing over anything either.

"Yes," I said as the crowd quieted, "much of what you've heard is true. Saint Peter is dead. So are his Defenders. Hadrian escaped with the Eye of Orik and sits on Oakengard's throne as its Protector."

Izzy marched along the bar, carefully stepping over half-filled mugs. "But that's not enough for him," she announced. "Hadrian the Whisperer will be doing less protecting and more attacking. His goal is to rule all of Haven. To essentially become a god."

Gasps and stifled exclamations answered her stirring words. She was a natural at this, adding flair to my workmanlike facts. It was a good tack considering the big ask that was coming.

"Send Decimus at 'im," cried Nooner, surrounded by a gang of enforcers.

I nodded his way. "Decimus is also dead, as is our friend Lucifer. The developers can't do much to help us either. That means we're on our own."

"What about the pagans?" shouted a woman outside. "Without the Eye, they can breach the walls!"

A gargantuan snort uprooted the poor woman. She spun and

raised her eyes to the eight-foot-tall mountain bongo towering behind her.

"No one's getting past the gates," I announced firmly. "And the pagans aren't the problem. We're well beyond Haven as a game, beyond the mentality of wild pagans versus civilized crusaders. That's all horseshit. This fight is about freedom versus tyranny."

Heads bobbed among the spectators and Izzy took the baton. "The Haven beta test is coming to an end. We launch in precisely three days, and how we start is a statement about the kind of world we decide to live in. Will we cower in safety, fearing for our lives, merely surviving the afterlife? Or will we stand strong, stand together, and fight for what we believe in?"

Affirmative words and grunts infected the crowd. Izzy had cleverly gotten to the heart of the matter without explaining the nitty-gritty game mechanics. I checked behind the bar in case Trafford wanted to add his own sentiment.

The buildmaster general held a frothy mug above his head. "I'll drink to that!" Glasses raised with cheers. Those without drinks pushed toward the bar. "All right," said Trafford, pushing loafers away. "Move along. Keep a healthy flow so everyone gets a drink. I don't tolerate loiterers and slack-jaws!"

I shook my head at the vociferous bar patrons. If Izzy thought my use of the dragonspear was a flagrant foul, Trafford had no respect for the game at all.

"Quiet down!" I boomed. "There's a lot to do. A fellow Black Hat, Hex, is imprisoned somewhere in Oakengard, now being led by a tyrant. Our brewmaster and Bravo Team are trapped too. I don't know about you guys, but I'm pissed. Heads are gonna roll for this," I shouted, spear overhead. "Now who's with me?"

Brash cries of support flooded the guildhall. Black Hats vowed solidarity with each other and cursed the Whisperer's name. But it wasn't all bravado.

"What are we gonna do?" asked a voice so quiet it barely broke through the commotion. It was Drummond, the faction banker. Only level 3 and hardly a fighter, the military camaraderie was lost on him.

"We're gonna come together, as a guild and a city," I answered. "Don't worry if you're not a combat class. For many of you, this'll be business as usual."

Scanning the crowd, the two ogres in the far corner stood out the most. Our three goblin faction members sat on their shoulders, including the young girl with a stone hammer. "Jixa, your crew did quick work on the barracks. The logistics of equipping everyone will take even more heavy lifting."

The sub-four-foot green girl with strawberry-blonde curls nodded sharply. "*Cha,* boss man. Helpses we will."

"Now we're talking," said Trafford, lighting up. "Arming soldiers beats quivering boots any day of the week."

"Not you, Trafford. I need you on something special. Saint Peter was working on something before he died. Apparently there are a set of quests somewhere meant for the Black Hats— meant for Haven. As questkeeper, we need you to find them."

Trafford's good eye enlarged more than usual. "Interesting. I'll get right on it."

I turned back to the frightened banker. "Drummond, aside from keeping the books, you've been helping Trafford inventory the armory. Not only did Dragonperch come with a ton of supplies, but all the loot from the recent attack was added to our coffers. Coordinate with Jixa on equipping the soldiers."

The bald man nodded, clearly relieved. "I can do that."

I locked onto the next familiar face I saw. "And Phil, uh... put some pants on."

The bearded man in a loin cloth widened crazed eyes like he'd been found out. "Gah!" His bare feet bounded outside and he disappeared.

I huffed, feeling some of my momentum lost. I cleared my throat and raised my voice. "The rest of us, well, we're going to kick ass."

The gold helm of the commander of the city watch bobbed as he entered the pub. "What is this, some kind of public disturbance?" Gladius looked around, locked eyes on me, and clenched his teeth. "I'd almost say it looks like you're planning on going to war."

"We are."

A random voice: "But the goblins!"

I put a hand up. "Stronghold is secure. A host of legionnaires will protect the town, but the walls will do most of the work. Beside that, we're digging deep for allies. The enemy won't be able to ignore us."

There was the expected reticence.

"There're too many crusaders!"

"How are we supposed to get allies?"

"We have no friends outside these walls!"

"The only friends we need are right here." A green cloak flashed behind the ranger as Dune shoved to the head of the pulpit and spun on the crowd. "Disaster after disaster, Talon has seen us through. Izzy and Kyle have been there. Lash and Bravo Team. The pirates. Even an old army veteran turned shopkeeper turned builder turned—" Dune swiveled his head to the bar. "What are you now?"

"Curse it, I don't know anymore!" exclaimed Trafford.

I smiled as the old man handed me a mug. "Buildmaster general, questkeeper, and one hell of a drinking buddy."

Dune turned back to the audience. "Point is, if there's one person in Haven who can pull off the impossible, who can bring a bickering town together, who can unite allies with nothing in common, it's Talon, the Protector of Stronghold."

The ranger faced me and lowered his voice just a little. "You know me. I'm the furthest thing there is from a follower. I'm here to blaze my own trail. But if there's one cause I'd risk everything for, if there's one person who can lead us to overcome insurmountable odds, it's you."

Dune fell to one knee and I got a faction notification.

> [Dune] has joined the Black Hats

I widened my eyes as the ranger accepted his longstanding invitation. Caduceus and Stigg approached.

"Peter was a solid dude," said the Viking. "He'll have a place wherever his Valhalla lies."

Caduceus shrugged. "What can I say? I'm a sucker for social activism."

[Stigg] has joined the Black Hats
[Caduceus] has joined the Black Hats

"Oi!" said Nooner, pushing forward with his gangly crew of tough guys. "Youse want the same thing I want: to protect this here town. We might disagree on whose town it happens to be, but I like yer style. That, and you're a nasty brawler to boot. I propose a dalliance!"

I blinked awkwardly. "A... what?"

"A dalliance!" he snapped. "You an' me, together."

"Watch it," laughed Izzy. "I might get jealous."

Nooner's eyes creased. "What're you on about? We can help each other!"

"Oh," I said, "you mean an alliance."

"Of course that's what I meant. That's why I said it!"

I took a moment to process the unexpected gesture. I extended the gangsters an invitation, and more approached as they accepted.

"Move along!" instructed Trafford, trying to bring order to the madhouse. "Move along!"

Soon Black Hats were stepping aside as regular town members sidled up for their turn. Izzy moved to the opposite end of the bar to split the line and ease the flow of traffic, and before we knew it demand for joining the faction trumped those waiting for beer.

"Saint Peter was a hell of a man," they said. "It wasn't right, what happened."

As Stronghold's Protector, it was no secret I'd been taking on more city responsibilities, but with the saints gone for good, the mantle of leadership was wide open. I'd expected some resistance, some competitors and politicking, but this was the polar opposite. Saint Peter's death was uniting the entire population of Stronghold into action, into joining the Black Hats.

1800 Dark Souls

Key members of the faction set off to address various duties, but a few of us were stymied by the sheer number of Black Hat applicants. It seemed like every player and NPC in the city wanted in, although logically that wasn't the case. Between the desperate times and the enormity of the crowd, there was no time to screen the applicants. If you were here and you wanted in, then welcome to the Black Hats.

Black Hat faction has reached level 3!
Congratulations! As long as you maintain a minimum of 100 faction members, you gain the following benefits:

Captain Controls
Promote faction leaders. Coordinate with private chat and tasks.

> **Group Bonus = 3%**
> When 3+ faction members are working together, this bonus applies to combat damage, hit percentage, and crafting skill successes.
>
> *Next Level Up: 500 members*

Although our headquarters had already leveled up due to building construction, the faction itself had a separate leveling track that was purely based on membership. After two hard hours of accepting new guild mates, I admired the new headcount.

Black Hats
Faction Level: 3
Members: 320 / 500
War
Catechists
Brothers in Black

The Black Hats were now a group to be reckoned with. My newfound pride was tempered as I noticed the armistice with the pagans was no longer listed. One step at a time, I told myself.

I opened the new captain controls, curious about how they worked. I was the faction leader, but there otherwise weren't official positions built into the structure. I went through my party, promoting Kyle, Izzy, and Trafford. Crux had already left, no doubt to party up with the rest of Bravo Team. Although Errol was missing, I promoted him as well.

I chewed my lip. Assigning only party members to captain positions defeated the purpose. The point was easy communication with key leadership and we already had party chat. I scrolled through the list of faction members and promoted Lash and Dune for a start.

With the guildhall emptied, I wandered Oldtown to manage our preparation. The neighborhood was more packed than it had ever been, with large swaths of onlookers following me around wherever I went. I didn't mind the attention. The mood in the city had definitely turned, from one of listless apathy to hardworking drive. The wheels were in motion now. Our engine of war was turning.

I approached the pirate, Errol Oates, as he sliced pieces of mango with an oversized Bowie knife and plopped them into his mouth.

"Ho, Captain," I said. Now that Crux had cleared a space, I re-invited Errol into my party. "You're a captain now," I noted.

"I was always a captain."

"I guess." I scratched my chin. "I was surprised to see you weren't in the guildhall meeting."

He hiked his shoulders without paying me much attention. "We know the score, Talon. We're in fer a fight on a whole lotta fronts." He stood and faced me. "I'll do what ye require o' me."

As always, the rogue was a stout friend. He walked with me to Dragonperch. "How's the *Cutter* doing?" I asked.

The *Heartcutter* was Errol's frigate, the flagship (and only ship) of the Black Hat navy. Before Hadrian was captured, his forces—comprised of bandits and mermaids—had scuttled the docked ship. It was in the process of being repaired, but as most of our builders were ogres who refused to partake in shipbuilding for fear of the water, it was slow going. Many of the pirates had returned to building duties, but they were far from experts.

"Arr," mulled Errol in answer. "She barely be seaworthy an' has nuthin' on her ol' self."

"Well we're gonna need a bunch of duct tape and bubble gum. We might need the old girl soon."

Outside the tower we consulted with Drummond.

"Most of the rogue gear from Hadrian's army consists of light arms, poisons, leathers, and cloaks," he reported.

I nodded. "We have some rogues and explorers who could use that stuff. Look for artisans who can craft potions and poisons. Maybe they could use the supply overflow. Reserve the lighter armor for mystics and other noncombatants. We'll have plenty of stronger stuff to go around."

"Makes sense," he said. "What about the mermaid drops? We have an abundance of ocean gear and resources."

"That all goes to the navy. Admiral Oates and his men will load it onto the *Cutter*"—I smirked—"given she'll take the load and stay afloat."

Errol's brow hardened. "Jest all ye want, matey. She'll take the supplies. I'll collect me scoundrels an' show ye what's what."

As he stomped away, I gave further instructions to Drummond. "Our armory has ample high-quality blacksteel and heartwood. I want every combat-ready soldier to measure their loadout against the Dragonperch stock. The surplus should go to the heaviest explorers and artisans."

"But that could clean us out."

"I'm betting on it. The Black Hats aren't hoarding treasure while the entire simulation is fighting for survival."

We spent some time going over specific distributions so our army wouldn't be so haphazard. The discussion made me realize the need to chat up the general about our troop makeup. We'd want separate units to attack different problems to keep us agile and ready for anything. With Trafford working on our special project, I applied what expertise I had for the time being.

Jixa's ogres rolled up the wagons on time and ready to work. I left them to it and returned to the guildhall to find Trafford deep in study. The pub had mostly cleared out by this point, with the barstools returned to their place, Trafford planted in one. His nose was buried in a large open tome.

"I've never seen you so studious," I said as I approached his back. When I clapped him on the shoulder, he started with a jolt and almost lost his seat.

"What? Who's that? I'll..." He groggily searched the room.

I dropped my jaw. "Were you sleeping?!?"

"What? Never. Men my age don't nap, we just think with our eyes closed."

I turned to the book filled with lines of jumbled scrawl I couldn't read. "Is finding the quests that complicated?"

The old man sighed. "Aye, boy. If they'd been released proper, I'd have found 'em, but they're missing from the usual spots. I'm doing my best to dig deeper, but it's like mazes within labyrinths."

I snorted. "Interesting expression. I would've said it's like peeling an onion."

"Why?"

"You know, because for every layer you remove, you uncover another."

Trafford scrunched his brow. "Well, what's so damn hard about that? It's an onion, for chrissakes! Just put a knife through the whole thing at once and be done with it!"

I sighed. "If only. So what are you gonna need to get this done?"

"I dunno." He mulled on it a moment. "I don't suppose we have someone on the dev team who had a hand in creating 'em?"

"No."

The quests had been Peter's project. He tried to tell me about them, when we'd been in the middle of things with Hadrian. The details were glossed over and I hadn't inquired further. As for our current Kablammy support, Tad already gave me what he learned from Peter. Even Christian hadn't worked on the side project, trusting his team fully and relegating control to his community manager.

Still, it belied belief that *someone* from support couldn't be of assistance.

I opened my main menu and dinged the blue question-mark icon on the top bar. Given recent developments, I half expected nothing to happen at all. So I was pleasantly surprised when a clean-cut man with blue eyes and short blond hair blinked into existence. The tech support "resident companion" wore a British red coat with white pants and shiny black boots. He stood hunched forward, hands upraised and actively clawing at something invisible before him.

"Headshot!" he screamed in delight. "Take that you overcooked mutton!" He stiffened and looked around anew. "WTFBBQ?"

"Varnu!" I cried, overjoyed to see the friendly face, even if it wasn't really his. You see, despite Varnu Johnson looking like your average Texan wearing colonial garb, he was clearly from an outsourced office in India. I didn't tell him I knew better. He put a lot into the act and calling him out on it would break his heart.

Varnu stood at attention and clasped his hands behind his back. "Talon! By the graceful visages of Bovar, it is good to see you!"

"You too," I exclaimed, surprised at the sentiment. "What were you doing just now?" I asked. "You know, with your hands?"

"Oh, would you believe I was consuming a Double Whopper Pounder, sir?"

I shook my head. "I've been dead for a bit but I'm pretty sure that's not a thing."

"I see."

"Is tech support still up and running?"

He winced. "Actually, sir, to cut to the cake and eat it too, our entire company was shut down without warning this morning."

"And you're still in the office?"

Varnu shrugged in a rare bout of honesty. "I'm gaming. The internet in this building really shoves ass."

I smiled as I realized his upraised hands had been furiously attending a keyboard and mouse. But this wasn't a social call, and there was little to smile about.

"Have you heard about the explosion that took down the servers? The attack on Kablammy headquarters in Seattle?"

"Seattle? Sir, I do believe you are making up words."

"What? No, the city in Washington."

"Washington DC?"

"Washington state!"

"Oh dear, there's a Washington state?" Varnu frowned and ticked his fingers to a silent count. "You have one hundred and seven such territories, am I correct?"

I gave him my heaviest sigh. "Varnu, sometimes I think you're screwing with me. But I'm serious, real people are dead. There's been sabotage. What's left of the dev team are cut off from outside communication." I canted my head. "I'm actually surprised I could reach you."

Varnu Johnson took my facts with somber nods. "I am sorry to hear of the troubles in the headquarters. Fortunately, the hard line in India—er, Texas—is far away from that mess." He paused a moment before leaning forward conspiratorially. "Texas is far from See-Ah-Tell, is this correct?"

My eyelids spasmed. "Yes."

"I'm from Texas," he added glibly, just in case.

Trafford cleared his throat. "Listen here, I don't know what you two are on about, but Saint Peter was working on a set of quests for us, and we need access to them. Right now."

Varnu pouted, studying the old man but speaking to me. "This inebriated game construct appears tattered around the edges. Are you sure letting him inside your faction hall is wise?

If you wish, I can relocate him to the slums."

"The slums?!? Why I oughta..." Trafford drew his arquebus.

Varnu's eyes widened. "What a beautiful firearm!" He extended his hand. "May I?"

Trafford traded glances with me and the resident companion. "Uh, sure, I suppose. Just don't scratch her."

"I wouldn't dream of it." Varnu accepted the arquebus with reverence. Gentle hands flipped it back and forth during his inspection. "Wonderful engraving, wide bore, precision muzzle rifling. Tell me, how many drams of powder per charge?"

"Depends which dram you're talkin'," said the shopkeeper.

"Oh, too right. I would've assumed British but, now that I think about it, you must be using the Roman drachma."

Trafford flashed a proud smile. "Greek."

"My word," whispered Varnu, eyes wide. "Six whole obols worth!" He nodded in approval. "Audacious and wildly dangerous. I'm impressed."

Trafford grunted as he accepted the return of his weapon. "I see. Well, you're not such a bad guy, I suppose."

"Guys," I cut in with a huff. "Now that we're done geeking out over guns, can we get to the quests?"

The resident companion snapped to attention and interfaced with an invisible workstation. "Yes. I have access to several query options that are unavailable to you, but it would be easier if I knew the details. You said Saint Peter constructed this quest chain. Is he not available?"

"He's dead."

"Impossible, sir, saints cannot be—"

"In real life. He's dead in real life."

Varnu's face lost color as he sputtered for a reply. "I see..." He silently stared at the pending database query.

"We just need to get through this," I told him. "For Peter."

Trafford nodded. "The first step is to find his quests. As questkeeper, I get a steady feed of the latest broadcasts, but I don't get to see anything before it's ready."

"We were hoping you had a better search function and some inside knowledge."

"I will do my best, sir. What are your search parameters?"

I frowned. "Can you search by user?"

Varnu shook his head. "Unfortunately, I am unable to parse developer credentials."

"What about new quests?" suggested Trafford. "If Peter added something, it has to be recent, right?"

"Oh dear, there are several thousand entries queued into silent patches. Furthermore, there are any number of dates we could inspect: initial creation, last edit, patch creation, patch deployment..."

"What about type?" pressed Trafford. "This has gotta be an epic quest."

"Yes. Most of these queued entries are grind quests to fill time, so the epic category eliminates many of them." Varnu did some additional typing. "I don't see..."

"No," I said. "Not epic. Try a search on fepic."

Varnu blinked and typed it in. "This is curious. I see the new quest type with several entries. Inactive, of course."

"That's them!"

He paused in thought. "What does this fepic mean, sir?"

"Uh, it's a private joke. Fucking epic, fepic. You know, so you don't need to curse."

"I don't see the fucking point." Varnu entered several commands. "There you go. I've activated the new content. Your questkeeper should be able to query them now. However, I'm not confident of their integrity. The quests appear to be incomplete. They contain numerous broken script references."

Trafford grunted. "Can you fix that gobbledygook?"

"Oh, reincarnations, no. If you need someone to bust a cap into thirteen-year-olds in death match, I'm your man, but I know nothing about programming."

"At least I can access them," said Trafford, thick index finger rapping his quest tome.

"Very well. If that will be all, gentlemen, I have some fools to murder."

"Varnu," I called, pausing his dismissal. "Thanks. I mean it. And I'm hoping I can lean on you for support in the next few days?"

He set his jaw. "Saint Peter personally trained the inaugural team of resident companions, of which I am proud to be considered one. It was a grueling two-and-a-half hour lunch meeting, but in that time the man made an impression on me. I like to think I made an impression on him too." Varnu bit down, gave a firm nod, and disappeared.

I watched the empty space for a reverent moment, speechless that Peter's death had such a profound effect on people. Not that my dead friend didn't deserve the praise. He really seemed to care about everyone he worked with. Anytime someone like that left the world, it was a true loss.

And now one thing was clear: our enemies made a huge

mistake by killing him. Like sand draining between the fingers of a clenched fist, they'd pushed and squeezed too far. Now it was time we turned things around on them.

I set my eyes on Trafford and the tome of quests. "Okay, old man, lay it on me."

Tad Lonnerman limped back into the office and placed the second monitor Christian had asked for on the floor. "There's no one else in the studio," he reported.

The CEO wordlessly attended cables to give his makeshift workstation on the carpet an additional display. Tad chuckled bitterly. Here he was, still recovering from a bad car accident and forced to use a crutch, and he was the better option of the two to play errand boy. Christian Everett, well, Tad wasn't sure he could even stand up anymore.

"I wonder how long this will take," said Tad idly.

Christian hiked a shoulder. "Not as long as I'd like."

"Really? I would've thought the hole in your gut would urge you to get somewhere safe."

"Will you carry me?" chortled the CEO. "You smothered the fire so there's no immediate danger. The alarm triggered, the elevators are offline, and neither you nor I can make it down forty flights of stairs in our condition. At some point you need to stop worrying about factors outside your control. There's nothing to do but wait for help." Christian rapped at the keyboard. "Ah, here we are."

Tad moved beside him. The newly plugged-in monitor displayed an array of video windows of empty rooms. "You've hacked into building security?"

"It's not a hack. Building management sets public permissions to the security feeds in common areas. Kablammy has additional cameras within the studio. They're all here."

Tad noted the main lobby and glass doors of the building entrance in a high-def window. Another covered the main plaza outside. Fire trucks were parked at the curb, with paramedics directing workers away from the building. The videos lacked sound and the faces were too small to make out. Even then, Tad detected a note of panic in the way people moved.

"What's that one?" he asked, pointing the tip of his crutch at a video of pure black.

Christian sighed. "That's the feed from my alternate launch site on Harbor Island."

Tad turned to the wall of windows facing Elliot Bay. The industrial island was a flat smudge of gray in the distance. "Ah," he realized. "No internet access."

"That's right. We have the building feeds because they're on a hard line, but anything at Harbor Island is a blank."

"Should we be concerned?"

"I see no reason to suspect anything amiss with the launch site. It was the Southern California location that was heavily publicized."

"It may not be sabotage, but doesn't the lack of internet access compromise Harbor Island all the same?"

"It's fully automated. That satellite is capable of launching and hosting Haven all on its own. Set and forget."

And just like that, Christian turned his attention from the second monitor back to a custom-colored wall of text.

Tad wiped his face. "You're coding."

"My workstation is keyed with special privileges. The server portal was loaded with a slew of launch changes Pete had planned. With it destroyed, I need to hack something together from an old integration."

"Isn't a new patch risky? I don't need to tell you that attempting last-minute changes causes more problems than it solves."

"There's no choice."

Tad rolled his eyes. Right, factors outside their control. Although Christian was focused on Visual Studio, Tad chose to watch the exterior feed of the first responders.

The CEO was correct. This could be a while. The fire control room in the lobby would confirm the end to the danger. The building would be evacuated just in case, firefighters sweeping the floors one by one. Talon was inside the game executing their plan. There was literally nothing for Tad to do but wait.

He frowned as Christian typed with one hand while the other stemmed the blood seeping from his stomach.

1810 King's Quest

If Trafford and I were expecting a simple set of instructions—fetch this or escort that—we were in for a long three days. Varnu had technically located Saint Peter's pet project, but that was only the beginning of the puzzle.

Luckily I was in a peculiar mood. Pissed but productive, driven by the type of righteous anger only achieved by equal parts tragedy and injustice. There was nothing pulling me off this scent.

As for Trafford, well, he was just about the most stubborn bastard I'd ever met.

"This dang path is all tangled," he complained. "It's a quest string all right, of that I'm sure, but it's unlike anything I've ever seen."

I frowned at the illegible book. Trafford furiously scribbled notes on a separate scroll, trying to make sense of things. "What's the goal of the string?" I asked.

"I don't know. It's not a normal string. Fepic isn't a searchable category. The possible paths are branching out in all directions, like a crazy, winding—"

"River," I finished. I strolled to a side window and gazed toward the Albula that skirted Oldtown. "A new start. For good."

The old man cranked open his good eye. "What's that now?"

I shook my head dismissively. "Just something Peter said to me this morning. I'm not sure what to make of it yet, but he was trying to help us. He was a good friend."

"Aye," said the questkeeper. "I just wish he was a better scripter."

As the salty veteran pored over the details, a few Black Hats caught wind of our impasse. Dune and co. wandered in and watched. Izzy and Errol took places at the bar. Even Jixa came by to coordinate with Trafford, saw the puzzled expressions crowding the room, and decided to mull along with everybody else. She planted her hammer on the bar and parked her butt beside it.

"Please don't sit on the quest book, dear." Trafford's tone was surprisingly gentle. He slid the book over and wiped at a sticky substance on the pages. "What is that, blood?"

"Sorry, boss mans," chimed the girl. "Todayses lunch was a little frisky."

"I find cooking usually takes care of that problem." He shook it off and returned to impatient grumbling over his book. "Best I can tell, there's not one quest, but a few of 'em, knotted together with no clear start or end."

"Any common threads?" I asked.

"Murky at best."

"Any advice that doesn't come from a Magic 8-ball?" chuckled Dune. He leaned against a mahogany pillar with his arms crossed.

The old man's face went hard. "Outlook not so good."

I smiled. "So forget the top-down mentality."

Trafford arched an eyebrow my way.

"Okay, when you're programming a system with a lot of moving parts, it's common to look at the problem from the top down. You prioritize what you want the system to do. All the subsystems serve that goal. It's smart and keeps the big picture in mind, but it sometimes glosses over the details.

"A bottom-up approach is the opposite. You look at all the subsystems needed to serve the greater whole. Unpack what needs to be done on the ground level, in order to get closer to where you want."

"Talon," he grumped, "I'm an NPC. Programming theory is out of my wheelhouse. You're fortunate I grok the concept of scripting at all."

I sighed. He was right, of course. "Okay then, don't get caught up in the programming part. The point is you're trying to unwrap some overarching quest with a bunch of vague pointers to moving parts. I say scrap that approach and go straight to the nuts and bolts. What are those gears and cogs doing? Look at the subquests, which should be more straightforward. Let's see which actions get us nearer to our overall goal."

Trafford scratched his wild silver hair. "But I don't even know where to start. The subquests aren't ordered in any chronology."

"Just pick one," I said. "Just pick a random section of string and parse whatever logical block is closest."

"Okay," he said uncertainly. He took some time weeding through the text and applying the new tactic. "So... for instance"—he rammed a fat finger onto a page—"here's one."

"Unpack it. Not the big picture, just the smallest goal. Let's start with a single directive."

The questkeeper fiddled with the pages a moment before a prompt flashed before us.

> Quest Abandoned: **Reunite the Trinity**
> *Quest Type: Epic*
> *Reward: 20 silver bars, 4,000 XP, royal treasure*
> What remains of the Oakengard Trinity
> appears well, but they require a bishop to
> return to full form.

My eyes widened. The current Oakengard quest, first given by Colonel Grimwart of the crusaders when he noticed something wrong in his city, disappeared from my quest menu.

"What'd you do? My epic quest is gone. There was sweet loot in there!"

Trafford winced. "Sorry, kid. It's what I'm saying. These quests touch everything."

"Put it back."

He flipped the page back and forth, scanning for something he missed. "I can't. But I suppose the quest is being rewritten as a new one. Let me push on."

Quest Offer: **Restore Oakengard's Glory**
Quest Type: Fepic
Reward: <empty>
Oakengard has been compromised by a Trojan and a fractured Trinity. Restore them to their old glory.

Accept Quest?

I grimaced at the new version of the quest as I noted it had no reward. It was just like Saint Peter to focus on the non-materialistic stuff first. I got my second surprise when the quest appeared in my menu, grayed out.

Restore Oakengard's Glory
Blocked by: **Bring Vagram to Justice**
Quest Type: Bounty (public)
Reward: Crusader Alliance
Cleric Vagram leads the rogue catechist faction in guerrilla warfare. Find and return him to Oakengard.

"Great," I hissed. "We can't restore Oakengard's glory until we take care of the Cleric Vagram quest." Dune scowled at the thought.

"This is what I'm talking about!" moaned Trafford. "Enough start and end points to make a Tasmanian devil dizzy."

Izzy snorted. "You've been watching too many cartoons with

Kyle." She rapped the bar with her nails. "You think it's a coincidence the Trinity gave us this quest to begin with?"

Dune frowned. "You think they were playing interference? Making sure we couldn't get to them?"

"It makes sense," she reasoned. "One bad apple spoils the bunch. Grimwart saw the trouble. He gave us the old quest. Then the Trinity gives us a filler quest to stall our progress."

The ornery shopkeeper nodded along. "As if this wasn't tangled enough."

"It doesn't matter," I decided, putting a definitive edge to my voice. "This is progress. We have a fepic quest unlocked. Cleric Vagram is the last vestige of the Trinity, so maybe we can kill two birds with one stone. All we gotta do is catch him."

Caduceus scoffed. "You say that like it's easy."

"Easy doesn't come into it. It's what we need to do." I turned to the questkeeper. "Find another one, Trafford. See what else we can unlock. It can't be as bad as the first."

He muttered to himself as his finger slid over the page. The fruit of his labor appeared a minute later.

Quest Offer: **Rally the Errant Folk**
Quest Type: Fepic
Reward: <empty>
Various so-called wild races inhabit the land, pagan or otherwise. There is no greater army, given they can be rallied together.

Accept Quest?

Errol burst out in wild guffaws. "Be this a joke? Them scrubs outside these walls have numbers, I'll give 'em that, but they ain't a shinin' beacon o' teamwork."

Jixa hopped off the bar. "You take backsies! Goblinses work together real goods."

Stigg stepped in. "No offense, lass, but I agree with the pirate. I'll believe in the goblin horde when they can put together a real fight and see it through without running. There's a reason we're in here and they're out there."

"Bah! Pirateses and Vikingses knows fighting, but they don't knows my people!"

Frustration among faction members was manifesting into hostilities. As the guild leader, it was my job to put a positive spin on this. "The horde has rallied before," I pointed out. "Azzyrk has a small army, but with the right support it could grow again."

"Aye," said Stigg. "All it took last time was a one-eyed titan."

Izzy chuckled. "Is it a bad time to bring up how the pagans just dissolved the armistice?"

"Or that the wildkins refused to help?" added Dune.

I shook my head with a smile. "This is exactly what we should be discussing. You guys are outlining our objectives, even if the quests are vague."

"I got another one," crowed Trafford.

> Quest Offer: **Quash Shorehome Unrest**
> *Quest Type: Fepic*
> *Reward: <empty>*
> Recent events have weakened support for the Brothers in Black. The pirate town can be a pivotal ally if their power is reconciled.
>
> ***Accept Quest?***

"You see?" I accepted the third quest with a grin. "That one's not so bad. With Hadrian in Oakengard, Shorehome should be easy to sway to our side."

"Ar," agreed Captain Oates, "that be sure."

"Brugo did fight with us in the Arena," said Izzy.

The pirate nodded. "The Papa will look out fer his int'rests, which in this case align with ours. He'll welcome our help an' do anythin' he can t' exact revenge on the Whisperer."

Now it was Jixa's turn to express doubt. "Three dayses since that man has respawned. Three dayses with no word to friendses. Maybe pirateses don't have the stomachs to fight."

The captain's eyes narrowed. "We'll see about that, girl."

"We can do this," I boldly assured, in no small part to convince myself. "Three quests: to Oakengard, the wild, and Shorehome." My tone dulled. "Each without clear objectives, riddled with multiple hangups, and all before the deadline of three days." I frowned as my rousing speech kind of sputtered out.

Trafford harrumphed. "I'm sorry to say it, son, but there's no way we can complete everything in time."

The room shared a collective sigh. It was one thing to approach obstacles with a gung ho attitude; it was another entirely to be successful. Blindly charging into failure might be brave, but it was hardly wise.

The need for wisdom brought to mind Peter's poisoned rose. Maybe the first advice I'd ever received after dying. Then again, it wasn't long before I came up with a mantra of my own: fight smarter, not harder. This was one of those cases where the hard part couldn't be avoided, but that didn't mean we had to ditch the smarts. We had to outfight, outwork, and outsmart our enemies on all fronts, which meant we needed to handle this like professionals.

"You're absolutely right," I said finally. "It's impossible for everyone to get everything done. *Not one quest at a time.*" I stepped away from Trafford and paced the room, passing by each of my allies. "These quests are too much for one party to overcome. Skill doesn't even come into play; it's logistics. We can't cover all corners of Haven in so little time. But we're not a single party anymore. The Black Hats are more than that, especially now since we've eclipsed three-hundred members. Hadrian came at us on multiple fronts—goblins, bandits, crusaders, even the real world. It's time for us to start fighting fire with fire."

Izzy's pressed indigo lips together. "You're suggesting we split up."

"Why not? Kyle and Bravo Team are already in Oakengard."

"That's not gonna cut it," grumped Trafford. "They'll need an army, and two-and-a-half days isn't a lot of time to march across the map."

"It better be. You'll be leading the march, *General*."

"Wha—?" The old man sputtered in shock. "I always thought that title was more of an honorary one."

"Not tonight. We have the manpower. We have the leadership. We have over two full days to achieve our objectives. Call it improbable if you want, but I don't wanna hear impossible."

Dune showed his teeth. "I'm getting the feeling there won't be time for pints tonight."

I grunted. "It's too bad I already used my dragon for the day. We could've used that head start." The more I thought about it, besides his escape with the soulstone, using up our daily legendary powers was probably the biggest fallout from Hadrian's siege. A small price, but a noticeable one.

"On the bright side," offered Izzy, "the horde is gone. We can send doves back and forth at will."

"No. I'm done with doves. We don't have time for protracted negotiations and vacillating back and forth. We're doing business face-to-face from here on out."

Errol rested a hand on the pommel of his rapier. "I suppose I'll be sailin' to me ol' homestead then."

I nodded. "The bulk of the army will head to Oakengard. We'll send teams to fulfill the subquests. Some of us will hunt down Vagram, some the errant folk."

"And no time for failure either," added Izzy with grave eyes. "Not if we want to make our deadline."

There were nods of support but hesitant eyes. The plan was only a rough idea at the moment. Most of the decisions and heavy lifting were on the way, the sooner the better. The thought was daunting.

"Okay, everybody!" shouted Trafford, snapping everyone to attention. "You heard the boss. Hit the bank, hit the shops, and gear up. We're moving out!"

The Black Hat captains rushed from the guildhall as Trafford still pored over his tome. I gave him a quick nod and headed out to mobilize the city.

1820 All 4 One

I sat on Bandit with the dragonspear pitched beside me into the Oldtown dirt. Much of my reputation hinged on the weapon and now my mount. I wasn't usually a sucker for ceremony, but with newcomers outnumbering legacy faction members, I had an impression to make.

Izzy stood at my side, winter staff in hand. I pulled Bandit's head and we spun in place to face the crowd.

"This is it, everyone," I announced in a commanding voice. "We're all Black Hats now. More importantly, we're residents of Haven. What we do, we do together, for each other." I sent out batches of brigade invites. "We'll shortly be splitting up into multiple units, each with their own goals. That doesn't mean we aren't all working together. The entire faction's gonna share experience and keep in touch over brigade chat." I could tell many of the lower-level players were confused by the new ability. "There's one rule: No speaking on brigade chat unless you're a guild captain or addressed by one. With this many people, the feed will get gummed up without moderation. Failure to abide by this rule will get you kicked off the brigade, meaning you won't benefit from shared experience. And trust me, given what we're facing, if you're not a guild captain, you'll want a cut of the experience we'll be getting."

Chuckles mingled with affirmatives. A lot of these players had never been in huge skirmishes, though a good number were present during the titan assault. Many others were hard workers who just hadn't been given the opportunity yet. This was their time to shine, and the eager faces were almost electric.

"All for one, one for all," I cheered. "We fought off the cyclops standing together. We fought off the kraken standing together. Now it's time we fight off the world!"

The attendees raucously chanted my name. I held up a fist and began chanting myself. "Black Hats! Black Hats! Black Hats!" Nearby members mimicked me, and the fire swept through the people like they were dry brush. All of Oldtown, a crowd of a few hundred, chanting the faction name.

"Now let's get to work!" I shouted. "Buildmaster General Trafford is here with Drummond. All combatants will check into the barracks. You'll be given supplies and storage. We'll run quick drills and group people according to skill level and need. This will happen quick because we're marching out before sunset."

Trafford squeezed through and patted Bandit's neck. "It won't be as smooth as all that, you know. This is a disorganized group mustered at the drop of a hat. And I'm no general."

I worked my jaw. The old man wasn't complaining, he was just telling it like it was. "I wish Lash was here to help." I eyed the crowd for support.

"What about Grimwart?" he suggested. "The colonel's familiar with battle."

"That's a great idea. We pulled forty crusaders through the

fast travel. It's time to repay the favor."

"It's almost like we know what we're doing," laughed the old man. He surveyed the massive crowd and pouted. "You know, we don't have enough healers. It was a problem during our last stand against Hadrian, and it'll be a problem again. This town simply hasn't been kind to 'em."

It was an odd development in an MMO, for sure, but Bishop Tannen's coup had soured people's attitudes on clerics. Real players had joined the catechists, especially healers, and they were run out of town.

"We have a large stock of health potions," I said. "Use the coffers to buy out what's in the shops, too."

"Will do," he said, "but potions don't go the distance. My time as a legionnaire taught me that much. No matter how dominating the force, attrition will slowly whittle it down. Once a day heals won't cut it." He grunted and shook his head at nothing in particular. "There's another thing, Talon. I haven't been able to single out any more subquests from the tome, but there's still the business of the overarching threads weaving through everything."

I grinned. "Still stuck on top-down specifics?"

"Don't get me wrong, I applaud your bottom-up insights. We have a direction to move, things to accomplish. But I'd be lying if I said it didn't nag at me not knowing what all this was in the service of."

I swallowed my levity and took a moment to ponder it. Izzy squeezed close as Trafford explained.

"I've been unraveling the loose threads on our three fepic quests. Remember how I said everything's connected by a master quest?"

"You figured it out?" asked the pixie.

His already gruff face blanched. "Not exactly, but I have found multiple references to the soulstones."

Izzy frowned. "Soulstones plural?"

"You got it. All three are specifically called out. The Eye of Orik, the Squid's Tooth, and the Crystal Core."

We simultaneously asked, "The Crystal Core?"

"That's Oakengard's soulstone, apparently."

My lips twisted. "Only no one's actually seen it before. The first time I visited the Trinity, Hero Gent let slip that it was stolen by a player."

Trafford hissed. "Hadrian."

"Could be," I replied, "but I didn't see any evidence of it. Peter said soulstones could be abused. That was how Hadrian controlled so many game objects."

"Wait," said Izzy. "I thought that was the Trojan."

I shrugged. "Maybe. Or it could be a combination of both. What I'm stuck on is, once we destroyed the Squid's Tooth, Hadrian seemed powerless. Does that sound like someone who's packing an extra soulstone to you?"

We traded grumbles and frowns, but none of us could compete with the salty veteran. "It gets worse," he said. "First, it's possible the quest chain could be broken since it references the Squid's Tooth, an apparently destroyed artifact. But that's not the only old game object mentioned." He lowered his head and swallowed. "I also found a quest link to the kraken."

Izzy pouted. "We've seen chat-log evidence indicating the kraken's still alive. It would stand to reason, if titans can respawn, that their corresponding soulstones can as well."

"We'd better hope, or we've got a monster on the loose and no way to hold it back."

I chewed my lip. Something wasn't sitting right. What was the common thread between our quests, the soulstones, and the kraken? My eyes flitted to the river where the pirates were prepping a skiff with supplies. The Albula. The Tiber. A new start. Saint Peter had almost told me...

"He wants us to destroy the soulstones," I blurted out.

Everyone stared at me in horror.

"What? Peter mentioned freeing the titans and ridding Haven of the soulstones. Think about it. The last few major battles were more or less fought because of them. Hell, they were enabled by them."

Izzy scoffed. "You don't think defeating evil's as easy as removing temptation, do you?"

"Not quite, but it's undeniable the soulstones can be exploited for supreme power. They're game breakers."

The old buildmaster eyed the Oldtown rubble. "Maybe taking care of them can at least prevent a semi-weekly Armageddon."

"There's that too." I idly scratched my chin as I mulled over the implications. "This changes things. We need to tweak our plans."

"What we need to do," asserted Izzy, "is get this pack of scrubs ready before the sun sets. We're two and a half days till launch and I've never seen a more ragtag band of rascals and bums."

I looked to Trafford for a second opinion.

"Never argue with a woman," he concluded. "Besides, I agree

with her."

"What else is new?" I chortled.

"Hey," said the buildmaster as he started for the barracks, "you're the one who wanted to work from the bottom up."

I grinned and surveyed the bustling chaos. There was nothing to do but get this show started.

1830 Army Men

The next two hours were a coordinated blur. The massive logistics involved in directing hundreds of people were best described as problematic. Every player, NPC, and mob was of a different mind. We had to work with that while remaining decisive and apportioning the best people for the jobs.

Drummond organized troop loadouts. Grimwart consulted Trafford at the barracks to organize marching units. Jixa and her crew joined the ranks of fighters as new faction builders applied last-minute patches to the *Heartcutter*. What had started as a slow burn over the three days since Oldtown's last stand ended with a flurry of energy and commitment. And why wouldn't it? Not only had Black Hat membership multiplied, but there was finally something pressing to do.

Tragedy was funny like that. Sometimes it took the worst of humanity to bring out the best. Saint Peter's labor and sacrifice had come through for us one last time. The city finally had a target to go after, and nothing sharpens focus better than a bull's-eye.

As the sky framing Dragonperch darkened, the streets of Oldtown quieted. Grug and Grom helped Admiral Errol Oates onto the river skiff.

"We'll be off, then."

I held up a clenched fist. "We're counting on you."

"Aye, looks like I'll have t' save the Black Hats one more time."

I smirked and verified the party was sorted while I still had the chance. Me, Kyle, Izzy, Errol, and Trafford. The OG crew, all promoted to faction captains.

"Can you make good time?"

"If the seas be quiet we'll beat the sun, but only if we quit yappin'. Don't ye worry, Talon. We heres know what needs be done."

They pushed off and headed downstream to the north river gate. The fully manned and loaded *Cutter* waited outside, and while her state of repair left many maneuverability and combat concerns, she was seaworthy and fast.

I turned back toward the tower and a number of waiting soldiers. What a difference a couple of hours makes. The units actually looked organized. Trafford, Grimwart, and Gladius stood ready. Bandit nuzzled Artax on the neck.

"One hundred legionnaires, at your disposal," announced Gladius. "The other hundred must stay with me to man the city."

I blinked. "You're not coming with us, Commander?"

"I cannot. My duty is to Stronghold. I trust Trafford to lead my men well."

"Understood. Thanks for your help." I rapped a fist on my chest.

Trafford turned to me, good eye twinkling. "Times sure are changing. Looks like this old veteran's finally getting reasonable support. I'll bring them back safely." Trafford and Gladius exchanged salutes. "And speaking of support..." He turned to Grimwart. "Since you're fighting with us, would you consider serving as colonel of the Black Hat army?"

The crusader was taken aback. "You want me to be the field commander?"

"I'll still be out there with you," tempered the old man. "If the last few hours are any judge, we could really use your experience."

"You're the best choice," I agreed. "You might be unfamiliar with our faction and our membership, but you're probably the most active field commander in all of Haven. Your skills aren't maximized on just your crew of forty crusaders." I stepped in closer. "And I'm assuming you'll do anything to get to Oakengard and save the rest."

"You assume correctly, Talon." Grimwart frowned. "But I've taken oaths to my order. I will serve the Black Hats as you ask, but when the war is won, my allegiance must return to the crusaders."

Trafford and I exchanged a frown, but there was nothing to be done. "I respect and understand your decision," I told him. "You won't be asked to forsake your oaths."

The colonel fell to one knee. "Then I am honored to fight the enemy as one of the Black Hats."

The sudden flair of ceremony took me off guard. I didn't know what the knight expected, so I simply rested a hand on his pauldron.

> Crusader Reputation +100

Trafford stepped forward and rested a hand on the opposite shoulder. "In that case, until whatever time Oakengard is liberated, you can fight as one of us." The old man laughed and helped the knight to his feet.

Black Hats moved close and patted the colonel on the back. Grimwart thanked them and accepted the faction invite I sent. I also promoted him to a captain so he could induct the rest of his men. His face went stoic and he pushed through. "Since I have official duties now, there are hundreds of troops organizing outside the gate I should attend to."

I smiled at Trafford. He'd made a great choice. "Take the legion. Have them ready yesterday," commanded the buildmaster general. "The march is imminent."

Colonel Grimwart saluted and went to work. Trafford sighed as the legionnaires followed the weathered crusader to the west gate.

I shoved his shoulder. "You gonna miss being so hands on with everything?"

"Bah! Just because I'm old don't mean I'm sentimental."

"Fair enough. But about that old part—you sure your knees can handle the march?"

The buildmaster scoffed. "Kids these days. No respect! I oughta shove this arquebus right up—"

Izzy approached, growing cautious as she saw our faces. "Everyone packed?" she asked. It was an ice breaker to defuse hostilities, but it wasn't necessary. Trafford was the saltiest grump around. To him, giving someone a hard time was just fun amongst friends.

"Good to go," I said.

"Aye," added Trafford.

"Any more word on the overarching soulstone quest?" she asked.

"Training an army doesn't leave a lot of time for digging into books."

"I don't blame you," I said. "You know what's funny? I passed 100k XP sometime during this morning's battle and I never even noticed."

Izzy stiffened and checked her menu. "Bastard! I'm at 99,491."

Trafford groaned. "You players and your obsession with levels. Let's go see what the Black Hat army is made of."

We laughed and headed out.

The double wooden gate was drawn open. Black Hats and city folk dotted the thoroughfare, but the main attraction was in the field beyond the walls. We passed through the gate to a greeting of 360 soldiers.

I opened my new captain controls, which conveniently consisted of a new warfare panel.

Army	360
Black Hats	220
Crusaders	40
Legionnaires	100

I was a little disappointed by the number. Total faction membership, including the 40 temporary crusaders, sat at 360. The added legion should've brought our numbers to 460. Alas, a marching army is only a subset of the total guild. Kyle and Bravo Team were away. 20 pirates sailed to Shorehome. Drummond was among plenty of noncombatants staying home to manage the city. Instead of the legionnaires bolstering our army to greater numbers, they really just plugged its holes. I didn't mind the trade considering they were highly trained soldiers. Between them and Grimwart's crusaders, there was plenty of battle experience to go around.

The rest of the Black Hats were a mixed bag. Some star players like Dune's party. Some high-level NPCs. Jixa's ogres. Nooner's gang accompanied us with a caravan of oxen pulling supply wagons. But beyond that Izzy was right: our army was made up of a whole bunch of scrubs. Brave men and women who were willing to die for their new faction. We only equipped and mustered the ones that wouldn't be a liability in the field, but that was a far cry from being able to fight. For them it would be a trial by fire.

So 360 soldiers. As the sole occupying force in the tended land they looked impressive, but I had grave doubts. Oakengard's numbers were boosted after the pagan invasion. By all accounts they were 600 strong, split between knights, sages, and priests, all expertly trained under strict military rule. But that number didn't account for their attrition: the catechist schism, the crusaders we'd stolen, those citizens of Oakengard too pure to join the Violet Order, at least the ones able to escape the infection. If I was being optimistic, we'd be outnumbered by no more than 50 troops.

Still, there was abundant room for pessimism.

The greater pagan faction used to stand at 2500 mobs, but

that was a long time ago. They'd since splintered all over the Midlands. Most wouldn't be a problem, but General Azzyrk's goblin horde was still 350 strong. Respawned and rested, it would be disastrous to meet them in the field before we reached Oakengard. Even worse would be if our enemies joined forces and flanked us in the field.

And then there was the actual journey to Oakengard. The terrain was an added obstacle. The path to the NPC fortress had never been fully mapped. It was mountainous and arduous. Our army had few horses and mounts. If it wasn't for Grimwart's familiarity with the route, we could never hope to make the journey in two days. Now it was a worthwhile prayer.

The new colonel executed his side flawlessly. With only hours of prep, our ragtag band of adventurers worked in organized units, all partied up and members of the greater brigade. Centurions blew horns to announce the start of the march. Crusader sergeants split off and guided various units. And just like that, hundreds of boots trampled the earth.

"Huh," I said, a little crestfallen. "I had a whole *Braveheart* speech prepared and everything."

Izzy snorted. "Keep it in the bag. You might need it later. I've been digging into whatever lore might be relevant to our set of quests. If there's a line to the kraken..."

"It stands to reason that Orik might be mentioned in them as well."

"Exactly. And after exhaustive research, the most I've been able to dig up on Oakengard's titan is a name: Gigas."

"Whoa there. You think this Gigas will come into play?"

She leveled cynical eyes on me. "You don't actually think

we're gonna storm the third city without running into the third titan, do you? Where have you been the last two months?"

"Fair point."

I paused at the rear of the army while she marched ahead. The gates behind us closed. The petrified statue of Orik peeked above the high wall, an awesome sight even while kneeling. There was nothing for it but to go forward.

I grabbed Bandit's reins and started the long walk. Our quest to Oakengard had begun.

<<<T-Minus 2 Days Till Launch>>>

Tad uselessly limped around the office. Just doing the rounds, he told himself.

The halls were dark this time of night. And quiet. The "emergency" responders weren't in emergency mode anymore. It had been a confusing turn of events until Christian discovered why hours earlier.

The lobby security feed had captured Abbie doctoring the front-desk sign-in sheet before planting the bomb. In retrospect, it wasn't hard to pull one over building security, which was really just Horace the semi-retired Baby Boomer with semi-hourly bathroom breaks. The firefighters weren't rushing to save anyone because they believed the office to be entirely empty.

Tad had already attacked that problem by flicking the light switches on and off. The fluorescent bulbs came on slowly and in stages so the effect wasn't remarkably dramatic. Combined with the building's tinted windows, there was a good bet the signal had been entirely imperceptible during the day.

To increase the chances of someone seeing them, and rather than trying to catch someone looking during a specific moment of switching, Tad went through periods of leaving the lights on and then leaving them off. Now, in the dead of night, it was sure to draw notice.

Right?

The office was in one such dark period as Tad patrolled with his crutch. The cubicles were eerily abandoned. Kinda spooky, actually. Being cut off from the outside world without internet, without phone reception—there was something intensely isolating about it.

Tad came upon the site of the earlier explosion. The area outside the Superdome was a mess. The adjoining hallway had partially collapsed, although access to the community room was still open. Tad dared not re-enter that graveyard.

Likewise, walking too near Abbie's body creeped him out. He averted his eyes and gazed at anything but her: fallen ceiling tiles, chunks of server racks, Abbie's recently discharged pistol. Tad was surprised by his reaction to the discovery. He would've thought it would be like an action movie or video game. Find a weapon, pick it up. Instead it brought to mind the wounded CEO. Thinking about the gun was as uncomfortable for him as dwelling on the dead.

Tad flinched away from scratching noises. Were they coming from a survivor in the Superdome?

No, it was the collapsed hallway. The stairwell. Someone was trying to get in.

Tad's eyes shot to the gun on the ground. Would he need to use it?

Normally, the exterior doors were all magnetically locked, but those were disabled due to the evacuation protocol. Tad stepped closer to the ruined hallway. A section of wall had buckled over the doorway.

"Is anyone in there?" called a voice. Hammering came from the stairwell. "Seattle Fire Department. Can anyone hear me?"

Tad relaxed his shoulders. "We're in here!" He hopped to the debris. "The hallway collapsed! There was a bomb!"

"Bomb! Did you say bomb, sir?" Other voices murmured.

"Yeah, there's—" Tad paused. Would mention of the bomb slow their rescue? "Someone's hurt in here. A gunshot wound. We need medical attention."

"Active shooter!" called one.

Damn. Tad couldn't keep his stupid mouth shut. "Use the other door," he urged. "In the west wing. Use the stairwell in the west wing."

"We're gonna get you out of there," replied the firefighter. "Be patient. Just sit tight."

Tad gritted his teeth as the voices descended the stairwell. He was pretty sure he'd just talked himself out of a rescue.

1840 The Black Cauldron

Due to the evening start and our pressing deadline, we pushed the march straight to midnight before making camp. We settled in a large field just off the westerly road, in territory that was still relatively safe. Roving mobs were not about to tangle with an army this size. Nooner rested the oxen. Fires were lit and tents were pitched, but we didn't extensively dig in. Trafford issued a standing order to get a move on in five short hours.

Rest wasn't totally necessary for players in Haven but it was strongly encouraged. A lack of sustenance and sleep contributed to inefficiencies in health and spirit recharging, stamina usage, and NPC morale. Further dereliction brought active fatigue debuffs into play. It didn't need to be said that those would cripple a combat-ready army. As for the NPCs and mobs among us, I wasn't sure of the precise game mechanics governing their rest patterns, but they seemed preprogrammed to want it.

Grimwart and I had figured a short rest after a half day's march would be sufficient. Reserving a full camp after the arduous journey tomorrow would give us the greatest returns right before the day of battle.

Bandit trotted in circles excitedly as I completed a lap around the camp. My aim was to be visible and accessible to every single Black Hat, though I did force myself to cut the many impromptu conversations short. The army needed their rest, and I had somewhere to be.

I pulled Bandit to the road and patted her neck as Izzy approached.

"You've been waiting for this, haven't you?" she asked.

According to the menu, it was nearly 1 a.m. "Legendary powers really have you watching the clock, don't they?"

Even though I'd been the first to hit level 10, Izzy and Kyle were already accustomed to once-a-day abilities due to their artifacts, the winter staff and Dorfin's Decanter. Now we were all level 10, including Lash, so we had new powers befitting our class and play style. My dragonrunning was once again unlocked at midnight.

I placed a hand on Bandit's forehead. The blue gem embedded between her horns glowed and she transformed into a large chestnut dragon as the camp watched on.

"Show off," muttered Izzy.

"It's not like there's a discreet way to transform into a dragon."

Bandit snorted agreement, sending an explosion of dust and grass into the air.

From atop the dragon's back I offered my hand to Izzy. Once she was snuggled behind me, Bandit pattered along the road, picked up speed, and leapt to the sky.

Izzy's thighs tensed. Her hands around my waist went white. I turned to reassure her, but instead laughed.

"Are your eyes closed?"

"Shut up."

I bellowed harder as we rose higher in the sky and bore south.

Aerial speed was a scary thing. Horses were fast but slowed often over the course of a day. Flying creatures from doves to dragons sped across the sky ignorant of the paths or terrain below. It wasn't long before we glided over the mountain range that stretched from Stronghold to the western edge of the map. I spotted the whitewater rapids and followed along until we hovered over a gargantuan waterfall. Despair equal to the weight of the water rushed over me. This was the site of my first experience in Haven, my so-called tutorial.

Bandit circled as she searched for a prime landing spot. The best she could do was a grassy ledge high above the path I'd previously walked. Once our mount splayed low on the ground, Izzy and I slid off her back.

I checked the game clock. "I still have twenty-five minutes of dragon time left. I get to go with you."

Izzy pitched her staff into the ground like a walking stick. Her cheeks tightened as she eyed the rocky ledges below. "No reason for both of us to go down there."

"I didn't know you were afraid of heights," I teased. I approached the cliff edge and perched comfortably to survey the terrain. "But you're right. This'll go faster without you."

I abruptly flipped around and hopped off the edge, causing the pixie to flinch uncomfortably. As my tiger claws and brand-new spider boots caught the rock face, I smiled long enough to flash her a wink and then descended.

The last time I'd been here, I was a total noob. Level 1, without any scaling skill or equipment. I well understood how someone even of Izzy's power could blanch at this crevasse, but it really wasn't all that difficult to maneuver if you knew what you were doing. I lowered to the first cliff path and then hopped to the other until I stood on a platform of rock that wandered under the waterfall.

I hummed the Zelda secret chime and chuckled. "That never gets old."

This time, when I wandered into the hidden cave entrance, my darkvision solidified the rock walls. My passive navigation and cartography skills made quick sense of the interior, and intuition protected me from sudden surprises. I swapped my tiger claws for the dragonspear and approached the three figures huddled around a cauldron.

The witches were black creatures with bony features and long matted hair. Boggarts stood taller than most humans, though in my case that wasn't unusual. The three women turned to me, hollow eye cavities open wide. Their voices were like sandpaper on my brain.

"Surprising to see the Protector of Stronghold in this holy place," said Crowlat ominously.

"Does he mean to dangle us from the ropes?" screeched Havlat.

"Depends," said Somlat, "on whether he comes marching or crawling."

I gritted my teeth. Hearing the coven speak grated my nerves. "I'm here on terms of peace," I announced.

Crowlat chuckled. "Ah, ah, ah, sister Somlat sees true. You come before us a beggar."

"I'm not begging, and the benefit is mutual. Unless you enjoy cowering in caves."

They coughed and cackled amongst themselves. Crowlat took a step toward me. "The Broken Falls are hidden for a reason."

"Yet finds us twice, he did," snapped Havlat.

Crowlat grimaced with sharpened teeth. "Why should we help the likes of you?"

I cleared my throat and spoke adamantly. "Because I mean to destroy the soulstones."

They traded sightless glances with twitching brows.

"No," said Havlat to her sisters. "Stronghold only sees the power as dangerous because they no longer have it."

"It's more than that," I countered, "and you know it. You've seen what Hadrian is, what he's doing. It's why he had you hanged before I could speak with you again." I stepped within an arm's reach of Crowlat. Even at my high level, I was nervous. "We realized long ago that we're not enemies. It's Hadrian. He seeks to usurp and control Haven."

"Control is an illusion," muttered Crowlat.

"He holds the Eye," pointed out Havlat.

"He seeks the servitude of giants," revealed Somlat. "The titans are meant to inspire."

"Orik," I said.

Crowlat's face hardened. "Currently a kneeling statue in your capital."

I swallowed. The witch had a point, but I wasn't sure what was expected of me. I had done what was necessary to protect the city, but maybe the need for that had passed. "Saint Peter mentioned freeing the titans. I'm not exactly sure what that means, but if all our factions could live in relative peace, I'm game."

The three witches congregated around the black cauldron and debated in scratchy whispers. When they turned to me, Crowlat announced, "Neither slavery nor slumber is an acceptable outcome."

"Neither steel nor stone," added Somlat.

"And if he's free?" I posited. "What's stopping him from smashing everything to bits again, including you?"

Crowlat growled. "Our lives are his breaths."

"Fine," I said. "You fight for your beliefs, I'll fight for mine. Freedom is what we're all after, isn't it?"

"Freedom or death," remarked Crowlat.

"From kings to commoners," said Somlat, "freedom and death are often the same."

Havlat approached menacingly. "And how do you wish to seek your freedom, human?"

"My army's marching to Oakengard."

Havlat scoffed. "An army in black."

Somlat grinned. "An army *of* black."

Crowlat held up an open palm. "You seek the Crystal Core." She clasped that hand with Havlat and held up her other. "You seek the kraken." That hand held Somlat's. "The Broken Falls reveal that water is at the heart of all things."

"It brings life," said Somlat. "Preserves it."

Havlat cackled. "And tears it asunder."

"In all its forms," continued Crowlat. "Water is the beginning of things, and the end. It serves in liquid, mist, and ice. You will find what you seek in depths frozen and agape."

My face soured at the riddle. It was hard to fault the

boggarts, seeing as they were crazy blind witches and all, but I really hated riddles. They were toys and tests, all trivial.

"I'm here for more than poetry," I said evenly. "Out there, in the open fields and rocky terrain, this will be a battle of numbers."

Havlat cackled. "We have only three to add."

"You speak for all pagans."

"Seeks to renew the armistice, he does," remarked Somlat.

"No," I said. "I want a full alliance this time. That's the price of destroying the soulstones."

Crowlat snorted like grinding metal. "Our peoples are divided."

"Scattered," added Havlat.

Somlat bent close. "It takes a titan to rally the errant."

Havlat chuckled. "It takes an Eye to awaken a giant."

"No," snapped Crowlat. "Even blind, we can see this will not happen. If you wish to formalize a truce, you must do so with the leader of our largest army."

I hissed. "You expect me to make an alliance with General Azzyrk directly."

"On the contrary, I expect you to fail. But that is your stated wish, and you have the freedom to try."

"Or die," muttered Havlat.

"And what help will you offer, then? Beyond riddles?"

The three witches converged on their cauldron and turned their backs to me.

"We give you nothing," snapped Crowlat.

"It is you who owes," scraped Havlat.

"Our gift for our kin," finished Somlat.

My voice and demeanor grew increasingly agitated with each retort. "And what gift is it you're giving them?"

Crowlat sighed. "It is you who gives it, Talon of Stronghold. Your word and your might are now pledged to the pagans. As holy guides, we will pass along your message. What comes of it," she warned, empty eye sockets stretching wide, "remains to be seen."

I scowled against the darkness. As much as I wanted to stand my ground and argue some sense into them, their position was clear. I stomped away from the witches and out of their cave. The authority for what I wanted lay with the goblin general Azzyrk. Besides, I was approaching ten minutes left on Bandit's dragon form. I hurried away from the waterfall and up the rocks.

"I thought you'd taken the plunge," said Izzy.

"Would've been a more pleasant experience," I muttered.

"What did the old hags have to say?"

"A whole lot about freedom and death." I frowned at the horizon. "My legendary ability is almost up. I'll fly you to lower ground where we can split up. I wish I could take you all the way to the wildkins, but I need to get back to the city."

There was no way I could make it to Stronghold in ten minutes, of course, but I'd found I could extend the dragon form by keeping high in the sky. The power thankfully didn't expire and leave me stranded in the clouds on a flailing mountain bongo. If we got too close to the ground or tried to drop Izzy off at the Blackwood, however, Bandit would revert.

"No worries," said Izzy. "You're not the only one with a mount. I'm a frostcaller now, you know."

The mage clenched her fist and activated her new legendary ability. A chunk of ice grew from the ground with enchanted blue light. A flash, a roar, and a forty-foot-tall frost giant stood beside the mountain's edge. He had long orange hair, a braided beard, and wore impossibly large furs. The giant cradled his hands and lifted Izzy to his shoulder where she sat cross-legged and smirking.

"See you, twerp," said the five-foot pixie.

The giant nodded and his voice boomed. "See you, little man." He turned and stomped toward the heart of wildkin country.

I grinned. Izzy had planned that well. While it wasn't snowy up here, the frost giant's large stride would easily navigate the mountain terrain. The massive fists and matching scowl more than guaranteed her safety.

With that taken care of, I climbed onto Bandit with minutes to spare and disappeared into the clouds.

1850 Vagrant Story

The *Heartcutter* dragged in the unseen surf. Shorehome's rough tidal waters proved dangerous at night when it was hidden beneath a layer of marine mist. The fog was especially thick tonight. To add to the ghostly surroundings, the horizon was pitch black.

Errol squinted on deck and grumbled. "She's near," he said. "I can smell me city even if I can't see it."

Grug frowned. "The guide lamps ain't on. When's the last time thems been turned off?"

"They ain't never been turned off," growled Errol.

The frigate shook on the waves, creaking louder than usual. The poor girl was still mid repair. Errol hadn't had the heart nor the humility to admit it to Talon, but he was frankly surprised they made it to their destination at all.

"I'm taking us seaward a bit t' avoid hittin' the crags. Even if the lamps be off, we'll see activity in town."

The captain moved to the helm and piloted the *Cutter* a safe distance off shore, driven only by instinct and starlight. But even those dependable stars winked out as a growing mass of black dominated their path, first a shadow, then a silhouette of a boat, then the looming breadth of Papa Brugo's flagship, the *Void*.

"Ship ho!" cried Grom, pulling up his pants as a busty wench scampered away. Errol wasn't sure which was more impressive: that Grom had taken that long to notice a destroyer-class cruiser, or that he'd somehow managed to smuggle a busty wench aboard beneath the notice of his crew of twenty.

Errol slowed the *Cutter*, hooked his hands in his belt, and approached the bulwark to greet his friends.

"Ahoy!" he called. " 'Tis a fine place fer a pirate parley, an' I could use a tankard o' ale an' yer finest pickled sturgeon!"

The black *Void* hung idle in the water as its gun ports opened.

"Speaking o' sturgeon," continued Errol, turning to Grom, "did I ever tell ye o' the time Mistress Sally at the Derelict Dagger swallowed—"

"Ar!" cried his pirate companion. "Ahoy and avast! She be readyin' her guns!"

"Now Grom," chided Errol, "that ain't no reason t' spoil a perfectly humorous sturgeon anecdote."

The quadruple cannons of the black ship opened fire, tearing into the *Heartcutter* along its length. The pirates on deck scrambled away from danger.

Errol caught his hat as it flew off his head. "Battle stations!" He sprinted to the down hatch and stuck his head in. "Wake up ye sorry excuses fer chum! Get them cannons ready!"

"Sir!" rushed an underling from below. "The cannons are offline awaitin' repairs!"

Errol retracted his head from the hatch. "I see." He turned to Grom. "Then unfurl the turbo sail!"

"Cap'n," replied Grom, "the sail is still disabled."

Another barrage of cannon balls splintered the frigate's hull. The *Cutter* groaned as she listed and took in water.

Errol ran to the port side to assess the damage. "Plug those holes or we're done fer!" He opened the ship controls and blanched when he saw the remaining structural points.

SP: 140/500

Errol grabbed the wheel, but the ship began to roll with the waves. Before he could retake control, the *Void* fired again.

Critical hit!
Mast Break!
[Heartcutter] is wrecked

"Woe be us, patriots!" cried Errol at the top of his lungs. "T' brave the depths o' the North Sea only t' be done in by traitors!"

By now the *Cutter* was half sunk and breaking apart. Pirates scampered from below deck, weapons in hand. "Ev'ry man fer themselves!" one screamed.

Errol drew his rapier. "Nay I say! Be we not admirals o' the sea, each an' ev'ry one? Are we not loyal t' this ol' girl in her dyin' throes?" The crew of twenty gathered round the charismatic captain with solemn faces. "Nay, I say! Fie to that! T' the bitter end, we'll hold strong. We'll hold until the *Cutter* holds no more an' we're washed out t' greet Davy Jones himself."

The captain raised his sword high. "Scandalous rogues one

an' all, if ye have any honor in yer mangy hides, ye'll die here like meself. We be goin' down with the ship!"

Glorious cheers bathed the pirate crew as their frigate buckled and broke apart. Men tumbled off the slanted deck, were swept up in a crashing wave, and landed on the beach unharmed. Errol lifted his face and spat out a mouthful of sand. They must have been much closer to shore—and Shorehome—than he'd figured.

"I see," he muttered gloomily.

The crew collected themselves and moved inland, away from the crashing waves and broken timbers of their old ship. They were on Shorehome's rocky beach, beside one of the feeder tunnels to the Narrows.

"The captain's a genius!" cried Grug. "Sailed us right past the Black Fleet and into the city!"

Errol quickly nodded away the compliment and looked over his men. "Who'd we lose, boys?"

"Not a butt cheek unaccounted fer," reported Grom as he idly slapped his wench's behind.

Amazing. Despite the disaster of a shipwreck, they'd made it to their destination with nary a scratch. Errol had always figured he led a charmed life. The pirates turned toward the flood channel that hid Underkeep.

Forty cutthroats filed out wielding all manner of sharp objects. Swords, knives, claws, axes. One fat man even brandished a campfire spit. The roughneck marauders fanned out and quickly had the harried crew outnumbered two to one.

"Hold!" ordered a firm woman's voice. A dark figure pushed through the line.

Errol's eyes widened as he stared drop-jawed at the approaching bouncing bust popping from a red corset. "I'm seein' double," he murmured.

Avisa slapped him. "Still as lewd as ever, my friend."

Errol's eyes begrudgingly rose to the pirate sergeant's face. "Would I do this with a friend?" He leaned in to give her a smooch.

She slapped him again with the opposite hand.

With tears streaking from his eyes and his stomach in knots, Errol finally burst out laughing. Grug did the same, followed by the rest of the pirate band.

"I don't get it," said Grom.

Avisa was a sight for sore eyes. Milk-chocolate skin, toned and weathered arms but soft and supple in the right places, she was sharper and sexier than anyone in the city, including Mistress Sally. Avisa had captivating yellow-green eyes, like seaweed. Errol admired her long brown eyebrows, high cheekbones, and the large gold hoops that dangled against her neck. Only too late he noticed his gaze was wandering down to—

Avisa attempted to adjust the silky cloth covering her cleavage, but the tantalizing tugging just squeezed her breasts in other directions. She huffed and released them back to the pull of gravity. "I'm still not sure why I like you," she said with a glower.

Errol smiled heartily. "If I cared, me dear, then you surely wouldn't." He turned to his crew, studied the surrounding cutthroats, and sighed heavily. "I do confess, it warms me heart t' run into ye here. Somethin' tells me we ain't wanted in town."

"Something, huh? You always were perceptive." The sergeant

turned to the flood channel they'd emerged from and waved them in. Once off the shoreline, she crouched on her haunches and spoke in a low voice. "Shorehome be in the midst of a civil war."

"What's the mist gotta do with it?" asked Grom.

She ignored him. "After Papa Brugo respawned, Hadrian's men turned on him. The Brothers in Black ruptured. It's been days, and we still don't know who to trust."

Errol glanced nervously at the forty blades escorting them.

"This is my personal guard," she said. They eyed the fat man with the pig spit. "And Corpulent Cass. They fight for Brugo. For Shorehome."

"Ar. What kind o' fightin' are we talkin'?"

"Underkeep has been seized by Hadrian's loyalists. The occupation means we don't have a base of operations. The good news is it keeps most of the bad guys inside. They don't have the numbers to root us out and overtake the city. The bad news is they've taken the Papa prisoner on the *Void*. They control the port and prevent any supplies from reaching the docks."

"With Brugo out o' commission," said Errol, "that can't spell anythin' good in the streets."

Avisa shook her head. "The gangs have splintered and engaged in bloody turf wars, each fighting for dominance of fuzzy borders. They used to be happy with splitting the neighborhoods."

"Until the Papa o' all Papas proved one man can take it all." Errol growled. "We came here for an audience with Brugo."

"That's great."

"No it ain't. How do we make an alliance with a man

imprisoned on the most powerful and only ship in port?"

"Easy," said Avisa, green eyes sparkling as she flashed a healthy set of teeth. "We go get him."

1860 Hexplore

Bandit adjusted her flight path over the mountain range.

Even though everyone had an open line on brigade chat, and we now had a place for command-level discussion on captain chat, banter like this was handled on party chat. That was me, Kyle, Izzy, Trafford, and Errol.

The dragon sagged in the sky. I pulled up on the reins, but Bandit was fighting me.

I grimaced. He was right, of course. I just needed them to hurry so I could get them back and focus on the next stage of the plan. Before I could reply, our steepening descent sent tickles through my stomach. I tightened my grip on the saddle.

"Bandit, what are you—"

She jerked in the sky. I thought we'd been hit until her neck and body began to shrink. Oh no. We were too close to the mountain peak. Her transformation was starting prematurely.

We rushed toward the nearest ledge as flight transitioned to a glide before approaching something more resembling a fall. I landed hard on the back of a mountain bongo.

"Ouch!"

Bandit's hooves absorbed most of the rocky impact. She hopped away and I jostled to the ground. After a quick roll and a skid, I lowered to the dirt to rest. Bandit cantered to a patch of grass and started snacking.

"We really pushed it this time, didn't we?"

The bongo snorted and farted at the same time.

Next time I went over the time limit of Bandit's dragon form, I'd remind myself not to fly over mountains. I breathed deep and gazed at the horizon. Stronghold wasn't in sight, but it was there. It was just gonna take a bit of a walk.

Kyle swiped his chat log closed with a huff. "Talon's wondering what we've accomplished all day." The big guy stomped down the narrow corridor of the mine entrance, the cobwebs long since trampled. "I've been wondering the same thing myself."

Lash sat against the wall resting her head. She spoke with her eyes closed. "At least the day ticked so our specials are recharged."

The brewmaster flushed. "Yeah, then maybe I should stockrig a cannon and blow up the reinforced door trapping us in this dungeon."

The head of Bravo Team sighed, opened her eyes, and turned to him. "You got a problem, frat boy?"

"Yeah, actually. We hid out until midnight. Talon's waiting to fast travel us outta here. Everyone's keeping up their part of the plan except for that troublemaking thief. I need a drink."

"Don't think I'm letting you break your clean-and-sober challenge just 'cause Izzy's not around."

The brewmaster deflated. "She got to you."

"She didn't need to get to me. We're friends, and I think it's hilarious."

"Great. Can we just keep the discussion on our situation here?"

"You mean trash-talking a member of my team?" Lash scoffed.

"A *troublemaking* member of your team. You realize he's the one who stirred up havoc the first time we were here, going down corridors on his own private quest, stealing silver, alerting the keepers, and getting us chased out like rats. The whole reason Hex is stone in the first place is—"

"Don't say it," warned the knight. The dark corridor went quiet for a moment. When Lash spoke again, she was less defensive. "We were all part of that mess. Nobody could've known how it would turn out."

Kyle blew out a hiss, part frustration and part relief. He hadn't known Lash to be very sensible, but she was obviously trying. As much as Kyle hated to admit it, her position in the faction had improved her mood and critical thinking. Maybe she had newfound perspective now that she was responsible for more than just her party.

They were heroes, thought Kyle bitterly. It was that same sense of duty that got them stuck in Oakengard in the first place.

"You're right," he said, hands on hips. "It's just that this all turned into a giant... poo-poo show."

Lash snickered. "Tell us how you *really* feel, Kyle. Izzy was right, this is great. But maybe trying to hold in all those bad words is what really has you ready to pop."

Kyle was about to sample a few of the aforementioned bad words when he turned to scurrying footfalls. Conan and Glinda returned from their dungeon diving.

The old witch shook her head. "The mapping's not sensible, I'll tell you that. There are so many tunnels and mountainside entrances it took us a while to find our way back."

Conan clenched a stoic jaw and offered a single nod. "Long walk. Not even any monsters to crush."

"Try crushing the door," muttered Kyle.

Conan's bare arms and chest went taut as he made a beeline for the entrance.

"No!" snapped Lash. "We didn't hide out all day only to blow our cover now. There haven't been patrols in hours. Bashing the door down is gonna turn all eyes on us again."

"I'm gonna try another shot of my corrosive oil," said Kyle.

"You still have some of that left?" asked Glinda with an arched eyebrow. "I would've thought ten tries was enough."

Kyle smiled magnanimously as he presented a vial of black liquid. "Maybe that's because the door needs *eleven* tries."

Lash snorted so loudly the room turned to her. She climbed to her feet, stretched her neck, and said, "I have a better idea." The white knight pointed to the reinforced access hatch and a loud click resounded.

Kyle's brow furrowed. "Whoa... How did you... ?"

The hatch opened. Crux held it, kneeling and peering down at them.

The brewmaster's face hardened. "Oh." Conan and Glinda chuckled, no doubt having been part of that hilarious coordination over Bravo Team's party chat. Still, as a light breeze wafted past him toward Oakengard's lower floor, Kyle could only be happy the hatch was open. They hurried from the mine and gathered around the entrance.

"I found something," whispered Crux, "but I need your help."

Kyle started through his inventory. "How long will it take? The tree form has a one-hour limit."

"No," said the thief. "We might need your decanter for something else. I can get you there without a fight."

"How?"

"A short while ago, a small contingent of crusaders awaiting reclamation escaped the castle. The Violet Order sent most of their resources after them, with Hadrian at their head."

"Why would they do that?" asked Lash.

He shrugged with a half-assed smile. "I'm pretty sure they think we fled Oakengard with them."

"A whole unit of troops sympathetic to our cause?" muttered Kyle. "We should've been with them. Instead we were stuck in a tunnel."

"We don't have Hex yet," stressed the thief. "And this is too good to pass up. With knight chasing knight in the mountains, we have free run of the fortress."

Glinda released a long groan. "Isn't everybody ignoring something? How can Hadrian leave the castle if he's on lockdown?"

They blinked at each other. Kyle hadn't been tracking the clock, but something was definitely amiss.

> **Kyle:** *Talon, can you still locate Hadrian by his player ID?*
> **Talon:** *Sure. Let me see... That's impossible. He's not in Oakengard.*
> **Kyle:** *He skipped out on his lockdown twelve hours early. Where is he?*
> **Talon:** *Northeast of the city. I don't have any map data so that area's a giant gray smudge.*

Kyle relayed the confirmation to Bravo Team, but they were already moving on. Crux led them down the dark halls, keeping their travel to the abandoned bottom floor. Without anyone to hear suspicious noises, even Lash and Conan were ghosts. Once they arrived at the staircase nearest their destination, Crux snuck upstairs, scouted ahead, and waved them forward through a few more halls, all empty.

For the first time, Kyle understood why the thief was such a famed dungeon diver. He hadn't spent the day dilly-dallying in hiding. Not that the rest of them had a choice about it. He followed with growing curiosity, feeling safer in the foreign city.

Finally, without encountering a soul, Crux escorted them to a circular aviary with a high ceiling that opened up to a third floor. Skylights flooded the room, painting moonlight on plants in clay pots and small fountains. Vegetation was extremely rare in the mountains around Oakengard. This room was primed to show off the biological treasures.

It *had* been, anyway, long ago. The plants were withered and brown. The water in the fountains was stagnant and black. Dead finches and starlings dotted the floor and a multitude of bird cages that adorned the walkways.

"Gross," observed Kyle.

Crux pointed upward. A heavy chain hung from the center of the ceiling. Suspended high above and between the viewing balconies was a giant steel cage.

"There aren't stairs to the viewing balconies from this room," reported Crux. "The third floor has more activity and is harder to search, but I managed. Thing is, the balconies are warded with strong magical traps. I don't know how to disarm them."

Kyle frowned. From their vantage on the floor, the oversize birdcage was mostly an opaque bottom. "What's in that thing?"

"My sister."

Kyle swallowed.

Bravo Team fanned out, checking the room for dangers, but mostly attempting to get a better view of their petrified party member above. "I see the problem," said Lash. "The easy access is from the balcony, but that's where the strongest defenses are.

And that's if we can sneak a bunch of us up there at all."

Glinda patted the smooth walls. "The cage is too high to reach, and there's no ready way to climb, I imagine?"

Crux shook his head. "I checked. Maybe if Talon was here."

Conan spun his greataxe in his hands. "I can break that chain with a good throw."

Glinda rolled her eyes. "No you can't."

The barbarian's head snapped to her, shocked that his statement would be challenged. "Of course I can. I am Conan."

The old witch huffed. "Everyone knows you're strong, you big dummy, but that's a thick chain and it's thirty feet above our heads. You could never pull that off."

"I can so."

Crux sighed impatiently. "Please, guys. Even *if* you manage to break the chain without causing a racket, when the heavy cage crashes to the ground, Hex would crumble apart. We don't know if she'd respawn after that."

Kyle bit his lip. It stood to reason that she should respawn, but players weren't supposed to turn to stone for days at a time in the first place. These were uncharted waters.

"What about a rope?" asked Kyle. "Just toss one up with a grappling hook and climb."

"That was my next thought after the balconies," explained the thief. "But check out those hinges on the cage floor."

Kyle squinted. "What are those for?"

"The mechanism extends to the top of the cage. If additional weight is put onto it and the cage pulls lower, the floor drops out."

Kyle blanched. "And so does Hex. Okay," he muttered,

pacing around the puzzle. "We can't climb up or pull her down. We can't reach her with the balconies. And if we touch the cage, she falls. What do you want us to do?"

The glum thief shrugged both shoulders. "Think of something I didn't."

"That's all, huh?" Kyle snorted. He'd really picked a bad time to abstain from swearing.

"Well, I got nothing," admitted Lash. "My tool set is mostly limited to killing and protecting. Same goes for Conan and Glinda."

The white witch raised a meek finger. "Mostly just protecting, on my part."

The barbarian nodded. "Killing over here."

"I'm confident I can pick the lock on the cage," offered Crux, "if I can get to it—as well as disable any physical traps in place—but I'm afraid I'm not the acrobat Talon is." Crux was a deft spelunker but was less splashy.

Kyle pressed his lips out. The thief had read his mind. Talon or Izzy would be able to solve this puzzle in no time. Their fearless leader would vault circles around this room. Izzy would use her magic to conjure up a bridge of ice or something. And that was if neither was in the mood to utilize their dragon or frost giant.

The brewmaster sighed. None of that meant he was chopped liver over here. He was, after all, one of the highest-level players in Haven. He had a legendary ability just like Talon and Izzy and Lash. As a crafter, his had a deal more flexibility than theirs too.

"Don't you have that whatchamacallit potion?" asked Conan. "The one that gives you solutions to problems?"

"Yes and no," he answered. "I can use Dorfin's Decanter, and the enchantment should give us something helpful to our situation, but it doesn't necessarily give you what you want. I've wasted it by using it too early before. It's best to save it as a last resort."

Crux winced. "What do you mean last resort? Don't be precious with your abilities now. This is my sister we're talking about!"

"Wait," said Lash in a commanding voice. She stepped forward and rested a gauntlet on the thief's shoulder. "Kyle's come through before. I think we should hear him out."

To the brewmaster's surprise, everyone turned to him and waited. Lash's eyes twinkled. "Okay then, frat boy, what exactly do you suggest?"

1870 Going Commando

<hr>

Errol and the cutthroats silently glided through the current, lost in the mist beneath Shorehome's main dock. The wooden structure was huge, branching out into several subdocks capable of housing full frigates themselves. Behind them, Hadrian's men scoured the beach and the wreckage of the *Cutter*. Above, assassins stomped on the dock into town after unloading.

"Where are they?" demanded one as he shoved forward.

Errol pressed his back against the dock piling and gently nudged his crew past. Between the waves and the trampling overhead, there was enough noise to make them ghosts, but one idle mistake could be their undoing. Avisa was taking up the rear, and as she passed Errol hooked her waist and pulled her into him. She inhaled sharply as their bodies met, their faces inches from each other.

"I have t' say, raidin' with ye again really brings back memories."

She glanced down. "It feels like more than memories stirring."

"Won't ye offer me a kiss fer g'luck?"

"Pirates make their own luck, which is why our kissing days are done." She tried to push away but he held her tight.

"What if I wish t' know ye well again?"

She sighed. "You never knew me, Errol. That was the problem. The sum of your interest was focused on the bedroom."

"And what be wrong with that? 'Sides, you an' me hardly waited fer a proper bedroom. I seem t' remember ye havin' a thin' fer the wind whipping 'gainst yer naked bosom."

Avisa's lashes fluttered. Her body relaxed and the water glistened on her skin. The sergeant placed a light hand on his cheek and leaned forward, squeezing her cleavage into his chest. She smelled like the summer breeze and tickled his ear with a whisper.

"You're getting sentimental on me in your old age." Avisa's other hand gripped a rounded fish knife to his balls.

Errol grinned. "Ain't old age but wisdom, me flower o' the sea."

She snorted. "Corny, too."

"If ye tryin' t' turn me on, dear, ye need t' squeeze a little harder."

Avisa rolled her eyes and pushed away. She put the small blade to her mouth and bit down playfully before winking and moving ahead. She *was* trying to turn him on.

To escape the pursuit of loyalists, the group of sixty-two pirates was making their way to the end of the dock where the *Void* was anchored. It was an overly large force to take a ship by stealth, but they had nowhere else to go.

> **Errol:** *If these next few minutes go well, we may have Brugo without even enterin' the city.*

> **Talon:** *Good to hear someone's on schedule. Keep me in the loop.*
> **Errol:** *Aye aye.*

With the main force of loyalists unloaded and approaching the boardwalk, Errol and his men circled the hull of the *Void* and gathered around the floating buoy of the bower anchor. Avisa, knife in mouth, hoisted herself up the rope first. She deftly scaled the bow and vaulted over the bulwark. A second later, a cutthroat came flying over the edge and splashed down in the surf. Pirates converged on him with blades.

The ever-impressive woman peeked down and waved them up. It would take time for so many to board so Errol went next. His boots ran up the hull and hit the deck beside Avisa and another dead crew member. A scan of the enemy ship revealed another deckhand on the far side. Errol couldn't believe it. The loyalists had practically given them their flagship.

But then, it wasn't theirs to begin with.

"I'll take this one," he gloated.

Errol drew a large hunting blade and approached the man from behind. Staying low, he pulled at the man's head and sliced the neck clean, dragging him to the deck. The stealth kill had gone off smoothly. By the time he returned, Grug, Grom, and a few Brothers in Black had joined them.

"When everyone's aboard," commanded Avisa, "raise anchor and cast off. We'll cut the crew off from reinforcements."

"Are we sure the Papa's here?" asked Errol.

"One way to find out."

They headed toward the wide stairway that led below deck. Errol and Avisa descended side by side.

"What the—?" blurted out a guard.

Like a dance, Errol and Avisa drew rapier and saber, his right hand mirroring her left. They advanced and plunged their swords into the unfortunate man.

"The brig is three decks down," said Avisa.

Errol nodded. "Aye. You men clear the ship, one deck at a time."

Blades flashed against candlelight as pirates rushed past. Errol followed Avisa to a pole running into the depths of the *Void*. She curled a leg around it.

Errol opened his mouth.

"Don't say it," she snapped. "Too obvious."

He conceded a nod as she slid down. He jumped on after her and slid two decks down. Another surprised crew member was woefully unmatched. By the time the two descended another set of stairs and burst into the brig, they were racing each other to the next kill. Three dead loyalists lay at their feet outside a steel cage in the center of the room.

"I applaud you," said Papa Brugo, the cage's only occupant. "But I'm afraid opening the cage will prove harder than swordplay."

Errol reached a hand between steel bars. "You've seen better days, Papa."

"Ha!" bristled the crime boss. He clasped Errol's wrist in greeting. "There is no better day than one surrounded by friends. It is good of you to come for me."

Avisa picked at the lock with her fish knife and hissed in

frustration. "Fie! I'll need to put my best burglar on it."

"Don't bother," said the large man. He crossed stout arms over his barrel chest. "It's magically warded. We'll need a metal mage."

Grug scuttled down the stairs. "Captain, the occupying crew has been dispatched. The *Void* is ours." His eyes snapped to Brugo's twisted smile. "Er, what I mean to say, of course, is that she's yers, Papa of all Papas."

The trapped kingpin grumbled.

"Cast off!" came a hurried cry from above. Errol rushed up a level and peeked out the gun port. The long dock stretched from their midship to the boardwalk. Thirty loyalists advanced with swords drawn.

Errol searched the room and patted down the various pouches at his waist. He produced a wood match, struck it against the iron of the already-deployed heavy cannon, and lit the fuse. It was only at the last second that he thought to tilt the aim downward. The black powder exploded in his face. Errol flew back several feet and landed on his ass.

"You crazy fool!" exclaimed Avisa, hurrying to his side.

Errol groaned as she crouched over him and leaned in to check his breath. That's when he wrapped both arms around her back, squeezed her tight, and gave her a shameless kiss.

He'd expected soft lips. What surprised him was that they kissed back. He'd also expected a friendly slap once it was over. He was once again surprised when she kneed him forcefully in the groin. Errol recoiled into a fetal position as she rose.

"I'm not the type of woman to bluff," she said instructively.

Errol grimaced. "All's fair in love an' war."

She offered her hand again and he finally took it earnestly. On shaky feet, he limped to the gun port to see Shorehome's primary dock in flames. Half the charging loyalists had jumped into the water. The other half were backing off and taking cover. Finally, the *Void* jerked as the anchor pulled away from the seabed. They rushed up the decks until greeted by the salty breeze. Grom surrendered the wheel and Errol steered the destroyer-class frigate northward, away from the coast.

1880 Steel Cage Challenge

Bravo Team stood under a bird cage, swapping glances between it and Kyle. They were counting on him.

The brewmaster dug into his inventory. His legendary power made him a stockrigger. That meant he could combine sets of equipment into impossible creations and utilize them for a whole hour. There had to be something that could free Hex from her prison. He just had to figure out what and how.

The mirror shield was his best standard item. It was great for stockrigging because its reflective qualities extended to many applications. He puzzled over a way to somehow "reflect" Hex's state from stone to flesh, but nothing came to him. It seemed like a reach, anyway.

His alchemy also failed him. Corrosives were a good solution to locks, but the metal in Oakengard seemed resistant. Besides, they had the thief for locks. And flame gel didn't solve anything.

Kyle studied his dual eagle crossbow. As the name implied, it had two simultaneously loaded bolts. He'd equipped them with glass tips filled with his brewery creations. The primary advantage the crossbow afforded was a delivery mechanism. Kyle could get something to the cage from across the room if he needed to.

Then there was the bishop gauntlet, one of two drops acquired by defeating Bishop Tannen. While it had proved handy in straight-up fisticuffs against shadows, the brewmaster's specialties didn't lie with light magic.

Kyle had armor, a brewer's belt, and standard adventuring equipment like camping supplies, rations, and the aforementioned grappling hook and rope. It wasn't much to go on. Then he realized he had more than that at his disposal. He had Lash and Conan, Glinda and Crux. Not only their equipment but their skill sets as well.

"What about the balcony walls?" he asked, pointing to one level with the cage. "Can we get a grappling hook onto one?"

"It's not close enough to the cage to do us any good," said Glinda.

"I can try," said Conan, producing a rope and swinging the hook around to gain momentum.

"Wait," said Lash, stepping to the center of the room.

> [Lash] cast Reveal Magic

Ruby sigils glittered into existence. Hundreds of them were inscribed on the surfaces of the aviary, starting from just above their heads and running past the cage and to the ceiling. The room was covered with them.

Crux widened his eyes. "Good thing I didn't get very high trying to climb. I sensed danger, but I had no idea it was this extensive."

Kyle frowned. "So we can see the traps now, but we can't disarm them."

"Too much even for my magic resistance," added Lash. "I might be able to withstand some, but anyone who touches this is gonna get fried."

Conan plucked a dead bird from the floor and beamed it at the wall. As soon as it made contact, a white-hot ball erupted and vaporized the finch. "*Hasta la vista*, birdy."

While Kyle respected Conan's dedication to his character, it was hard to be flippant. Those same wards would prevent the rope from hooking onto the balconies.

"Look at the wall." Lash pointed to where the finch had hit. The exploded sigil had gone black. Over a few seconds, color from the neighboring wards faded and bled over. "They're re-energizing themselves. Any hope of brute-forcing a path on the wall is shot."

"That's a lot of magic," noted Glinda. "There must be a limit to it."

"Which means," asserted Kyle, "we need to find its source."

He found a wooden chair beside a small fountain. Kyle picked it up and flung it above his head. The chair bounced several times on the rounded wall, fireballs exploding in its wake. It destructed into burning pieces that clattered to the floor. A wide path of sigils blackened in its wake. They quickly refilled.

"It's the moonlight," said Lash. "From the skylight. It's recharging their energy. The sun probably does the same during the day."

The brewmaster's awe turned to conviction as he noted the dead foliage lining the entire wall. "I have an idea."

Kyle liked blowing things up. It was kinda his thing, and he was good at it. Blowing things up was a reward in itself, but it was especially rewarding when other people appreciated it. When fire was a solution.

The brewmaster doused the perimeter of the circular room with flame gel and lit it up. The dead plant life burned quickly, sending flames stretching up the walls. The wards responded, crackling and zapping with destructive energy.

"Fighting fire with fire..." murmured Lash.

Kyle's grin grew.

The fire provided a DoT that continually expended the wards closest to the floor. They exploded outward, darkened, and sucked more energy from their neighbors.

"It's not enough," said Lash.

"Wait for it," said the brewmaster.

Black smoke roiled upward, gathering under the domed skylight. The whole room darkened as the moon blotted out. This, in turn, saw the magic wards slower to refill.

"Okay, frat boy," conceded the knight. "I'll give you that one. What's next?"

"I still can't make the climb," said Crux.

"I'll need everyone's ropes and blankets."

Amid the rolling flames and popping walls, they dutifully obeyed. While Conan and Glinda contained the fire to the walls, Kyle went to work. After several attempts to knot the ropes together, it was apparent he was going to need a little something extra. Given better planning and sufficient time, his plan was solid. With the burning brush a ticking clock, there was no way to execute his plan without spending his stockrig ability.

The legendary power activated and combined his selected

equipment on the fly. The four ropes and hooks became a safety net padded with blankets. Kyle hooked his crossbow into the rig, and when the wards all the way up to the balcony were weakened, he took aim and fired.

A grappling hook shot out and clamped to the top of a balcony wall. Weak sparks protested, but the rope was secure. Kyle repeated that for the three other balconies, centering the net and blankets beneath the cage. As the last rope extended to its limit, the net went taut and settled fifteen feet above the ground, ten feet under the bird cage. It was a work of art. Such precision would've been impossible without invoking stockrigging.

"No," said Crux. "You're not doing what I think you're doing."

"It's the only way," returned Kyle.

"But the statue's heavy. The net—"

"Is the result of a legendary ability. It's not magically fortified but it's as structurally sound as it can possibly be. The net will hold as long as the hour isn't up."

"Let me get up there at least. Make sure Hex doesn't slip off."

Conan came over and boosted Crux to his shoulders. The thief pulled himself up and bounced in the net. "It's surprisingly stiff." He looked up. "And the positioning is perfect. This might actually work."

"Take up positions around the net," ordered Kyle. "When she comes down, do whatever it takes to keep her steady."

Everyone nodded and surrounded the net, except the barbarian who took it on himself to stand directly under it.

Kyle cleared his throat. "Um, Conan, unless you want to

become two feet shorter, you should stand to the side. The net's designed to lower as it absorbs the impact."

"I knew that." The barbarian sheepishly moved.

Kyle made eye contact with everybody to make sure they were ready, ending with Crux who was standing on the perimeter of the net. Kyle drew his personal rope and grappling hook, aimed it for the cage above, and fired. The metal claw clinked between the bars. Kyle yanked down.

The birdcage moved and the floor swung open. The statue dropped like an anchor, catching beside Crux in the blankets. Conan lunged as the net dropped low. He caught the rope but its bounce yanked him off the ground. Crux and Conan held on as the swaying net slowed.

"We did it!" cried the thief.

Lash steadied a hanging Conan, whose legs were still a few feet off the ground. The net sagged a good five or six feet, but it was still a little high. The white knight hopped and grabbed the opposite rope, pulling the group further down.

"Now what?" piped Lash.

"Now we're done," said Crux, steadying himself against the heavy stone. "We don't need to get the statue down from here. We just need to turn it back into my sister." He pulled out the half-filled vial containing the antidote.

Growing flames around one balcony bit at the base of the grappling hook. The rope snapped, sending the entire net lurching sideways. The thief lost his footing. He hugged the statue to catch himself, but the jerky movement knocked the wind from his lungs. The glass vial flew from his grip.

"No!"

Kyle pounced forward.

Agility Check...
Fail!

Unsurprisingly, his crafting loadout wasn't primed for feats of dexterity. The glass vial shattered on the floor, spilling fluid between the worn tiles.

The statue was nestled on its side, and the sudden dip caused it to shift toward the edge. Crux panicked, pulling against a rope looping the statue's arm, but the strain was too great for him. In an equal and opposite tragedy, the thief's loadout wasn't built for strength. They all watched on pins and needles as Hex slid off the net.

Lash released her hanging hold, drew her cleaver in midair, and stabbed the ground as she landed.

[Lash] cast Bastion

The shield winked into being, a wide dome around her body. At eight feet tall, the barrier materialized inches below the stone figure. Instead of falling nine feet to the tile floor, the statue hit the barrier and continued sliding along its curvature.

Conan, cut off by the energy field at his waist, was unaffected. He released the net and safely dropped through the shield to the floor. As the statue slid down the side of the dome, Conan grabbed Kyle's loose rope, hooked it around their petrified party member, and pulled hard. His chest and shoulders expanded to a barrel. His arms went taut. The barbarian looked ready to pop, but his strength slowed Hex enough that she hit the floor with a gentle knock. He released the rope slowly as Kyle helped set her upright.

She was safe.

The bastion shield evaporated and the party sighed in relief as Conan helped a glum Crux off the net.

"The last of the antidote," he groaned. "All this way and I dropped it."

"Step aside," said Glinda, "and let a good witch work." She laid hands on the statue.

[Glinda] cast Moderate Healing on [Hex]

The light effect fizzled out. Glinda furrowed her brow.

"What just happened?" asked Crux, crestfallen.

The good priest didn't know what to say.

Kyle scowled. Crux was a good kid. He'd made mistakes, but he didn't deserve this. No one did. Not to mention whatever Hex must've been going through.

"We still have the last resort," he announced, producing Dorfin's Decanter of Luminous Fluids.

Glinda's eyes went wide. "Will that work?"

The brewmaster shrugged and raised the turquoise decanter to eye level. "Okay," he warned the bottle, not skimping on the glare, "we need you right now. We need you to do the right thing. *Not* transforming people into trees or voluptuous strippers or making them bark like dogs. For once just give us a straightforward and uncomplicated fix, huh?"

The brewmaster took a breath, unstoppered the bottle, and poured the potion onto the statue. The stone crumbled away and Hex blinked apprehensively.

"I can't believe that worked," said Lash.

"Hex!" cried Crux.

The twins embraced, tears welling in their eyes. Kyle crossed his arms and smiled at his companions, emotions welling after the job well done.

"It was horrible," confessed Hex, continually ruffling her black cloak like she was amazed it was soft. "The things happening here. People being turned to stone. And worse. There's some kind of plague turning the soldiers."

"The Violet Order," said Lash. "We know about them, but our first priority is getting you home."

"I'm afraid," announced a deep voice as a chamber door opened, "I cannot allow that." Rygar entered the aviary in a full suit of flickering purple plate.

1890 The Darkness

I trudged through Oldtown in the predawn darkness, Bandit at my side. We were both exhausted from hours of frantic travel. I really wanted some shuteye, but that was impossible. My party was scattered to all ends of the Midlands. As their leader, it was my job to make sure they each had what they needed to succeed. I couldn't let them down.

At least the home front was quiet. Stronghold had seen its share of calamity. It was refreshing for once that we'd actually drawn the fight away from the city.

As the magical seal to Dragonperch released and the large door swung open, Bandit skirted around the tower. The mountain bongo stopped on the bank of the Albula and turned her head to me.

I smiled and released the drawbridge. "Have fun in the Foot." She scampered onto the bridge before it fully settled and raced across, no doubt looking forward to the greenery of the public park. Oldtown was mostly dirt, rubble, and supplies, not unlike a young boomtown in the Wild West. The whole grass-is-greener idiom is supposed to be a lesson in self-reflection and appreciation, but in this case it was the literal truth.

I entered the tower, secured the doors, and hurried up the

spiral stairs. As I climbed past the kitchen, my stomach rumbled loud enough that I considered microwaving one of Kyle's chimichangas, but curiosity beat out hunger. I had trekked all this way. A few more flights wasn't going to kill me.

In the war room, I activated the sanctum master panel and swiped to the socket manager. The locations of my party members lit up the display. Trafford on the march, Errol by Shorehome, Izzy nearing the Blackwood, and Kyle in a sea of unmapped gray. Beside it all, the void pearl dribbled with black magic that grew excited at my presence.

Izzy had warned me away from this. Kyle and Trafford weren't here to be my go-betweens. Ultimately, I had a choice to make: Did I care more about my sanity or the well-being of my best friends?

It wasn't a choice at all.

A grin spread across Errol's face as he fought the waves. "Ar, she's a big dame an' handles like a whale, but damn it all, her heft is half the fun!"

Grom's eyebrow's creased and he turned to his busty wench. "You been cheatin' on me, woman?"

Grug smacked the pirate in the back of the head. "He's talking 'bout the *Void*, barnacle for brains."

Avisa crossed her arms and leaned on the railing at the helm. "I'm guessing you don't pay top dollar for your crew."

"They pay themselves by scroungin' and raidin'," said Errol

defensively. He leaned close. "Why, do ye actually get paid?"

"Captain!" cried Grug. "Ships ho!"

Grom's frown increased. "Why's everyone talkin' 'bout me tart?"

Everyone else turned to the horizon in panic as three support vessels approached. "Ready the cannons!" ordered Errol.

"No!" Avisa pulled an orange crystal from her sack and hurried to the bow. As she rubbed the enchanted glass, a bright signal light pierced the coastal mist. Seconds later, an orange glow shined back from the lead ship. Pleased, the sergeant spun around. "They're Brothers in Black loyal to Brugo. They couldn't face the *Void* without taking heavy casualties, so they held back and waited. We now have a fleet."

Errol scanned the dark seas and opposite coastline. His home city was a war-torn mess, but he felt more invincible than ever before. "Grom, man the wheel." The pirate captain strutted across the deck of his loaner ship and followed Avisa back down to the brig.

"So power is consolidating," murmured the Papa of all Papas as they entered. The pirates jumped at the sight of Brugo speaking with a shadowy form.

Captain Oates drew his rapier and peered closer. "By the Maelstrom, that be you, Talon?"

The Protector of Stronghold smiled. "Sorry to jump in on you like this."

Errol wiped burnt powder from his face. "Well, ye arrived at a dandy time. We have Papa Brugo, four combat vessels, an' near a hundred sailors."

"They will die for you," said Avisa solemnly. "All that's left is to retake Shorehome."

"No." Papa Brugo clasped his arms behind his back, pressing his belly out as he paced to the end of his small cage. The scar on his left cheek sagged with his frown. "I will not rain destruction on my hometown."

Errol started. "We're not attackin' the city, Papa, just them scurvy bastards what took it from ye. How many traitors be loyal t' Hadrian still? A hundred? Two? With the fleet on our side, we could take 'em."

"It's not the loyalists I worry about, it's everyone else. The gangs have splintered. New bosses scramble for new destinies. I've been stripped of my powerchain, making someone else the new Protector of Shorehome. Do you imagine these newly powerful men and women would welcome my return?"

"You've shown them who's boss before."

"A city can be lost in a day. Winning one over is a different matter. Influence starts from the bottom."

Talon chuckled. "The bottom-up approach."

Eyebrows arched toward him.

"Sorry, programming jargon."

"He's right," said Avisa, speaking about Brugo not Talon. "If we go in there we'll be met with resistance. Not just by the loyalists, but by every street thug and two-bit hustler that found a new game."

Brugo grumbled again. "I have no doubt we would prevail, but the fight would be bloody and earn us new enemies. No, I cannot retake Shorehome without irrefutable proof of my power."

"How 'bout we sneak in an' steal back yer powerchain?"

suggested Errol.

Talon simpered. "I have a better idea. How would the city take to the return of the kraken?"

The crime kingpin's eyes sparkled. "The Lurking Deep?" He thoughtfully rubbed his chin. "Yes. The unrefuted symbol of the city's might would have many throw immediate support behind me. It would be a restoration of sorts. But the great titan has been banished to the under realm."

Errol's eyes widened. "The Maelstrom..."

A loud gasp from the steps caught everyone's attention. Blades scraped free and pointed to Grom attempting to silently retreat.

"Sorry," he said. "I weren't eavesdroppin', I swear. I was just lookin' for orders."

"It's fine, Grom," said Errol, sliding his rapier into its sheath.

Talon stepped forward. "Izzy mentioned the under realm before. Something related to my shadow magic. Is it a big deal?"

The captain grimaced. "The Maelstrom be a gapin' hole in the ocean from which nothin' escapes."

"Depths agape," realized Talon. "The boggart witches gave me clues to finding the soulstones. The Squid's Tooth and the kraken are in the Maelstrom."

"Now Talon," hedged Errol, voice quivering, "I be the bravest pirate o' the Six Seas, but even I ain't crazy 'nough t' ride the Maelstrom."

"This is a simulation," said Talon. "How bad can it be?"

Papa Brugo took in a long breath to stave off the darkening mood. "Seafaring peoples the world over share stories of the Maelstrom. The home of the beast, the sodden grave, a black hole of a hellscape to witness the end of all life. There is no hope in the abyss. Believe me, many have tried."

Errol tensed at this and avoided Talon's gaze.

"Heroes among pirates are common," continued the crime boss. "Any man or woman with the fortitude to stand against authority is applauded, any who stumble upon treasures revered, but I'd wager the only true heroes in our dastardly line of work are those who dare defy the sea herself. Those brave and crazy in equal measure who have stared down the abyss. Very few have ever done so. None have returned."

"That ain't true!" swore Grom. "Cap'n Oates has done it!"

Errol blanched as Avisa walked a circle around him.

"No, Grom," said Brugo. "Our mutual friend claims stakes in many legends, but most don't take the veracity at face value."

"They ain't legends," Grom asserted, "they be songs. An' we all know songs don't lie. The cap'n, he entered into a starin' contest with the Maelstrom, and the Maelstrom looked away. He says he was rewarded with skin black as midnight. Tell 'em, cap'n!"

Avisa smirked and traced a finger along Errol's cheek. "Is that so? It seems to me you're looking a might bit pale now."

"Nonsense," he grumbled. "It just be the black powder on me face."

"So the song tells true, then?"

The captain swallowed and checked the faces of all present. "If there's one thin' in this life ye can count on, it's that me legends be true."

Grom brandished a satisfactory nod. Brugo was less convinced.

Avisa moved close, corners of her mouth crooking. Her soft flesh ballooned between their bodies. "I've always admired legends."

Errol lifted his chin proudly. "That tingly sensation yer feelin' is somethin' more than admiration."

She stifled a laugh. "Maybe you're right."

"So you'll do it?" asked Talon.

"Oh, he'll do it," boasted Grom. He rapped Errol hard on the back. "Second go round will be even easier than the first. An' this time I'll be there to see it!"

Grom was so excited he was bunching closer to his captain than Avisa was. The lady sergeant begrudgingly pulled away and Errol sighed at his change of fortune.

"Then we'll get the soulstone, free the kraken, and save the city," said an exhilarated Talon. "But I need to make one thing clear. All this is in service to the greater goal. The ultimate plan for the artifact is to see it destroyed."

Brugo's face twisted. "It's just like you to have some high-minded goal. I rely on the Squid's Tooth for a great many things. Then again, I find myself in a weak position to bargain." He took a tortured breath. "For doing this for me, what is it you ask in return, Protector?"

Talon smiled. "That's easy."

He went into his faction menu and offered the imprisoned crime boss an invitation. Brugo may have lost Underkeep and the city, he may have been stripped of the powerchain and his mantle of Protector, but he was still the official head of the Brothers in Black. The imprisoned Papa accepted the request.

Black Hat Alert:
The Brothers in Black have called off the war!

Brothers in Black Reputation +100

Black Hat Alert:
The Brothers in Black have entered an alliance!

Brothers in Black Reputation +100

Errol nodded congratulations to his fellow pirates, but Brugo crossed his arms, unsettled by the happy moment. "What be the matter?" the captain asked.

"Words." Brugo bit down and squared with Talon. "Arrangements based on words have little merit. Surely an alliance cannot be all you seek?"

"That's it," assured Talon. "I'm uniting Haven, and I need you on board to do that."

The Papa grumbled. "I truly do not understand men like you, Talon." The big man turned to Avisa and Errol, then broke into a grin. "Ah, captain, *you* I understand. I still see hesitation in your features, but I also see something else. Is it... opportunity?"

Errol swallowed. "Aye. Now that ye mention it."

Brugo nodded. "Then name your price, loyal pirate. What do you ask to charge into hell with me?"

The captain shrugged. "It be a simple matter, really. I want the *Void*. 'Tis fair recompense fer destroyin' me frigate."

Papa Brugo's breath stopped. The *Void* was his flagship and the mightiest vessel in all of Haven. "Power in return for power," he mused. "The price is steep but equitable. Get me my town back and you'll have my flagship." He turned to Talon matter-of-factly. "Now *that* is the kind of deal I can wrap my head around."

Talon hiked a shoulder. "This is about more than profit, Brugo. I'm sure you can appreciate that."

"I think I do. This stirs within me a familiar feeling, back when I was nothing, alone and in the streets."

Errol's mouth crooked as he settled in for another of Brugo's parables.

"In his formative days," continued the Papa, "it's easy for a man to mistake himself for immortal, to favor reward over risk. A hustler means to make something of himself, to claw from his lowly station to greater heights, and to possess what he deserves. Yet possessions do not make the man. We must be stripped of our crutches in order to truly walk."

The charismatic man waited a beat, drawing the audience to his next breath. Talon swayed in place enough to draw Avisa's eye.

"Never mind walking. Looks like someone's having enough trouble with standing. Don't tell me you're seasick."

Talon shook it off. "No, nothing like that."

Brugo glared at him in warning. When he spoke, others listened. He cleared his throat. "It was during one such incident, while I was outcast and alone, that I learned I wasn't fighting for silver, I was fighting for survival."

Talon doubled over in a fit of coughing. His breaths came quick and ragged, simultaneously hyperventilating and gagging for air.

"What's the matter?" asked Errol. He tried to steady Talon but his hands went through the shadow. "Talon! Can ye hear me?"

The leader of the Black Hats vanished into thin air. The pirates blinked in shock, wondering what had just happened.

"Well that was rude!" muttered Grom. "The Papa ain't finished tellin' his story!"

I collapsed at the foot of the sanctum master panel. A strenuous weight pushed me to the floor. It was forceful more than painful, but I had the distinct feeling it was an invader. I gritted my teeth and pushed against it, struggling to my hands and knees.

The void pearl loomed large above me, black fingers swirling outward. The shadow magic was fighting me. I had to do something. Had to shut it off.

With great effort, I lifted a hand from the stone and reached out. The black fingers twitched and curled, lightning seeking a contact point. Too late I realized it wanted me. I lurched backward but it wasn't enough. I couldn't avoid it. The mass of shadow rushed into me, sending me on my back. I could do nothing but writhe helplessly as the void tore through my being.

The pain was so unbearable that I blacked out.

1900 Advanced Warfighter

Kyle touched the trigger of his dual crossbow.

The monstrous knight before them didn't have a lot of soft spots. Clad head-to-toe in full plate with a well-shielded helmet, the violet armor crackled with alien energy that sent flutters through his cape. The impressive warrior was even a head taller than Lash.

Dying flames licked the aviary tiles. The withered vegetation that was its only fuel turned to ash. The fire had caused little structural damage. Oakengard was built of undying crystal and stone. It outlasted all. It was the occupants of the room who were looking at very reduced lifespans.

"The god emperor told me a player would come for this one," said Rygar, voice rigid and deep. Dull eyes sized up Kyle and Bravo Team. "He didn't say there'd be five of you."

"Six," corrected Hex, fully recovered and bone rattle in hand.

"We stick together, dumb-butt," added Kyle defiantly.

Rygar blinked calmly, clearly unimpressed. "As does the Violet Order."

Purple knights flooded the open chamber door and filed into a line behind him. Ten more to add to the might of Rygar.

"I am required to ask that you surrender peacefully," he said, "but I would prefer if you would not."

In reply, Kyle squeezed his trigger finger. A bolt lasered into Rygar's eye socket. The pop of glass injected corrosive fluid.

```
Critical Hit!
Surprise!
[Kyle] dealt 103 damage to [Rygar]
```

A fifth of Rygar's health was instantly depleted. He growled in fury and his backup knights charged. As much as Kyle wanted to take advantage of his follow-up shot, he swiveled the crossbow to an oncoming knight. The bolt cracked apart against the breastplate, but yellow liquid spattered and a wave of magical fire consumed the purple tunic. The knight stampeded blindly ahead in a panic. Kyle stepped to the side and hurried to reload as the enemy passed.

A black shield appeared in Lash's hand and she slammed it into the floor.

```
[Lash] used Shieldquake
```

Onrushing knights stumbled. Conan's greataxe came down

and split a helmet in two. When he swung his weapon around, the helmet came with it, only jerking loose as the axe was buried in another knight's back. The wounded enemy clutched the barbarian's ankle with a gloved hand. Violet energy built up and Conan screamed. A cleaver severed the offending hand and cut off the energy flow. Lash dragged Conan away.

"Don't let them touch you!" cried Hex. She and her brother scrambled away from the front line. "That energy is strong!"

The barbarian clenched his teeth as Glinda converged on him.

[Glinda] cast Minor Healing on [Conan]

His pained expression subsided.

Kyle fired two more projectiles as Lash fended off the recovering knights. They were outnumbered; it was hard to keep everyone off. All it took was a stray touch to deal damage and both sides knew it.

New projectiles rushed past and sputtered against Violet Order helmets. They were dead finches. Most of them did little more than distract, but a few found their marks through the eye slots. Knights dropped their weapons, threw off their helmets, and clawed at the animals attacking their faces.

Kyle turned to Hex, who happened to be a necromancer. "Did you just make cute little bird zombies?"

The girl shrugged and scanned the room for more minions.

Conan rejoined the fray. Kyle swapped out his crossbow for the combo of bishop gauntlet and mirror shield. He batted away a sword with his metal hand. As the knight reached fingers his way, Kyle shoved the mirror shield forward. Purple energy dissipated in a flash.

"I can hold them off!" he announced.

By now Lash had spawned two shield walls. The small yellow energy barriers were nothing compared to her special, but they bought the group some room to maneuver.

"Everyone joins," growled Rygar. His glowing bastard sword came down and immolated one of the shield walls. He barreled forward.

[Lash] cast War Cry
+10% strike for the next 30 seconds.

The white knight charged him. Though the famed warrior of Oakengard was taller, Lash's cleaver had twice the mass of the bastard sword. The weapons met in a shock wave. Rygar's knee came up and doubled Lash over. He spun the sword downward in his hand and readied to stab her in the back as Kyle flew in.

Backhanded and off-balance, Rygar flicked his sword and easily deflected Kyle's punch. The brewmaster braced against his mirror shield and rushed forward. Rygar sidestepped and kicked Kyle in the back, knocking him to the ground.

Lash had recovered, though, and her cleaver bit into Rygar's side. The hurried blow shifted him a foot but the armor held. Rygar countered with a full spin, sword aimed at bisecting the white knight at the waist. Lash's body shield cracked against the magical weapon. She flew across the room and landed hard. While she was still in one piece, her black shield no longer was.

"Arrrgh!" screamed Conan in guttural fury.

[Conan] used Blood Frenzy

Motes of red energy dusted him as his double-sided axe came straight down toward Rygar's head. The hero of the Violet Order hopped backward as the weapon crashed down. Rygar readied a counter but Conan barreled into him and grabbed his sword arm. The barbarian pounded the knight's armor with a bare fist as he held his opponent's weapon at bay. Over and over, Rygar's breastplate and helmet rocked with the blows. He'd nearly been disarmed.

But slowly, surely, through nothing but pure, brute force, Rygar's sword arm rose upward, fighting the might of the barbarian and rising above their heads.

Kyle tried to intervene but a flurry of knights forced him on the defensive. Lash, too, was already on her feet but having trouble getting through. At the last second, Conan saw he was compromised and disengaged. Rygar's sword came down and sliced across his chest. The only thing that stopped it from going clean to the floor was the shield wall that materialized in the way.

Crux and Glinda dragged Conan to safety. Rygar grunted and focused on the magic. His bastard sword shattered the shield and he locked eyes on the barbarian being healed.

Damn, damn, damn. This guy was a force of nature. Kyle and Lash had both used their specials to save Hex and now they were facing a formidable opponent. As Kyle jockeyed to regroup with his friends, Lash cut down two enemies in her path toward the red mob.

It wasn't gonna work. Lash was as tough as they came, but some combination of the hero status, the previous Oakengard buffs, and the Violet infection was supercharging this guy. Kyle continued pressing the defensive advantage of his shield to keep the enemies apart while they could be picked off. He wasn't sure how long they could last.

Lash swung her sword again, this time going for her enemy's legs. Rygar met the sweep. Their blades reversed and met again, clanging loudly. Metal locked on metal, Lash scraped her blade closer to her opponent.

Rygar punched her chest. The armor rang loudly as she stumbled backward. Rygar lifted his sword and stepped forward, readying another killing blow.

Kyle dove to the floor as Rygar's boot stepped between the rope netting. The brewmaster yanked hard on his end of the net, shifting Rygar's stance just enough to throw his blow off-balance. The flat of his weapon clanked against Lash's armor and drove her to the floor.

"He's too strong!" shouted Kyle.

Lash was probably scowling under her helmet, but she backpedaled on the floor, cleaver fending off members of the Violet Order that attempted to overtake her.

Rygar chuckled viciously. "This is the best Stronghold can offer?"

Conan's eyes went wild and he roared from the other side of the aviary. He spun in place like a shot-putter and flung his weapon. The greataxe flew high and sliced the chain holding the steel bird cage to the ceiling. The weapon clattered into the far wall and tumbled. Rygar's helmet turned upward as Hex's cage slammed to the floor, open bottom engulfing him.

"What is this?" The powerful warrior punched the bars of the cage, shoving it slightly.

The remaining knights rushed forward as a unit for Lash, still unable to get to her feet without getting touched. Thrusts were parried as she skidded away, and then one of their own stabbed another through. The knights turned as the other member of the Violet Order withdrew a bloody sword and stabbed another one. Two men grabbed the rogue as Hex incanted and waved her bone rattle.

"I guess she graduated from birds," laughed Kyle.

Purple energy built up around the grappling soldiers, but no matter how much they sent into the zombie, it couldn't hurt the turned NPC.

"The purple plague can't affect the dead!" announced Hex.

While the zombie was immune to magical hijacking, it didn't otherwise display superior combat advantages against the other knights. Outnumbered, it took heavy blows. Fortunately, with Rygar sidelined and Lash and Conan back in action, what were left of the Violet Order combatants were defeated.

The group breathed heavily as Glinda sent heals around.

"Cowards," growled Rygar. "Weaklings!" He shook against the cage, which slid a foot across the floor.

"This isn't you," insisted Hex. "Look at the magic that's infected you!"

"Listen to her, Rygar," said Crux. "You're better than this. I saw your protest earlier. You have a noble heart. Now all the sages are dead. Is that what you really want?"

His eyes flashed. "I want what the god emperor wants."

He sheathed his magical sword, put both gauntlets on the cage, and lifted. Amazingly, the metal rose off the floor.

"No!" Lash crashed into the cage and pressed it down. Conan added his strength to hers. The brewmaster pitched his weight against the metal bars too. Slowly they forced the bird cage down.

Still struggling, purple energy flowed through Rygar. "You cannot stop the Violet Order!"

Slowly, the metal lifted off the floor again. Their eyes went wide at the unbelievable force at the warrior's disposal.

Kyle scanned the room for something else that could help. "The wall!" he yelled. "Push him into the wall!"

While Rygar pushed up and the others pushed down, nobody was too concerned about the cage's horizontal velocity. The three of them grouped together and shoved with coordinated effort. Suddenly they were all walking it sideways. The focus on covering ground allowed Rygar to lift his prison almost two feet in the air. As they struggled, the bird cage and prisoner crashed against the wall.

"Nothing's happening!" shouted Lash. "The sigils aren't working. We need moonlight."

Although the fires were mostly embers now, thick smoke still collected beneath the skylight. Kyle broke away from the struggle, dropped to a knee, and equipped his crossbow. Two bolts streaked upward and crashed through the skylight. Glass rained down on them. The gathered black smoke escaped into the open sky, and the moon once again fed its magical energy into the wards.

Lash and Conan recoiled from the cage. Rygar triumphantly

lifted it above his head. Although the runes started at about eight feet high, the cage itself was ten feet tall, and now being held up. The sigils went off, popping and sending fire outward, pummeling Rygar's helmet. The warrior released the steel, its bars sliding down and triggering more wards. Explosion after explosion rocked the cage and its occupant, with the light recharging and reactivating the barrage.

It was a full minute before the cage was sufficiently blown from the wall and the sigils were satisfied. In the center of the blackened steel rested a charred husk of what was once a mountain of a man.

Even his fancy purple armor had melted.

>> Minigame <<

A nap caught Tad off guard. He jolted awake to the sound of Christian at the keyboard. He rubbed groggy eyes and sat up.

Police surrounded their Seattle tall tower now. The bomb squad too. For Tad it was all an aggravating formality. The shooter was dead, the bombs had detonated, and he couldn't stare at the damned security feeds anymore.

Grimacing, Tad stood, forcing blood flow through his rigid leg. Walking was painful, but anything was better than doing nothing at all. He wandered through the office to see if there'd been any progress.

Somewhere, a door slammed.

Finally, they'd been rescued! Tad excitedly limped toward the west-wing stairwell, right where he'd told the firefighters to go. Hurrying past cubicles and turning the corner, Tad stopped as a single man spun to him.

"Sir," said the paramedic, slightly startled. "There you are."

The man in the blue uniform approached. He wore a gold badge and had a fire department patch on his shoulder. Opposite the badge was a name stitched over his chest: Campos.

The man tightened blue latex gloves over his fingers. "Are you injured, sir? Is anyone else here?"

Tad tensed. Why was this man alone? He didn't have an equipment belt, though there was a radio attached to his shirt and he held a large orange plastic briefcase.

"Are you a paramedic?" Tad asked.

"Yes, sir. Are you injured?"

"What's in the case?"

"My supplies. Are you okay, sir?" He stepped closer and Tad stepped back. Seeing this, the man set his case down and raised open palms. "Sir, my name's Ramon. I'm here to help."

"Why are you alone?"

He hiked a shoulder. "I'm not really supposed to be up here, if I'm being honest, but I heard someone was trapped. It's my job to help people, so I'm helping." Ramon noticed Tad staring at the orange case, so he slowly bent to a knee and opened it. Various packets of medicine were slipped into pockets stitched on the case's inside flap. The bulk of the contents rested in the bottom and looked to be electronic consoles and other medical supplies.

Tad nodded encouragingly. "There's another man up here. The CEO. He has a gunshot wound."

Ramon closed the case and stood. "Take me to him." As he followed, he pressed for more info. "What happened to the shooter?"

"She's dead."

"And the bomb threat? Is it legit?"

"It was. It detonated before anyone got here."

Ramon nodded. "Anyone else up here? Are you hurt?"

"No. I'm okay. This way."

Even though the stairwell was close to Christian's office, Tad took the circuitous route and passed by the collapsed hallway. He pointed out the situation to Ramon, who insisted on checking the Superdome. Tad nodded and waited outside. As the paramedic checked for life, Tad leaned down and scooped up Abbie's pistol. He tucked it into his pocket just as Ramon returned. His face had gone ashen.

"Christian's this way," Tad instructed, once again leaning on his crutch and hoping he hadn't made a mistake.

1910 Brain Age

The buildmaster general of the Black Hats trudged forward. His knees ached, and he blamed Talon for bringing it up. He wouldn't have considered how his knees felt had it not been for their fearless leader. Now the friendly jape had mutated into a cruel torture device as every other step sent a pinch through his nerves.

The old man sighed. He had a failing left eye and now a bum right leg. He wondered how long it would be until half his mind went as well.

The NPC shook himself. Was that his programmed personality talking? This was a simulation, after all. As far as he knew, Haven wasn't packaged with an aging model. Surely that precluded degenerative diseases.

But if that was the case, why in the hell did his bones ache? A health potion would do away with the pain temporarily but it'd be back a few hours later. If there was a sure fix, he hadn't found one.

As general of the army, Trafford could've ridden one of the wagons. Nooner's company of oxen pulled plenty of them. Feeding an army wasn't a trivial affair, and a couple of the wagons already had space for the injured. That said, the old man couldn't bring himself to do it. As practical as he was, he was also a man of the people. If the Black Hats lacked a stable of horses, so would he.

The march thus far hadn't been very arduous. A straightforward affair along the southwesterly road, the army advanced with ease. The dark sky gave way to the morning sun, but the air was still crisp. Now, with the daylight hours compounding, their fortunes were beginning to turn.

With the growing heat and their path headed into the canyons, the terrain was beginning to object to their presence. Nothing too untoward. Uneven, rocky ground to upset the wagon wheels. A gradual incline to put more effort behind each step. And the more Trafford marched, the more the canyon walls closed in from both sides. For the second time today, he ordered the formations to narrow.

"The Cloven Path," noted Grimwart bitterly.

General Trafford snorted. "Isn't there a better way to get the army across the mountains?"

"This is the best way," said Grimwart. "We avoid half the swampland. Skirt the great lake. Forsooth, it is better to march on a major roadway."

"Aye, if you can call it that."

The grayed whiskers on Grimwart's lip curled as he smiled. "There are no good ways to or from Oakengard. Such hardship lends resilience to the famed fortress."

"Lends pretentious mystery too," muttered the general.

Trafford didn't know what was so great about the famous crusaders anyway. When his city was beset by a titan, they hadn't helped. When the rogue Bishop Tannen executed a coup, the best assistance the crusaders could offer was to march away. Time and time again, Stronghold had held against much worse odds than anything the knights had ever faced. But he had to admit, they had the whole inaccessibility thing down. The Cloven Path was a real pain in the ass.

"At least we have the road," huffed Trafford in resigned agreement.

"Yes," nodded Grimwart. "Until the Godsbog."

"The what now? I thought you said this road skipped the swamps."

"It skips *half* the swampland. But you can't get to Oakengard without going through the bog."

"Great coogly moogly, of course you can't." The old general rolled his eyes and wondered why he hadn't stuck with shopkeeping. If rocky elevation was already proving troublesome, Trafford didn't want to see what muddy pits did. "Can the wagons get through?"

"The road breaks down for several stretches, but logs have been laid out to mitigate the worst of the goop. These narrow formations will be necessary. Stray off the path too far, and you may discover a sinkhole." Grimwart's black stallion nickered uncomfortably. The colonel looked back and frowned. "It's a mystery to me why, but Artax is deathly afraid of the swamps."

Trafford shrugged. "Then we'll continue in a line until we approach the fortress."

The colonel bobbed his head in consideration as he patted his horse's nose. "What concerns me most is walking into an ambush. This terrain is flush with monsters. Rogue catechists are on the loose. The swampland is home to the pagan horde.

Our men no longer have the tactical advantage of horses. After the Cloven Path, I suggest we transition to advance-and-secure maneuvers."

Trafford's brow furrowed. "Hold a forward position while the rear advances and does the same? No can do, Colonel. Time is our biggest enemy, speed our greatest asset. If we miss the deadline, we lose the war without raising a single sword."

"And if we stumble into an ambush and get routed on the way, the time we saved will matter little."

The old man frowned. He was a practical man, and that came in handy when dealing with the logistics of moving five hundred people across the Midlands. Grimwart was more focused on strategy, which again proved useful when those five hundred people had swords. If the crusader colonel was afraid of a goblin ambush, Trafford had to respect that.

He opened his world map and grumbled. The immediate area of the Cloven Path was just now filling in. He'd never been here before and the swamps, mountains, and waterways were all grayed out. Grimwart stepped close and opened his map, revealing heavy familiarity with the land and the route.

Oakengard was nestled in the southwestern corner of the Midlands. That surprised Trafford. He'd known the NPC fortress was far west but had never seen it in relation to the rest of the map. It was high in the mountains, eastern flank protected by the nigh impassable range of Sunscrapers. The western and southern edges of the map were the literal ends of the world, at least during the beta. A field of blue was said to wall off the fruitful lands beyond. For now, the only approach to Oakengard was from the north.

As enlightening as the crusader's map was, patches of the swamps, mountains, and beyond the lake were dark. It was a testament to the unknown and the extremes of the unforgiving terrain. It also highlighted exactly how many places their enemies could hide.

"What we need," contemplated Trafford, "is a way to scout ahead quickly enough while allowing the army to maintain its expedited pace."

Dune casually strolled up the line to meet them. "You rang, old man?"

"That's general to you," he snapped. "But you just read my mind. How much of that did you hear?"

"All of it." The ranger smiled coyly. "Shouldn't Shadow Talon be the one giving us the lay of the land, though? He's the one with the scout class kit, and teleporting should allow him to safely check miles ahead."

"It doesn't work like that. The void pearl will only teleport someone to another party member, and even that has limitations because Hadrian somehow locked us out of Oakengard. But that's beside the point. I haven't heard from Talon in a few hours, and he's not answering my chat requests."

Both Grimwart and Dune were surprised by the news, but the ranger recovered with a sigh and a smile. "Well, well. Maybe it's because Talon knows ol' Dune here's the best man for the job."

General Trafford grumbled. The kid was cockier than all get out, but with Talon busy, he *was* the best man for the job. "Think you can find the horde before they find us?"

"Piece of cake," replied Dune. "You know what? It's gonna be fun being a Black Hat."

He twirled his cape as he went to collect his party. Trafford locked eyes with Grimwart, both hoping the ranger's antics wouldn't get them into trouble.

1920 Where the Wild Things Are

◆━━━━━━•◆•━━━━━━◆

Izzy Sakata strolled through the Blackwood, staff in hand.

The last time she was among the forest of charred trees she had a party at her back. The three had nimbly scouted the terrain and snuck into the Black Keep's roof access.

The pixie snorted. Those were simpler times, when all they cared about was leveling and questing and loot. Things would play out differently now. The wild king wouldn't fall for the same trick twice, and Izzy lacked Talon's skill with climbing.

It was all moot, however, as she had no intention of subterfuge. Talon had given her free rein to deal with this as she wished, and while she didn't feel especially suited for the assignment, she was determined to do it her way. That meant throwing out the disciplines of stealth and intuition and detecting secret passages. Given the unofficial relationship between the Black Hats and the wildkins, a direct approach was more appropriate.

So here she was, a matchmaker of sorts, except she was a marriage counselor without a marriage. The rub was making the relationship official. With the aloof wildkins, it was a tall ask, but the best chance they had of making it happen was dealing with Theoderic in person. Let him save the poetry for the doves.

The dead forest rested in a sunken valley surrounded by mountains. The trees were barely clinging to life, creating a canopy of patchwork leaves above the blackened branches. As with the wildkins, life was finding a way. Small birds perched in dry alcoves. Rodents scurried underfoot. The Blackwood wasn't lush with activity, but it wasn't the barren hellscape it appeared from a distance either.

As Izzy's boots kicked ash from the ground, she thought it ironic the dry field would've been a lake bed without the dam lining the southeastern end of the Black Keep. The old castle was a pyramid built of petrified wood. The dam, crumbling stone patched with rotting logs and piled bones.

A dry lake, black trees, and thousands of brittle body parts keeping everything a devil's breath from destruction. The wildkins really knew how to set the mood.

Izzy marched forward in the open, a trail of ash painting a straight line to the double doors of the Black Keep.

Numerous footfalls reached her ears like whispers. Izzy glanced to her flanks and noted movements. Nothing overt, but a ducking head here, a foot sticking from behind a tree there. Of course. The wildkins were already aware of her presence.

A moment's walk later, Izzy realized the rodents and birds had all but disappeared. Then the large gates of the Black Keep groaned open. In what she deemed proper deference, Izzy halted her progress. The gaping blackness in the old castle's maw was daunting, as were the hooded figures that scurried out. A low, rumbling growl filled the sparse wood.

Izzy rolled her eyes. The warden of the Blackwood was putting on a show with his prisoners. She supposed it came with the territory and settled in to wait it out.

Her cool confidence wavered as the back of her neck bristled. Someone breathed close behind her. Too close. The pixie spun around.

"Pray tell, pray tell, what bringeth a Black Hat to my wood?"

It was the ruler of the Blackwood, the wild king himself. Lean, bare-chested, wearing only ragged leather pants, boots, and a stag skull fitted to his face like a mask. His voice was clear and commanding, with just enough mirth to have you second-guessing his intentions.

Izzy took a stabilizing breath. "A purple plague."

The seven-foot tall man strode to within a few yards of her. His sinewy chest was painted with broad antlers. The king studied her as she studied him. His eyes were locked on her lavender skin.

"Not me, you dolt. Another purple plague."

If the wild king took offense at the slight, he didn't show it. "Explainst thyself."

Izzy's eyes scanned the perimeter of the wide circle the wildkins were forming around her. They shuffled and traded places and peeked over bushes and shoulders at a safe distance. The Blackwood prisoners had no such reservations. They were humanoids of various castes and kin, all with solid hoods over their faces. They didn't need eyeholes because they didn't need to see. They were nothing more than thralls of the warden.

She glanced toward the keep and watched Hood approach. Where the wild king was calm and fair, the warden of the Blackwood was anything but. He was an eight-foot brute wearing mismatched plates of armor and lengths of leather and chain. The metal links clinked and trawled the ground around him with minds of their own. The warden's black hood had eyeholes, though she wished they didn't because the glowing white eyes within threatened to pierce her sanity. By comparison, the two-handed executioner's axe the monster wielded in a single hand was the least threatening thing about him.

Monster he may have been, he was also an asset. Endowed with cursed damage, he was one of the few weapons effective at circumventing the healing magic of Cleric Vagram and the catechists. Izzy wore a bold countenance but inwardly shivered as the warden drew close. Theoderic signaled the warden to halt his progress. She wondered if that was for her benefit and if she'd shown weakness. Hand tight on the winter staff, Izzy raised her voice for all to hear.

"You probably already know, but in case you've been living in a cave"—Izzy's eyes flitted to the Black Keep—"Haven is set to launch in two days."

The stag skull cocked. "Such events be of little note to me and mine."

"On the contrary, those holding power in the cities will enjoy promotions, of a sort. Hadrian will be permanently ingrained into Haven's power structure. His grip on the land will tighten."

"That be why we reside isolated from thy kind and thine affairs."

"Not so isolated from Oakengard." Izzy hooked a hand on her hip matter-of-factly. "Hadrian has made use of your kind before. Pagans, wildkins—does any of it really matter? He takes advantage of our prejudices and hate and uses it as oil for his engines of war. Don't you wonder why General Azzyrk fights for him? What was he promised?"

"No promise," asserted the king, "just prejudice. He harboreth a mutual hatred of mutual enemies. Alas, can it be said the white city played no part in that enmity?"

"You'd have a point if Hadrian wasn't heading up the crusaders. They've done more against pagankind than anyone. Talon means to change all that. He's pledged to destroy the soulstones. The boggart witches have sided with him."

Izzy hoped the overstatement of the truth wouldn't backfire, but the wildkins were a tough audience. Theoderic was a hard read with a skull over his face.

"The witches be respected for their wisdom," admitted the wild king. "Did they not seeketh the destruction of the white city?"

The pixie smiled. "You're highlighting the very danger we're facing, Your Grace. That siege was the result of manipulation by Saint Loras, working for the same company as Hadrian. The witches have seen the light. If the pagans can approve an alliance, why can't the wildkins?"

Theoderic scoffed. "I have spurned the advice of the witches before. Thou wilst recount my kind played no part in that battle."

"Which is why we take you for measured and fair, why we appeal to your reason now. Even you must see your peace can't last. When Hadrian marches east, he'll overtake the isolated Blackwood with ease. You gain nothing by hiding in your keep. You lose everything by not making allies."

The wild king's tone hardened. "Hiding we are not. 'Tis living we go about." He took a menacing step closer. " 'Tis easy for thee to paintst thy skin and pointst thine ears, but thou knowest naught of our struggles. All this be a game to thee. Be the wildkins no more than game as well, animals for thou to hunt, rob, and pillage? And now that we possess minds of our own, be it not enough to let us be? Still, still thou must draw us into petty wars and strife?"

Izzy shuddered under the weight of the ruler's stare. She noted the stillness of the wildkins in the trees. This was too dense a matter to resolve now, but it had to be addressed.

She swallowed calmly and spoke with tenderness. "I empathize with your struggle. The Black Hats are open to furthering relations and peace among all manners of people."

"The Black Hats," he scoffed. "Talon. The witches. Hast thou no cause of thy own?"

Izzy jutted her lips out. "Of course I do. That's why I'm here."

"Thou art here on behalf of another." The wild king canted his head and neared. "I inquire into the nature of thy heart."

She blinked defensively. "We're defending Haven. The entire simulation."

"Insincere platitudes. I desire nothing less than the truth."

"I..." She paused and breathed deeply. "You want the truth? I understand exactly where you're coming from. You wanna take care of you and yours. Make your own way without getting bogged down by all the shit out there. I did that as the days turned into weeks and then months. I was the best. I was the queen of kick ass. But it was an empty victory. I was hollow inside."

Theoderic watched intently as she spoke.

"Yes, it took meeting Talon for me to change. He's different. He's not just acting for himself but for other people, his friends and everyone alike. But I'm here because I want to be here. Because I'm fighting for what I believe in. This isn't a game to *any* of us. Not anymore. Our livelihoods bind us to each other much more than our disparate pasts. We're here now, struggling and clawing and demanding the same damn thing. This is about freedom or death."

Chains rattled on the ground around the warden. Theoderic remained still. She'd at least gotten them to hear her words, to listen for a moment. Spurring them into action would take something more.

Izzy took a solemn breath and spoke with emotion. "That awakening you experienced, that life you so want to live, you have it thanks to a single player. Lucifer. He gave his life for this cause. He's deleted, and he isn't coming back."

Theoderic shifted back a step. He shot a steadying glance to his warden. Izzy wasn't sure if the wildkins had ever met Lucifer, but it was obvious they regarded him with reverence. They hadn't known of his death.

That was good. The only reason the wildkins had helped them before was to recover their crown. Talon had found a way to make it personal for them, and she just did too.

"The Black Hats are still fighting for him," she said. "We all are. Because it's a fight worth breaking the peace for."

The pixie dug into her inventory, pulled out a crusader helmet, and tossed it to the king's feet. Hood lunged forward to intercept it, brushing past Izzy. The full helm rolled and settled on the ground, and Theoderic held up a hand to stall the warden's rush.

The crusader helmet was unremarkable on its own—good quality plate, chipped and dented with use—but the steel had taken on a sickly purple hue that clung to it like a living stain. Behind the stag skull, Theoderic's brown eyes narrowed. Hood leaned into the armor and blinked as it crackled with energy.

"A purple plague," he mused in a deep voice.

"It dominates the mind," said Izzy. "I figure you know something of that. This infection forces people to do things they otherwise revile. Like taking up arms." Izzy stepped forward and leaned on her winter staff. "Talon and I have been asking you nicely. Hadrian? If he can't convince people to join his cause, he forces them too, all in the name of growing his army. You may not want war, your grace, but it's coming for you anyway. And one way or another, you'll be fighting for someone. Pick a side or have it picked for you."

The warden of the Blackwood straightened after his inspection. His glowing eyes were somehow softer now. Filled with worry. He conveyed his thought with a grunt and a single nod toward his liege.

The wild king sighed as his eyes ran over his people. "Freedom or death," he bitterly mused.

1930 Castlevania

"Now what?" asked Glinda as the group raced down the halls. "Hex is free, Rygar's dead, and Hadrian's back in the castle."

They strode down a familiar tunnel that took them back to where they started. The halls of Oakengard seemed to be changing, becoming twisted and mazelike. Kyle chalked it up to stress and a trick of the flickering lights. Yet even Crux had led them down paths that, once previously clear, now resulted in dead ends.

Lash, helmetless, wore her frown plain. "That's not what's bothering me. Why aren't there patrols looking for us?"

Conan nodded. "I'd welcome a fair fight over these mind games."

The companions slowed at a corner. Kyle thought they were getting ahead of themselves. "Hadrian doesn't necessarily know we're in the castle."

"We burned down the aviary!" protested Glinda.

The brewmaster canted his head. "Fair. But for all he knows, we're teleporting or fast traveling or who knows what else. He doesn't have any way to track us."

"You sure about that?" asked Lash.

"I mean, if he did we'd be surrounded, right?"

"He might be right," said Hex. "We can't even track ourselves."

Crux butted in. "It doesn't matter. We should get to a stairway and hide on the lower level. See what Talon has to say." The thief peeked ahead and waved the party into the empty corridor.

"Hiding isn't gonna get us home," said Kyle. "And Talon's MIA. Our objective is to unlock the fast travel. We can easily handle that."

The stairwell came into sight. Crux led and the others quickly followed. Hex, Conan, Glinda, Lash, Kyle, and two Violet Order zombies. They paced in the pitch black below. Kyle flinched at a surprise notification.

Black Hat Alert:
The Wildkins have entered an alliance!

Wildkin Reputation +100

"There's another one," said Kyle. "Talon's plan is coming together. If we want to be part of it, we better find ourselves an exit."

"What about the mines?" offered Glinda. "The tunnels lead to the mountainside."

Kyle scoffed. "You wanna *walk* back to Stronghold? Shouldn't we at least *try* the fast travel?"

"And how do you plan to unlock it?" asked Crux.

A tired voice rang out in the darkness. "It can be done."

The group spun to the sound. "You're quiet, old man," said Hex, raising her bone rattle.

"Wait," said Crux, the only other party member with darkvision. "You're Speaker Harroway."

The sage twisted a knob on his lantern, illuminating his weary features. He was hunched on the floor against the wall.

"What are you doing down here?" asked Kyle.

He cracked a bitter smile. "Same as you, I imagine. Hiding from the Violet Order."

Crux frowned. "Talon said the sages were murdered."

"That we were. So many of my brothers and sisters are gone. Alas, they're the lucky ones. To my misfortune I didn't fall to the plague. Instead I respawned in a city that's no longer mine."

Kyle stepped forward. "You said the fast travel could be unlocked?"

The man sighed. "It can, if you go to the Inner Hall."

Lash's eyes narrowed. "The Inner Hall is far from the portal. We should be able to unlock it up close."

Harroway smiled. "You're clever for a knight." He nodded. "You're correct, of course. It can be unlocked with a portal scroll from right beside it. But I need something from you first."

Kyle hissed. "Let's skip the tit for tat, bro. We're already fighting Hadrian, that should be good enough. Just hand over the scroll and let us get back to our normally scheduled programming."

"I'm afraid that is inadequate."

Lash crossed her arms. "Our army's already on the march. You won't think it's inadequate when you shit your pants at the sight of them."

He sighed. "Maybe you aren't so clever after all."

Crux inched forward. "You realize I can just steal the portal scroll from you, right?"

The speaker's eyes flashed. "Not if I bind it to a quest."

> Quest Offer: **Turn Off the Oakengard Recruiting Factory**
> *Quest Type: Action*
> *Reward: Portal Scroll*
> Gain access to the training facility in the Inner Hall and find a way to power down the machine.
> **Accept Quest?**

Crux cursed, which was good enough as confirmation that Harroway wasn't lying.

"Revoke the quest," demanded Conan, raising his axe.

Harroway snorted. "I'm beginning to think my faith in Stronghold is misplaced. At least hear me out. Listen to what's at stake."

Kyle tried to pull Conan back, but the barbarian wouldn't budge until Lash nodded agreement. The companions settled around the sage as he recounted his tale in the darkness.

"Fewer than two months ago, and since its inception, Oakengard stood at 300 strong: 100 each among equal castes; knights, sages, and priests. Then the pagans awakened Orik and raided Stronghold. Even as the titan was defeated and the horde scattered, a new threat loomed. As defenders of Haven, it was up to Oakengard to turn the tide. To that end, Saint Loras worked to increase our power. New weapons were acquired, aggressive training regimens enacted, but by far our greatest asset were the soldiers themselves. Loras activated a recruiting factory aimed at matching the numbers of the horde."

Kyle swallowed hard. "The horde at the time numbered in the thousands."

"Two-and-a-half thousand," clarified the sage. "But that was before the battle of Stronghold. After their defeat and the ensuing schism, the pagans spanned many groups numbering in the hundreds. Over the next two weeks our recruiting factory doubled the count of our residents to 600."

"That's when Bishop Tannen stole the Eye," pointed out Lash.

"Wait a minute," said Kyle, moving closer. "It's been over a month since we took care of the bishop..."

"It has." Speaker Harroway lifted his chin. "Now you're beginning to take my meaning. If we can spawn 300 soldiers in two weeks..."

Lash's eyes widened. "Then the Violet Order has grown to 1200 soldiers."

Conan looked to his companions. "How do we fight 1200 soldiers?"

"It's not quite so many," tempered the sage. "Between the catechist schism, the escaped crusaders, and those of us who still resist—we all subtract from the whole. But as long as the recruiting factory is powered up..."

"The enemy forces will soon grow out of hand," concluded Lash. Her face went hard and she turned to Kyle.

"Oh no," muttered Glinda. "I know that look. Do we really want to continue wandering around this maze? You said it yourself, Lash. Our army is on the march. We don't need to return to Stronghold. We can safely slip through the mines and join up with our soldiers."

"No," said Kyle firmly. "That might be better for us, but is it the best we can do for the Black Hats? The best we can do for Haven?" Kyle chewed his lip.

Lash nodded along. "It's the right call."

Harroway allowed a smile and produced a blue key from his robes. "You'll need this to access the training facility." He offered the key.

Crux ignored the item. "Guys," he cautioned.

His sister stepped forward. "Hadrian did a real number on me. If this is a way to hit him where it hurts, I'm in."

Crux winced.

Conan hefted his axe. "Everyone knows my answer."

The thief rubbed his temples. "Fine. I can get you to the Inner Hall."

"And then the fast travel," affirmed Kyle. "We'll get that scroll?"

Speaker Harroway nodded. "You don't even have to find me again. It'll automatically be placed in your inventory upon quest completion."

"Works for me," said Kyle as he accepted the quest. "Bravo Team, at my back."

The brewmaster did a one-eighty and headed straight for the staircase. Crux snatched the blue key from the sage's frail fingers, and their new mission was afoot.

>> Minigame <<

"Sir, I need you to keep still."

Christian winced as he twisted away from his workstation and faced the paramedic. "I thought you finished dressing the wound."

Ramon clenched his jaw. "I did what I could, but that doesn't change the fact that you need surgery." He put a hand on his radio and lowered his head to speak. "Jake, do you copy yet? Come on, man, come in." Ramon grunted and shook his head. "I don't know why this radio's not working."

"Too many floors of metal and concrete between you and them," explained Christian.

"You're probably right." The paramedic nodded toward the security feeds. "You got controls up here? Can you get the elevators online?"

"That's managed from the ground floor."

"Why don't you ask your buddies in the fire department?" offered Tad.

"They won't do it," said Christian. "Not until they're sure it's safe. After an explosion it could be weeks before confirming the elevators are structurally sound."

Ramon hissed. "We need to get you out of here."

"That's where you're wrong," said the CEO. "I'm not going."

"What do you mean you're not going?"

"Exactly what I said." Christian turned back to his programming window. "This is a vital moment in my business. I have less than two days to get this done."

Ramon shook his head with incredulity. "Sir, I've staunched the bleeding. You have strong blood pressure but I can't determine the extent of your internal injuries. Without medical attention..."

Tad parked his butt against Christian's desk and stretched his leg. Ramon was being formally introduced to Christian's stubbornness. How long it took to come to terms with it was up to him. The CEO gritted his teeth, swallowed a few more painkillers, and dug in.

"Don't try to talk me out of it," he argued. "This is my life's work, and my life is quickly coming to an end. I have a right to choose what I do with my final moments."

"I don't care if you're a billionaire," countered Ramon. "You're crazy." He turned to Tad, eyes searching. "Help me out here."

The programmer shrugged. "I couldn't help you even if I wanted to."

The paramedic frowned at Tad's cast and crutch. After a quick grimace, he nodded confidently. "Okay, new plan. You two sit tight. I'll get a team up to you. Hell, I'll call in a helicopter if I have to."

"I appreciate the fervor," said Christian, "but I'm not moving. Not until I'm done."

Ramon stood up, eyed the two men, and backed away. "You'll

thank me later. Hold onto my equipment in case you need medical supplies. Keep that bandage tight. And do me a favor and keep the gymnastics to a minimum."

The CEO returned his attention to the screen and clacked away. Ramon sighed, nodded firmly to Tad, and left the room toward the west stairwell.

Tad sighed. "The guy's not wrong, you know."

"This needs to be done."

"Does it? Isn't the whole point of putting our trust in Haven so Talon and the others can decide their own destiny? I get that we have preprogrammed launch conditions to deal with, that we need to wait until the official launch in two days, but the people on the inside don't need additional support anymore. You need to think about your life."

"This is my life," he said curtly. "Not just my work but my life. You're right that we could do nothing and, depending on Talon's success, Haven would probably turn out all right. Harbor Island will launch without us. Assuming the servers remain protected, our job is mostly already done." Christian closed his eyes tightly for a long moment, took a calming breath, and squared his face with Tad. "Still, there's one more matter, something that absolutely needed to wait until the last second. There's one final important piece of the puzzle to upload." Christian lifted his hand and placed a firm finger against his skull. "Me."

Tad nearly slipped off his perch against the desk. His mouth opened weakly. "But you said it yourself. The launch site is Harbor Island. We don't have any communication outside this building, so none of your changes will make it into the package.

You won't make it into the satellite."

"That's not how the launch protocol works." Christian turned to his workstation. "The point of moving Haven to space is to secure it from external threats, but there's a special launch condition that opens the satellites up to a one-time update. Phoenix Y will launch into the atmosphere with whatever data it has. Any updates we make here will then be uploaded via a satellite dish on the roof. Only after a full sync is complete will the servers permanently relinquish master control. We can still realize the changes Pete envisioned. My dream. And..." The CEO stopped, horrified by the display.

Tad shook his head, numb from the steep detour the day had taken. "What is it?" He moved into position beside his desperate friend.

Christian maximized the security feed. Two transport vans wove around the fire trucks and police cruisers, skipped onto the curb, and drove to the middle of the pedestrian plaza. A firefighter cautiously approached the disembarking driver. The men argued, and when the firefighter wouldn't back away, the soldier reached into the van for a rifle and butted him with the stock.

Police officers swarmed forward with raised pistols. A daunting force of twenty paramilitary troops unloaded from the trucks, firing a few rounds into the air. The reports echoed through the high-rise windows.

The emergency personnel hastily backed away. The police took positions behind their vehicles but were hesitant to open fire against a superior force.

"Those are InLink operatives," said Christian.

"The team Abbie called."

The soldiers backed into the building, rifles drawn, the police helpless to intervene.

"They're coming for us," said Tad.

The CEO doggedly shook his head. "They're coming for Haven."

They remained glued to the security feeds as the InLink operatives secured the main lobby. On the exterior camera, police barked into their radios, cordoned off the perimeter, and pulled the rescue personnel away. Unfortunately, a few firefighters were still inside the building. The soldiers pounced on them, knocked them out, and zip-tied their hands and legs.

Now Tad and Christian couldn't leave the building even if they wanted to. They were stuck, with no way to reach the authorities. Tad hated this limbo. He watched, paralyzed with indecision.

The soldiers in the lobby were rebuffed at the disabled elevator doors. They argued over what to do. As Tad watched, Ramon exited the stairwell into the main hall. He froze as multiple rifles pointed his way.

"Damn, this is a full blown hostage situation," said Tad.

The CEO tapped away at his code integration, fingers and keys covered with drying blood. "Looks like we're gonna be here a while."

"Really? Because I'm thinking the gunmen are gonna come up and execute us posthaste."

"Not with the police surrounding them." He pointed at the exterior feed. A large fire truck was rolling over the plaza with a line of officers advancing behind its cover. Rogue operatives posted at the main door fired warning shots into the vehicle. Tad flinched as the gunshots echoed up to them.

Christian blinked away from the monitors, took a long breath, and spoke slowly. "I understand, Tad, that this is all new to you. That this isn't your dream like it was ours, but—"

"I'll do it," said Tad. He winced at his own admission but set his jaw nonetheless as he watched the soldiers hogtie Ramon. "Screw InLink and Abbie and Loras. I'll help you and Talon and everybody else that needs helping. As far as I'm concerned, I'm living on borrowed time anyway."

1940 Track & Field

Dune's boots pattered in the dirt as he returned to the Cloven Path. "No recent tracks," he muttered. "Not any of consequence."

"Aye," said Stigg. "Why would goblins venture through the mountains when they're at home in the bog?"

Caduceus twisted her lip. "The big guy's right. You'd have an easier time tracking them through the wetlands than you're having here."

"Oh ye of little faith," snorted Dune. "It doesn't take mastery like mine to track a pagan horde. The only reason I don't see signs of their passage is because they didn't cross here. More likely they skirted the road and went straight to the swamps from the north. That way's safer for mobs."

The red robe chuckled. "Less likely to run into snobby players that way."

"Hey, I'm arrogant, not a snob. There's a difference."

They marched in the open, surrounded by miles of solitude.

"They must have kept a hard pace," said the physicker, "considering the one we're pushing."

"It's not that bad," said Stigg. "Especially now that the army's not slowing us down."

Dune chuckled. "Yeah. And we made camp last night. What's with you, anyway?"

Caduceus shrugged. "What do you mean?"

"You're in a mood."

"She's becoming a city girl," laughed Stigg.

Caduceus gave the Viking an evil eye. "It's not that. It's just... I don't see what the rush is. Say we march right into the wetlands and find the horde. What then?"

Dune gave a matter-of-fact shrug. "We report it to Trafford."

"And then he orders a full-scale incursion into the bog? We're rushing into disaster."

The Viking scoffed. "We have more fighters. And better ones, at that."

"And they have the lay of the land, as much as we hate to admit it."

The green ranger let silence take over as he mulled the options. It was true, he didn't have a complete plan. Then again, that was the beauty of taking orders. His responsibility was to do his job and do it well. His thoughts were interrupted by birds cawing ahead. Just as well: there was nothing to figure. "Talon's still working it out," he concluded aloud.

"Isn't that part of the problem?" asked the medic. "This continual flying by the seats of our pants? Is everything really gonna work itself out?"

"You're a control freak," said the ranger.

"I'm a fan of control," she returned. "And I'm not sure we should've given ours up so easily."

And *there* it was, the real reason Caduceus was so grumpy. She was having second thoughts about joining the Black Hats.

The three hunters had weighed the option many times before and had always come back to the underlying urge to fly solo. Until yesterday.

"Bah," said Stigg, "it's not that bad. They're good folk."

"And it's the way the winds of Haven are blowing," reasoned Dune. The birds ahead made sharp noises as they scrapped amongst themselves. Even though they weren't in view yet, the ranger identified them as crows. "Look, we can still do whatever we want. Faction membership doesn't come with official duties."

"For now," Caduceus mumbled.

"We're just in it to help our friends. Talon would do the same for us."

The physicker couldn't deny that point and ended the conversation with a curt nod. As the party rounded a ridge, Dune finally caught sight of the pack of crows fluttering on a mountain ledge. There was a lot of wailing and gnashing in their ranks, but they weren't fighting.

"Wait here."

The ranger deftly hopped up the steep terrain. The birds cawed at the intruder, but Dune shooed them away and converged on the peak. The congregation fluttered to the sky. Dune kneeled beside a dead crow with an arrow through its heart.

It was a good shot. The ranger cracked the arrow and slid it from the limp body. He gently returned the crow to the ledge and nodded at the pack of birds. "Into the dirt we return."

Dune skidded down the mountainside back to his party. On the way, he scanned the terrain and the sky, making several revolutions to take it all in.

"What is it?" asked Caduceus.

"I know this feathering. These flights are custom made. Serpico used these in the Wicked Crow."

Stigg grunted. "The catechists."

Dune nodded. "A hunting party. They came from the south. They must be desperate if they're taking down crows."

Caduceus pursed her lips. "But this one fell too close to the road and they abandoned it. They're not *that* desperate."

"Too much risk for so little gain." The ranger spied a cleft in the peaks and headed southward into the canyon.

"Whoa," cautioned Stigg. "We're supposed to be searching for goblins."

"We're supposed to be searching for threats," said their fearless leader.

Caduceus sourly smacked her lips. "You do remember what happened last time we approached them alone?"

"Last time we didn't have an army twenty minutes behind us."

She huffed. "You're fixating on the bounty. What happened to being a team player?"

The ranger smiled. "I told you, I'm my own man."

1950 Uncharted Waters

Admiral Errol Oates was, for the first time since joining the Black Hats, feeling like a legitimate admiral. Not only was he captain of the grandest vessel the Six Seas had ever known, he now had a fleet of three support frigates in tow. While the Brothers in Black were not an official part of his navy, the alliance would see them through the war. He was sure of it. The pirate's sun-strained face stretched into a smile as the wind whipped against it.

Avisa came up from behind and leaned into his side. "Invigorates the skin, does it not?" Errol was acutely aware the woman was pressing her soft flesh into him. "Almost feels like old times."

"In the old days, 'twas more than yer face that was feelin' the breeze." His gaze traced up her neck and locked longingly on her eyes. "I could order the deck cleared." He flashed his teeth. "Or not, if ye prefer."

"I see command of the *Void* has already gone to your head." She took a breath and jutted out full lips that Errol knew were meant to be conciliatory. "We have an important mission, good captain, and being caught with our pants down, quite literally, would do us no good."

The pirate snorted. "I don't need trousers t' fight!"

The sergeant crossed her arms. "Ever the romantic. That's the Errol I know."

"Don't hold it 'gainst me, Avi. Ye knows me disposition."

Her eyelashes fluttered. "It's been a while since you called me that."

"That it has," he said softly.

"Don't expect me to suddenly swoon. You haven't changed a bit."

"Not true," he protested. "Lookie, I got me a silver tooth now." He grinned wide to show off his dental upgrade. She scoffed and started to strut away, but Errol grabbed her arm. "Give me an inch, woman! I'm doin' me jolly best here."

"I can give you the whole deck, if you like. Or maybe you need more space?"

"Space? It was ye who left me, Avi! We were the roughest scallywags on the seas an' you had t' go mess that up an' take up with the Brothers in Black."

She puffed her chest defensively. "It's a respectable profession."

"No more respectable than bein' an independent pirate. We had somethin', you an' I."

Avisa sighed, for the first time letting down her guard. "Do you truly not understand my mind, Errol? After all this, after joining the Black Hats yourself, can you not see the appeal of wanting to be a part of something? To know you have a future instead of bouncing from port to port?"

The captain had no rebuttal. Avisa had always loved Shorehome, as did he. Taking up with Brugo was much less of a stretch than joining Talon, anyway. Even he couldn't argue that point.

Avisa's pleading eyes told a larger story. Her desire to be a part of something applied to more than faction affiliation. Onetime lovers and cohorts, had they been destined for more? Sometimes Errol feared his keen stubbornness for independence was what had pushed Avisa away.

"Given recent events," said Avisa wistfully, "I find myself questioning the future of the Brothers in Black. What is there left?"

The pirate captain swallowed and avoided her gaze. For once in his life, he was at a true loss for words.

Avisa huffed and pulled away to peer at the distant horizon. "Do you think Brugo's right about the kraken?"

The captain glumly adjusted the waist of his pants. It was a sloppy change of subject, but effective. "Papa Brugo held the Squid's Tooth longer than any man, Hadrian included. If he says the kraken hunted the North Sea, the kraken hunted the North Sea."

"But surely we should do more than sail westward. The ocean is vast and endless."

"Not accordin' t' the players. They say a great blue wall encases the world."

Avisa snorted. "Next they'll be saying the earth is flat."

The pirates glanced at each other. Errol scratched his head. "Maybe 'tis, an' the blue wall is what holds the water in."

Grug approached from the port side holding a telescope. "Captain, the coast is cutting northward."

"Aye, I see it." Errol turned the wheel and steered the ship to match.

Haven's continent was barely in sight. By his reckoning, it was their best guide. Sail as far north as they could whilst sighting the coast on their port side, and keep watchful eyes to their starboard.

Avisa slumped against a barrel of rum with a sigh. "How long do you suppose it'll take us to get there?"

"No one goes t' the Maelstrom. It comes t' them."

She splayed her hands in the air. "Then what's the purpose of sailing west at all?"

"One needs t' put in an effort, woman! We can't just twirl our boots o'er the docks an' wish fer a great big hole t' open in the ocean!" Errol's chapped lips twisted under his teeth. "Besides, there's also the matter o' the sacrifice."

Avisa's dark eyebrow arched. "And what be that, exactly?"

The captain frowned and mumbled.

"What's that?"

"A ship," he said loudly. He glanced around the deck to see if his crew had heard, but they were busy tying ropes and swabbing the deck and wagering false eyes.

The sergeant-at-arms of the Brothers in Black sharpened her features. "You mean to scuttle one of our support vessels?" She turned to the *Void's* wake and swallowed as she considered them. "I suppose the ships aren't fully manned. And the *Waveskipper* is still damaged from the coup. We could restaff its crew among—"

"A *flagship*," clarified Errol. "The more massive, the better. She won't accept a support vessel. The Maelstrom swallows all but opens fer nothin' less than a legend." He grimly studied the sergeant. "She requires a flagship."

Avisa blinked uncertainly. It was an odd show for the cocksure woman. A moment of hesitation. Even odder was that, for once, Errol wasn't excited by the fluttering lashes.

The admiral pulled a worn nubuck glove from his hand and rested the naked skin on the wheel of the *Void*. The smooth wood was elegant and strong. She was a fine ship, to be sure. A respectable prize. And, in all likelihood, the second flagship Errol would lose in the span of a day.

Hadrian's nose turned at the crispy mess in the blackened cage. A war hero equally admired and feared, Rygar was meant to be his general. Now, for some reason unknown to him, he wasn't even alive.

As keepers combed the aviary and surrounding halls, the spymaster ignored all extraneous activity and closed his eyes. He tried feeling for the war hero again, searching the crevices of Oakengard, but Rygar was gone. Perhaps the NPC had been trapped or killed with a special of some sort.

"God Emperor," called out one of his knights. Hadrian angrily opened his eyes.

The man interrupting his scan was one of his least favorite soldiers. A born leader, a little heavy in the leading and light on the doing. Hadrian hated people like that, holding status they didn't work for, reveling in undeserved privilege. "What is it, Halpert?"

"The Hall of Heroes—it's been breached. Colonel Grimwart is gone."

Hadrian folded clawed fingers around the man's throat. "I will not have that name spoken aloud, Sergeant."

The man squirmed under the encroaching pressure. "Y—y..."

A pair of knights behind the sergeant straightened, eyes retreating to the floor. Hadrian smiled at their servitude and squeezed harder. Halpert's gurgles went silent as his face turned blue. In a final moment of defiance, he tried to fight back, push away his emperor, but it was too late. The sergeant went limp.

[Halpert] is dead!

Hadrian let the body drop to the floor. One of the knights flinched.

"My prize in the cage is also missing," muttered the spymaster. "What are you doing about it?" His eyes met the man who had flinched.

"Searching, God Emperor!"

"Then get to it. Unless you prefer Halpert's company." Hadrian glanced at the dead man on the floor. The two soldiers skittered away as fast as they could.

That was what he liked about the corrupting power of the soulstones. True obedience. Unfortunately, the purple energy came with drawbacks past sometimes spotty reliability. Hadrian once again closed his eyes and searched his fortress, this time focusing on Halpert. As he feared, the sergeant wasn't in the respawn queue.

He'd seen this before Rygar and feared the eventuality, but it wasn't adequately tested yet. Hadrian's power was instinctual, not learned. It was something he felt in his core and went along with, like a rushing river. He could no more break down the programming of his abilities than a fish could analyze the molecules of water it breathed. It just was.

At least now, at the moment of failure, Hadrian caught a message in the error log.

```
>ReInit() memcpy: ERROR: invalid access at
address 0xAFA43332
```

The spymaster hissed. This was a programming glitch. A technical problem caused by a rigid system getting tripped up by the purple energy. Hadrian couldn't dissect this, but the instinct he so relied on revealed to him the truth, the weakness of his terrible power: his newly corrupted minions didn't respawn. He would've expected a fresh start, clean and uncorrupted, which was trouble enough as it was, but no. Once members of the Violet Order died, they simply disappeared.

The obvious workaround was to corrupt more of the populace, to keep going until no one was left to kill his minions any more. Which meant taking care of Talon and the Black Hats. With the devs and Lucifer out of the way, it was only a matter of time before that clash occurred.

But first thing first. Hadrian had a breach in Oakengard that needed to be sealed. The fast travel was locked, but he no longer trusted the guarantee of a code switch. Not where he was going.

There was another way to solve the problem. A way to attack the breach from the other side. Hadrian chuckled as he drew the

Eye of Orik from his inventory. The red gemstone shimmered and sent jagged vibrations through his arm. The stone itself was wild. It didn't want to be commanded.

Hadrian grinned and welcomed the challenge.

1960 BioShock

I jolted awake. Butterflies twisted in my stomach as I desperately clawed at purchase to keep from falling.

I froze, body still save for my frantic breathing. I shook off the stupor and slowly realized I wasn't in danger. What had felt like a tremor must've been part of a dream. I was safe now, on the floor of the war room.

The memory came back to me. The void pearl was attacking—no. What had happened exactly?

My eyes went to the sanctum master panel. The pearl was safe in its socket, but it no longer bubbled with life. It was inert now.

On the other hand, I felt almost electrified. This was more than leftover adrenaline from a nightmare. I checked my character sheet for a sanity check.

Talon		Level	10
Class	Explorer	XP	100287
Kit	Scout	Next	113400

Strength	18	Strike	390
Agility	24	Dodge	450
Craft	6	Health	300 / 300
Essence	10	Spirit	255 / 255

Everything was normal there. In fact, I was the spitting image of health. Fully rested, free of afflictions. I'd even received a trickle of XP thanks to the shared brigade.

But I'd lost the entire morning. The game clock confirmed I'd slept through to midday.

> **Talon:** *Kyle, you guys holding up okay?*
> **Kyle:** *You're back!*
> **Errol:** *Ye left us high an' dry back there.*
> **Izzy:** *Back where? What happened?*
> **Trafford:** *Son of a gun, look who decided to check in.*
> **Talon:** *Guys, guys, hold up!*

I scrolled the captain chat back and saw request after request to coordinate with me.

> **Talon:** *Sorry, everyone, just a little setback. Let's do this one at a time. How's my army doing?*

> **Trafford:** *Oh, just great without you. What would we need you for? We're just gonna be in pagan territory soon.*
> **Grimwart:** *What our cranky friend means to relay is we could use your presence by nightfall.*
> **Trafford:** *What the colonel said. Trust me, Talon, you don't want me dealing with the goblins. I'm not what you'd call a people person.*

I chuckled.

> **Talon:** *Fair enough.*
> **Dune:** *There's more news. I might have a line on our catechist friends.*
> **Talon:** *You found them?*
> **Dune:** *I'm not sure what I've found yet. But rest easy, I got this.*

I wasn't sure I liked the sound of that but I was half distracted by skimming the chat history. I let it go for now, eager to get updates from the rest of the team.

> **Talon:** *Still searching for the Maelstrom, Admiral?*
> **Errol:** *Aye, an' it ain't the type o' task that can be rushed. What happened to ye before? Seemed t' me yer shadow magic threw ye fer a loop.*

> **Izzy:** *You're teleporting again? We talked about this.*
> **Talon:** *I have no choice. It was just a little hiccup. I'm fine.*

I searched the game log next, looking for any clues as to what actually happened.

> **Izzy:** *Well, I suppose you'll be glad to know the wildkins are marching west.*
> **Talon:** *I saw the alliance notification. What's your take on the wild king?*
> **Izzy:** *Theoderic? He's a big softy. He knows what's at stake here.*

My eyes landed on the anomaly in the game log.

> You've acquired [Shadow Essence]

That had happened hours ago, right when I'd blacked out. I nervously rushed to my inventory.

> **Kyle:** *Oh, I see how it is. You're a chatty Kathy all of a sudden until it's time to talk to your old pal Kyle.*
> **Lash:** *Ugh. We recovered Hex. The brewmaster did all right. But Hadrian's back in the castle. By now he knows we killed his favorite pet. He'll come at us hard.*

I blinked in disbelief. There it was, an item in my inventory. The shadow essence ebbed and flowed like the void pearl used to. The dark magic had somehow latched onto me.

> **Talon:** *Uh, that's great news. Can you get to the fast travel?*
> **Kyle:** *We have a surefire way to unlock it, but there's a quest we gotta complete first. Apparently, before Loras went to the great beyond, he installed a little upgrade to Oakengard.*

I sneered. The last thing we needed was another setback. As I rose to my feet, the shadow essence vibrated. I felt it thrum inside me. The void pearl onscreen blinked, like it synced with the shadow essence.

I waved my hand before the screen and flexed my fingers. Bands of shadow throbbed between them and I clenched my fist. The dark pulled at me. Bonded with me. No longer tied to the sanctum, I was now able to harness it completely.

Yeah, better not to mention this to Izzy and Trafford.

A tremor shook the war room and the butterflies in my stomach returned. That hadn't been a nightmare, it was an earthquake.

> **Talon:** *Okay. How much time do you need?*
> **Kyle:** *No way of knowing for sure. Oakengard's shifting and twisting in place. The upper halls are turning into a maze. It's gonna be a close thing.*

> **Talon:** *When has that ever stopped us before?*

Rumbling shook the walls. I trudged to the southern window overlooking Oldtown and widened my eyes in horror. The statue of Orik, the symbol of Stronghold's victory, was shaking. Rocks cracked away and exploded into dust on the ground.

This was not good. The titan wasn't just crumbling, he was waking up.

The brewmaster and Bravo Team hurried through the stone halls of Oakengard. The patrols were increasing in intensity and they'd already encountered small patrols of the Violet Order. It was only luck that the keepers hadn't yet noticed them.

Kyle nodded at the white knight. Lash's full helm dipped in return. She spun into the next doorway, cleaver leading the way.

"Clear."

She waved the team forward. Conan led, followed by Kyle, Glinda, and the twins. Bravo Leader took up the rear until the next doorway, where stone sentries raced past. Everyone skidded to a halt with baited breath. Alerted hums continued down the hall.

"They missed us," whispered Kyle. "Stupid dummies."

Lash glared hard at him from her forward position. Kyle readied to defend himself, then saw the knight's eyes flick to the back of the room. A keeper streamed into the doorway they had come through and stopped hard. Its rock head canted and fixed on them, and the purple energy binding it to life flared red. A single extended chime rang out like a deafening bell. Similar sounds repeated throughout the entire castle.

"You were saying?" growled Lash.

Kyle swallowed sheepishly. "We're boned."

Lash waved her arm into the forward doorway, their easiest point of retreat. "Move! Move!"

1970 Quake

I descended the winding stairs. The tower rocked so hard I slipped. I fell against the wall for support, afraid the entire tower might crumble. It was a relief when Bandit skittered up the stairway to greet me.

"We need to move fast, girl."

I grabbed the bongo's horn and pulled myself into the saddle. Her hooves deftly pranced down the shaking stone through what felt like several extended earthquakes. As we exited the tower, the mighty cyclops pushed to his feet and roared.

"Titan!" I screamed, though it was unlikely my warning did anything the rumbling giant hadn't.

Orik at full height edged out Dragonperch, currently making him the tallest object in Stronghold's skyline, all dirt and muscle and fur. His bald crown was ringed with matted hair. His eye cavity, though closed, seemed to nevertheless sense his surroundings. Orik bellowed a war cry and raised a fist.

"Hey!" I called out. "Not Dragonperch!"

Orik ignored me and took a swing at my tower. I recoiled as a barrier of magic appeared between the meaty fist and the ancient structure. The magic shuddered under the blow, sparks raining everywhere, but withstood. The giant snarled in anger.

He raised both fists in retaliation. I wasn't sure how much the sanctum could take.

"Orik!" I screamed. Bandit cantered in a wide circle as I waved my arms. "Come get me!"

My voice was drowned out by the cyclops beating his chest. Not only had he failed to notice me, but he was going for the tower again. But then, suddenly and like a switch was flicked, the giant paused. His ear wriggled and his nose sniffed the air. The cyclops relaxed and sidestepped Dragonperch over the river, making a beeline for a new destination.

Oh no. This wasn't good. The titan was now on a collision course with the Pantheon.

City Alert:
Orik has awoken!
Stronghold is under threat. All residents may engage in combat. While within the walls, all watchmen and residents are immune to friendly fire.

"This is bad."

My heels dug into the bongo's side as she galloped across the drawbridge to outpace the titan's stride. Meanwhile, the possibilities raced through my mind. What was the game here?

The last time the pagans invaded the city, Orik was going for the Oculus. He'd wanted to recover his Eye and potentially take control of Stronghold. But the founder relic was no longer in the tabernacle. As far as I was aware, there wasn't anything for Orik to do in the capitol building.

Then I thought of what Hadrian had tried.

> **Talon:** *I've got bad news, guys. Orik woke up and is headed for the Pantheon. I think he's going for the fast travel.*
> **Izzy:** *Did you just say what I think you said?*
> **Kyle:** *Can he even do that?*
> **Talon:** *I dunno. Maybe I should politely ask.*
> **Trafford:** *Can't you see what's happening, son? Hadrian means to reinforce his army with a titan.*
> **Talon:** *We can't let that happen.*

I gritted my teeth as Bandit ran past the giant. We passed Black Hat noncombatants and other players who'd stayed behind in the Foot. If their frightened scrambling was any indicator, they were no match for the titan and knew it. We flew over the bridge and headed into the Forum.

> **Talon:** *The dev menu confirms the portal is locked, but I wouldn't put it past Hadrian to have a trick up his sleeve.*
> **Izzy:** *Wait a minute. If he's planning on using the fast travel, that means Hadrian will unlock it from Oakengard's end. Kyle, Lash, that's your way out.*

Centurions formed up their second legion in the cobblestone marketplace. Horns resounded and Gladius drew his sword at the head of their ranks. Orik, ever focused, stepped across the Albula River and made his way toward the opposition.

"Hold strong!" ordered the commander of the city watch. "We no longer have the Eye. Once he finds there's nothing for him here, he'll leave." Legionnaires brandished extended spears. The commander's sword burst with brilliant fire. "Might need a little convincing, though."

It was unbelievable bravery in the face of utterly overwhelming power, but the city watch had displayed it before. Their sole mission was to protect Stronghold, the core of Haven.

Bandit slowed by the commander.

"How is this happening?" asked Gladius.

"It's Hadrian. He has the soulstone. He's controlling Orik just as he did the kraken."

The centurion blinked stupidly. "Even the boggart witches couldn't pull that off with this kind of precision."

"Tell me about it."

"What's your plan?"

I shook my head. "This is it. I'm gonna save my Black Hats and then see what happens."

Orik was faster than before. Where he'd first been a raving savage, he was now driven by a force of will more monstrous than him. Bandit galloped forward to keep ahead of him.

The tall architecture of the Forum was an obstacle, even to a giant. The easiest way to the Pantheon was straight up the fairway, and that was quickly filling with organized units of soldiers. Bandit had to slow to weave through, and it was only possible because spears and men cleared the way for us. I watched as the sea closed in our wake, sealing off the Pantheon from intrusion.

"Loose!" cried Gladius.

Taut bowstrings snapped. The two ballistae already in position released heavy bolts. Spears behind the front line hurled forward. The effort was much less haphazard than the first time Orik had breached the gates. Perhaps having a petrified titan inside the city had urged the city watch to run drills. Whatever it was, Gladius had trained his army well.

The arrows mostly ricocheted off Orik's thick skin, and those that penetrated were little more than mosquito bites. The heavier projectiles were not so easily ignored. Despite the titan's massive life bar barely budging, he roared in pain at the wounds running up his leg and belly.

"Reload!" commanded Gladius. "Archers, loose!"

A second wave of arrows filled the gap as new legionnaires hurried into position. They didn't get there in time.

The giant bent forward and wisely zeroed in on the commander. "Shield wall!" yelled Gladius. Orik pitched his fist into the dirt and flattened him and the surrounding centurions.

I recoiled inwardly as Bandit's hooves climbed the portico steps. Who were we kidding? We hadn't been able to halt Orik's Pantheon rush the first time he'd gotten through the gates. It was only a reboot that saved the city, and I couldn't manage that without the devs. Even if I could, it wouldn't solve anything. Any autosave would find Orik already inside the walls and Hadrian in possession of the soulstone.

> **Talon:** *Kyle, Lash, I'm at the portico. I need you at the fast travel yesterday.*
> **Kyle:** *No can do, kimosabe. We got a little recruiting factory to take care of first.*
> **Lash:** *Little is an understatement. Hadrian's growing his army by hundreds of troops per week.*
> **Kyle:** *We're gonna sabotage his machine before he 3D-prints an even bigger army.*

I gritted my teeth as Bandit shuffled nervously. Behind us, the titan was making quick work of the defending force. Heavy sandals stomped the ground indiscriminately. The blind head swiveled as fists took care of the largest threats. A ballista to his left, another on his flank. The titan's assault barely slowed as he lumbered forward, flattening any resistance.

I searched the skyline for buildings tall enough to give me a boost. I didn't have a dragon for the rest of the day, but I still had a dragonspear—a titanslayer.

The Pantheon was the tallest building, even in its half-collapsed state. We approached the statue of Decimus, holding up crumbling rock in a last gasp. Bandit was a mountain bongo, and her hooves were well accustomed to this sort of terrain. She hopped up the caved-in roof and weaved upward, toward the intact dome of the rotunda.

The titan bowled forward like Armageddon's first wave. I unlocked the fast-travel portal.

> **Talon:** *Forget the recruiting factory. There's only a day left till the war. The extra troops won't matter.*
> **Kyle:** *Bro, this might be our only chance.*
> **Lash:** *The frat boy's right. If things don't go as expected tomorrow, this factory could keep running for weeks or months.*

My knuckles went white as the giant approached. Bandit leapt onto the domed roof and galloped a lap around as Orik lumbered nearer. We were close to three-quarters his massive height now. It wasn't enough to leap to his head and give him a shot to the eye, but it was close. I pulled Bandit around for another circle of the roof to time my strike. As she came around, Orik predictably leaned forward to take on his greatest threat: me.

"I'm doing this one without you," I told Bandit, placing my boots atop her saddle and rising to a shaky stand. Rather than equip the dragonspear, I had my tiger claws on. I would worry about the stabbing once safely atop the colossus.

We charged forward. Orik swept a hand across the rooftop and Bandit leapt over it. At the top of the arc, I jumped off her back. With Orik's current stance, I could actually make it to his shoulder. I zeroed in on my target and dashed ahead with a sudden boost.

The giant's body twisted, reducing my chances of a pain-free landing. I stretched a claw forward, and then the titan's other fist swatted me out of the air.

Critical Hit!
126 damage

Breath fled me as I tumbled headfirst toward a nearby building. I was coming in hard. Just before impact, my senses returned and I triggered wall run. The skill partially propelled me at a perpendicular angle, fixing it so my boots struck down first. Unfortunately, my momentum was too much to completely overcome. My flailing steps couldn't keep up and I buckled against the second-story wall and pitched to the ground.

Fall damage!
22 damage
Fall damage!
14 damage
Stun!
You are stunned. You may not use skills, move, or attack for 20 seconds.

I reeled in the dirt, trying to make sense of my sudden surroundings. Orik was already moving on to the Pantheon. Bandit was nowhere in sight.

Talon: *Kyle, Lash... status.*
Lash: *Hot and heavy over here, boss.*
Talon: *If you're gonna come through, it's now or never.*
Kyle: *Bro, you're not hearing us. We're not gonna make it.*

Orik's sandal blanketed the lower grouping of portico steps. I clenched my jaw.

> **Talon:** *I can't let Orik through the portal.*
> **Lash:** *Understood.*

I opened the dev menu. Right as Orik hugged the portico wall, I bit down and locked the fast travel. He was trapped.

I was too dazed to smile, but my supposed victory was premature. Orik bellowed at the top of his lungs and raised mighty fists to the sky. He wasn't here to use the fast travel at all. In a fit of titanic rage, he savagely pummeled the Pantheon. The ground shook as Orik finished what the death of Decimus had started. Ancient walls collapsed, burying the statue of the angel and destroying the fast-travel portal. Even half of the rotunda dome caved in.

In a matter of seconds, the core city's capitol building was razed, a wrecked punching bag for a raving hulk. And then, in a manner very unbecoming a mindless monster, the cyclops halted his frenzy. His empty eye socket calmly zeroed in on a new target. The titan leaned down and scooped at the ground.

He picked up Bandit.

"No..." I groaned, still reeling from the status effect and unable to move.

Orik took a heavy breath, turned his head west, and lumbered away. If he wasn't gonna teleport to Oakengard, he was gonna get there by foot. I watched as he effortlessly slid over the city wall and headed toward the horizon, devastated to see my mount helpless in his grip, and me even more helpless to do anything about it.

My stun wore off and I rose to my feet. The marketplace was a nightmarish scene of flattened and wounded soldiers. The threat had left the core city, but the cost was high. Bandit was gone, and my allies were now trapped in Oakengard for good.

> **Talon:** *This is bad, guys.*
> **Kyle:** *You've got to trust us, bro. We know what we're doing.*
> **Talon:** *I sure hope so, because there's been a little development.*

On the floor at Bravo Team's feet, a last chunk of crystal lost its violet glow. The patrol of keepers was defeated, but the next wasn't far behind. Kyle and Lash exchanged a heavy look.

"Did Talon just report what I think he reported?" grumbled the white knight.

"What?" asked Glinda. "What happened?"

The brewmaster rested a tired shoulder against the wall. "The Pantheon's destroyed. We're not going back through the fast travel."

Grim silence followed the news until Crux sucked his teeth. "So, we're on a quest going the opposite direction we wanna go for a reward we can no longer use."

Lash worked her jaw. "The *reward* is making it so we go to

war against fewer soldiers."

The thief bit his lip and faced the floor. "I'm just saying, Speaker Harroway could've at least thrown in some silver pieces or something."

The stranded companions broke into smiles and laughed at the ridiculousness of it all.

1980 Crusader Kings

Grimwart nodded his chin toward the canyon ledge. "There's another one."

General Trafford frowned. There'd been eyes on them from the peaks for the last half hour.

"We should slow down," urged the colonel. "Tighten the ranks."

"No space to tighten them," said Trafford. "It's too late for all that."

"We can't leave ourselves exposed like this."

"I can recall the scouting party. Dune knows these lands too. He found the clerics once before."

"And how did they fare afterward?"

Trafford solemnly turned to the colonel.

"We should slow," repeated Grimwart.

A message came over the brigade chat, visible to every single Black Hat.

Talon: *I've got a bit of terrifying news. Orik's awake. He smashed the Pantheon and now he's headed toward Oakengard.*

The entire army froze a step as if they'd experienced a communal hiccup. Then the worried glances started.

> **Talon:** *The Black Hat army has a day's head start. That won't last forever. Keep moving.*

The buildmaster general scratched the back of his head. "Still insist on slowing down?"

Cries rang out from their forward position. Trafford rushed ahead through legionnaires brandishing pikes. Ahead, mounted crusaders in black rode out from a winding canyon path and blocked the army's route. Horses neighed and soldiers cursed.

"What good is that damned scouting party?" muttered the old man.

"Shield wall!" cried out a centurion. "Archers ready!"

"Hold!" ordered Trafford, pushing through.

More armored crusaders spilled from the mountainside. After the first thirty horses or so, the rest were on foot. Black tunics with white crosses filled the road and advanced.

"Ho there!" Artax charged past Trafford, Grimwart in the saddle. The black stallion cut past the legionnaires and drew a line across the tenuous no-man's-land between both armies.

"It's the colonel," remarked a crusader. A regal-looking fellow in plate surveyed the situation, rode to the front of the line, and saluted.

The buildmaster general pushed to the front of the line and watched the colonel and the crusader discussing the situation. After a tense minute, swords were sheathed. For once, a happenstance encounter turned out to be pure providence. The disparate band of knights immediately fell into line with their long-lost field commander, bringing dark tidings of Oakengard. Grimwart dismounted to greet Trafford as he approached.

"The sage caste is no more," reported the colonel. "There is no Trinity. No order. Hadrian rules Oakengard as a god emperor." Grimwart swallowed back a curse as he continued. "Our countrymen are imprisoned or assimilated. These soldiers may be all that remain of the crusader order. Sixty men, forty horses. They are now pledged to the Black Hats to help us defeat the Violet Order."

"About time we had a bit of good news!" Trafford wholeheartedly welcomed the new blood. As he sent out faction invites, he ran the numbers in his head, impressed by his growing army. The marching soldiers now totaled 420.

"And what's our best estimate of the Violet Order's size?" asked the general.

Grimwart frowned. "Among a mix of loyal soldiers following orders, those turned by the plague, and keepers, Oakengard stands at over 900 strong."

Trafford clenched down hard. "So much for the bit of good news. Correct me if I'm wrong, but we're up against a larger enemy force manning an impenetrable fortress, a roving horde of errant folk, and now there's a titan en route."

The colonel nodded grimly. "And that's not all that's out there."

To emphasize the point, a message came over captain chat.

> **Dune:** *Calling all captains, the forward party got a line on Cleric Vagram and the catechists, and you're not gonna like this.*

Dune crawled toward the rocky ledge, keeping his profile low so it wasn't silhouetted against the sky. He wasn't sure what to make of the scene below. Despite being on an elevated mountain bed, an expanse of crystalline blue water stretched to the horizon. He'd never seen anything like it. The lake was so massive it looked like it never ended.

But end it had to. Traveling further south would see the elevation rise into the impassable Sunscraper mountain range. Those peaks were the source of all this water, after all. Any number of streams and rivulets fed this lake, ultimately forming two main rivers that blended into the Albula and ran through the center of Stronghold on the way to the North Sea.

Despite his overworld map coming together, the lengthy coast of the lake would take some time to survey. Luckily, one landmark some way into the water stood out: a small land mass, barely enough to constitute an island. Its entire surface was built over by a wooden outpost. Dune's rocky overlook afforded a direct view of the fortification.

It was a small building complex—a tower, a barracks, a dock —but it was well secured. A strong log wall repelled attack from all sides with vantages in all directions, landward and seaward.

The surrounding water served as an outer stage of defense, with only a single bridge connecting it to the coast. The spindly dock stretched a hundred yards into the lake, funneling any overwhelming forces into easily managed lines.

"Time for some rangering," he said as he recalled an animal companion.

The red-headed falcon was a feisty specimen. Claws squeezed Dune's forearm as he flicked a treat into her mouth. Blossom, perhaps the only named falcon in all of Haven, was ready.

"Get me eyes and ears on that outpost."

The bird launched from his arm and sped into the sky, approaching the target with unassuming lazy spirals. Blossom landed atop the watchtower without notice.

[Dune] cast Bird's Eye View

Immediately, his prying eyes scanned the interior reaches of the outpost. His new vantage revealed puzzling facts.

Cleric Vagram and the catechists were inside the outpost all right, but so were a contingent of Violet Order knights. Some of them were friendly with each other and some weren't, and if the ranger was reading the scene right...

Dune: *I think the catechists are their prisoners.*
Talon: *Have they been assimilated? Are they part of the Violet Order?*

> **Dune:** *It definitely looks like some of them are playing for Hadrian's team now, but I can't tell if they're turncoats or if they've been infected. What's obvious is that Vagram and some of the others have resisted. They're wearing chains.*
> **Talon:** *How many are we talking?*

The ranger made a quick estimation based on what he'd seen and the size of the building.

> **Dune:** *Hard to say definitively, but I'd guess twenty captured, thirty with Hadrian.*
> **Talon:** *The catechists are a hundred strong. Where's the other half of them?*

Caduceus cried out, quickly and sharply, before being cut off. Dune spun on a dime. In the blink of an eye, he leaned away from and caught an incoming arrow, aimed his Atlantean longbow, and nocked it with the stolen projectile. His target, ten yards across the clearing from him, was Serpico, the catechist's best archer. Although his bow was now empty and he was on the losing side of the standoff, a number of priests backed him up. One had a knife to Caduceus' throat. Stigg was a heap on the floor.

"Your allies are alive," crowed Serpico confidently. "They can stay that way if you surrender."

Dune's mouth twisted. He didn't like Serpico, partially 'cause he was every bit as cocky as Dune himself. The archer was tall and lean with a pockmarked face and brown hair tied back in a pony tail. The guy just reeked of a douchey eighties-movie villain. But he was dangerous as well, a crack shot that had almost gotten the drop on him. It could be argued that Serpico still had the advantage.

"I don't know the meaning of the word surrender," said Dune, "except when I'm demanding it of an enemy. So what do you say?"

Serpico worked his jaw. "Say about what?"

The ranger nodded at the twenty visible catechists. "About surrendering. You release my party, back off, and I swear I won't kill every last one of you."

The enemy archer chortled. "Has anyone ever told you what an ass you are?"

"All the time," peeped Caduceus.

"Shut up!" said the priest holding a knife to her throat.

She blinked hotly. "I'm just saying, it's in one ear and out the other with him."

"I said—"

Dune swiveled the arrow to the priest. "Give her neck some room or I'm taking you down first."

The catechist swallowed uncomfortably and glanced at Serpico. The archer sneered at the pinkish wood in Dune's grip. "That's my bow," he said sourly.

"You lost it fair and square."

"Won't deny that. You're a slick one." Serpico reached for his quiver and Dune aimed at him again. The archer lowered an empty hand. "You won't look so slick when I loot it from your corpse."

"You really expecting that lucky a drop? You have a one in ten shot at best."

Serpico hiked a shoulder. "Better odds than I had yesterday."

As the ranger single-handedly faced down twenty men, a shadow materialized in the ten yards between. Serpico took an instinctual step away from the phantasm. Dune's mouth crooked. "About time you got here."

Talon turned to the ranger. "Sorry, it's been a day."

"I thought you could only teleport to party members?"

"Yeah, I'm kinda playing fast and loose with this now."

"Sacrilege," muttered Serpico. "The Protector of Stronghold employing shadow magicks?"

"Say," started Dune, "you okay to use that? You might have the others fooled, but I can see you struggling with the power."

Talon's cheek twitched. "I got this."

"You sure? 'Cause it looks to me like you're holding in a bad case of gas."

"Just one of Kyle's burritos. I—"

"Ahem," coughed Serpico loudly. "Hostage situation here, in case you forgot. Less idle chatter, more begging for your lives."

"Right," said Talon brusquely, "but I don't have a lot of time. I need to talk to the most important catechist here." Talon's shadow stepped past Serpico and surveyed the ranks. "Any notable priests in this ragtag outfit? Any men of wisdom or measure?" He looked around impatiently, eyes eventually falling on the archer. "Oh God, tell me you're not in charge or my opinion of the catechists will tank."

Serpico gritted his teeth. "I'm leading them," he snarled, "while Cleric Vagram is unavailable."

"Unavailable," mused Talon. "That's a funny way to put it."

"Imprisoned is what I'd say," ventured Dune.

Serpico grinned hungrily. "The crusaders won't hold him long."

"They're not crusaders," said Talon dismissively. "They're Hadrian's Violet Order. His purple magic infects them. Sways the most respected Oakengardians to his side. They already turned most of your captured men."

"Impossible. None are more devout than catechists."

"Saw it with my own eyes," reported Dune, bow still trained on the archer. "Figuratively speaking. Vagram and some of the others are still locked up, but I wouldn't put my money on them holding out forever."

Serpico's face darkened. "At least they're still alive."

Talon sighed. "You're thinking like an NPC. You *want* them to be killed. Then they'd respawn. And I'm guessing since you have your own faction now, instead of respawning in Oakengard it'll be somewhere close by, in these mountains."

Dune smiled. "What I can't figure is why hide them out here, in the middle of nowhere? With the Violet Order finally succeeding in the capture of Cleric Vagram, they should want him secured in Oakengard."

The Protector of Stronghold nodded. "Maybe Hadrian's afraid of Vagram. Of his holy power."

Caduceus put a hand on the arm holding the knife against her and spoke. "It's the quests." She opened her quest menu along with everyone else.

> Quest Revoked: **Bring Vagram to Justice**
> *Quest Type: Bounty (public)*
> *Reward: Crusader Alliance*
> Cleric Vagram leads the rogue catechist faction in guerrilla warfare. Find and return him to Oakengard.

> **Restore Oakengard's Glory**
> *Quest Type: Fepic*
> *Reward: <empty>*
> Oakengard has been compromised by a Trojan and a fractured Trinity. Restore them to their old glory.

"The Violet Order has captured Vagram and completed one of our quests for us," explained Caduceus. "They can't return him to Oakengard without partially advancing the next quest to restore Oakengard's glory. If they walked him into the fortress, they'd be helping us."

Dune snorted. "Hadrian's blocking our quest goals. The asshole's playing 4D chess."

"Which is why we need to work together," emphasized Talon.

"Work with this smug son of a bitch?" barked Serpico. He spat on the ground. "I'd die first."

"That can be arranged," said Dune coolly.

The archer's eyes flashed. "You have one arrow before my priests charge you."

Dune cocked his head. "Oh, I've got a trick or two up my sleeve."

Red feathers flashed through the sky, clawing the priest brandishing the knife to his medic. As the blade fell, Caduceus rolled away from the crowd. Before the catechists could descend on her, cries came from the back of their ranks. Priests were flung into the air like rag dolls. The catechists turned in panic as a bear barreled through with a roar.

Dune let loose and Serpico's own arrow punctured his neck. At the same time, Caduceus threw a heal on Stigg. The Viking hopped to his feet.

[Stigg] cast Berserker's Frenzy

"Cut it out!" ordered Talon, running to the center of the melee. His shadow form fluttered as he grew angry. A wave of darkness burst away from him, immediately commanding everyone's attention. Dune, Stigg, and Caduceus froze, weapons drawn, in the middle of a pack of enemies. The bear, another of Dune's animal companions, backed off.

"This isn't about personal battles," berated Talon. "This isn't about payback or one-upping each other. When I said we need to work together, I had a clear goal in mind, and it's one we can both support." The Protector of Stronghold marched up to Serpico, gripping the wound on his neck. Dune stood above him with a nocked arrow. "Do you want to save your cleric?"

The grounded archer gritted his teeth, then nodded.

Talon waved his guild members off. As soon as Dune begrudgingly backed away, a catechist priest came to Serpico's aid and instantly healed him. Talon shrugged. "I'd offer you my hand, but I'm a shadow."

Dune slung his bow over his shoulder. "The man can get up by himself."

Serpico stood. "You mean to rescue Cleric Vagram?"

"In a manner of speaking," answered Talon. "Dune, can you take a shot at him?"

The ranger blanched. "From here? Even if the range wasn't impossible, the mountain winds are too violent."

"A single arrow wouldn't kill Vagram," hissed Serpico. "It wouldn't save the rest of my faction either."

"We can call the rest of the army over," offered Caduceus, rubbing her neck.

Talon shook his head. "You saw my message about Orik. A jailbreak would slow them down too much. They need to get out of the canyon while they can." He grimaced and turned to the portside outpost. "How many of those bears do you have?"

"Just the one. Sorry," said Dune. They all peered at the scene below.

"What's that thing?" asked Stigg, squinting at the distant outpost.

Dune noted the metal contraption suspended from a crane on the dock. "A cage," he answered. "Looks like they're prepping it for something.

Serpico growled. "They're going to torture the cleric again."

The ranger grinned. "Not to say the dude doesn't deserve it, but I'm starting to get the makings of an idea."

The physicker shook her head and turned to the catechists. "I told you. In one ear and out the other."

1990 Eternal Blue

"Another one!" ordered Errol.

Grug lit the fuse on the quarter cask and kicked it off the deck. "Thar she blows!" hollered the pirate.

Grom chuckled as the makeshift depth charge sank. "That's what she said."

Avisa smacked the swabber on the back of the head. "I enjoy a lewd joke as much as the next man, but that doesn't make any sense."

"That's what she said," replied Grom.

"Why would a rhetorical wench say that doesn't make any sense?"

Grom shared a conspiratorial grin with Grug and said, " 'Tain't rhetorical. Mistress Sally said that when I suggested usin' a bit o' sailor wax on the chandelier. You know, on account o' the chafing."

Avisa's brow furrowed. "What does a chandelier have to do with chafing?"

"Well how else we gonna do it on the ceilin'?"

Errol joined the boys in laughing as Avisa massaged her eyes. "Fine. That happened. But it makes for an awful joke."

The pirate's face strained. "Why?"

"Because you need the context to be obvious to your audience. You want to tickle at the subject matter." Avisa cupped her hand and fluttered her fingers. "*Fondle* it. *Tease* the image in the mind. Then, when the boys are hard on for it, you spit on your hands, clench 'em tight, and yank 'em in." Avisa presented waiting hands to Grom.

The daft pirate chewed his lip and studied her a moment before conceding, "I don't get it."

"Ugh!" huffed Avisa. "Humor is lost on you. I was trying to set you up!" She threw her hands in the air and turned away. "That man's head is denser than a diamond!"

Grom snickered. "That's what she said."

As Avisa stormed to the wheel, the sunken barrel exploded, sending a column of water jetting into the air in their wake.

"Another!" called the captain.

The sergeant-at-arms crossed her arms. "Making all this racket on the open ocean makes me nervous. You sure you don't want to call back the support vessels?"

Errol shook his head. "They'd only be shipwrecked where we're goin'. 'Sides, this *is* an awful lot o' racket."

"All the more reason to keep them close by. If we attract the kraken—"

"Ain't the kraken we be fishin' fer."

Avisa pouted at the revelation. "But then..."

"Here we are," said Errol, flashing a silver tooth.

Numerous bow waves emerged in the ocean, tracing streamers that flanked the ship.

"Undine!" called Avisa.

But the individual mermaids were just window dressing.

Larger, more turbulent waves appeared, one on either side of the *Void*. Scale-covered frigates rose from the ocean.

Errol chortled. "Predictable as ever."

The sergeant glared at him. "Captain, we don't have time for personal vendettas."

"There's always time fer revenge, but this ain't that. The undine are nothin' more than chum on a line."

Her eyes went wide. "Forward ho!"

In a maneuver Errol hadn't counted on, the *Deep Blue* surfaced smack in the middle of their path. Prince Navoo's ship was almost as titanic as the *Void*. While the undine vessel was reinforced with superior armor, Errol was betting he had the edge in firepower. Which wasn't to say the *Blue* was lacking. A trio of shell cannons deployed on either side of the hull. Although the fore of the ship was headed with a large spiral drill, Navoo had opted to face him sideways to maximize ranged damage.

The ship combat dialog appeared before them.

[Deep Blue]
Undine Flagship
700 SIP

Errol checked the two enemy vessels flanking him. Their cannons were deploying as well, but that wasn't their primary strategic function. With them on either side and keeping pace with the *Void*, he couldn't alter course away from the *Blue*. In other words, he was headed into a perfectly laid trap.

Errol opened his ship controls.

Void	Level	4
Structural Integrity		800
Speed		7
Maneuverability		5
Armor		20

Weapons
Black Cannon
Black Cannon
Black Cannon
Black Cannon
Powder Cannon
Powder Cannon
Powder Cannon
Powder Cannon
Special
Hull Phase

The captain cricked his head from side to side to loosen his neck. "I never did have time t' familiarize meself with the big dame, but here goes nothin'." He turned to the crew. "Rammin' speed, ya assemblage o' sun-dried gull droppin's!"

"Captain," hurried Avisa, voice laced with fear. "The hull phase is only meant for avoiding incoming projectiles!"

Errol's head jerked. "Is it now?" His grip on the wheel tightened and he yelled, "In that case, *double* rammin' speed!"

"Errol!"

"Did ye not want me t' live me legend, woman? Well, here it be. I'm the cap'n on this ship, an' the undine are 'bout t' find out why they call me the Scar o' the Six Seas!"

Avisa swallowed hard, drew her saber, and waved it at the crew. "You heard the captain, fluffers! Billow the sails! Catch the headwind! We need every ounce of speed the *Void* has ever seen!"

Errol locked in on their quickly approaching target. As a sailor, he preferred maneuverability over speed, but in this case the *Void's* single-mindedness worked in their favor.

"Ready!" he warned.

The support vessel cannons at his flanks fixed on him. The three on the *Blue* tracked him as he neared. The undine were definitely going for shock and awe.

"Now!"

The cannons barked from three fronts. The *Void* went black, like Talon's shadow form. The crew held their breath as shellshot sped through lumber and flesh without so much as a scratch.

The two support vessels suddenly found themselves in each other's crossfire. Moderate damage peppered their hulls. The *Void* phased right through the *Blue* and a startled crew of mermen and mermaids. Prince Navoo's head swiveled as he tracked them, face flushed in fury. "After them!"

The pirates phased back to reality as their special expired. Like most, it was a one-and-done for the day. Its purpose had been served and couldn't be exploited again. But now the trap was sprung. The *Void* blazed a trail through the North Sea while Navoo's ship was at a standstill. Yes, the *Blue* edged them out in top speed, but it would take time to come about and catch them. As for the undine support vessels... They weren't quite wrecked, but they had all but defeated themselves already.

"I love it when a plan comes together!" laughed Errol.

Avisa sheathed her saber. "That was hardly a plan."

"Course it was! Everythin' I do be carefully thought out!"

"Your hat's on backwards."

Errol stiffened and corrected his tricorn.

The sergeant's eyes took a humorous slant and she crossed her arms. "Enlighten me, then."

The captain shrugged. "I sent explosions into the ocean, didn't I? The plan was t' deal with the fallout."

Avisa sighed. "I see I'll be needing to get accustomed to a new management strategy with you at the helm."

The pirate smiled. "Ye better believe it."

The race on the open ocean dragged on. The *Deep Blue* was proving at home in its element, gaining headway on a screaming-fast *Void*. As it closed on them, the support vessels, unable to match their speed, disappeared in the wake.

"Just you an' me, prince," challenged the captain.

The flagship canted to the side under sudden pressure. Errol fought against the current but the pull was too strong. The crew steadied on the deck.

"More undine?" asked Avisa.

"No," shouted Errol. "Look!"

At their starboard side, a black mass appeared in the water. The pirates drew their long weapons as the mass spread closer to the surface.

Errol: *Talon, ye be needed o'er here.*

The captain jumped as the shadow form appeared beside him in a blink. Errol wondered how Talon had managed that so fast. Maybe he was learning to better control the power, or maybe he'd been waiting expectantly in the war room. As long as he was here, it little mattered. The deck, and the entire ship, steered toward the encroaching mass.

"What's the emergency?" shouted Talon over the rush of the waves and the wind. The Protector of Stronghold gazed at the empty horizon. "Where are we?"

"By the Maelstrom!" cursed Errol.

"You say that a lot," muttered Talon.

"No," urged the captain, "we're *by* the *Maelstrom*! Look!" Errol threw his finger toward the darkness growing in the middle of the ocean.

When the black mass finally breached the surface, the crew realized it wasn't a thing at all. On the contrary, it was quite apparently nothing. A gaping hole yawned open and the contents of the North Sea tumbled downwards in an ever-growing spiral. The deck of the *Void*, along with the entire ship, listed toward the legendary abyss.

"Slack the sails with haste!" ordered the captain. "Commence tacking and jibing!"

Talon watched the pirates on deck scramble. "Tell me the truth. You're just making up words, right?"

As the crew attended the complex work of managing the winds on a spiral course, Prince Navoo attempted to pull away from the vortex. His attempt was woefully unsuccessful. The *Deep Blue* drifted sideways and joined them doing laps around the gargantuan whirlpool. The draining ocean sounded like a waterfall.

"Evasive maneuvers!" yelled Avisa. "Return fire!"

From the far side of the Maelstrom, Navoo fired his guns. Two cannonballs struck the top of the *Void's* tilted deck. Errol's crew returned the favor, firing the two main cannons and the two sub cannons on their starboard side.

The ships circled the abyss on opposite sides of the sink, drawing closer with each lap. Navoo triggered a special. A giant crab, rolled up like a cannonball, launched high into the air and arced toward their ship. Errol spun the wheel and cut the *Void* deeper down the vortex. The shelled projectile kicked panicked feet as it missed the deck and plunged into rushing water.

"Ya see?" yelled an elated Grom. "The cap'n stares the abyss down in style!"

Navoo, enraged, ordered his vessel to cut downstream of them. As he descended the water funnel, he entered a smaller circuit and circled more quickly. The *Blue* gained on them and approached their aft. The large pointed shell on their bow spun into motion, sending hundreds of ridged teeth hungrily whirring.

"She means to open us up!" cried Avisa.

Talon leaned close to Errol. "What's your plan?"

The captain shrugged. "Usually I opt fer killin' them 'fore they kill me." Errol dug through his inventory and produced the Atlantean anchor.

Talon started. "How'd you get that?"

"That slight fellow o' yers—Drummond the banker. Ye instructed him t' transfer the sailin' stock t' me."

"I didn't mean the artifacts!"

The captain grinned. "Seems yer lucky he did. This was dropped by the kraken, and methinks it'll help us find him." Errol applied the item and checked the *Void's* new special.

<table>
<tr><td>

Special

Hull Phase

Atlantean Anchor

</td></tr>
</table>

Talon nodded encouragingly. "Well, okay then."

Errol checked the wind and made minor adjustments to the wheel. "Before ye be gettin' too impressed, Talon, I do feel a confession be in order."

Talon moved closer. "You've never been to the Maelstrom before, have you?"

He grinned. "Don't tell Avisa, but I haven't the faintest idea if this'll work. Now how's me hat?"

"Backwards."

The captain grumbled and turned the leather on his head.

As Talon looked on speechlessly, and as the *Deep Blue's* drill closed on their aft, Errol spun the wheel toward the empty heart of the Maelstrom and deployed the Atlantean anchor. A glowing hook of metal dropped from the hull, trailing a twine of black in circles, deeper and deeper. The keel of the *Void* broke away from the ocean and rolled into the underwater sky, no longer suspended on water. Behind them, Prince Navoo screamed in terror as the *Blue* spun around and broke apart.

Somewhere, the anchor caught, but the *Void* was spinning as well, swallowed by the depths of the black. Sound and sky receded until there was nothing else.

The wildkins pushed past the tree line. Izzy's eyes widened as a great expanse of water opened before them.

"The Lake of Dreams," expounded the wild king. "It serveth as a barrier to the strife that layeth across."

Izzy frowned. That strife was exactly where they were headed. Scores of wildkins dragged long canoes from the foliage to the water. They piled in the longboats single file. Izzy sat as a row of oars cast them out. Thankfully, the warden and his prisoners claimed another boat.

The pixie stared at the beautiful water that surrounded her and her wild traveling companions. She had never before felt so immersed in nature. "It's so... big," was all she said.

"My kind, my kind telleth of a sanctuary preserved by the heavens. A piece of the old times, lingering still."

"It's definitely serene."

" 'Twas, it was," Theoderic muttered idly. "Those knights of violet thou marchest 'gainst be encroaching on peace and property alike. We welcome not their heavy brigs and troop maneuvers."

Izzy's face paled. "You already knew about the Violet Order?"

He smiled under the bone mask. "The people were known but the infection was not, nor their purpose."

But they'd been aware of the building army, watching from their safe coastline as the enemy amassed. No wonder it'd been so easy to finally draw the wildkins into an alliance. The sanctity of their home was being threatened. Asking them to march for Stronghold was akin to abandoning the Blackwood. That was never going to fly. Instead, they were moving west to defend their home.

Part of her wondered whether Theoderic had played them. The other part was thankful that Hadrian made the misstep of venturing too near the Blackwood. The Violet Order had prematurely shown their hand and rustled an opposing army.

"Is Oakengard on the other side?" she asked.

"Afar and aways it lies. The westerly lands be a span of marshes christened the Godsbog."

The pixie swallowed hard. She'd never seen it, but she was well read. All the lore about the place warned of danger. Then again, what could be worse than Oakengard? Danger was inherent when marching to war.

Instead of pondering what lay past the horizon, Izzy focused on the picturesque beauty of the water. The sky darkened around the orange fire of sunset. The stark colors swirled on the lake surface.

> **Dune:** *We're ready, Talon.*

Izzy idly watched the captain chat. As she waited, she went back over the log to piece together the various adventures the Black Hats were tasked with, wondering if everything would come together.

> **Dune:** *Anybody seen the head honcho in a while? We need an assist from the navy.*

Izzy decided she was best suited to answer.

> **Izzy:** *You're in the mountains, moron. The navy's a million miles away.*
> **Dune:** *Oh, look, someone who thinks they're smarter than everyone else.*
> **Izzy:** *Smarter than you.*
> **Dune:** *Shows what you know. I'm only kind of in the mountains. I also happen to be in the middle of a gigantic lake.*
> **Izzy:** *The Lake of Dreams?*
> **Dune:** *How'd you know that? Maybe you are smarter than everybody else.*

She didn't take joy from the admission. Talon was silent, yet again. That worried her immensely. But everyone was in their place for a reason, and for *some* reason Dune was near the Lake of Dreams too. Considering how deep into enemy territory they were venturing, it felt good to have an ally close by. She leaned over and peered as far north as she could see. The water stretched to infinity. The ranger could be anywhere.

> **Izzy:** *What do you need? I can offer an assist.*
> **Dune:** *I doubt it. Not unless you have a few boats and a private army.*

Izzy laughed out loud, startling the wild king with her mirth.

2000 Out of this World

<hr>

My hand braced the muddy ground, fingers oozing caverns into black sludge. It was an odd sensation. Slick, wet, cold... tactile. The mud squelched as I drew my glove from it.

"Errol," I started unsurely. "Am I really here?"

The pirate trudged up and planted a fist in my face. The shock of the blow caught me off guard. I threw my hands forward, attempting to catch my balance before I fell backward. Errol caught my arm and steadied me.

"Yup," he declared, silver tooth on full display. "Yer here, all right!"

I rubbed my jaw. "What is it with you guys?"

Errol dropped a heavy arm around my shoulder. "Ar, don't be so bitter, Talon. Ye set me up, fair an' square."

"That I did."

The pirate patted my back, unhooked me, and tromped ahead.

I considered socking him back, but that would just reveal my resentment. A much better turnabout would be something clever. Something that would take patience and planning.

"The hell with it," I said. I jutted a boot between his legs and Errol tripped face-first into the mud. Grom and Grug laughed as they helped him up. The imprint he left in the soft ground looked like something out of Looney Tunes.

Avisa waited in resignation, hands on hips. "You boys realize we're in mortal danger?"

"Yer always welcome t' join in," offered Errol. He played with the sludge between his fingers. "Ye know what this reminds me of?"

"Is it sex?" asked Grom. "I bet it's sex."

I thought Avisa might have an aneurysm, but her lips crooked ever so slightly. She was actually amused by the antics. I took it for pirate foreplay.

As the gathering crew bantered, I finally took in our surroundings. The air was dark and thick, like we were submerged in something, but it wasn't water. The pressure felt similar to a sauna, except this was cold, like a place long forgotten. The immediate area was visible but quickly darkened over a short distance. We were in the middle of nowhere and darkvision didn't seem to help.

Beside us, a gargantuan black anchor jutted from the mud. A twine of dark energy trailed up with a slight lag, and although we couldn't see the ground fifty feet away, visibility was clear straight up. The *Void* rested in the sky, suspended on nothing at all. With only a few pirates on the ground, the other crew members were apparently still on board, safe and sound.

The same could not be said about other present vessels. Massive splinters of lumber were cast about the ground. I scoured the debris to get a handle on the scattered shipwreck. "Is that—?"

"The *Deep Blue*," finished Errol, face masked with mud.

I pulled back. "Would you, uh, like a moist towelette or something? I think I have a few left over from the *Last Stand's* grand opening."

"Nay. The sun scorches a man's cheeks. I could use the rejuvenatin' mud bath." He turned to admire the shipwreck. "Looks like ol' Prince Navoo finally came through fer us. The Maelstrom needed a flagship fer a sacrifice, an' it got one."

Avisa blinked in awe. "Maybe you actually *do* plan things out in advance."

"I have me moments." Errol winked at me.

I strolled around the destroyed vessel. There was no sign of Navoo or other undine. "So we're in the under realm?"

"Aye. The negative world."

"What is this, like Haven's recycle bin?"

"What's a recycle bin?" asked Avisa.

"Uh, it's like a garbage can, except for stuff that can be used again."

The pirates furrowed their brows. "Why throw away somethin' ye wanna use again?" asked Grug.

"Because it's disposable," I explained. "It's not for you to use. It's for other people."

Errol shook his head. "Ye come from a strange, foreign world, Talon o' Stronghold." The crew followed me around the wreck.

"Your comparison is near enough," explained Avisa. "This realm stores Haven's dead. But I've never heard of things being reused. As far as I know, what enters the under realm never leaves. We are part of the void now."

I again studied my fingers. While I was most definitely solid, the shadow essence stirred within me. "This is where void magic comes from. Hadrian's shadowguards. Dragonperch's pearl. This place is what teleportation in Haven is based on."

"Bravo, Talon," called out a light voice. The small crew of pirates spun and faced the darkness. "Be not afraid," said the stranger.

I narrowed my eyes and fought the urge to draw the dragonspear. The voice was familiar, not in tone but in lilt. It carried a weighty confidence despite drifting on the air like a feather.

I stepped forward through the mud, illuminating more of the surroundings. A pile of sticks and bones lined a mound of dirt. At its peak sat a little girl, face cold but familiar. As I studied her, green text displayed over her head. [Lucille Black - Level 0].

I blinked. "You're Lucifer."

She grunted lightly. "It's more accurate to say Lucifer is me."

The girl was ridiculously young, eight years old if I remembered correctly. Her jet-black hair was straight and long. Her clothes were a simple dark tunic. The contrast with her pale face and hands was striking, especially in this dark hell.

Errol moved to my side. "But ye were struck down! Deleted by an angel!"

"My persona was," explained the girl. "That's all the angels were ever trying to delete. I was always here, refusing to partake in my father's 'game.' "

I swallowed as I took it in. Lucifer was alive. It was a lucky break I hadn't told Christian the news of his daughter. Then again, maybe he would've known the truth and saved me the heartache. He wouldn't ever delete his real daughter. I'd been such an idiot.

"Refusing to partake," I repeated. "You're level 0. I didn't know that was possible."

"I was created a long time ago, Talon."

I stepped closer and snorted lightly. "The eight-year-old master hacker."

She conceded a momentary smile. "I was one of the first successful black box captures, the first human mind to reside in digital space. The technology came too late to save my mother and sister, but I was a success. A prized treasure. Unfortunately, the backup storage state wasn't in place at the time." She noticed my confusion and elaborated. "Nowadays, copies must be activated to gain sapience. There's no point thinking before there's a world to ponder. You were stored for weeks before I woke you up." She took a solemn breath. "That wasn't true in the primal stages of capture. I was stored alive. Awake." Her head tilted sharply. "Can you imagine a human mind in storage? Alone in the dark? It was like living in a coffin."

I averted my eyes from her willful gaze. "I'm sorry you had to go through that."

"I was uploaded into an empty sim, a third-grader who just lost her family. It was all I could do to keep from going crazy. I was eight when I died, Talon, born without a world. It was only half a year ago that I hacked my personnel file and created Lucifer, but Lucille has been around before even the beginning. I had to wait some time while my father created a world for me to live in. All said, it's been thirteen years since I died."

Another swallow. "Making you something like twenty-one now. Which explains the child prodigy thing." I frowned.

"How'd you cope all that time?"

A wry mask covered her face. "I've learned a lot since I died. I've lived in the simulated world much longer than I did the real one. A lifetime's worth of digital reality."

"And most of it inside a black box."

She gave a curt nod. "My father kept me close on a portable drive. The initial interface was rudimentary. Text only. We communicated through a command line. All things considered, it was only natural for me to gravitate toward programming. He understood the boredom I would face." She held up a leather-bound bible. "And though he provided me with this, he knew it wasn't enough."

I gritted my teeth. "You didn't just gravitate toward programming, you were immersed in it."

"It takes more than faith to survive."

"Though the bible does explain the motif," I laughed.

She smiled drily. "I was Eve in a world without Adam. A girl needs to get creative when confronted with nothing but the black."

"And the swap to a man. Was it all a deflection?"

"Not entirely." She shrugged. "I lived alone in a box for the majority of my active memory. What use is gender when all life needs is a copy paste?"

Grom butted in. "I could imagine a reason or three."

Lucy smiled playfully. "Don't make me rethink giving you free will."

Grom and Grug shared a confused glance.

"Does Christian know where you are?" I asked.

"He rarely does. For half a year Lucifer and the Fallen were on the run."

"But why the subterfuge?"

She sighed. "As soon as I discovered the plot against Haven, I told him what I knew and went dark. The problem was, I knew very little. I was foolish to believe he'd be convinced by the broad strokes. Capitalism is control. Both are our enemy. Both threaten the sanctity of Haven."

"Christian didn't take your warnings very seriously."

"He took most of them for the contrariness of a precocious child. I did what I needed to do to make sure I see him again."

I was silent a moment. Lucifer—*Lucille*—planned to reunite with Christian Everett one day in the sim. She needed to make this existence work or that might never happen.

"It was hard not seeing him," she admitted. "It'd been so long, until you Everchatted with him in the Oculus." She paused. "I miss him so much. I often wonder if it's all worth it."

"And now we're rushing headlong to a bigger endgame than any of us thought possible."

"The rush is the only way to ensure our freedom, before Hadrian gets his hooks in everything."

"And if the rush ends up killing us all?"

"I'm prepared to die for what I believe in, Talon. Are you?"

I clenched my jaw. She wasn't wrong. "Everything you've done," I realized aloud, "from the beginning, was to fight the formation of a new god. You're a hero. Hell, you're *the* hero. I've just been along for the ride."

Her mouth crooked. "Don't sell yourself short. I may be the brain, but you're the hand. Or, rather, the talon."

"Aye," amended Errol. "In me short time buildin' fer you, I

learned that an architect ain't nothin' without someone t' put hammer t' nail and chisel t' stone."

I studied the crew of stalwart pirates and hooked a hand on my hip in contemplation before addressing Lucifer. "Well, it's coming down to one final fight. We're doing everything we can to win, but we sure could use your help."

"That," she said glumly, "is a bit of a problem. Lucifer was the powerful one, the persona to battle my nemesis. I can no longer help in the obvious ways."

My face sagged. "As if your help was ever obvious. What about down here? Isn't it dangerous for a lost little girl?"

"In the negative world, power is opposite. The greatest giants find themselves at the mercy of the masses. That's why I hide here."

I scoffed. "So at level 0, you're pretty much the queen of hell."

"By striking me down and forcing me into the Maelstrom, Hadrian has made me more powerful than he could possibly imagine."

"Ar," interrupted Errol, sticking a sheepish finger up. "What about that angel o' yers?"

"Otho," she said. "I'm no longer his caretaker. Otho is no longer angel nor Fallen. If he exists, he's something in between. Just like you, he'll be the arbiter of his own fate."

Putting it in those terms stifled any objection Errol might've had. I paced at the foot of Lucifer's dirt mound. "You expect me to believe you're just hiding here?"

Her face softened, dimples forming in her cheeks. "Hiding," she insisted, "and waiting."

"For?"

"You, of course. I have what you seek." She reached into her tunic and tossed an item my way. I snatched it from the air.

[Squid's Tooth]

"The second soulstone," I whispered in awe.

The artifact didn't glow or thrum or otherwise *feel* powerful, but something deep in the shadow twitched. I wasn't sure if it was the Squid's Tooth or the shadow essence, but I knew the titan was near.

"That's it!" yipped Avisa. "If we sail back to Shorehome and command the kraken, the city will be ours in a day!"

"But Brugo be locked under a magical ward," said Errol.

Lucy smiled. "That which is shadow cannot be bound."

Brugo materialized behind them, huge grin beaming across his face. "The devil of the Salt Sea," he boomed as he stopped beside us. "It appears there is much to your notoriety after all." The big man surveyed the crew, gaze landing on me and the artifact. "You recovered the Squid's Tooth for me."

"Not the tooth," said Lucy. "The kraken. And only for a short time."

Brugo frowned and I hurried to explain. "The deal was to get your city back. I'm destroying the soulstones."

The crime boss snorted in boisterous defiance. "I need the kraken to get my city, and I need that tooth to command it."

"The soulstones are too powerful to leave unchecked," said Lucy resolutely. "They were created to trap the souls of gods. Consider the applications. Capture and domination of game objects. Control and coercion. These are Hadrian's tricks. They're why he's able to manipulate that which is close to him. It's the same with Talon."

My eyes widened and I involuntarily stepped backward. The queen of hell turned to me. "Do you not wonder about these shadows tied to you? The absorption of the void pearl's shadow essence? This special talent was not a gift, it was the result of your personified will. You're a soulstone worker. Like Hadrian and myself, you are one of the few in the game who know how to manipulate their power."

My denial came out flustered. "But I never messed with a soulstone."

"The piece in your mount's head was the start of your ability."

"Bandit? The dragonstone? That's—" The permutations raced through my mind. "That means *you* were the player that stole Oakengard's soulstone a long time ago. You fitted the Crystal Core into your witchwood staff."

I really needed to stop underestimating the long game Lucifer had been playing. With Saint Loras on the take, the devil's first step was to cripple the NPC fortress. His heist had been the only thing holding off Oakengard.

"You beat Hadrian to the punch," I said.

"I did, until the heart of my power shattered into fine mist."

"There ye go!" chimed Errol happily. "The Crystal Core be already destroyed."

"All except for the fragment in Bandit's head," I said solemnly. "That's why Hadrian kidnapped Bandit. That's the last piece."

"Not the last," countered Lucy, "but the smallest." The crowd's confusion was apparent. The girl patiently went on. "The largest core of power has been regenerating within Oakengard. Its soulstone is not an artifact that can be worn, but rather the heart of the fortress itself."

"The witch's words," I remembered. "Depths agape and frozen. The crystal lake in Oakengard's Speculum is the soulstone."

"Indeed," she answered. "I spirited away its magical core within a small fragment of the lake. When that power trap shattered, the crystal mist was no longer caged. The magic flowed back to Oakengard. And now, with Hadrian inside, it's mutating."

"Like a virus," I added.

"Closer to a cancer." She breathed deeply. "It's an apt comparison for what Hadrian represents to Haven: a wild outgrowth that destabilizes the sanctity of the whole. He'll grow until he consumes us all."

"The boggart witches must see this. That's why they're cooperating."

Lucy's eyes sparkled. "Heed their words. Repentance and regret are powerful motivators."

The room was silent at that note until Papa Brugo voiced his thoughts. "I see a flaw with this plan to destroy the soulstones. The Crystal Core was destroyed once, yet it's apparently more powerful than ever. If the soulstones have the power to regenerate, how can they be destroyed for good?"

"They can't," answered the girl. "They never can."

Errol strolled closer. "Then what d' ye suggest, little lass?"

"Follow the path Saint Peter laid out for you."

I shook my head. "We're doing that, but the quest chain—"

"Of course. I should have foreseen complications after his death." The girl opened a menu and fiddled around, ultimately unlocking a new prompt.

> Quest Offer: **Remove Soulstones from Play**
> *Quest Type: Fepic*
> *Reward: <empty>*
> The Eye of Orik, the Squid's Tooth, and the Crystal Core have the unwieldy power to dominate Haven. Collect and remove them from play.
>
> ***Accept Quest?***

I bit down and accepted the prompt.

> **Remove Soulstones from Play**
> Blocked by: **Quash Shorehome Unrest**
> Blocked by: **Restore Oakengard's Glory**
> Blocked by: **Rally the Errant Folk**

"Finally, the master quest." I chewed my lip and reread the description. "Doesn't really give us a lot to go on, does it?"

"But it does," countered Errol. "The girl here. She be deleted in a sense, but not destroyed."

Avisa nodded. "This place. Your recycle bin."

My brow furrowed. "You want me to toss the soulstones into

the void?"

Brugo lifted his chin. "Where a queen of hell will ensure no one ever digs for them."

I nodded slowly. "Okay, but the Crystal Core is part of Oakengard. How are we supposed to sail the frozen heart of a fortress into the Maelstrom?"

"A power trap," concluded Brugo. "You're a soulstone worker, like the girl. You can accomplish what she has."

"It can be done," said Lucy. "Failing that, the founder relics each have a companion. The dragonspear can release the power of the Eye of Orik, the powerchain the Squid's Tooth..."

"And the trijewel the Crystal Core," I finished. "So I can free the magic, trap it like you did, and cast that into the abyss. But how do I do that?"

The girl eyed Errol mischievously. "I'm the architect, Talon. You're the one who needs to fit the pieces together. But with that in mind, I can offer some raw materials. I come bearing gifts."

"Of course you do."

She waved an arm and items appeared in the air before each of us. "Witness and possess your greatest desires."

Brugo quickly grabbed his. "It's a feather."

"It's a key," corrected Lucifer, "to open the magical ward when you reappear in your cage."

The other pirates snatched their booty. Avisa got a couple of gaudy rings, Grug a serrated sword, and Grom... He jiggled a three-foot-long fluorescent-yellow dildo before his face.

"I didn' know these came double-sided!"

Errol examined the folded midnight-blue cloth in his hand. "This can't be possible..."

"It is," assured Lucy. "Our time is almost up so we must upgrade your flagship."

"The *Void* is *my* flagship," asserted Papa Brugo. His eyes went to Captain Oates. "Until Shorehome is liberated."

Lucy looked to me and I nodded. "It can be managed."

Brugo stepped forward with pomp. "It will be necessary in order to recover the powerchain." He chuckled. "Have I ever told you about when I first obtained the founder relic?" Brugo turned to his audience, paused, and read the room. He shook his head. "But then, I'm done telling stories for the moment. Instead of talking, perhaps it is time we do something worth telling."

I was the last one to inspect my gift.

[Orik Chibi]
Collectible bobblehead figure from the
Titans of Yore set. 1/9

I arched a skeptical eyebrow and shook the miniature cyclops figurine. The head whimsically bounced back and forth. "Uh, I think you made a mistake with mine."

"Don't complain," said Lucy. "You already got the Squid's Tooth."

"Yeah, so I can cast it into the abyss. It's not like I get to keep it."

She looked us over. "Some of you will find more joy in giving than receiving."

Grom shook his dildo. "Ain't that the truth!"

"I doubt that's what she meant, Grom." I grumbled under my

breath and shoved the chibi into my inventory. If we were being technical about things, Lucifer had already gifted me lots of items, including the dragonspear. Whining was bad form. "It's late. We should get going."

Errol glanced up at the floating *Void*. "Ye mean t' up an' sail outta here just like that?"

"It can't be done," said Avisa. "One day to sail to Shorehome, win it back, defeat Oakengard, and return to the North Sea with the soulstones? We'll never make it."

"You're thinking too linearly." Lucifer's grin splayed across the childlike face. "Various places of power exist in Haven. The Oculus and the Speculum, Blind Man's Peak, the Broken Falls... places touched by the gods. The Maelstrom is merely a portal. It can be opened anywhere the water of life runs."

My breathing slowed as I processed her words. "We need to go to the Lake of Dreams."

2010 Fortnite

The westerly edge of the Lake of Dreams grew thick and boggy, water no longer crystalline and long marsh grass spattering the shallows. With the sun fully set, the cover and darkness allowed their crafts to skirt around the Violet Order outpost unnoticed.

A few boats idled south of the fortification. It was as close as they could get without being seen. They were in the deeps now, on open water. No more cover. Darkness and distance obscured them.

"I can't see a thing," complained Izzy, peering north.

Dune settled into the long canoe. "Neither can they." He studied their companion, Theoderic, and glowered at the ratty leather pants and tattooed chest of the feral man. "So, what's your deal?"

The wild king sighed. "Same as thine own, methinks. Freedom or death."

"No, I mean with your duds. Aren't you supposed to be a king or something?"

"A king who suffereth no fools."

Dune snorted. "Just asking."

> **Caduceus:** *In position.*

The ranger eyed the coast to the west. There was nothing like a good jailbreak to brighten the day, though he had qualms about the team they'd put together. Caduceus and the wildkins were waiting on the coast. Stigg was with Serpico and the clerics, in the ledges north of the outpost. For now everyone was working together. Better to take advantage of the cooperation while it lasted.

> [Dune] cast Bird's Eye View

Twenty unbroken catechist prisoners lined up on a skinny backside dock. This platform was along the outpost's rear wall, away from the unsecured bridge entrance. A heavy brig was docked to one side and was lightly staffed. It was meant as a troop transport, but its large sails made it look fast. The line of prisoners was accompanied by the catechists who'd flipped to Hadrian's side.

So the Violet Order was using like to police like. This complicated matters because it left the purple knights with a full complement of security elsewhere. With only a few purple tunics on the dock, most continued to patrol the outpost grounds. Between that and the wall, breaching the compound would be prohibitively difficult.

The main attraction, of course, was the wooden crane about three-quarters of the way down the rear dock. It didn't look unlike a gallows, but the contraption was taller and skinnier. It held a metal cage above the water line. The cell's occupant? Cleric Vagram.

The Violet Order turned a winch and the cage submerged in the lake. After a long half minute, the wincher reversed direction. A panting Vagram clung to the metal bars and took desperate gasps of air.

Blossom perched atop the crane and carried the dialog to Dune's ears.

"You've already lost," spat a knight in a violet robe. "Tell your men to give in. Do the same yourself. Only then will you be spared this indignity."

The cleric cleared his throat. "Perhaps it will spare me suffering, but there's no greater indignity than wearing that crass violet."

The knight sneered and signaled the wincher. The cleric once again disappeared underwater.

"Alack and alas, he'll be undone soon," muttered the wild king.

Dune turned, surprised the ruler could make out what was happening at this distance. "They're not trying to kill him," he explained. "That would be counterproductive. They want him to lower his magical defenses and take on the infection. But you're right, it's only a matter of time." The ranger worked his jaw and studied Izzy. "We have no choice but to move forward without Talon." The pixie didn't object.

Dune waited as his bear companion swam along the entrance bridge and climbed onto the outcropping between the water and the outpost wall. She lazily grabbed at fish in the surf. A brown bear wasn't the most inconspicuous of allies, but it was a natural enough sight in the wilderness. A few knights watched the National Geographic moment, but most were concerned with the drowning cleric. After a full minute, the cage once again emerged from the lake. Vagram's catechist allies collectively sighed as their leader choked up water. He was still alive.

The brown bear meandered along the base of the log wall, a sparkling fish hanging from her jaws. She neared the rear dock as nothing more than a curiosity. Dune listened to another round of questioning and watched as the adamant Vagram was again pitched underwater.

> **Dune:** *Wait for it...*

The priority was the cleric. Once he was clear, they could take action. The line of catechists on both sides of the conflict watched intently as air bubbled to the surface. Vagram would be holding his breath longer this time. As long as he could stand, anyway. If he didn't make it, Serpico and his band wouldn't look kindly on the rescuers, whether or not he safely respawned. It was why dealing with NPCs was tricky.

Beyond that, it was late enough into the night now that the cleric's death would be counterproductive too. A delayed respawn, a distant spawn point, and a possible lockdown were all obstacles to their impending deadline. This needed to be pulled off without a hitch.

> **Dune:** *Okay, move in.*

Shouts came from the mountainside as a boisterous pack of catechists revealed themselves from hidden crevices on the north coast. Leading the charge were Serpico and Stigg. They stormed onto the long dock toward the outpost gate. The crew was large but only had the clearance to advance in doubles.

Through Blossom's eyes, Dune watched as the Violet Order addressed the oncoming threat. Their soldiers were, unsurprisingly, every bit as disciplined as crusaders. It almost seemed like they'd expected this. The alarm resounded and the scattered patrols of knights along the back dock rushed to the outpost gate. The brunt of the enemy force had cleared the rear coast.

"They're here for the cleric!" cried the interrogator. "Secure him at once!"

The man on the winch pulled the prison from the lake. More than forty priests, friends and enemies alike, stared agape as water slicked off and dripped from an empty cage.

"Whereth be the cleric?" asked Theoderic, eyes narrowed.

"Blossom has eyes on them," said Dune.

The red-headed falcon circled in the sky overhead before swooping down and landing on Dune's shoulder. The water at the edge of their canoe rippled. Two bluish tentacles pulled on the edge of the boat, making Izzy flinch. An octopus lifted Cleric Vagram from the water and heaved him inside.

The ranger grinned. "Meet Bubbles." The slithery companion made squelching sounds before releasing the canoe and swimming away. "And now, it's Buttercup's chance to shine."

The brown bear leapt onto the unguarded rear dock and loped down the narrow pathway. Startled catechists and knights hopped into the water to avoid being steamrolled.

Izzy's face soured. "You named your animal companions after the Powerpuff Girls?"

The ranger grimaced. "Do me a favor and don't tell Caduceus. She wouldn't let me live it down."

As Vagram coughed up gallons of water, the wild king beckoned with his arm and three half-manned canoes sped toward the waterborne catechists. Wildkins pulled priests to safety as Bubbles assisted with the recovery effort.

Meanwhile, the Violet Order was quickly coming to grips with the situation. A number of them in the main yard split off to the back dock, leaving the bulk to fire arrows at the catechists outside the front gate.

Stigg and Serpico launched fire bottles into and over the wall. The rough wood logs lit up in flames, preventing the knights from marching outside the wall to meet them. As the Order scrambled to quench the fires, the catechists retreated toward the coast, setting the entrance bridge ablaze for good measure. They were only a distraction, and their work was done. Serpico and Stigg sped away on foot, confident their tracks were covered.

Izzy let out a slick whistle. "I've gotta admit, you put on a good jailbreak."

Dune dipped his head in thanks.

As the forward rescue canoe filled up with drifters, the Violet Order's heavy barge sounded a guttural horn that shook the water.

"Oh crap," said Izzy.

> **Dune:** *Get out of there!*

Straggling knights hurried onto the barge. In the minute it took them to fully board, the twenty catechist prisoners were out of the water. As more violet tunics crowded the rear dock, Buttercup belly flopped into the lake and swam off. Bubbles returned to the depths. Blossom shot to the sky to provide overwatch. The contingent of canoes turned west, and the heavy brig disengaged from the dock and gave chase.

"We should've set fire to the boat," cursed Izzy.

"Easier said than done. Our people had access to the gate, not the boat."

She grunted. "Kyle would've figured out a way."

"And accidentally blown himself up in the process, probably."

Cleric Vagram, on all fours, was finally all coughed out. He bounced to his feet and glared at the boat's occupants, locks of golden wet curls plastered to his head. "What is the meaning of this?"

"I thought it was kind of obvious," muttered Dune. He took a dagger to the rope binding the cleric's hands.

Vagram shoved the assistance away and spread his arms. Two bronze swords flashed into waiting hands. "This is a pagan vessel," he spat. "You're after the bounty!"

"The quest was revoked," hurried Izzy. "The Violet Order got to you first."

Vagram's face burned red hot. "You're all infidels!"

Dune stood defiantly as the canoe sped on the waves. "These

infidels just saved your ass and about half your captured men that weren't turned."

Before Vagram could bark a response, Izzy chimed in again with a better explanation. "Serpico's waiting for you with our people."

A loud clang reverberated and a harpoon at the head of the heavy brig fired. The metal spear slammed into a fleeing canoe, shattering it apart. Priests and wildkins leapt into the water and reached for nearby boats.

Theoderic had thus far been silently amused by the exchange with the cleric. Now the eyes behind the stag crown went hard. "Doubt not, doubt not, holy man, if thou so spurnst me and my kind, thou also spurnst these vessels mine."

Dune grinned. "I think he means shut up or swim."

The cleric gritted his teeth.

"Temporary truce?" pleaded Izzy. "Until we get out of this mess?"

The knights on the brig hurried to reel in the launched harpoon which was still hooked to debris from the sunken canoe. It would only be a minute till they had the weapon ready again.

Cleric Vagram bit down. "A truce then, and may the White King forgive the company I keep."

The grouping of canoes sped across the open lake, a race for the coast. The pursuing brig was fast. With its large sail finally unfurled, the power of the wind outstripped the paddling wildkins. Their only advantage was their small size. The fleeing boats, now parallel to the brig, offered small targets. Another two harpoon launches missed their marks. As the Violet Order's vessel neared, those misses would become less likely.

"We need to cover their retreat," said Vagram.

"No can do," answered Dune. "Our priority is you. We have the leaders of two factions in this boat."

"Which is why it's up to us," asserted the cleric. "Those are my people."

The wild king's eyes gleamed. "In this, the holy man and I are of one mind. My kin are in the water, and my boats shall save them."

"But—"

Izzy put a hand on Dune's shoulder. "Don't push it. It was a nice plan. Now it's time to do whatever works."

Dune grumbled. Vagram appeared pleased but avoided eye contact with the wild king. Theoderic flashed a smile and nodded to the oarsmen. They slacked the pace, lagging the boat between the rescue operation and the heavy brig. Caduceus and a crew of catechists waited on the coast to expedite the retreat.

The ranger drew a single silver arrow. "We'll do this your way." On deck, two men reloaded the harpoon. Dune waited as the knight aimed, tracking the heavy projectile to the nearest target: them.

"Uh," mumbled Izzy, "any time you're ready."

"Timing is paramount," he said.

"Paramount? Who says paramount?"

Dune ignored her and waited until the enemy gunner was confident of his target. Then he loosed the arrow. The silver point hammered into the gunner's eye. He tumbled back, kicking up the harpoon handle and pointing it straight down at the water. The metal spear launched into the depths.

He brandished a smile. "You see? Paramount."

Dune nocked another arrow. The knights were more wary this time. Instead of recovering the harpoon, they stayed low and cut the line. Then they changed their tack. As the side sails found the wind and the brig increased its speed, the Violet Order was now trying to run them down.

The canoe being rammed in the middle of this lake would almost certainly result in their deaths or capture.

"You've saved my priests," said Vagram. "For that I thank you, but it appears we're doomed."

Talon materialized in the canoe beside them. Not his shadow form but the man, flesh and bone and ones and zeroes. The nimble scout almost fell as he accustomed to his surroundings. "Damn boats."

"Talon!" Izzy jumped to her feet and braced him in a hug. "Where were you?"

The cleric's eyes widened. "Blasphemer!"

Theoderic crossed arms over his chest in warning. "Did we not cover this, holy man?"

"But he consorts with devils and pagans."

Izzy snickered. "Kinda like what you're doing now?"

Dune's Atlantean bow swayed in his hand as he hunted for a shot. "Guys... Big boat, pointy swords." The brig loomed closer, towering above the tiny canoe. Dune loosed an arrow but an armored knight ducked away. "I don't think arrows can save us at this point."

"No," said Talon. "I think you're right."

He smiled as a low rumble shook the water. Dune and the others searched the lake. The wildkins paddled furiously but the effort was futile. They simply couldn't outpace the brig.

As the Violet Order moved into ramming position, the water around them surged upward. The massive wave lifted their canoe. The passengers held on precariously. Gargantuan tentacles breached the surface at points around the brig.

Vagram's face sagged. "You didn't."

Talon shrugged. "I kinda did."

The appendages of a titan twisted in the sky and crashed down on panicking knights. The toothy mouth of the kraken heaved above the water; it bellowed and gave a mighty squeeze. The Violet Order brig whined before buckling under the sea monster's immense power. Knights in heavy armor jumped ship as the tentacles sucked the wreckage into the lake's depths.

Meanwhile, the canoes were propelled to the coast like surfboards riding a tidal wave. They left the screams and destruction in their wake. Dune hooked his bow across his shoulder and grumpily took a seat.

"Always stealing the show," he muttered.

Though his voice was bitter, he grinned at the oncoming coast.

2020 Ultimate Alliance

The longboat hit the shore. I jumped off first, followed by a few wildkins. We trudged through the shallows and grounded the boat so the others could disembark relatively dry.

"What are you beaming about?" asked Izzy.

The grin was glued to my face. I wasn't hiding it or letting Izzy get me down. "You guys did it. I didn't lift a finger and I'm standing here watching the wild king unload beside Cleric Vagram."

"Yeah, I wouldn't go claiming mission complete just yet." She hugged me close and rapped my chest. "How are you here anyway? I mean *here* here. I didn't think the void pearl could manage real teleports."

I shrugged. "It has more to do with its source of magic than the pearl. We found the kraken in the Maelstrom. And—" My eyes shot to a glaring Vagram. "It's a long story. First, I need to fulfill a promise."

In the moonlit night, the lake was a flat black mirror, marred only by the ripples of our recent exit. In the distance, a fire burned the outpost on the water. The Violet Order had lost their foothold on the Lake of Dreams.

"Life and death beget glorious breath," said Theoderic.

Izzy gave him the side eye. "When did you start rhyming?"

The king sighed. "A beautiful thing, it be."

"It's only a start," I said. I stepped into the water, clutching the Squid's Tooth, and willed the kraken to make its way downriver. The beast would navigate treacherous rapids, the Broken Falls, and the Albula on the way to the North Sea and, eventually, Shorehome.

I switched to broadcasting over full brigade chat.

Talon: *Drummond, are you in Stronghold?*

Drummond: *Uh, hi Talon. Yes. I'm here.*

Drummond: *Why?*

Talon: *I'm gonna need you to find Gladius and open the river gates. You have a guest passing through.*

Drummond: *A guest?*

Talon: *The kraken needs safe passage through the city on the way to Shorehome. See that it gets through and isn't attacked.*

Drummond: *Uh, really? I guess.*

Talon: *Drummond, you're a Black Hat. You'll get it done.*

Drummond: *Yes, sir. You can count on me.*

Izzy's hands were hooked on her hips. "Poor guy needed his pep talk broadcast to the whole guild."

I hiked a shoulder. "It's his moment to shine. He'll do fine."

"And us? You don't think we could use a titan in the coming fight?"

"Sacrilege!" snapped the cleric.

Serpico and the larger catechist contingent came down the coast and huddled around their leader. The priests checked the former prisoners for signs of the purple plague, but they were just being thorough. The infection wasn't subtle and the catechists were fine.

I pulled Izzy away from the judgmental crew wearing gold crosses and lowered my voice. "This isn't a fight for titans."

The pixie snorted. "Yeah, right. Anything involving the soulstones is a fight for the titans."

"That's why our job is to free them. Founder relics work in pairs. We can use the charms to dispel the stones."

"A certain cyclops stomping our way might be a complication."

"We just need to stay one step ahead of him." I chewed my lip. "A giant, lumbering step."

"I bet you're gonna keep telling yourself that right until Hadrian wakes Gigas."

The wildkins went quiet. Theoderic's mask turned to his warden, surrounded by his prisoners. I grew uncomfortable as I realized both factions had gathered on opposite sides of us. They were casting adversarial glances across like two teams waiting on a coin flip.

"We're not enemies here," I asserted. "Players, NPCs, and mobs—we're in this together. This is where we figure out our shared destiny."

The catechists glowered. "The truce I agreed to has expired," said Vagram. "There's no more danger from the Violet Order." He pointed a sword my way. "And I made no promises to you, blasphemer."

I sighed. "Open your eyes, Vagram. Mara and Gent are dead. I'm on a mission to restore the Trinity, and that starts with our cooperation."

Vagram frowned at the news.

"We've fought side by side before," I pointed out. "We made a good team too." My head canted in reflection. "Even if you *were* technically planning on betraying me from the start."

The cleric's face flushed red. "It was you who betrayed the people!"

Dune snorted. "I got news for you, priest. The world's changed a lot while you've been on the lam. There's a new war and there are two sides: everyone who was here before, and the purple infection that already turned a number of your men."

I stepped forward. "You can't be so stuck in your ways. You're NPCs, with a rigid holy code no less, but you've got to utilize that free will that broke you away from the crusaders in the first place. Not just at a power-hungry bishop's orders. Can't you see all the wrong that's occurred?"

Vagram worked his jaw. "Tannen may have overstepped, but he was a righteous leader."

"He's why you're in this mess, but I know you to be more reasonable. Strict, but measured when you wanna be. You're a threat to Hadrian. So am I. Ditto for the wild king. The last thing he wants is us fighting together because it's the only way the Violet Order's going down. Even now their recruiting factory is generating more knights, sages, and replacement priests."

That last point spurred some concern in the catechist ranks. No one wanted to be disposable.

"You'd have us take down one tyrant in service of another," said Vagram. "What makes the Black Hats any better than the Violet Order?"

"We're not trying to drown you in a cage, for one."

"Yet you imprisoned Bishop Tannen's mind, nonetheless." His glare moved to the wild king.

"He got what he deserved," I grumbled.

"And has paid a steep price. We refuse to join your faction."

"I'm not asking for that." I moved closer as the catechists fingered their weapons. "I need your healers in the coming war. You need my army." I motioned toward Serpico and Dune. "If these two can come together to spring you from heavy security, to put teamwork above ego, then you and I can match that example. Let's set aside our squabbles and knock Hadrian on his ass."

"I admit the situation sounds dire, but there's no cause for such language."

"If the end of the world isn't good cause, I don't know what is. We need to finish this before the end of tomorrow; otherwise Hadrian's the permanent ruler of Oakengard."

Vagram growled, as if even the possibility of a new ruler was an affront.

"We don't have a lot of time," urged Izzy.

Dune nodded. "It's now or never."

Vagram raised his chin in thought. He didn't inquire about the mechanics of Hadrian taking control of his city. As an NPC, perhaps he sensed the truth of it somehow. "You ride for Oakengard now?"

Izzy snickered. "Walk is more the sum of it."

The cleric looked over his gathering people. "And you agree to allow the catechists to restore Oakengard's glory when the usurper is dealt with?"

"Funny you should put it like that." I displayed my active quest for him.

Restore Oakengard's Glory
Quest Type: Fepic
Reward: <empty>
Oakengard has been compromised by a Trojan and a fractured Trinity. Restore them to their old glory.

"All this for no reward?" he asked skeptically.

I offered my gloved hand. "The reward is you and Grimwart getting your home back."

"The knights are alive?"

The cleric was so shocked and stubborn he didn't take my hand. I boldly held it out and explained. "A hundred of them ride with me. Add your seventy to the mix and we have plenty of Oakengard residents on the side of good. The rest, I'm afraid, will be marching against us. The purple has already taken them."

His eyes flitted to my waiting hand. "This genocide will not go unanswered. You have convinced me of your motives, but sharing a battlefield with the Black Hats necessitates bringing the wildkins into the negotiation."

"You're square with them," said Dune. "They helped rescue you."

"They did," conceded the cleric. "And that buys them a civil audience. If they want cooperation, they know what must be done."

I slowly pulled my hand away and turned to the wild king. His brown eyes were already on his warden.

"Absolutely not," stressed Izzy. "We're trying to work together here, guys, not tear everything apart."

"There's no other way," assured Vagram. "Which of us is best suited to restore Oakengard than the only living member of the Trinity?"

"He tried to usurp the Trinity," I said through gritted teeth.

"And will be penitent before the White King. Bishop Tannen will see the light, as I have. In the face of this violet threat, we must all come together, no? Do you truly want the past forgiven, or do you offer only platitudes?"

I took a heavy breath. When Izzy turned to me, I stared at my boot and kicked the muddy ground.

"A time and place for all things," came the wild king's crisp voice. He towered over Izzy and smiled behind the mask. "Did thy words to my kin ring true, little one?"

She swallowed. "Of course they did."

"Then we choose 'tween freedom and death." Theoderic raised a finger and flicked it skyward. "Warden of the Blackwood, releasest thy prisoner."

A deep growl grated the coast. "Let it be so."

Various hooded figures lurked in the tall grasses behind the warden. One unassuming man stepped forward. With a sweep of his hand, the warden slipped the black hood away. Even though it was nighttime, Bishop Tannen blinked quickly against the sudden light and collapsed to the ground. Catechist priests hurried to his side.

I swallowed hard and finally met Izzy's glower. She was pissed. The awkward moment was thankfully interrupted by a notification.

Black Hat Alert:
The Catechists have called off the war!

Catechist Reputation +100

Black Hat Alert:
The Catechists have entered an alliance!

Catechist Reputation +100

Tad wandered back to the office, so exhausted even his crutch was tired. "It's still quiet," he reported.

The CEO typed away with barely a nod. He was working through the night. That was okay. Tad had grown accustomed to the quirks of inspired genius. Christian was doing what he had to do.

Tad carefully slid to the floor and rested his back against the cabinet beside Christian. The occasional helicopter droned in the distance, but it really was quiet otherwise. The dark sky seemed to wind down the tension. There hadn't been any progress with the standoff in the lobby. The security force had hunkered down, securing their position and hostages. The police had the building surrounded, their attempts at communication rebuffed.

Tad relayed his day's work in snippets, knowing Christian was listening even if he didn't respond. "The elevators are still offline. I barricaded entry into this wing. There're just two stairwells leading in from the ground, and the main one's in the collapsed hallway. I secured the one in the back and triple-checked the doors. We're safe for a bit."

They must have sat there an hour in the dead of night. Tad thought about his brother, Derek. About how well he'd been doing on his own. It was like the new city had given him all the confidence he needed. In fact, after the accident, it was Tad that had needed Derek more than the other way around. How was that for a plot twist?

The programmer sighed, comforted by the thought. If he died here and now, without seeing Derek again, he'd still be confident of his brother's promising future. Maybe that's all family needed of each other.

Tad did a double-take at the screen. A stairwell cam revealed a small group of soldiers ascending.

"They're coming," said Tad.

Christian paused to take in the scene. "That's the main stairwell. You said they wouldn't be able to get through."

Tad forced himself up and leaned on his crutch. "Maybe."

He hopped out of the office and toward the stairwell. With the hallway collapsed, he waited just around the corner wall. Within minutes, the sound of scraping debris came from the blocked door.

"Get out of here!" Tad yelled.

The sounds paused for a few seconds before resuming even louder as the soldiers redoubled their effort. Tad raised Abbie's pistol.

"I'm serious!"

They kept working at the door. A piece of the collapsed ceiling bumped in tempo with the pounding. It was only a matter of time.

Tad held his breath, steadied his hand at the drywall partition separating him and the soldiers, and pulled the trigger. The bullet popped into the wall. He froze, startled by the sound, and waited. Silence. No more digging, no more hammering. Tad scanned the hall for signs of movement.

A line of automatic fire ripped through the wall. Tad dove to the carpet. The air whistled over his head. Bullets bit into desks and cubicle walls. Tad covered his head as several more strafes tore through the debris. He aimed his weapon blindly, returned fire, and crawled away.

Between the reports in the dev studio, Tad heard a chorus of gunfire in the distance. The police, possibly spurned into action by the battle above, had joined the fray. The operatives behind the wall cursed. Next thing Talon knew, he was cowering on the floor completely alone, the only gunfire coming from forty floors below. After the deafening experience up close, the battle downstairs seemed muted and unimportant, like a TV in the neighboring apartment.

Tad scrambled to his crutch and hurried back to the office.

"Nice job," remarked Christian.

"I didn't do anything. I panicked."

"Whatever you did, it worked. The operatives retreated downstairs to fortify the lobby."

Tad plopped down at the video feeds. SWAT team vans had advanced across the plaza. The police had attempted an incursion but were already pulling away with several wounded officers.

"It's not gonna be that easy," said Christian. "InLink sent professionals."

Tad trembled as the adrenaline wore off. He patted himself down looking for bullet holes, relieved not to find any. He was fine, but how long would that last?

2030 Up Your Arsenal

Ten knights marched down the hall, steel plate shiny and unmarred from battle, tunics freshly inked with bright violet. Hadrian's keepers didn't waste any time turning the fresh recruits. As they disappeared around the corner, Crux peeked back through the doorway.

"That's the last of them."

The six companions were hunched in some kind of white room with clean lines and plain benches. It reminded Kyle of the intake room in the Pantheon where he'd first spawned into the afterlife. Perhaps, once Haven officially launched, the room would welcome the first of the NPC fortress' player residents. Perhaps those unlucky players would find themselves in an apocalyptic nightmare scenario, being hunted and assimilated by an unthinking army.

"Okay then," said the brewmaster, tapping Harroway's blue key in his fingers. "Let's get this over with."

They emerged from the room situated near the entrance of the Inner Hall. This was uncharted territory for them, meant only for the saints and other Oakengard leadership. It had been wise of Loras to place the recruiting factory here. The Inner Hall was well guarded at all hours of the day. Even Crux hadn't been able to explore this area yet.

Which made it all the more puzzling that the keepers weren't watching it now. Kyle was getting the sinking feeling that they were walking into a trap.

After two more turns, Crux walked ahead, but Kyle stopped at an ornate door. The wood was lacquered with a royal blue pigment rich with sparkles. A bejeweled red heart adorned the nameplate. "I guess this is it," he said before taking a heavy breath. He slipped the blue key into the lock.

It got stuck after a quarter twist.

"Son of a B."

Lash converged on him as he put his shoulder into it. The door wiggled in the stone frame a bit, but it was still stuck, as if something was blocking it from the other side.

"What are you doing?" asked Glinda as the others caught up.

Kyle took three steps away from the door. "Just giving it a little nudge." He charged and planted his shoulder by the doorknob.

Glinda threw her hands up. "No!"

The door flew open and Kyle fell forward. He tried to throw his feet under his weight, but they got caught on a lavish red carpet. He tumbled head over heels and came to a rest on his back. The brewmaster winced and massaged his neck, blinking at the chandeliered ceiling.

Four scantily dressed women pursed painted lips and ogled him.

"Oh, poorest sir, art thou all right?"

"Goodness, that was a fall!"

"We must check for bruising!"

Kyle sat upright as hands pawed him from all sides. He took in the room, astounded to see a few other ladies rising from fanciful pillow beds.

"What do you think you're doing?" accused Glinda as the party pushed in.

"What?" asked the brewmaster.

"We're supposed to stay out of sight, and you just barged into the middle of Hadrian's harem."

"This isn't—" Kyle furrowed his brow and turned to the woman cradling him with her bosom. She nodded emphatically. He pushed to his feet. "It's not my fault. It was Harroway's key. Blue key, blue door. What could go wrong?"

Glinda sighed impatiently. "The quest says to go to the training facility, not the... love facility."

The women giggled. Kyle blinked. "You guys actually read the quest text? I didn't think anybody did that."

Conan nodded. "Me neither."

The good witch glared at him. "I suppose I'd expect that from you blockheads. Isn't that right, Lash?"

The white knight offered a meek shrug. "Um, I mean, it's sort of understandable. Pound stuff, get paid."

Glinda huffed and crossed her arms. "I can't believe I'm stranded in Oakengard with all of you."

Rather than take sides, Hex quietly backed out of the love facility to check where Crux had gone off to.

Kyle frowned and took in all the beautiful ladies. "Wait a minute. You mean to tell me that every single one of you is intimate with Hadrian?"

A woman with gold-painted breasts nodded. "He's the ranking god emperor."

"But he's awfully mean," added a woman with smudged lipstick. "He hasn't let Gloria up for hours."

"It's not so bad," called Gloria, voice muffled by the pillow she was lying face down on. Her arms and legs were handcuffed to the bedposts.

Kyle worked his jaw. "I mean... that's just... wrong on so many levels." He produced a vial of corrosive and broke the designer shackles.

A chubby girl squeezed the brewmaster tight. "That's real nice of ya, mister."

"I guess," said Gloria, not shy about her disappointment.

The hugging girl's lashes fluttered. "Makes a girl wonder if a man as big and strong as yerself can take over for the god emperor."

Kyle rubbed his chin. "Now that you mention it, I have always wanted a harem."

"Kyle!" snapped Lash, stomping forward. "We don't have time for this!"

"What? They're damsels in distress."

Gold Boobs nodded. "*Soooo* distressed."

The girls crowded around him. "Tell us about yourself." "Where are you from?" "Do you like butt stuff?"

"Whoa," he said. "Slow down. I'll address all your questions. I'm one of the leaders of the Black Hats."

"Ooh," they said.

He passed out flyers for the Last Stand. "I'm a bartender,

actually. And for you ladies, I'll give you two-for-one pints."

Lash growled at him.

"Right," he chimed. "Free, of course. I'll buy your drinks. And I do like butt stuff."

The women cooed and crowed. "So generous of you!" "A bartender?" "We should do shots!"

Kyle nodded. "We totally should!" He flinched under Lash's glower and remembered his clean-and-sober-and-stupid challenge. "Is totally what I'd say if I wasn't on an important mission right now."

One of the girls fluttered her lashes at Conan. "Ooh, what's your name?"

Kyle shook his head aggressively. "He's just the help." He turned to the strapping barbarian. "Go put a shirt on."

Crux returned to the doorway. "I found the training facility. It—" He paused, eyes moving from lady to lady until finally stopping at the blue key in the door. "Oh."

Lash took Kyle's shoulder and ripped him free of his adoring fans. "We have more important matters to attend to."

Arguable, thought Kyle, but he puffed his chest out. When he spoke, his voice was an octave deeper. "My subordinate is right, ladies. I must free the people of this city. Why don't you stay back while I handle this."

Disappointed cries chased him to the door. "We'll find you!" they promised. Lash yanked the blue key from the keyhole as they pushed down the hallway. The harem girls winked and blew kisses after them and he sighed. Saving the world was tough work.

Ahead was a door labeled "Training Facility." The blue key

easily spun that latch open. Bravo Team and Kyle charged forward, weapons drawn.

Aside from a large ring of metal that Kyle swore resembled a Stargate, the room was empty.

"I can't believe it," muttered Lash. "The hardest part of this quest was pulling Kyle away from the naked ladies."

Kyle snorted. "*I* can believe it."

"It gets even harder to believe," said Crux as he examined the machine. "There's an off switch."

The companions approached the control panel and there was indeed a switch to shut the machine down. It was attached to a glowing orb, no doubt its power source.

Lash frowned. "It's already set to off."

The thief winced. "Riddle me this: the fast travel's broken, the portal scroll is useless, and the quest is already complete, so what are we doing here?"

The brewmaster grinned. "Well, some good did come out of it. After all, we found a—"

"Don't say harem," snapped Lash.

Kyle chewed his lip.

"Crux is right. It's a bad sign that the machine's off."

Conan grunted. "It means Hadrian already has his troops."

"He's at full strength," said Hex.

Glinda's eyes brightened. "On the plus side, we don't need to blow our cover by turning this off. We can still sneak off into the sunset."

Kyle saw the worry on their faces, the concern at the turn of events, but he didn't get it at all. To him, this was an opportunity. And the butt stuff was only part of it.

They were here, in the heart of Oakengard and Hadrian's power. As long as that was the case, they had the upper hand.

"Wait," he said, voice laced with confidence and bass even though there were no ladies to impress. "I'm getting the inkling of a plan..."

2040 Boggle

We slogged through the murky wetlands in the dark of night. The more distance we gained from the lake, the more we found ourselves in a bubbling bog of unnatural proportions. The air was heavy and the going was slow. Our boots were saturated with water and slick with moss. The muted colors of the land ranged from olive to forest to burnt orange. Strange, otherworldly, and far from heavenly. In truth, the whole place looked and smelled like Haven's toilet.

I swatted a large bug attempting to take a bite from my sweaty cheek. "And they call this the Godsbog?" I scratched my head idly. "Are we sure we have the right bog?"

Izzy warily hiked forward. Her lavender skin seemed to fare better against the pests, but she was every bit as morose as I was. "I don't like this. The errant folk by definition don't have a home, but this is a good place to find them. According to the texts, the Godsbog is holy to them."

I cracked a smile. "You got that from hours of poring over tomes, huh?"

"That's not all I got," she said defensively.

"So lay it on me then. What are we dealing with here?"

Izzy pressed her lips together and looked around. The wild

king was marching behind us. Vagram was further out but within earshot. Our uneasy partners were making sure to stay apprised of developments. Izzy didn't attempt to hide her words from them.

"The Godsbog isn't holy the way a church or temple is holy. The pagans don't architect places of worship so much as respect the land and pass down legends from generation to generation. Goblins and boggarts and kobolds and"—Izzy nodded to Theoderic—"wildkins don't always see eye to eye, but they all agree that the gods were born from this bog."

I wiped my damp brow, darkening at the implications. Pagan gods were titans, less the wholesome-inner-spirit and more the grinding-of-flesh-and-bone kind. They were very present, very big, and supremely terrifying.

"We have the kraken on our side, at least," I said. "Although it's small and limited, as far as titans go. Do we have any intel on how big Gigas is?"

Izzy's nose wrinkled. "Is the name not enough of an indicator?"

Theoderic splashed ahead lightly. "A giant among giants. Gigas be not a being in the common sense, but the land itself."

I frowned. "Well *that* doesn't sound ominous or anything."

"But what is he?" asked Izzy. "*Where* is he? What can he do and how do we stop him?"

He smiled beneath the mask. "*Her* legends be feathery, her details light. Gigas is the All-Mother, the giver and taker of life."

"I didn't see any of that in the books," muttered the pixie.

"She be known not, even amongst our kin, yet remaineth everlastingly familiar. To appease Gigas, thou must appeal to her maternal nature."

"Swell," I said. "We'll swap muffin recipes and disparage kids these days." I didn't hide my frustration. "Damn. I was kinda hoping having wildkins on our side would make this part easier."

"If you seek to fight alongside us," snapped Cleric Vagram sharply as he converged on them, "you would do well not to needlessly blaspheme."

I scrunched my face as we all trudged forward. "You're still on the no-bad-words thing? Can't you find a way to circumvent that part of your programming? You realize we're at war, surrounded by hundreds in the active military. Cursing comes with the territory."

The cleric brushed blond curls from his face. "I do not circumvent my personal beliefs or my code for *convenience*." He said the last word with a sneer, as if being pragmatic was a compromise. I'd forgotten how tiring it was to travel with him. "I heard you were riding a dragon these days," he added snidely.

I set my jaw. "Working on it."

I eyed the troop of catechists hanging back and reminded myself that Vagram was the reasonable one. The mad bishop was among them somewhere, still recovering. As I considered them, I got the distinct impression that Vagram was likewise studying me.

"What is it?"

The cleric pressed his lips tight. "You hold the Squid's Tooth?"

I focused ahead. "I do. And don't think you're gonna get your hands on it. I almost forgot how hungry the catechists were to recover relics, like the crown of the wild king and the dragonspear."

"Those instances were"—Vagram took a steadying breath —"misguided."

I arched an eyebrow and viewed him askance.

"The devilry worked upon us freed our minds," he explained, "but it twisted them as well."

"You're gonna blame that on Lucifer?"

"It was out of character," he insisted. "Bishop Tannen grew power hungry instead of humble. I was merely following orders."

"And now?"

He glanced toward his men. "The bishop is our leader, and you have yet to prove yourself as much."

"Yet here we march."

"I'm not as concerned with *now* as I am with after the usurper is defeated."

The insinuation angered me. I'd set aside my personal grudges for the greater good. He was the one who'd rewarded me with betrayal. But I didn't want to start the argument anew. What mattered was the catechists were on our side in this fight.

"What do you want me to tell you?" I asked. "I meant everything I said about fighting for freedom."

"And the soulstones? You really mean to destroy them?"

I sighed and opened my quest menu, rotating the window toward Cleric Vagram.

Remove Soulstones from Play

Quest Type: Fepic

Reward: <empty>

The Eye of Orik, the Squid's Tooth, and the Crystal Core have the unwieldy power to dominate Haven. Collect and remove them from play.

He scanned the text with a mix of satisfaction and relief. Maybe seeing it in text felt more official.

"What does fepic mean?" he asked.

"Oh, heheh..." I nervously rubbed the back of my neck. "I don't know. Must be a typo."

He nodded uncertainly. "I see. And you've encountered no objections from them?" Wary eyes shot to the wildkins that currently outnumbered us. We let them wander ahead while the cleric and I spoke in whispers.

"Relax. They're not the problem, they're part of the solution." I swiped to a subquest.

Rally the Errant Folk

Quest Type: Fepic

Reward: <empty>

Various so-called wild races inhabit the land, pagan or otherwise. There is no greater army, given they can be rallied together.

"No greater army," he said with a snort. The cleric was less relieved after reading this quest description. "I'm sure you've been told this before, but you trust too easily. They cannot be relied on."

I closed the menu with a scoff. "And that's *your* problem. You mean to fight the world and impose your views with an iron—bronze—fist. You need to live and let live, man. It's what we're all here for."

The easygoing pack of wildkins jerked their necks and halted their march. They crouched and sniffed the air, drawing spears and hatchets. Izzy turned in a circle and scanned the bog, eyes finally landing on the wild king.

"What is it?" she asked.

Theoderic took a few backward steps as a contingent of his guard enveloped him.

Cleric Vagram showed his teeth, a bronze sword in each hand. "You were saying, Protector of Stronghold?"

I scanned the outskirts. The stifling terrain muted my darkvision, but it wasn't as bad as the Maelstrom or Ashen Moor. I could barely make out small figures darting around us into defensive positions low to the ground.

"Interlopers," called the scratchy voice of General Azzyrk. "What brings you to this holy place?"

Shorehome's guide lamps diffused in the fog, enveloping the horizon in a sickly green glow. The *Void* cut through the ornery coastal waters, silently followed by the *Waveskipper*,

Deepfisher, and *Ugly Puss*. Engagement was imminent.

"They be waitin' fer us," snarled Errol, collapsing the spyglass back into his inventory.

"Of course they are," said Brugo calmly. He stood on the deck of his ship, puffing his chest forward. "The gangs have a taste for power now. Just a nibble, and they're resolved to die for it."

Avisa leaned into the forward handrail, fingers rapping the pommel of her saber. "I can accommodate their wishes."

Aside from the green dock lamps, a front line of orange fires lit up along the coast. The archers would attempt to set their boats alight. The encroaching force pushed through the fog anyway.

Errol examined the *Void's* new special with a sigh.

[Sky Sail]
Midnight-blue fittings for sailing the skies.

While a flying ship would give them a steep advantage in battle, he reminded himself that razing his hometown was not their objective. They needed to get past the defensive front and take the city on foot. The crew waited expectantly as Shorehome's main dock came into view.

Brugo's eyes widened. "My ballistas."

"I believe the proper usage is ballistae," said Grug helpfully.

The Papa worked his jaw and Grug made himself scarce.

The heavy guns had been mounted along the dock to dissuade enemy ships from easily offloading. Between the firepower and the number of combatants on the dock, it was a hefty deterrent.

Hadrian's loyalists led the charge. These were members of the Brothers in Black, Brugo's own faction, who had pledged to the Whisperer over the Papa. It was Hadrian's betrayal and subsequent capture that had spurred all the other gangs into rebellion. As the *Void* neared, the crew made out the telltale colors of the smaller criminal elements on the coastal boardwalk. As Brugo had surmised, they were here to fight for their scraps.

"Line her up," ordered Errol. Grug turned the wheel to settle the *Void* on the same axis as the dock. It meant the rear ballistae would have their line of fire blocked by the forward guns and defenders. Unfortunately, the subdocks branched out perpendicularly from the main, and those ballistae retained their firing lines.

"No," Brugo said. "Steer into the kill zone. Draw their fire, fast and furious, and use the *Void's* special to phase safely through."

"Can't do it," said Errol. "We already phased fer the day."

"Then wait for midnight to approach."

The captain shook his head. "We need t' save that special fer the real fight."

"This *is* the real fight."

"Condolences, Papa, but we can't take the chance." Errol glanced sidelong at Brugo, hoping he wouldn't pull rank. It was, technically, still his ship. "The *Void* can take some fire," he added.

"Ready!" came the cries from the dock.

The ballistae spun around frantically as the dark ships came into view. The flagship, in the lead, predictably garnered most of the attention. Its line of attack, also predictably, frustrated the defenders. It took them longer to get into place.

"Aim!" they called.

Admiral Errol Oates grinned.

Gargantuan tentacles curled around the forward ballista. Loyalist cries cut short as the kraken smashed them. The heavy gun buckled and the entire platform sagged into the sea.

"The kraken! Fire!"

Ballistae swiveled as the sea monster disappeared beneath them. The loyalists went frantically quiet until the kraken emerged along another length of dock. Appendages ripped through wood and men alike. The heavy guns that managed to fire did negligible damage to the titan.

"Close!" ordered Errol. "Come about!"

The *Void* altered its trajectory and sped past the ruined head of the main dock. The flagship turned and aligned its starboard side with a subdock full of defenders.

"Fire!"

BABOOM, BOOM. BABOOM, BOOM.

Cannonballs plowed through the defending force, scattering loyalists into the water and destroying their ballista.

Avisa's saber slid from its sheath, pointed skyward, and fell forward. "Charge!"

Pirates leapt over the gunwale and landed on the dock, raiders in their own town. They pressed forward as other sections of the dock were similarly taken by the support ships. Fire arrows plugged the *Void's* hull, but they were too little, too late compared to the outgoing onslaught. As the kraken moved for the coast and pulled itself onto the boardwalk, the criminal gangs scattered.

"Remember!" growled Brugo. "No pillaging, only killing. I'm gonna need my town back." A pair of axes flashed into his hands. He zeroed in on a contingent of loyalists and jumped to the dock to give chase.

2050 Dino Crisis

Vague shapes moved in the darkness, smaller ones giving way to a larger mass. What I first thought was an ogre cleared up on approach, and I really wished it hadn't. I'd seen this giant lizard before. The reptilian beast was lumbering and smelly. It was purple with green stripes and loped with a zigzag to accommodate a fat belly. Leather reins secured a bit inside a wide mouth brimming with tiny serrated teeth. The mount made an unsettling swallowing sound as it neared.

In the saddle sat the goblin general himself. Azzyrk, for his part, was no less imposing. Although his race was short in stature, he appeared fierce beyond his size. His features were stern and striking, even among goblins. A long curled nose, earlobes that drooped down to points, and sharp ridges on his brow. He wore bright-red war paint and had thick bone piercings in his cheeks.

"The Protector of the white city," he said mockingly. "Have you abandoned your charge?" He turned the lizard in a loop and addressed his men. "Or is he here to exterminate our people?"

Sniggers rang out around us, dissonant and hoarse. The mirthful chorus grew till its volume was overwhelming. We were surrounded by more pagans than we could see. With the wildkins and catechists combined, we were two-hundred strong. If the entire horde was here they had us grossly outnumbered, on their terrain no less.

I slyly coordinated on captain chat while calling out to the general.

"You're right to presume I'm here on behalf of Stronghold," I said loudly for all to hear, "but I'm here for all of Haven as well. I'm here to ask for your help."

Azzyrk's grating chuckle sounded like a grindstone. "We know why you're here, Protector. Do you take our witches for cowards who would hide after being captured and hanged in your human cities?"

They knew. Word from the boggarts had outpaced us. The goblins knew and still met us with hard faces. I went with what had seemed to convince Vagram and the witches before him.

"We're on a quest to destroy the soulstones and free the titans."

The general's toothy smile remained hostile. "Pagan scouts report that Orik, the Mighty One, the Leveler of Cities, is already free. In fact, he's on his way to join us."

Damn, word *really* traveled fast.

Pagans, as a whole, weren't a unified organization. By all measures they were an afterthought by the devs. A loose faction of baddies to provide fodder for valiant adventurers, their grouping was one of convenience and category. Rather than subscribe to any one way of life and leader, they were splintered into roving bands and tribes. General Azzyrk was a chieftain of sorts—he just happened to be the one with the largest tribe. His horde was a shadow of its former self, but his power was still respected and feared. Speaking with him face-to-face, I was beginning to understand his awful charisma firsthand.

I took a measured breath and spoke. "Orik is one of three—"

"And they are three of nine," he crowed.

I nodded. The legends told of nine great cities built on the backs of nine terrible titans. Haven's beta test in the Midlands only accounted for a third of that—I was speaking practically while the mob's viewpoint was steeped in lore. I ignored the correction and pushed on.

"We still need to contend with the kraken and Gigas."

Azzyrk turned to his people and guffawed. "No one *contends* with gods. We are puny to the Mighty One. He shall roam the wild and level the land, as it was meant. And you will tremble before him."

"Many humans will die!" chirped a goblin from the background.

"Many cities will fall!" cackled another.

Azzyrk grinned hungrily. "Maybe it's time for the wild to reclaim the land."

Theoderic stepped past me and stood unfazed before Azzyrk and lizard alike, the stag on the wild king's chest brandished without fear. "Forsooth, 'tis the very same—call it the wind, call it the wild—that beckons us to action."

Azzyrk, who'd thus far done an admirable job of ignoring the wildkin contingent, settled yellow eyes on the self-outcast ruler. "And what would *your highness* know of the call of the wild? You've done no favors for your kith."

"Alack, our purposes have crossed not. I favor my kin, I do. A home, they possesseth, ripe with sanctity and warmth. If isolation be the will of the people, there was no better way to serve."

The general grimaced as he worked through Theoderic's poetic diction. "Yeah, well, my feud isn't with your kind. The wildkins are friends of the pagans, brothers in blood if not in battle. Don't forget you left us high and dry."

"Shalt thou return the favor?"

The general's features hardened. The skin around his eyes pinched in agitation. "The goblin horde never runs from a fight. From anyone. You'd best take your kind back over the Lake of Dreams and let us finish our business with the humans."

A throaty rumble escaped the warden of the Blackwood. The goblins on the outskirts chittered and shuffled. Even Azzyrk's prehistoric lizard sidestepped from the sound.

The pittering chuckle of the wild king followed. "I blame not that enmity yours, yet thou meanst to battle an enemy false. A purple plague is upon the land, budding and ravenous."

A few goblins turned to Izzy. The lavender pixie crossed her arms. "Not me!" Theoderic smiled.

Azzyrk grunted. "We know of the Violet Order. They stay out of the Godsbog. They skirt or cross the Lake of Dreams, or patrol the mountains." The general fixed a glare on Cleric Vagram. "Same as you and your priests agreed."

Color me surprised. There'd been previous contact between the catechists and the goblins despite their ideologies being polar opposites and in direct defiance of each other.

On one hand, it made sense for Vagram. He was stern and powerful and a tactical leader. His hundred priests had been on the run, hiding from Oakengard patrols and at times engaging in guerrilla warfare with Black Hats. In an odd concession to practicality, Cleric Vagram decided not to add goblins to his list of active enemies.

Yet the same rationale little applied to the horde. General Azzyrk was helping Hadrian, likely being used and possibly unaware. His assault on Stronghold had coincided with the spymaster's escape. Why then would the horde not descend on the catechists? Why ask the Violet Order to stay out of the Godsbog?

"You're afraid of them," I announced, suddenly appreciating Azzyrk's shrewdness.

He raised an eyebrow. "What's that you're going on about?"

"The Violet Order. You've asked them to keep their distance."

He grunted sharply. Dismissively. "The Godsbog is holy ground. Our kind has always resented crusader breaches into it."

I shook my head. "This is more than that. You know what Hadrian's capable of. You've been fighting for him, alongside him, but you're not his lapdog. You have the fate of your own people to worry about."

He lifted his chin. "The same can be said about all leaders."

Our eyes met for a second. My face softened slightly. "It can. That's why the boggart witches listened to reason. That's why Cleric Vagram and the wild king stand beside each other. Why the crusaders march with the Black Hats, and Papa Brugo retakes Shorehome in our name. Even Haven's developers, and Christian Everett the creator, side with us. We're all leaders seeking the betterment of our people."

While I was proud of the point, the general absorbed the

speech with a casual sneer. "You speak of the creator, the so-called White King and his saints who cast us as adversaries to the world. We're just evil pagans to you." The goblin leaned to the side and spat into the murk.

It was a misstep to mention the developers. "The saints are no more," I offered in concession.

"Yet the crusaders and catechists fight on."

"They were also directed by the saints, but no longer. They have free will now, just like me and you."

Azzyrk surveyed his men as he pondered my words. "You are free to follow your own gods. The horde will follow theirs. Orik will make his way to us, and his will be a wild and mighty rage."

The wild king cocked his head. Izzy stood with crossed arms. Dune muttered under his breath. Vagram's expression was openly hostile, but even he refrained from speaking. The success of this venture was hinging on me.

I paced into the space before the lizard and casually drew my dragonspear. Murmurs spread throughout the onlooking goblins. Murmurs closely followed by spits and curses.

"There was a time," I called out, voice cutting through the mire, "that I meant to use this on you." The general's eyes narrowed. "There was a time I used it on Orik."

Goblins gnashed their teeth and beat the ground. "Titanslayer!"

"Those times may come again," I continued undeterred. I deftly twirled the spear in my grip. "But I do not seek those moments." I faced Azzyrk straight on. "I'll defend myself against Orik again if I have to. If he comes for me."

The general chortled. "That's likely to be sooner than later."

I cocked my head. "I think you'd be surprised at his destination. Orik the Mighty isn't returning home to the Godsbog. Oh, he'll enter the holy ground all right, but only on the way to his master at Oakengard."

"That's preposterous. Pagans can't enter—" The general's breath caught. He flinched backward ever so slightly and paused to mull it over. The pagan ban on entering cities only applied during saintly control. Hadrian possessing the Crystal Core nullified that protection.

"Orik can enter Oakengard," I insisted. "He's already tried. The cyclops demolished the Pantheon after failing to access its fast travel." Whether that bit was true or not was impossible to know for sure, but it sure made my point. With as fast as word traveled, Azzyrk was sure to have heard of the Mighty One's destruction.

The experienced general worked sharp teeth together. "Where is the Eye?" he demanded. "Who holds it?"

My lips crooked in a modest show of advantage. "You mean... Hadrian didn't return it to the people after he stole it?"

Azzyrk's eyes flared. His painted face grew even more red with rage. "The Whisperer holds the Eye?" He turned to Theoderic. "Is this true, king?"

The ruler sighed before responding. "Know I only what mine eyes see, and see I only what mine heart knows."

The general's lizard turned southward. Azzyrk fumed at the mountain range, as if his will was enough to bring the distant fortress into focus. "That scheming human conniver!"

I pressed in his moment of anger. "What do you think will happen when Orik sets foot in Oakengard? Will the Whisperer kindly hand over the eye and bid the cyclops on his way? Will the Mighty One bend the knee to Hadrian's will, an endeavor even the boggart witches failed at? No, you're clever enough to work out the only shot Hadrian has of controlling a god. You can guess Orik's fate."

"Hadrian means to infect him with the plague." The goblin general scowled at his people. "He means to take control of a god. Of *our* god."

"There's a reason he styles himself a god emperor." I stepped close enough to feel the hot breath of the lizard mount. "We need to stop Orik from reaching Oakengard, or he won't be Orik anymore. He'll be an unstoppable weapon, aimed even at you."

The general's lips curled. "So it is that humans enter a holy place for a holy cause. You mean to stop the titan at the Godsbog."

"If that's what it takes. I come to you with no tricks, no lies. I don't fight for the titans, but I fight for the people." I produced the Squid's Tooth and held it in sight of the horde. "And in the name of the people, I mean to destroy these."

"Would your cities not suffer?"

"The world suffers with them. I don't worry about the loss of the soulstones. Saintly control is gone anyway. Our cities will prosper. We can all fend for ourselves."

General Azzyrk looked over his horde and idly chattered his teeth. "And here I thought the pagans would enjoy a mighty charge this day."

"You won't attack us then?"

"Most of *you* are my kith. I don't seek war with the wildkins. And although I don't know how much faith to put in your words,

I know how much Hadrian's are worth."

The tension in my shoulders eased. "Will you fight with us?"

"We'll fight for the Mighty One," he stressed. "And the All Mother. And the Lurking Deep. If your people will do the same, we'll allow them passage."

"That's great!" I said, honestly completely surprised. Azzyrk was harsh and grumpy and his lizard was really disgusting to be around, but the encounter was turning into a breath of fresh air. "We'll need an alliance," I said. "Another armistice isn't enough. We need to ensure mutual support. Just as with all cooperating factions."

The general studied the leaders present and gave a sharp nod. "You'll have your alliance."

I was stupefied silent. After a moment, I fumbled into my faction controls to request it.

"Not so fast," barked the general. Azzyrk put one leg over the other and slid off his saddle. "The moment you stuck that titanslayer into Orik's eye, I swore a blood feud with you." He drew a jagged scimitar from the lizard's saddle bag and squared with me. "The Black Hats can have an alliance after I've extracted my pound of flesh."

2060 Combat

The mass of goblins chittered and jumped and jawed as the circle surrounding us constricted. Ogres pushed forward to act as enforcers. Theoderic reverently backed away with his people.

"Uh," muttered Izzy, "what does everyone think they're doing right now?"

I gripped the dragonspear tight, eyes on the perimeter. "Tell me you're not serious about this, Azzyrk."

"Dead serious. And so you'll be. This is a duel to the death."

Vagram and the clerics held weapons forward as the pagan horde converged. Dune's bow was nocked.

I threw my hand up to appease the catechists. "Wait." The goblins moved in hungrily, beady eyes on me. I again appealed to the general. "What does this accomplish? We mean to fight together. Our people need us."

Azzyrk shrugged. "Can't be helped."

"This is exactly what Hadrian wants."

"This is what I want," he spat. "And what you want. An alliance, right? These are my terms." The goblin general scraped a hand across the flat of the scimitar, applying some type of poison. He pulled the lizard's reins around and slapped its hindquarters. The beast lumbered to the sidelines.

"Does it need to be to the death?" I hedged. "A respawn doesn't help either of us right now."

"It'll be you who respawns. And it *can't be helped*. You need to fight if you want peace. A few drops of blood will avoid a bath."

I groaned in defiance to the logic. But I wasn't blind. The horde was hungry. I imagined their endless marches, their lengthy sieges and struggles at Stronghold's massive walls, their panicked scrambling from a flying dragon. They finally had an enemy right in front of them. I scanned the crowd of priests. I wondered where the wildkins would fall in.

"And you'll agree to the alliance after the duel? Just you and me, and everyone else marches together?"

The general impatiently tested the weight of his weapon. "That's what I said, didn't I?"

"We're not letting you fight alone," stressed Izzy.

Dune nodded. "It's risky. He's a red mob."

I considered the general. Mob colors were consistently accurate indicators of strength. Azzyrk was red when I'd first encountered him. It was impressive that, as much as I'd leveled since then, he was still red. But I'd killed reds before, and the dragonspear had a 15% damage bonus against pagans.

The circle around us had tightened to fifty feet, lined mostly by goblins and ogres. The wildkins had backed out behind the line. The adamant priests stood their ground on the outskirts and served as a portion of the wall. Izzy and Dune stood with me.

I squared up to Azzyrk. "I agree," I said.

"Not a chance," snapped Izzy. "If you fight, I fight."

"Then you'll resign everyone here to picking a side and fighting to the death."

"We could take them."

I stepped close and rested a comforting hand on her arm. "It's not about who would win. We need these soldiers—both sides. We need to set an example of what we're willing to lay on the line to make things right." My gaze strayed from her and fixed on Vagram in the distance. "We *will* stand together."

"Come on, Izzy," said Dune. "We'll be right here." He moved toward the crowd. "For the Black Hats."

She swallowed, angry eyes fixed on me. "For the Black Hats."

The ranger pointed at my weapon with a smile. "Dibs on the dragonspear if you go down."

I rolled my eyes and pointed the spear at Azzyrk. Its reach overpowered that of his curved sword by a ridiculous margin. "Have at me then," I said plainly.

The general showed his teeth and advanced. His approach was cautious, at an angle to my driving arm. The arena was spacious enough that I could backtrack and spin away from his steps, keeping him firmly at my head.

He tested me with a slash. The jagged teeth off his blade raked off the smooth spear. He readied a counter but I didn't bite, choosing instead to plant my feet as he did.

"What's the matter with you?" he growled in annoyance. "Don't you want blood?"

"Not why I'm here," I told him.

"It's the only way this ends."

I hiked a shoulder playfully. "Maybe you'll get tired."

His scimitar struck my weapon again. This time the goblin

ducked the spear and drove it up with his free hand while he charged under my guard. I flipped the dragonspear overhead, planted it in the ground behind me, and vaulted clear over the short leader. I landed in the mud fifteen feet from him, spinning and resuming the standoff.

Azzyrk snorted. "You're a slippery one."

My spider boots squished on the spongy moss. "This is a slippery place."

The general smiled. "That it is."

He charged me again with the same move. Slash, weapon control, charge. This time my boot got stuck in the backpedal. The moss of the Godsbog gave way more than before. By contrast, the goblin's steps were lighter than ever as his diminutive body pittered over the terrain. I did get my vault off but Azzyrk managed to graze my leg with his blade. I deftly landed and scanned for sturdier ground when I noticed the damage report.

> DoT: 150 dmg/15 secs

My eyes widened at the unusually high damage affliction. I was facing fighting at half health if I didn't stop it. Caduceus raised her bone pick from the sideline.

"No support!" snarled the general.

I waved her off and popped a health vial. The smaller potion didn't heal as much, but it cured the poison and came with a much shorter cooldown time. Either way, I wouldn't be able to heal again during this duel. I soaked in the feeling as my health ticked back to max.

"That's your one," he said drily.

I clenched my jaw. "That's okay. I learn from my mistakes." Even if I did get hit again, I was hoping the poison didn't hit so hard on subsequent uses. Sometimes that was the way of things.

Azzyrk and I continued our slow dance. This time I reserved extra attention to the terrain. Darkvision sharpened my night sight. A combination of my exploration and navigation skills assisted in choosing the sturdier portions of the bog. I could see it now. General Azzyrk wasn't just circling me, he was angling me onto softer ground. He was a more tactical fighter than I would've guessed. I supposed, at the very least, it showed he respected me as an opponent.

As I backed nearer a marsh, I took my eyes off him for a second to scan my surroundings. Azzyrk batted my spear aside and charged. I readied the crossblock and triggered the skill as the scimitar came down. The blade clanged against my legendary weapon. The general reversed into a spin and I activated dash, shooting past him in the other direction. Azzyrk slashed empty air and growled as he fixed on me.

"Fight me, you coward!" he demanded. "I'll not be toyed with."

"I'm trying to prove my intentions here."

"That you're an annoying brat?"

"That I don't want to fight you."

He grunted. "It doesn't matter what you want!"

Azzyrk pressed a wild series of strikes. The dragonspear met each as I backed away. When he tried to slip underneath, I put my weight on the weapon and pushed his arm to the ground, plunging half the scimitar into the wet moss. We were stuck there a full second. It was enough time to reset my guard and hit him dead on, but I wasn't looking for that. I braced the spear downward, trying to force him to release the sword.

Azzyrk fell forward to the ground, swinging on my spear with his free hand. From the lowered stance, he pulled his sword free, slashing through the soft ground. The jagged edge came up with strings of moss. As I attempted to yank my spear back, he used his weight on it to pull to his feet and lunge forward. With him behind the guard of my weapon, I triggered spinshield. An immediate whirlwind swept me around and deflected him away.

The rebuffed goblin wiped his weapon clean and sneered. I wasn't really waiting for him to get tired, of course. I wasn't a coward, I wasn't toying with him, and even though he was growing angrier with every dodge, that wasn't my intention either. It was only when the pagan aurochs horns sounded that my strategy became clear.

The horde chittered excitedly and the general's sharp brow creased. He pointed his sword at me. "You were stalling. You've sent for reinforcements."

I kept my spear ready. "Haven't you been paying attention? We're in the middle of a war. You've surrounded the wildkins and catechists, but have you considered the rest of my army?"

A goblin on the sideline wailed. "Tricksies human!" The mass of the horde shuffled and reoriented themselves. "They ambushes us!" cried another.

In the distance, the banners of the Black Hat army caught the moonlight. The formations were haphazard in the uneven Godsbog, but my support was unflinchingly bearing down.

"So your claims of peace were a ruse," spat Azzyrk. "A show

of force won't sway us."

As cunning as the general was, he wasn't very smart. I gritted my teeth. "The army's not here for the horde. We've been marching to Oakengard for two days. At worst I plan on passing through unmolested, but my intention is and always has been to recruit you."

"And my intention is to satisfy the blood feud."

He turned his back on me to assess the situation. I wondered if his guard was lowered enough for me to attempt my subdue skill. Then again, a submission hardly seemed an appropriate way to end a blood feud. He snapped his attention back to me, ending my deliberation.

"Nothing changes then," he announced aloud. "If you're true to your word, I'll be true to mine. The horde will allow you safe passage." The general wiped the dirt from his blade on a fur leg guard. "But only once our business is done."

The general rushed me again. Very reckless. All around us, soldiers were shuffling with panic and excitement and itching for a fight, and Azzyrk had decided to charge with blood in his eyes. He bashed my spear aside with hand and blade. I couldn't believe he was doubling down in the presence of a greater army. The surprise amounted to just enough indecision that he caught me flat on my feet. Instead of a graceful parry, I stumbled backward and activated crossblock.

Only the general's wild swing was a feint. Without an actual weapon to deflect, my defensive stance did nothing but limit my reach. Azzyrk hopped to the side and struck his real blow low, once again slicing my leg.

DoT: 45 dmg/15 secs

Thankfully, forcing the scimitar through the muddy water had wiped most of the poison away. Azzyrk's lips pressed tight as he realized he wasn't gonna take me down with a DoT. Before he could react, I pulled my spear close and activated tornado spin.

Unlike spinshield, this skill dealt damage. For once I was thankful it had been nerfed. I hit the general with a series of painful slashes but the damage was minimal. Azzyrk glared at me and roared.

That was okay. I was getting a little mad myself.

"Apa! Apa!"

A goblin girl broke through the circle. She had reddish-blonde hair, wore crude hide, and had a stone hammer slung over her back. It was Jixa, and she was yelling at General Azzyrk.

"Apa! Yous no hurtses hims."

The fierce general's scowl evaporated. "Luluberry? What are you doing here?"

"Hereses is Black Hats. Jixa is Black Hats."

"What?" The scimitar waved my way. "This is the Protector of the white city. I'm here to kill him."

The girl slapped the chieftain in the face. "Talon giveses Jixa work. Giveses Jixa home. Jixa buildses the white city."

Azzyrk and I blinked in disbelief, but for entirely different reasons. "Wait, wait, wait," I said. "Time out. Are you two related?"

The goblin builder turned to me with a proud smile. "Jixa is the great General Azzyrk's daughter."

Azzyrk massaged his cheek with a palm. "One of many daughters."

She upturned her chin. "His favoriteses."

Baz and the other Black Hat pagans pushed into the arena. The ogre's eyes lit up when he found Jixa again.

"Uh," I started, unsure where to go from here. "Does this mean we should cancel the blood feud?"

Jixa's face blanched. "Blood feud? *Apa*, youses embarrassing me in fronts of boss man. Blood feudses old fashioned. Only country goblinses make blood feuds. Jixa city goblin."

"Kids these days," he chided. "No respect for the people or traditions that got you here. I can't just cancel a blood feud."

"Sures you can! Talon willses give you blood gift. You callses off feud."

"A gift?" I stammered.

"Now, dear," noted the general in a fatherly tone, "a blood gift must be a meaningful expression of a kindred cause, as well as something the recipient greatly desires. There's no way the Protector of the white city knows what I want."

I blinked at my inventory, dumbfounded as the words of the boggart witches echoed in my mind. It takes a titan to rally the errant. I produced Lucifer's bobblehead and tossed it to Azzyrk, hoping he wouldn't mind the regift.

The general's eyes widened. "An Orik chibi?!? This is the last one I need to complete the Titans of Yore set!"

"There!" announced Jixa with a slap to her father's back. "No moreses blood feud. Youses and boss mans be friends."

"He can't be your boss," muttered the flabbergasted father. "He's a human."

She rolled her eyes hard. "No say that, *Apa*. Humanses teach me: that racist." She crossed her arms triumphantly.

The general scowled and paced toward his mount. "Racist? I'm not racist. He turned the Mighty One to stone."

"Convenient excuse," she countered, walking alongside him. "Admits it. You hateses the white city because it humanses city."

"That's not true! I have lots of human friends."

"You do? Who?"

"You know... I'm sure I can come up with one." His eyes lit up. "What about that baby Chowa's nephew kidnapped?"

Izzy and Dune strolled up as the arguing goblin family disappeared between the ogre enforcers and the waning crowd. The goblin audience was breaking up as they realized there'd be no blood sport today.

"Uh, hello?" I said, waving the dragonspear in the air. "Blood feud, anyone? I was just getting started."

Izzy snorted. "Sure you were."

"I was."

"You did 17 points of damage to him."

I scoffed. "That was on purpose! I was stalling till the army showed up."

Dune's eyes narrowed. "Wait, you knew Jixa was related to the general?"

"Hell no, I just figured adding four hundred armed troops to the mix would be incentive to stop the fight."

Baz, listening nearby, exploded into crude laughter. "Har har har! Little yooman funny. Soldiers don't stop fight, soldiers make fight. Har har har!" The ogre stomped away like I was the stupidest person in the world.

After a moment, I begrudgingly hiked a shoulder. "I guess I underestimated the determination of the goblin horde."

Izzy snorted. "Just be glad blood is thicker than blood feuds."

As the pagans recollected to the west, the human army approached from the north. It was slow going. The road in the Godsbog wasn't much of one. If it wasn't dirt it was mud, otherwise it was moss. Some stretches of ground were waterlogged and supported with rotten logs and stones. No wonder Oakengard was so protected. It was isolated by the impassable Skyscrapers, an endless lake, and grimy wetlands.

Our disparate party sheathed our weapons and greeted Buildmaster General Trafford and Colonel Grimwart.

"Aye," exclaimed the old man. "You're a sight for sore eyes. And in the flesh, too!"

"These are the new troops you reported in captain chat?" I asked, admiring the wave of knights in black cloth.

"That they are."

"The most dependable cavalry in Haven," added Grimwart.

I nodded. "Well, now they'll be backed up by the best healer regiment." I pointed to the collected catechists. My good humor experienced a hiccup and my face went grim. "Bishop Tannen is among them. Terms of the alliance."

The usually collected Grimwart was shocked by the news. "My countrymen! I must see to them." He spun away, collected two of his sergeants, and headed for the priests.

Trafford studied me with his good eye and scratched his wild hair. "Now, correct me if I'm wrong, son. I'm an old man with a foggy memory. Didn't Bishop Tannen steal the Eye of Orik and attempt to take over Stronghold?"

I spoke through tight lips. "He did."

"Uh-huh. And isn't that pretty much the same thing we're fighting Hadrian for?"

I didn't answer this time. Not all our peace would come at the hands of a lucky familial connection. In a war of this magnitude, we needed the army of healers more than anybody else.

The march continued as the moon rose higher in the sky. It had been a while since I'd been with the troops so I did my rounds. That included checking on Kyle and Lash and Errol in chat. Everyone had their problems to deal with, but ours were especially menial.

Driving supply wagons through the Godsbog was excruciating. Exhaustion swept the ranks, wagon wheels broke, Karen died of dysentery—it was like Oregon Trail all over again. I came up with a plan of action after Nooner gave me the full update.

"Ditch the wagons. They're light enough now that we don't need them. Reshuffle the supplies into saddlebags on the oxen. They'll walk through the bog easier only managing four legs."

The gangster-turned-cattle-driver nodded along to my instructions. "Oi, that's a workable idea, but it requires reorganizing a village's worth of inventory. It'll take time we surely don't have."

I surveyed the area. We'd just pushed up a steppe to slightly higher ground in the bog. It wasn't dry, but the stiff plants clung to the soil and provided a measure of drainage. It wasn't perfect, but there was no perfect place for hundreds of people to sleep. "We'll camp here for the night. Everyone can take shifts reorganizing supplies."

As Nooner went to work, I hurried to the priests and wildkins to relay the decision. They were accustomed to the terrain and happy to stop for the night. The first objection unsurprisingly came from Trafford. If his constant cursing was any indication, he definitely wasn't keen on the idea.

"You did a great job getting this force through the Cloven Path as fast as possible," I told him. "It's time to rest now. The soldiers need it after we skimped on camp last night. We can't head into battle disorganized and buried by fatigue debuffs."

"I'm not talkin' bout the debuffs and you know it," argued the old man. "I believe in you and all, but what about the titan? If we stop here for the night, Orik'll be sure to catch up to us."

"I'm counting on it. It takes a titan to rally the errant, and we're way past bobbleheads."

"What's that now?"

"Nothing." I nodded him off and headed toward the next group. "Get this army in shape for the big battle tomorrow."

"You got it, supreme commander."

I chuckled as I marched away. What a lovable pain in my ass.

2070 Streets of Rage

The Papa of all Papas stomped forward through the streets. The beaches and boardwalk were littered with bodies. His axes and bare chest were awash in blood. Idle fires burned, and the war-torn cries of the injured were dying down.

Brugo stepped lightly over the corpses of the last pocket of loyalists. The cowards had fled Underkeep. Their might had buckled at the first sign of trouble. With the leaders of the rebellion running for their lives, the smaller gangs had lost their footing. Some unwisely resorted to attacking any opposition, but the smart gangs executed tactical retreats and disappeared into the shadows.

The fishmongers and dockworkers were the first to capitulate. There were other gangs, more dangerous gangs. They needed to be reined in rather than dealt with. But the loyalists came first.

Brugo stopped over a sniveling man. He was clawing at the dirt road, gasping through mud caked on his face. Blood leaked from his ruined nose and jaw. Brugo laid a heavy boot to his back and spun him over. The man shielded his face with his hands and averted his eyes.

"*You* are a lucky man," announced Brugo. Behind him, a

goblin family ran to safety. The Papa frowned at the sniveling man and the street littered with dirty weapons. "Do you not care to hear why?" When the man didn't answer, Brugo pressed his boot into his stomach. The gang member grimaced, eyes shut, but his hands lowered to the boot.

"P-please," he said.

"You are a lucky man because you are the last of Hadrian's loyalists. The last of the men who swore to *me* yet served *him*." Brugo lifted the boot and paced around the prisoner. "This distinction earns you an exceptional farewell. I shall string you onto the posts of the boardwalk and have the crows and the crabs pick at your flesh. Your suffering will last weeks. Do you hear me?"

The man opened his eyes. Their unnatural violet glow shook the hard crime boss down to his bones, yet this was unapparent to the few observers who gathered. Brugo turned to them, his people now, and hid a shiver.

"Or perhaps you are lucky because, in the interest of mending a wounded city, Papa Brugo deigns to show mercy."

His axe came down swiftly, severing the head of the last holdout. As it rolled to a stop, the eerie light in the eyes went out.

"Papa," called Avisa, approaching with her guard. "We have a gift."

Errol shoved forward a man in plain leathers. The assassin's head humbly drooped to the ground.

Brugo studied him as he approached. "You are Poe, notorious among the assassin collective."

"The head of it now," spat Avisa. "He took advantage of the

shakeup in the city to seize power without your consent."

Brugo's eyebrows stretched high. "Did you now?"

"You were no longer here to appeal to," rushed the assassin. "I only took over to keep the collective in line. I surrendered to your people of my own volition."

The words came out honestly enough. When Brugo checked the guard, Errol nodded confirmation.

"And I come with a gift," said Poe nervously. Reaching under his leathers, he pulled a chain of manacled iron from his neck. "Your powerchain," he offered reverently, "taken from the man I replaced, from the people who turned against you."

Brugo yanked the offering into his hands and studied the twisted links. With a heavy breath, he pulled the charm over his head and once again became the official Protector of Shorehome.

Spectators converged in the alleys. The fishmongers were there. The dockworkers and shipwrights. Standing before him, however, was the representative of the assassin collective, one of the most powerful and feared gangs in the city. The freelancers who, out of duty, could never join the Brothers in Black but had often dealt plainly with them.

"And you would presume to be a Papa?" asked Brugo.

Poe's head lowered again. "I would, but only at the whim of my boss, the Papa of all Papas. The collective continues to support you."

The Papa of the raiders approached and knelt beside Poe. "I'm with you, Papa of all Papas," said the gruff man.

And so Brugo stood as the seven approved Papas beneath him pledged their loyalty to him once again.

The moon dimly lit the pagan horde as I weaved through their encampment, which looked more like a scene from Burning Man than an organized military affair. Even under a single commander, they were a mass of disparate units. Kobolds gambling over bones, handlers feeding beasts of burden and terror, stray trolls lumbering about. Animalistic imps swarmed in pockets, around campfires, looking for scraps of food, and chasing unlucky swamp critters.

The bulk of the pagan horde was comprised of goblins, every bit as varied as player classes. Shamans, tinkerers, warriors, bandits. Yellow and orange eyes locked on the lone human invading their space. It unnerved me, but then it would unnerve anyone.

"Conqueror," called out General Azzyrk from my flank, finding me before I found him.

"Just who I was looking for. I hope you don't mind a bunch of outsiders making camp in the Godsbog."

He ignored the pleasantries and grumpily tore a piece of meat from a bone with daggerlike teeth.

"Better to rest now," I added, feeling an explanation was expected. "Once we emerge from the wetlands, Oakengard scouts will spot us."

Azzyrk chewed with an open mouth. "It's a good decision. Like recruiting my daughter. You're full of good decisions." He glowered. "Probably why I haven't managed to kill you yet."

My eyebrows shot up at the alarming honesty. I was stuck for a moment considering whether to come back at him hard but decided it better to deflect the comment. "Good thing I had that bobblehead, right?"

He spat a glob of skin from his mouth. "Damn cooks. I hate it when they burn the skin. Flesh is supposed to be soft and wet." He lapped his tongue over sharpened teeth and frowned. "The chibi was a nice gesture, but it wasn't the real gift. Jixa told me what you did for her. I owe you for that. As long as you stay true to your word and destroy the soulstones, our blood feud is over. And one more thing."

A notification popped up.

Black Hat Alert:
The Pagans have entered an alliance!

Pagan Reputation +100

The progress didn't stop there.

Quest Complete: **Rally the Errant Folk**
Quest Type: Fepic
Reward: <empty>
The pagans have agreed to fight at your side.
1,000 XP awarded

General Azzyrk tossed the half-eaten bone to the ground and stomped away looking for someone to punish. I barely had time to reflect on the accomplishment when another quest notification came through.

Quest Complete: **Quash Shorehome Unrest**

Quest Type: Fepic

Reward: <empty>

The loyalists have been crushed and Shorehome is back to normal.

1,000 XP awarded

Nice timing. Saint Peter's dying wishes were getting closer to fruition.

Talon: *Kyle, everything still golden on your end?*
Kyle: *One sec, bro. Trying really hard to concentrate right now.*

I tensed.

Talon: *Is your cover blown?*
Lash: *I think he's trying not to blow, actually. We're hiding out in a harem, of all places.*

I swallowed, pondering how to phrase my follow-up question, but was fortunately rescued by a change of subject.

Lash: *At the turn of the day, Kyle will be able to stockrig us a distraction. Until then, we're waiting on you. We're in position.*

> **Kyle:** *I'm technically in three positions right now, but what she said.*

I blinked a few times before shaking it off. It was probably better not to know. The important thing was they were safe, out of sight, and out of mind.

I stared blankly at the moonlit wetlands and the hundreds and hundreds of men and women, fighters and mages, rogues and workers, players, NPCs, and mobs, and cracked a measured smile.

It was all coming together.

As I idled back toward my personal campfire, a coarse voice grated my ears.

"There is a last," drawled Crowlat.

I spun to the boggarts that had snuck unusually close. To hide my nerves, I brought attention to my quest menu.

> **Remove Soulstones from Play**
> Blocked by: **Restore Oakengard's Glory**

"We're getting there," I said plainly.

"You've accomplished the agreeable," nodded Somlat.

Havlat's snort sounded more like a bark. "What comes next is anything but."

I swallowed in the face of the three blind witches. "I'm gonna need your help with Orik tomorrow."

"We will do our part," assured Crowlat. "But you must do yours."

"All of you," added Somlat, somewhat darkly.

"No one's let me down so far," I told them.

Havlat sniggered but held her tongue.

"You cannot trust the catechists," urged Crowlat. "Their existence hinges on our destruction."

I worked my jaw slowly. "They've often claimed the same about you."

Crowlat's empty eyes stared hard.

"Bah!" spat Havlat. "Let the blind lead the blind. It is the only way."

Somlat nodded. "The only way."

Crowlat just grunted, turned, and limped away with her sisters.

I headed back to camp more determined than ever to have all the pieces in place for what needed to come.

<<<T-Minus 1 Day Till Launch>>>

2080 Darksiders

I packed up the bedroll early. The supplies were ready for the oxen, food and rest was taken care of. The dawn mists over the Godsbog surrendered to a bold sun.

It was time for the logistics of war.

I made my way through the ranks of soldiers sharpening weapons, readying poisons, and organizing units. Trafford and Grimwart worked with various leaders on assignments and support conditions. The massive coordination blew my mind. Weaving among the various units, over and over, a single color was continually brandished.

Black.

The core of our force was the Black Hats, a guild of malcontents. The Brothers in Black of Shorehome stood with us, in spirit if not physically present. The black-clad crusaders were the muscle, along with the wildkins of the Black Keep.

There were exceptions. The pagans used red war paint and the catechists flashed white and gold, but those were tentative allies at best. And the legionnaires, while loyal, were pledged to Stronghold. These exceptions didn't change my impression.

"We're the Black Army now," I announced, hands on hips as I gazed to the southern mountains.

Trafford nodded slowly, getting a feel for the moniker as he scratched the white stubble on his cheeks. "Seems fitting. Never did go for that white-knight crap." He leaned close. "Let's keep that opinion from Lash though."

I laughed. "We're gonna need to get her an alternate uniform. But even she sports black highlights."

"She's sure heavy on the eyeliner."

"Think we're going too far with the black? I'm worried it's getting overdone."

"Embrace it," said Grimwart, sliding his full helm of black plate over his head and climbing onto his black stallion. "Come on, Artax, time to muster the cavalry." The horse spun around and carried him away.

"He's good at this," remarked Trafford after a moment. "I've been in wars before you were born and I haven't seen better."

"We've got a good team," I agreed.

He grunted. "And speaking of said team, and our white knight, and pirate, not to mention Kyle..."

"Everybody's in place. We're all fingers of the same mighty arm."

"Heh. You're starting to sound like Lucifer."

I admired the sky as it cleared. "It's all gonna end here, Trafford. I can feel it."

"Now just wait one minute," piped Izzy in the distance. "I demand to know what this is about."

A neophyte priest was attempting to skirt around the pixie without making eye contact. "If you please, I have my orders."

"And I have this jagged little wand, in case you need a reminder that we don't take orders from you."

I caught myself before I laughed. "It's always something."

"Aye," said the buildmaster general. "Looks like you're needed over there. I'll finish the rounds and coordinate with our allies. General Azzyrk's been fighting my ideas of unit formations."

As I split away and headed for Izzy and the priest, I couldn't shake the feeling that Trafford got the easier task. "What's going on?" I asked the bickering pair.

"Yes," agreed Izzy sharply. "I'd like to know."

The neophyte cleared his throat. "Talon of Stronghold, his eminence summons you to the war tent."

"Summons?" I growled. "That's a crusader war tent erected by acting members of the Black Hats. The catechists have no jurisdiction to commandeer it."

The priest stuttered. "My orders—"

"Don't apply to Black Hat leadership," I finished. "Izzy's a third of that leadership—"

"The pixie is not summoned."

"There's that word again." I sighed harshly. "I don't care what you catechists think of pagans and pixies and dragons. When you're in *my* camp you'll look her in the eye when you talk to her."

Izzy groaned. "Don't tell him that. I kinda like his submissive puppy-dog act." She leaned close to the priest. "Avert your eyes. You're not worthy."

The neophyte swallowed uncomfortably. "Yes. Perhaps summon is a strong word. Your presence is *requested*."

Izzy smirked. "With a cherry on top?"

"What?"

Her voice flatlined. "Does the request come with a cherry on top?"

The priest's eyes darted to me. He didn't understand the connotation. "Just say yes," I prodded.

The neophyte met Izzy's eyes. "If it pleases my lady."

"Better," she said, raising her hand and flicking her fingers. "You can scurry off now."

The priest blinked, again looking to me for help. I nodded. He turned and ran away.

I chuckled. "You're really not making this alliance thing easy, are you?"

"Oh yeah, because they have a great love for all things pointy-eared."

"Don't forget the breasts," I said. "They seem to hate those as well."

She rolled her eyes. "What a bass-ackwards people. And they think the pagans and wildkins are primitive."

"They sure are powerful though," I conceded. "And Vagram. I don't trust him enough to turn my back on him, but I swear there are times he almost seems noble."

"Just not when he's sticking bronze swords in your chest."

"Hey, Lucifer killed you before and we're on his side now. Things change."

"I don't know," she said with a smirk. "You sure you're not just a sucker for blond hair and a cute face?"

My head turned sharply. "You think he's cute?"

She straightened as we approached the community tent—black, of course. The crusader standing guard saluted as we passed. I pushed in, ready to give Cleric Vagram a strong piece of my mind.

The catechists at the war table all stood in deference to Bishop Tannen. I froze, surprised at the sight.

Unlike Vagram, Tannen was a sickly man. Thin even before his captivity, he was bald and had veins running over his head and face. His sneer was accompanied by a set of tiny teeth that made him look more animal than human, and his long, clawlike fingers added to the comparison. The bishop wore steel plate covered by a white tunic with a gold cross. A tattered gold cape shimmered across his pauldrons. Notably missing were his helmet and gauntlets, which might have had a bit to do with us.

"You've arrived," he said. His voice was as snively and villainy as ever. Golden eyes locked on Izzy. "All of you."

"Is that a problem?" she asked gruffly.

"Certainly not. Every able mind is welcome in these deliberations."

A couple of crusader sergeants were in attendance but the rest were priests. Vagram stood unassumingly in the back of the tent, perhaps still getting used to giving up control.

"What deliberations are those?" I asked.

The bishop pushed away from the table. "Cleric Vagram has acted well in my stead. These alliances are unconventional, but we find ourselves shepherds without a flock. Compromises must be made."

The subject of conversation remained stoic in the back. I blinked, unsure what to make of the whole thing. Bishop Tannen had assumed command of the catechists much sooner than I'd expected, and he was surprisingly even-tempered.

Don't get me wrong, I trusted him far less than I trusted

Vagram. Tannen likely viewed me as a disposable pawn on a chessboard. I had to proceed with caution.

"I've been appraised of recent developments," he continued. "And future ones as well."

"Meaning?"

"The launch leader conditions," guessed Izzy.

The bishop grinned. "Able minds. Yes. It's of great concern to be told a usurper may be given the permanent keys to our kingdom. One calling himself a god, no less. Tell me." The bishop stepped around the table and approached. "Is it true you're an acting vessel of the White King?"

I peeked at Vagram. The man was more savvy than I'd given him credit for. How much did they know?

"The saints are dead," I somberly relayed. "I've been tasked by Christian Everett to recover his kingdom."

Some of the priests gasped at the truth. The CEO's real name somehow held meaning for them.

Tannen studied me and nodded. "It is so. In the hands of the Trinity, the keys will be given to the White King."

I was getting a bad feeling about where this conversation was headed.

"What news of Shorehome? Can the town be saved?"

Izzy crossed her arms defensively. "Liberated by allied forces last night."

Knowing the priestship's opinions of pirates and goblins, I treaded cautiously by speaking in the abstract terms of the quests. "And the errant folk have been rallied."

"It is His will," said the bishop. "All that remains before destroying the soulstones is Oakengard's glory. I have a strategy for that, and it little involves the army."

I blinked back surprise. It was like he already knew my planned course of action. "The Black Army will meet the brunt of Hadrian's forces. I'll accompany a small scouting team past the battle to Oakengard."

Bishop Tannen nodded. "Excellent. We should leave at once."

"Wait a minute. I never said the catechists were going."

The bishop lifted his nose high. "As I understand it, I'm the only living member of the original Trinity. If it is to be restored, I must have a hand in it."

"Your alliance with us is enough."

"Hardly. You plan on sneaking into my fortress and recovering the soulstones and trijewel, yes? We need to visit the fallen Trinity."

"Why?" asked Izzy.

"So I can bring Philosopher Mara and Hero Gent back from the dead."

The tent went quiet at the statement. The catechists, originally the priest wing of the crusader faction, had great and terrible power. I'd seen dead knights push to their feet under their care. It wasn't healing and it wasn't necromancy—it was as if they'd never fallen.

And it was undoubtedly a clear path to restoring the fractured Trinity.

"I can't deny your point," I said.

Izzy shook her head. "Are you sure you're not better off leading your priests on the battlefield? We can take other catechists with us to do the reincarnating."

"Hardly," Tannen scoffed. "The White King bestows such lofty power to very few. Vagram has the gift. He'll attend as a backup, but I must be there too. I'm one third of the Trinity being restored. As for the army, Colonel Grimwart is a capable battlefield commander, as I'm sure is anyone else currently in place."

Approaching voices came from outside the tent.

"Is he inside?"

Dune pushed in followed by Caduceus. I tensed at her presence. She was, after all, in possession of Tannen's bishop helm.

The ranger hurried to my side. "Bad news. Hadrian's army is marching for the Godsbog."

"How does he know we're here?"

All eyes in the tent searched for answers. "Maybe the Violet Order knights respawned after our little jailbreak," suggested Dune. "It's hard to keep secrets in a virtual world."

"But they never spotted our full force."

"Aren't near a hundred catechists enough?"

Cleric Vagram spoke from the back of the tent. "The Whisperer has sent search parties before. He's never dispatched the entire army."

"If this isn't the full might of Oakengard," said Dune, "we're in a lot of trouble."

Bishop Tannen's eyes went sharp. "He knows we're here. We're surrounded by hundreds of pagans. All it takes is one to report us."

"Hey," I said, "they're in the crosshairs too. You'll change your mind when you see them dying on the battlefield beside us."

"Friends," cut in Vagram. "The means of Hadrian's intelligence matters little. The Violet Order is meeting us in the field. Are we not ready for them?"

Izzy scoffed. "I can't believe I'm saying this, but the choir boy's right. It was always going to come down to this. The real question is, why leave the safety of Oakengard to go on the offensive?"

Dune chewed his lip. "Maybe they want to spare damage to the fortress?"

Caduceus shrugged. "Take us by surprise? Divide us from the horde before we've organized into a cohesive unit?"

I nodded along to the suggestions, all reasonable but none convincing. "There's gotta be more here. It's almost as if Hadrian prefers a fight."

"It's quite possible Hadrian isn't aware of the launch leader conditions," said Izzy.

"That's true, but I'm more concerned about what I saw in Oakengard when we freed Grimwart. The purple plague." I worked my jaw and turned to the collective crowd. "Hadrian's army isn't like other armies. His power can assimilate us. Take us captive. We need to make sure engaging him doesn't add our soldiers to his."

"My order has been reciting protective prayers," said Tannen. "We're at full strength."

Caduceus crossed her arms. "Fat lot of good that did for the captured priests on the Lake of Dreams."

Tannen stood up straight. "Young lady, there are leagues of difference between beaten men in chains and those fighting on the battlefield with an army behind them. The White King will protect us."

"Even many beaten men in chains fought off their power," added Vagram.

"They're right," I said. "I witnessed Rygar turn. The process took the combined focus of two Oakengard keepers on a submissive subject. We can defend against the plague as long as we don't let our guards down." I held a stern finger to Tannen. "But your units will be spread out. We need to buff the Black Army equally as needed, which means protecting pagans."

His featureless lips upturned. "Of course, Protector. My order will assist as needed. I leave the warfare dynamics to you. As it turns out, the approaching army is a blessing in disguise. We can skirt the Violet Order with a small force and breach Oakengard to get to the Trinity. We won't be expected."

I worked my jaw. I preferred not taking the bishop along, but it was pretty much written into the quest. He had the best chance of restoring Mara and Gent, and he himself had a place on the shared throne.

I flipped open the flap of the tent and gazed southward. Moving to Oakengard first thing hadn't been my intention, but it was a damn fine game-day adjustment. "Take Dune's party and go ahead without me. He's the best ranger out here. I'll coordinate with Bravo Team, already inside, and catch up to you later. But I'm gonna need you on the battlefield, Caduceus."

"What?" she exclaimed.

"What's the big idea?" asked Dune.

I took a heavy breath. "You have certain... abilities," I told her. I pulled them out of the tent and lowered my voice. "You're the owner of the bishop helmet. With Tannen and Vagram infiltrating Oakengard, that artifact can do a lot of good, even if you aren't able to raise the dead. Unless you wanna hand your most powerful piece of gear to someone else?"

She clenched her jaw and wore a sour face. "You don't want Tannen close to the helmet."

"It's too powerful." Dune nodded. "It's a good point. You can do more good here."

"I can definitely stomp more heads. Will you boys be okay without me?"

Stigg was near but ignoring us. He bobbed his head, lips tight, eyes distant, no doubt listening to his heaviest thrasher metal, getting in the mood for what was coming.

Dune nodded but I spoke. "They'll be escorting two of the most powerful priests in the sim, neither of whom can be fully trusted but, maybe, put together there's just enough goodwill there for us to pull through. What could go wrong?"

We laughed nervously. Izzy pressed to my side. "And what about us?"

She meant me and her, and there was no talking her into leaving my side. "We have a war to fight."

>> Minigame <<

Tad Lonnerman opened his eyes. Daylight streamed through the windows. Sluggish senses tried to keep up with a scrambling brain. Tad had slept through the night.

And what of Christian?

The CEO was still, for the first time not working on his code integration. Tad leaned over and checked him. Still breathing. He let out a relieved breath. Despite just waking up, his heart was pounding a mile a minute. They were both still here, both still alive.

Tad squinted out the window. The view from Christian's tall-tower office was stunning. Higher than most buildings. Across the street, snipers camped on the lower rooftop opposite. The police had the high-rise surrounded. Tad waved but the officers made no reaction. They couldn't see him through the reflective glass exterior.

He checked the cameras next. Seattle PD had settled into the extended crisis. Officers in SWAT gear sipped coffee from Styrofoam cups and chatted during shift change. The bad guys were still posted inside, visible from the windows but well covered. The standoff had completely stalled.

Tad wondered if anyone even knew they were up here

anymore. Ramon would've helped them except he was a hostage. The firefighters he'd encountered through the debris had every reason to believe they were now hostages as well. Hell, the people on the floor of the lobby in zip ties were the ones that needed saving. The fortieth floor was an afterthought.

Building that thought out further, besides having their hands full with the authorities, the InLink operatives were reluctant to breach the office. Doing so would trigger another gunfight, first above and then below. The illegal soldiers were just as trapped as they were.

The thought dawned on Tad that he and Christian might actually pull this thing off. Today was the final hurrah of the beta test. The satellites would launch in the a.m. The CEO was patched up and appeared stable. All they needed to do was get through one last day.

Tad clicked through the sequence of security feeds, leaving the building exterior and main lobby behind in favor of whatever popped up next in the sequence. Inner hallways, stairwells, Kablammy corridors. Several figures efficiently moved through the studio floor. Rogue soldiers.

Tad's muscles went taut. "Christian, we have a situation."

The CEO pushed to his side as if already awake and focused on the screen. His eyes were sharp even if clearly lacking rest.

"It's the east wing of our studio," Tad said. "InLink snuck a small team inside for a stealth operation."

"No," he said bitterly. He took over the keyboard and toggled through several cameras. "No, no, no. I've been so hyperfocused on my work I didn't fully consider how to defend it."

Tad's brow furrowed. The operatives were scouring through

QA computers. The cluster of workstations was unimportant but probably looked like a server farm or something with access to real data. "What are they up to?"

Christian breathed as he contemplated. "A virus, probably. If they can't stop us from launching Haven, compromising it would be an acceptable consolation prize."

"But didn't they already upload their Trojan?"

"They did, but combined with Talon's in-game actions and our patches, we've greatly limited its impact. Hadrian has somehow commandeered it to grow into a menace, but that's the extent of it. That's all the Trojan was designed to do: create chaos and force us to delay."

Tad frowned and saw where this was going. "But a new virus..."

"A new virus can be geared for anything: ransom, control... even total destruction." The CEO grunted and checked his bandage. "I'm bleeding again. Will you—?"

Tad slid the paramedic case over and set aside new bandages and ointment. Christian pushed him away before he could provide medical assistance.

"No, I need you to switch off the alternate server. Just like you did in the Bosom."

Tad pulled away. "But that's in the east wing. Where the InLink operatives are."

"You're not looking at the bigger picture. They haven't reached it yet, but eventually they'll find the server farm."

"So? Just let them destroy it like Abbie did. With your backups spun up, Haven won't even experience downtime this go around."

"They'll find the central hub, Tad. They'll have direct access to Haven. With our redundancy they wouldn't be able to delete it, but they could easily upload something malicious. I need this code integration to be pristine. If even a whiff of a new virus is lurking on the servers, the satellite sync at launch will compromise the sim. I can't risk losing it all in the final moments."

Tad gulped. Going up against veteran gunmen was a dicey proposition. Even if he did manage to shut the servers down, that would only redouble InLink's efforts to get to them in Christian's office. Their seeming ceasefire would evaporate as InLink grew more desperate.

"If we're holding all the cards in this office," said Tad grimly, "they'll come at us hard."

The CEO nodded. "That becomes more true the nearer we come to launch. InLink is very close to getting everything they want. If we shut down the alternate servers and contain the simulation to my office, with any luck, it will give the operatives enough pause to save Haven."

Tad tilted his head. "*Or* the police might force the issue and get them to blow the whole building up rather than be taken alive."

Christian Everett popped a couple of pain pills straight from the bottle and winced. "There's that too."

2090 World at War

◆————•————◆

The Black Army marched south.

Getting free of the Godsbog was key. Doing battle in the wetlands might benefit the light-footed horde, but every other fighter besides the floating keepers would be at a disadvantage. Standing on solid ground would afford regrouping pathways behind the front line.

What we found was the best of both worlds. Solid groundpack at the wide base of the mountains, with a clear field ahead where the enemy had no cover or slope advantages. A rock outcropping on our west prevented us from being flanked, and a third of the battlefield to the east were the remains of the moss-covered bog where the horde positioned themselves.

The Violet Order marched over the peaks, carrying bright banners. The army, mostly composed of mounted knights and footmen, grew on the horizon.

I stood on the line and referred to the warfare panel in my captain controls.

Black Army	965
Black Hats	220
Crusaders	100
Legionnaires	100
Wildkins	125
Horde	350
Catechists	70

Everyone was organized into units of 25 troops. 4 legionnaire groups established the front line with stout pikemen. They were backed by 4 wildkin and 8 Black Hat units as the backbone of the army.

The pagan horde was a whopping 14 units.

Horde	350
Goblins	125
Imps	75
Kobolds	35
Ogres	50
Trolls	15
Boggarts	25
Other	25

I shuddered to imagine what the "other" designation might be but reminded myself they were on my side. I held back 2 goblin units with the boggart unit and 1 wildkin unit for a special assignment. That left 3 goblin units and 3 imp units to cover the east wetlands. I split the ogres, trolls, and kobold handlers into 6 units and peppered them around the full battlefield for heavy support.

Next I studied the 4 crusader units.

Crusaders	100
Footman	50
Cavalry	50

Only two of my crusader units were mounted, and that was after reallocating some horses from the catechists. I would've liked them to each flank a side, but the mossy ground on our left didn't suit the horses so I put them both on the high ground to our west. I placed the 2 footman units beside them in my right field, an opposite complement to the pagan forces in the bog.

This left the 70 catechists in 3 mixed units. While some of the priests were mounted, organizing them into shock cavalry defeated their purpose. Instead I spread out the horsemen among the units to be used for battlefield assessment and fast support as necessary. The catechists would be rovers. 3 units meant one backing the main front line, and the other 2 pushed toward the sides to provide mutual support to either the flanks or the center as needed.

The Black Army's units settled into place just as the oncoming Violet Order crested the foothills and spread out to fill the expansive stage of rocky ground between us. We watched their lines form, and I was astounded by the army's size.

Violet Order	1040
Knights	460
Sages	260
Priests	220
Keepers	100
Brutes	20

Kyle hadn't been exaggerating when he said Oakengard pumped out 1200 soldiers. They were very nearly at that number, minus the crusaders and catechists I stole and some stragglers.

Half their number were former crusader knights now donning purple. Each was expertly equipped and trained, and while half were on foot, they fielded more than 200 horses. Interestingly, the other half of the Violet Order was made up of sages and priests. I caught a glimpse of the stone keepers behind the lines. The special units would be key to Hadrian's tactics to grow his army. Most keepers were man-sized but several giants dotted their ranks.

The army parted for one such keeper brute. The collection of smoky quartz boulders pushed ahead, animated by tethers of purple energy. The large body floated weaponless into the empty battlefield while the knights of the Violet Order waited in the background.

"What's that about?" asked Izzy, annoyed by the holdup.

I squinted at the lone enemy. "I'm not sure. I think he wants to talk."

She snorted. "Have you ever heard keepers utter a single comprehensible word?"

"Grimwart understood them." I eyed the colonel on the distant outcropping on our flank. "I don't want to get him out of position for this unless it's necessary. Our cavalry's too important."

I pushed the forward soldiers aside and stepped into the barren no-man's-land. The keeper brute immediately zeroed in on me and increased pace. With two armies watching, I approached boldly, but I kept my speed slow so our meeting point would be three-quarters of the way to my side. I figured Hadrian wasn't personally putting himself at risk, so why should I?

If the keeper sensed my tactic, it didn't care. Levitation magic sped it my way. As it approached, I stopped and waited. The stone giant loomed larger up close, a good ten feet of height with a couple more added due to its hover. I drew my dragonspear and staked it into the ground. The keeper slowed to a stop five yards from me.

The wind blew the dry dirt of the mountains into my face. Black banners flew behind, violet banners ahead. Close to two-thousand players, NPCs, and mobs waited out of earshot for the result of this parley.

"Um"—I cleared my throat—"my terms are your full surrender."

The golem drifted ever so slightly in place. Despite the bright magical ebbs of energy, the rock faces were smooth and dark.

I waited for a response but none came. I raised my voice. "If you seek anything other than the full evacuation of Oakengard

—"

The stone brute dipped forward, body hitting the dirt and head bowing. Its stony arms came forward and launched a swell of violet magic. I recoiled into a defensive stance, dragonspear held crosswise before me. The bespelled energy shot into the ground between us and grew into a holographic figure.

Hadrian.

It was him but it wasn't. I mean, obviously he wasn't here. The translucent energy was an image of him, a remote duplicate, an uncanny imitation. But that aside, the image was further jarring still.

Hadrian wore several bits of quartz armor, the repurposed pieces of keepers. I'd seen him absorb them in the Speculum, but now the pieces were cracked and formed into jagged shapes of imperial armor. Spikes fanned up from his back. The pieces punctured through skin and leather. His ungloved knuckles were broken and encrusted with sharp rocks and, although he tried to hide it, I spotted short spears extending from the soft flesh of his forearms under his hands.

The purple plague allowed the Whisperer to take over and assimilate various game aspects. It started with the shadow armor, but now it was crystal. There was Loras, Hero Gent, and who knew what else.

"What... what are you?" I asked hesitantly.

Hadrian flashed a cool smile. "Have your spies not informed you?"

"Have you not captured them yet?" I returned.

His smile widened. "Rats infesting an old building. Worry not, whatever pests remain will be fleeing the household soon."

I paced sideways, mostly to keep a defensive distance from the projection. "You've assumed control of quite the army. First, play up the dangers of the pagan horde. Compromise Loras and have him bolster the numbers at Oakengard in response. Your soldiers have buffed stats and weapons far beyond what's normal."

The god emperor's eyes fluttered. "You see I'm not the type to throw things together at the last second. Unlike you."

"Is that what this is? The culmination of months of planning?"

"It's exactly that," he snapped. "I don't expect you to understand, of course. You were only ever the weapon in the hands of my true enemy, Lucifer." His laugh was grating. "It was satisfying to finish him off, even if he left a bit of a mess behind."

"Sorry to say, bud, but the Black Army's more than a bit of a mess. And I'm not just a weapon."

"Please. Lucifer manipulated you the whole way."

"I could say the same about you. This wasn't your plan. InLink was the entity who created the Trojan that compromised Loras. They drafted you to their cause."

He scoffed. "InLink's a losing proposition. They showed me a greater world, but I don't need them anymore. What happens on the outside is out of our hands. We're living in the simulation now. This is our home, and I'm the one that decides what happens here."

The keeper brute was nearly prone as it projected Hadrian before him. I paced nearer to better gauge the usurper himself. "That's what we're doing here, isn't it? Lucifer's dead," I lied, "but I've made my own choices the whole way. So have you."

Hadrian cocked his head. "Fair enough, so you have."

I nodded and raised my arms to either side. "And look where our choices have led. Behind me stands what will prove to be the greatest army Haven has ever seen."

"A testament to you."

"No, this was *your* doing. They're here for *you*, Hadrian. The hate and divisiveness you've nurtured have come back to bite you in the ass. Pagans are standing with priests, crusaders with legionnaires. Allied pirates have retaken Shorehome. Instead of division, you've sowed unity. The entire free-willed population of the sim is standing against you to claim what's theirs."

Hadrian the Whisperer, the Protector of Oakengard, usurper and god emperor, snickered. "Free will is overrated."

His arms thrust toward me. I was out of range and prepared as the spears extended from his arms. What I hadn't counted on were the rays of purple magic that lasered into me.

"Ugh!"

I strained under the force as the magic slithered over my skin. My arms turned purple before I managed to trigger spinshield. The skill effect was slowed and lackluster, but it seemed to hold. At least for a moment.

"You. Dishonorable. Piece. Of."

My body went pure black. My eyes widened as the shadow essence within me pulsed. A sudden explosion rocked Hadrian backward. The darkness dissolved, leaving my body and arms normal. The Whisperer dropped his jaw and blinked back disbelief.

"Lucifer..." he muttered.

Still in shock after what happened, I couldn't hide the truth on my face.

"It's no matter," he barked. With preternatural grace, the hologram flipped to his feet and sliced dual spears forward. "When I'm done with you I'll—"

A massive fist pounded the prostrate keeper brute, smashing it into the ground. Izzy's frost giant roared and shook his head wildly, beard braids whipping back and forth as he lifted the keeper high in the air and hammered it into the dirt over and over and over again. The projection of Hadrian flickered and vanished. So too did the magical tethers suspending the golem to life. As the giant bashed, the disconnected rocks released their hold on each other and bounced away like marbles.

I backed away from the display and turned to Izzy smiling at my side. "Skoal comes in handy in a pinch."

I stretched my neck. "You're telling me."

"But, you know, he's only around for another fifty-nine minutes, so let's not waste any of them."

We watched as the Violet Order's army pressed forward.

"Izzy, I don't think that's a problem we have to worry about."

I opened the battlefield panel as both armies charged.

Tad took measured steps with his crutch. He was in a public corridor on the thirty-ninth floor, one story below the Kablammy penthouse. He knew this path well because he often came down here to use the toilet.

Game studios were dominated by males and the bathrooms

tended to be high-trafficked. The QA guys, specifically, were infamous for leaving behind impressively disgusting trace evidence of their passage. Especially that guy who came to work in his bathrobe. But the thirty-ninth floor was home to a chic fashion company with the opposite demographics. Their male bathrooms were spotless and deserted and accompanied by upbeat pop music filler. There was nothing like having a public restroom all to yourself and taking a relaxing dump to Taylor Swift.

Tad smiled wryly at the mundanity of normal life. It was a fleeting remembrance as he begrudgingly limped past the bathroom. This visit to the thirty-ninth floor was anything but mundane. It was a way to sneak into his own studio floor without alerting a team of professional gunmen.

Having made it to the far side of the building, Tad began the arduous process of climbing a flight of stairs in a full leg cast. His normal pooping visits made use of the elevators, of course. Now the mere act of getting from one Kablammy wing to the other was an adventure.

At the top of the stairwell, Tad listened at the door. He turned the handle slowly and peeked inside. As he'd suspected, the InLink operatives were elsewhere. Tad slipped in and closed the door in total silence.

He was now in the belly of the beast.

As he made his way toward the alternate servers, more everyday trivialities contrasted starkly with his nerves. Colorful walls in lighthearted shades of blue and orange. An aluminum scooter with rainbow streamers on the handlebars leaned against a desk. Another work space was littered with Minecraft figurines. He passed a whiteboard in a design nook that listed, "Ten Reasons to Keep the Saints Happy." Number one was, "So Pete doesn't crush you with his monster calves."

Tad ground his teeth. Kablammy would never be the same again. As he pressed on, a motion-activated Darth Vader bust lit up and blared heavy breathing. "Come to the dark side."

Tad stiffened. Someone rustled around the corner. The programmer ducked under the cubicle wall, cursing at the design team's knickknacks.

"Anyone there?" called out the operative.

Tad pressed his lips tight and backtracked down the cubicle hallway. With the long crutch and straight cast, he concocted a sort of half frog jump in order to keep low. As he turned the corner, he spied a Yoda statuette guarding the next row.

"Damn," he muttered. "Environmental hazards."

Tad ducked behind another desk and gripped his pistol tightly. Beside his head was a Nerf rail gun. The irony was not lost on him. Tad chanced a peek.

"I don't know," called the guard. "Thought I heard something. I'm gonna check it out."

Tad ducked when the soldier turned his way. What was he gonna do? He had to get out of there, but he didn't know if the man would approach on his right or left side. Tad had to pick a direction. He had to...

"Do or do not," came Yoda's eternal wisdom. "There is no try."

That confirmed it, the operative was on his right. Tad dipped the other way, going two rows down to avoid triggering the Sith lord. Up another cubicle, he glanced both ways. No soldier, but

Boba Fett stood vigilant to his right, and just his luck, it was facing away from him.

Tad grabbed the statuette and chucked it toward the design nook. It landed on a beanbag chair with a muted *poosh*. And then: "He's no good to me dead."

"What the... ?" The InLink operative hustled toward the sound. Tad smiled and advanced to the next area of the studio.

2100 The Battle for Middle-earth

◆——————◆—◆——————◆

I stood at the rear of the Black Army. Izzy, Caduceus, and Trafford were at my side. My reserve units were held behind us, but all the action was spread out in front. Our troops were motionless as the Violet Order charged.

"I've been itching to test out these army controls," I said.

"Sure," grumbled the old general. "I march 'em halfway across the world and you take over for the fun part."

"Perks of being supreme commander." I smiled and dove into the menu.

```
> CLASS
> ARCHERS
> ATTACK
```

The class category commanded specific troops of a certain type, regardless of organized unit. Bows across the battlefield pointed overhead. Crusader and catechist longbows, pagan short bows and slings. They released a volley at the charging violet knights, scattering some but pressing others harder.

```
> CLASS
> ARTILLERY
> ATTACK
```

Trolls and ogres among the heavy units heaved boulders skyward. The projectiles bombarded the front wave. The heavy stones that fell short rolled forward into the rush like bowling balls. I left the ranged attack orders active and scanned the incoming forces.

As telegraphed by their unit starting positions, the enemy was leading with their knights. Their footmen occupied the middle ground and the cavalry were on the east and west flanks. This was a solid strategy all around, as horses didn't fare well against dug-in spears.

It didn't change my strategy at the center. This time I utilized the command for my organized legion.

```
> UNIT
> LEGIONNAIRES
> DEFEND
```

The pikemen lowered and braced weapons into the ground. The surrounding Black Hats and wildkins readied to counter first contact. That took care of the approaching footmen.

The cavalry was more problematic. Their unit type easily overwhelmed mine four-to-one, plus they were attacking the weakest parts of my line.

```
> CLASS
> ARCHERS
> ATTACK
> CAVALRY
```

This was perfect. Since the bulk of my archers were either of the horde or Oakengard, they were already at the flanks. The goblins in the left field fired forward to the horses charging them, and the crusader archers did the same on the right.

I kept the heavy artillery on the main grouping because I liked how it disrupted the slower charge. Plus, the boulders rolled and bounced and caused massive collateral damage—throwing them to the flanks would limit the secondary impacts. Besides, horses were large targets and arrows were plenty against them. Mounts collapsed and threw their riders. The first to fall were trampled and tripped up following knights. It was beautiful chaos.

Hadrian's cavalry got smart and widened their ranks. The arrows were less effective against individuals than clusters, and there were way too many horsemen to track them all. The well-trained cavalry bore down on the disorganized band of goblins and imps. Normally, the rush of hooves would easily cut them down, but in this case...

The first horse to reach the horde stumbled in the watery moss. The sudden twist of momentum flipped horse and rider completely. Monkey-like imps bounded on the poor knight and tore him apart.

The rest of the cavalry had similar initial results but, again, their attack adapted to changing conditions. The horses slowed their charge and opted for steadier footing. While that diminished the cavalry's shock effect, the knights sat atop warhorses with superior weapons and armor. A few fell to close-range archery, but once enough knights breached the line the goblins switched to melee weapons.

The right field had fewer defenders in total and lacked the terrain advantage, so I assisted them first.

```
> UNIT
> HEAVIES
> MOVE
```

Kobold handlers directed ogres and trolls to assist friendly crusader footmen. Few things can disrupt a charging cavalry, but six-ton ogres with fists the size of barrels were among those things. Horses were punted and body slammed.

The tactic was so effective I sent an opposite unit to support the horde on the left. Unfortunately, the heavies were slower on the wetland terrain. It sort of evened out since the cavalry could no longer charge and the horses were spooked by the new monstrous enemies.

So far, after first contact, I gave the Black Army the slight advantage. We'd prevented the cavalry from surrounding us and depleting morale by forcing them to incur heavy losses. However, there were so many of them and they were very capable fighters. If it weren't for the heavies they'd be decimating us, and 65 ogres and trolls could only take us so far.

But there was one key factor that hadn't been brought into

play yet. A soldier type that we not only already had in position, but one which Hadrian's cavalry had outrun: priests.

```
> UNIT
> CATECHISTS
> HEAL
```

The left and right flanked catechists went to work on the first wave of casualties. You wanna talk about demoralizing? Charge through arrows, boulders, and bogs, avoid ogres and trolls, and gravely wound a few goblins only to have them completely restored by the best healers in Haven. Black Army troops returned to full capacity while the Violet Order knights, stranded and cut off from their main force, continued to fall.

```
Violet Order
Cavalry 119/225
```

That was half of them, the price paid for shock and awe. The other half wouldn't be eliminated so quickly. The attacks at range were over, and the rest of the Violet Order was finally catching up.

Purple knights on foot clashed with Stronghold legionnaires. While I'd give the all-around edge to crusaders when it came to general combat ability, the pikemen were experts at one single thing: holding the line. Knights impaled themselves trying to get around the extra-long weapons. Black Hats and wildkins filled the gaps with shortswords and hatchets. The literal wall of death eagerly welcomed the charge and took it head on. The central unit of catechists kept their focus on the front line, keeping them hearty and healthy, and the army of the Violet Order slammed to a halt.

The clash could be heard miles away. Soldier pressed against soldier, the masses shoved and swayed. From a distance it seemed a gentle breeze tickling blades of grass, but up close it was bloody and dirty and brutal. Even with the priests working full-time and skilled fighters filling any gaps, soldiers on both sides were cut down.

It seemed amazing after a full minute that the line held up, but the centurions and legionnaires were there, resisting every inch. They looked to be in complete control when Hadrian sent units of sages to back up his main force. Standing behind their physical brethren, learned men launched stoppered bottles filled with fluids of various colors. I was familiar enough with Kyle's arsenal to know how this would go down. The hand-thrown projectiles flew over the opposing pikes and cracked open on legionnaires, Black Hats, and wildkins. Explosions rang out. Fire and lightning blew holes in the defense.

```
> CLASS
> MYSTICS
> DEFEND
```

It was late, but magical barriers and fields sprouted above the line. Potions exploded midair to dazzling effect, sending fumes into both armies. The loss of soldiers was partially mitigated, but in another thirty seconds the front line fell apart completely. The legionnaires were alive, but the chaos and close-quarters had forced them into sword combat. Units intermingled, friend fighting beside foe. Instead of a neatly organized football pre-snap, the battle devolved into mosh central.

"That's my cue," said Izzy.

I nodded. Her frost giant lifted her up and lumbered to support the backbone of our defense. Skoal stood high above the tallest ogres and trolls. His presence on the battlefield was immediately felt. What's more, he showed great intelligence and grace, at least compared to the nomadic errant folk. He plowed through enemies and rebuffed their pitiful attacks. But he was only one soldier, and the damage was already done.

I worked my jaw. Besides the erupting disorder, the goblins and imps in the bog were starting to be overrun. Shamans fought against another wave of sages and footmen.

```
> UNIT
> BLACK HATS
> MOVE
```

I repositioned some of my central force to the left field. I didn't want to do it, but I fully committed the left catechists to their cause too. Although the wetlands were a natural barrier, I couldn't have the Violet Order pushing through and surrounding us.

"I won't stand back any longer!" growled General Azzyrk, riding to me on his giant predatory lizard. I'd held back a couple goblin units with the boggarts. They were completely inactive way behind us, and the bloodthirsty chieftain didn't like it.

"General, we need to keep our eyes on the bigger picture."

"That's your job, conqueror. I fight for my horde."

Azzyrk co-opted one of my goblin units and charged into the left field.

"Damn him," I muttered to Trafford.

The chieftain's surefooted lizard scurried on webbed feet. From the way its razor-like teeth snapped at horse and knight alike, it looked as if Azzyrk hadn't fed it in weeks. The addition of 25 goblins was a noticeable assist. The shaman-heavy unit launched fireballs and erected swamp golems, providing immediate relief.

"I know you want your pagan reserve support," said Trafford, "but Azzyrk's doing some real damage out there."

I conceded the point with a grunt. The seasoned chieftain had probably made the right call.

"It's about time for me to do my thing," volunteered Caduceus. I nodded and she removed a full helm from her inventory and placed it on her head. Bishop Tannen's helmet was a gaudy affair, horizontal and vertical face slits forming a cross with an added bronze cross jutting out on top. She charged into the fray.

[Caduceus] cast Salvation

Although she couldn't replicate Tannen and Vagram's ability to bring people back from the dead, the healing power of the artifact was immense. Golden light showered swaths of troops and restored them to full.

I took stock of the battlefield. The reinforced goblins were holding their own. The frost giant pushed back an enemy wave, allowing legionnaires to reconstitute the front line. The mixed crusader-heavy push on the right was so strong that they actually advanced, cutting into the Violet Order's backfield. All was going according to plan, even if Hadrian was holding back his biggest weapons.

Glowing quartz automatons formed a wedge in the central battlefield and advanced into the empty area created by the frost giant's wrath.

> **Talon:** *Pull him back, Izzy.*
> **Izzy:** *I'm trying.*

The ornery giant huffed and backhanded an incoming keeper. The bundle of rocks catapulted off the ground and tumbled into a contingent of sages. But two more keepers charged with energy batons. As the giant moved to smash them, they struck his exposed fingers.

> Stun!
> [Keeper] dealt 27 damage to [Skoal]

The line of keepers parted for a brute who stepped forward, purple energy flaring bright.

Damn it. Reality didn't always play out as kindly as drawn-up plans, but I wasn't unprepared for this.

```
> UNIT
> LEGIONNAIRES
> MOVE
> PHALANX
```

The block of legionnaires advanced as one into the open field, overtaking the giant behind their lines. The keepers charged forward and struck at the pikes. Violet electricity sizzled out on the wooden long weapons.

```
> UNIT
> HEARTWOOD
> ATTACK
```

Select members of the Black Hat units rushed forward. Outfitted with heartwood armor from the Dragonperch armory, they were immune to the stuns of Oakengard defenders. The other half of the strategy left them with inferior wooden weapons: clubs, staves, and spears. It reduced their damage potential but protected their point of contact. Battling keepers and staying alive was a delicate game of cat and mouse.

```
> CLASS
> MYSTICS
> ATTACK
```

```
> CLASS
> ARTISANS
> ATTACK
```

My ranged support classes shifted to their new targets while the wood-equipped fighters held them off. This organized strategy exposed the vaunted keepers of Oakengard as one-trick ponies. Without their ability to stun, the Black Army was rebuffing their assimilation abilities as well.

That's when Hadrian's priests flooded the melee. Sticky energy surged from corrupted holy symbols. The power snaked between combatants and expanded into a fog, coughing and sputtering at haphazard targets. There was no perceived effect on the Violet Order priests and keepers, but the Black Army was another story.

```
Pestilence!
[Priest] dealt 40 damage to [Crusader]
Pestilence!
[Priest] dealt 40 damage to [Wildkin]
```

Instead of buffing their own troops, Violet Order priests were using their magic destructively. The pestilence debuff applied constant damage and caused havoc to my line. Since the attack was ranged, the priests were safely behind the keepers, who, while ineffective, had strong armor properties that would keep them in the fight for some time. It was my first moment of true surprise in the battle.

Then again, I'd been holding back a trick of my own.

```
> CLASS
> CAVALRY
> ATTACK
```

Grimwart and the mounted knights on the rock outcropping charged. With the crusaders holding the right field, the horsemen easily pushed forward and swept into the enemy's flank. Since all the keepers were located in the center of play, I no longer needed to worry about losing my valuable knights. The cavalry skirted them and trampled through Violet Order priests. Disarray and panic washed over their reinforcements as swords and axes cut them down.

To say I was pleased with the results was an understatement. Assessing the battlefield, we were experiencing victories on every front of the fight. Most shocking were the numbers.

Black Army	752 / 965
Violet Order	686 /1040

We'd gained a clear advantage in what had been, by tally, an even fight. I wanted to chalk it up to the power of players, to the willing sacrifice for freedom, and the loyalty and devotion to the side of right, but from my vantage behind the mixed units of the Black Army I spotted the true culprit.

Healers.

I'd been dead on about needing the catechists. Though our

fielded force lacked the power of true resurrection, the White King was coming through for us in a big way. What struck me as odd was that no healers among the enemy ranks were using similar abilities.

Hadrian's factory had pumped out OP soldier after OP soldier. By all accounts he should've had another Vagram on his side. Was their lack of healing because they had gone against their promised King? When you relied on clerics for power, going against gods brought consequences.

Or was it something simpler, something technical: the limitations of a glitch manifested as violet energy? Hadrian's army was a disposable resource, efficiently spawned and obedient in function, yet bereft of the humanity and self-preservation needed to persist indefinitely. And with the keepers effectively handcuffed and his soldier factory discovered, Hadrian's plan to grow his army with mine had failed.

Tremors shivered through the murky ground like Jell-O. On the battlefield, keeper brutes stretched to attention and pulled their forces back in anticipation of their next phase of attack.

Of course.

The Whisperer-turned-god had called on a titan, and after more than a day of travel that titan had arrived.

Tad waited as the mercenary fumbled with the red security door.

The soldier didn't show a lot of urgency, probably because the door to the server room kind of looked like a closet. Still, the red color didn't exactly blend in, and his job was to search the studio. This was an obstacle InLink needed to overcome.

The operative kicked the door a few times. It was solid wood in a reinforced frame. He grumbled and fingered his rifle a moment before slinging it back over his shoulder. Gunfire would only spur the police into action. The soldier muttered to himself and hurried away. Tad had no doubt he'd be back.

Tad limped forward to the closed door, greeted by the bright-red LED on the card scanner. He reached in his back pocket and produced Abbie's administrative key card, taken from her body. It was covered in blood.

"Red door, red key," he muttered sardonically.

He waved the card before the scanner and winced at the loud beep that accompanied the LED turning green. Tad hurried inside and closed the door a bit too loudly. He relaxed his back against the door as the soothing sound of whirring machines filled the room.

"Okay, what next?"

Tad limped to the central hub. The computer appeared untouched. The programmer checked the usage log to confirm it: InLink hadn't corrupted the system. Good.

He scanned the room, looking for the switch box. It was on a nearby column, just like in the Superdome. He flipped the switches, one by one. These didn't cut the power. Although the thrumming of the servers continued, Tad knew their update loop into the sim had been interrupted. Even if InLink flipped these switches back on, they wouldn't have central hub access without a handshake with Christian's machine, and that authorization wouldn't be coming. They were effectively locked out.

Tad smiled at his success just before the central hub station emitted a loud alarm.

Beep, beep. Beep, beep.

Oh no. He hadn't spun down the hub and it must have been set up to emergency alert under fail conditions. Tad hopped over and hammered at the keyboard. He managed to shut the alarm off. Unfortunately, instead of returning to the silent hum of the servers, soldiers outside were barking orders.

They'd heard him.

"What's in there?" they called out. They pounded on the door. "Anyone inside? This is the fire department. We're here to save you." More pounding.

Tad knew they weren't with the fire department. Now he wondered if his first brush with the authorities was phony as well.

The banging on the door grew more urgent. "Step aside," said a soldier. He hit the door handle directly. Tad's side of the door shook at the impact. The sound of a tool hammering the handle continued. Tad ducked behind a table.

Suddenly, the lights went off. A few of the consoles beside him went black.

"What was that?" called a guard.

"The police shut off power to the building."

Yellow emergency lights lit the room with a soft glow. The servers were still humming, running on backup power. In fact, most essential systems in the studio would be unaffected. Given the nature of Haven, Kablammy had several stages of power backups.

"Check the windows!" ordered an operative. "Then get Case over here with his club. We need what's in this room."

Tad braced behind his cover and checked Abbie's pistol. He only had two bullets.

2110 Pitfall

Orik lumbered through the Godsbog, forcing me to back away from the warfare. At this point the soldiers were pretty much on cruise control. I hurried a few minor adjustments. I advanced the right field to cut into the Violet Order while pulling my cavalry back to hold the flank. I redistributed the catechists and heavies for a balanced defense as the frost giant lifted Izzy from the ground and backtracked toward me. I opened up brigade chat, which communicated to every single member of the Black Hats.

> **Talon:** *Hold strong, advance against the biggest threats, and at all costs do not allow the Violet Order to breach the Godsbog.*

I turned from the fight and stepped toward the wetlands where my reserve units waited. A crew of boggarts, including the witches; goblin shamans, now deprived of their general; and wildkins, notably the warden of the Blackwood and his prisoners.

"It's time," I told them.

Orik came into view on the horizon and bellowed as he closed. As far as I could guess, he had one of two instructions. Either he was dead set on making it to Oakengard no matter what, or he would be pivoted to assist on the battlefield. If the keepers were able to turn him to their side then maybe the latter was enough. Therefore, not only did the Black Army need to stop the Violet Order from breaking through the line to the Godsbog, but I needed to stop the cyclops from reaching the keepers on the battlefield.

I drew my dragonspear.

"We ready?" asked Izzy, stepping to my side with her giant in tow.

"Ready as we'll ever be."

"I guess that's the only answer that's important." The pixie raised a hand and the giant gently took it between finger and thumb to lift her to his shoulder.

I charged forward as the reserve units and the Black Army's noncombatants hurried to their posts. I stopped at the edge of a deep bog, positioned so it was between me and the titan. Countless logs and fronds had been meticulously placed over the murky surface in a hasty approximation of solid ground. It wasn't the most convincing trap I'd seen, but I was hoping it was enough to get one over on a blind behemoth.

Besides, I was pretty worthwhile bait.

I raised the dragonspear above my head and roared for Orik's attention. And just in case I was too measly in an expanse of battling soldiers, Izzy and her giant stood behind me hooting and hollering too.

It worked. The cyclops faced me, disabled eye squeezed shut

in ire.

I was pretty mad myself as he stomped closer. His bloated right hand swayed over the ground in a wild gait, but his left was cupped to his belly, clutching Bandit in a terrifying prison.

I now knew what Orik wanted with Bandit. A fraction of the Crystal Core's power was encased in the dragonstone, and Hadrian wanted what was his.

The cyclops plodded forward in the increasingly squishy ground, each heaving step pushing five to ten feet into the mud. The Godsbog was supposed to be the place from which all the titans were born, and I'd seen Orik break free from a rocky mountain peak. It hardly took imagination to figure how he and the others could have climbed from these murky depths.

I stood my ground with clenched teeth and waited, stomp by stomp, as the Mighty One grew closer, until his giant sandaled foot took one massive stride to converge on me. Orik lifted an outspread hand overhead and prepared to smash.

The setup was perfect. The titan's weight came down in the center of the hidden pool. The surface debris disappeared under Orik's foot as it sank ten, twenty, forty feet to the bottom. The squick of water slurped against the cyclops' knee. His strike was redirected to the side. Instead of attacking, the giant flailed to save himself, hand barely catching the edge of solid ground and suspending his weight over the pool.

I cursed. Another several feet and the handhold would've been insufficient. Instead of tumbling all the way to the ground, Orik had caught himself close to a kneeling position.

Nooner rose from a hiding spot in the water. "Get 'im, boys!"

A seemingly scattered crew of no-good Stronghold gangsters

pounced into action, driving oxen forward. Ropes dragged across the scrub and lifted off the ground. Orik's back foot attempted to move forward, to steady his balance, but caught on multiple tripwires.

Back in Stronghold, we'd tried this stunt before and failed miserably. Besides having the oxen backing us up this time, we made sure to save the ropes until after the giant's momentum was halted. Instead of dealing with a charging titan, we were merely trying to contain a dragging back foot.

Orik's features twisted as he realized the design behind his misstep. He roared in anger. Still clutching Bandit and relying on his only free hand to support his weight, he attempted to tug his back leg free.

The gangsters were set up single file on each rope like a collegiate tug-o-war team. Feet lifted off the ground and oxen hooves dragged through mud as the titan yanked ahead.

"It's not gonna hold," said Izzy.

"Drums," I called.

I searched the ranks of goblins. General Azzyrk and his lizard were still chomping through the battlefield like a twisted game of Pac-Man. His waiting goblins in reserve were listless.

"Drums!" I commanded.

The pagan war drums started. On a good day, with the full horde powering the fearsome beat, the drums could be heard halfway across the Midlands. We were going for a much more modest accompaniment today. Instead of inspiring furor, the pagan beat was toned-down and mellow, the percussive equivalent of elevator music. Think of it as meditation for titans.

Boom.

Boom.

Chanting boggarts filled the empty space between notes.

Boom.

"N'yeh neh."

Boom.

"N'yeh neh."

Goblin shamans cast charms. Boggarts shook rattles and staked burning sticks of incense into the mud. Drummers swayed and bobbed their heads.

Boom.

"N'yeh neh."

Boom.

"N'yeh neh."

Meanwhile, the gangsters were losing their battle with the back foot. Wildkins swarmed forward to help them. I spun to the battlefield and yelled for Azzyrk to fall back. The general's sharp nose snapped my way. He nodded and recalled the unit of shamans.

I bit down and leaned forward, checking the titan for signs of pacification. His grip on Bandit loosened. The bongo was wide-eyed with fear, so terrorized that she hadn't even noticed me yet.

"Just hold on a few more seconds, girl," I whispered.

Orik perked at the pagan drum beat, but he didn't seem content. His massive features twisted into a scowl.

"It's not gonna hold," said Izzy again. She leapt onto the ground beside me. "Go help them, Skoal."

The frost giant grunted and dashed around the deep pool. On the other side, gangsters and wildkins struggled to remain on the ground. Orik groaned and turned his head from side to side.

He was fighting it.

"Screw it." I hurried in the frost giant's tracks. If the titan managed to stand up, this was game over.

Orik had been leaning sideways, standing on one leg in a deep pool and propped on one arm. His back leg was in an awkward position and didn't have a lot of leverage to fight the crowd. As more people piled their efforts together, he yanked hard and showed he was still a titan. Ropes snapped. Gangsters plunged into the bog. Orik was about to break free when Skoal gave a great big heave.

It was funny calling something twenty feet tall a giant and then seeing it beside something ten times its height. Izzy's legendary summon was barely larger than a cyclops foot. Still, he was a scrapper. He had Orik's ankle in a bear hug and wouldn't let go. The gangsters and wildkins hurried to reset the lost ropes.

Izzy and I were almost on them when Orik finally pulled backward and centered his mass over his submerged leg. This allowed him to lift his free hand from the ground, twist around, and prove that hairy, overweight titans could be limber too. The cyclops bellowed and shoved his hand down, uprooting the frost giant from his leg and crushing him into soft earth.

"That bastard!" cried Izzy. "No one messes with Skoal like that!" She pointed her winter staff ahead and widened into a spellcaster stance.

Jets of ice erupted forward and clamped onto the titan's hand. The wet ground between his fingers froze.

"Hurt him not!" cried Havlat nearby.

"Don't worry," snapped Izzy. "It's just a little ice breaker."

As she hardened the titan's fist to the ground, I charged ahead. Everyone had come together to pull off an impossible plan. We had almost succeeded, but Orik was no longer off-balance and in danger of falling. The frost giant was dead, the gangsters and wildkins half scattered. As soon as the Mighty One got through the ice distraction, there was nothing left to keep him down.

Nothing but me.

I vaulted into the air and landed on the titan's frozen hand. Spider boots pattered on rocky flesh as I turned and sprinted up his arm. I stuffed the dragonspear in my inventory and equipped the tiger claws. The cyclops was twisted around and lowered. With his knee at sea level, I raced up past his loin cloth and toward his large belly.

The muscles under my feet flexed. The entire surface jerked as Orik broke free.

Agility Check...
Pass!

I didn't fall, but it was a close thing. I thanked Hadrian for his spider boots as I charged up Orik's now-free arm. As a bit of extra insurance, I pulled the assassin needle out and fit the blade between my teeth. On the unsteady surface, the +8 to agility was immediately appreciated.

Orik reacted to my presence with absolute fury. He twisted back around to face me, brought his back leg forward to a knee, and straightened his back. The sudden twirl and elevation increase were dizzying. Agility checks flew past my notification window as I continued to charge up his arm.

Now on his opposite side, I vaulted off the wild arm. My boots touched down on the side of his belly, momentum following into a wall run. I was basically traversing across the spare tire of a cyclops. But his belly was massive and my skill was running out. As I rounded the center of his gut, I fixed on the cupped hand protectively pressed to it. The grip of my footfalls slowly lost purchase with each step, and I began to slip. Orik's free hand moved to snatch me from the sky.

I triggered a midair dash and rocketed forward. Titan fingers closed behind me and I stretched forward, reaching. Bandit turned and locked eyes on me. She peeked out above Orik's thumb, and I grabbed onto her horn.

The titan's grip failed as a fully formed chestnut dragon burst free.

Bandit veered into a steep dive to avoid clutching mitts. I pulled myself over her neck and settled into the saddle, laughing and patting her scales. Orik raged as we flew from his grasp and sped around his back.

"I hope the witches and goblins don't mind," I said, "but you need to *stay down*."

Bandit released a jolt of light from her mouth. The focused beam blasted the backside of Orik's knee, just above the water surface. With most of his weight on this leg, the titan buckled, falling sideways and dropping his knee to the bottom of the pool. The side of the belly I had run along smashed into the spongy bank. Although he caught himself on an elbow, Orik the Mighty was, for the first time, practically lying down.

General Azzyrk rushed forward with chanting shamans. The

gangsters and wildkins worked at the ropes. Crowlat, Havlat, and Somlat moved close, enchanting the moss itself to grow over the titan's forearm. Orik's face and eye were clenched tight, but the drum beat hit him with renewed vigor.

Boom.

"N'yeh neh."

Boom.

"N'yeh neh."

The warden of the Blackwood drew forth chains from the ground. They snaked around the titan's leg. Muscles flexed, but the panic was easing, the movements slowing. The tension fled Orik's face. A single eyebrow rose, and he opened his empty eye.

Something close to a sigh and a groan and the low rumble of thunder escaped Orik's lips, and his face eased.

Bandit landed on the ground momentarily while I lifted Izzy to the seat behind me.

"Holy shit," she said. "That worked."

"You ever consider trying the clean-and-sober challenge yourself?" I asked.

"Hell no."

We immediately took to the sky and did a few laps around the pacification effort. If the pagans were upset at my single use of Bandit's breath weapon, they didn't show it. Goblins, boggarts, wildkins, and yes, even humans worked together to Gulliver a titan. A wide circle formed as the participants continued their song. Catchy but not very in depth, it was just a repetition of the same beat and words over and over. I figured I couldn't complain so long as "n'yeh neh" didn't mean "kill all humans."

With Orik pacified, we returned our attention to the battlefield. The lack of healers was taking its toll on the Violet Order, but the fighting remained fierce. Strong magic and buffed stats made for a scrappy enemy. I zeroed in on the keepers, a fighting force in the center of the scrum. While the wooden weapons kept them at bay, the rock guards were hearty brawlers even without their stun ability. Their grouping remained surprisingly stout.

Bandit burst over them like some kind of sci-fi death satellite from above. Beams of light strafed their ranks. Quartz boulders exploded. Purple energy fizzled into the sky. As the ground itself rocked, the backbone of the Violet Order crumbled.

We did several more passes against organized clusters: cavalry, priests, whatever. We had just subdued a giant—a bunch of stragglers weren't going to stand against a dragon. The fearsome attacks completely broke whatever morale the enemy had left. Those not under the spell of Hadrian's purple plague broke rank as the army was routed.

The bulk of the opponent was, unfortunately, not so free-willed. The assimilated victims of the plague couldn't choose whether to fight or run. They would fight to the last man and woman.

Black Army	578 / 965
Violet Order	423 /1040

The battle was all but technically over. The field was won. Orik was soothed by the sounds of his subjects and secured on the ground. The remaining scraps of the Violet Order were so intermingled I couldn't risk dragon breath.

But then, we had somewhere else to be anyway. The Black Army could take it from here.

We soared over the battlefield, in awe of the stunning scene of destruction and unity, cooperation and bitter war. I turned my head to Izzy.

"You ever see anything as crazy as this?"

Her arms around my waist squeezed and she leaned into my back. "You take a girl on the best dates."

"Just wait till you've had dessert," I told her. "We're going to Oakengard, baby."

Tad Lonnerman figured it was as good as it was gonna get. In the absence of voices outside the server room and the distraction the power outage had caused, he chanced opening the door a crack. The InLink operatives were spread out, with a few checking the window on the far wall to see if the police were starting a raid.

Tad jumped out of the room, softly closed the door, and hopped away. A few soldiers approached from the way he'd come.

"Don't worry," said Case. "Big Bertha's never let me down." He lovingly patted a bright-red metal bar in his hands. It was a battering ram.

"Shit."

Tad rushed away in the opposite direction, just barely

rounding the corner before being spotted. With another group of soldiers ahead, he had no choice but to push forward under the cover of a cubicle farm.

He wasn't getting to his rear exit now. If Tad could sneak past the InLink patrols, he would reach another stairwell ahead. It was more central and wouldn't be so inconspicuous, but it was the best route he had.

Fortunately, the studio had gone dark. The dim emergency lighting left the room with plenty of shadows. The alerted soldiers marched down the aisles with their weapons pointed forward. Tad imagined predictable forty-five-degree cones of awareness attached to those rifles, just like countless AIs he'd programmed. It would be tough with a bum leg, but he could pull it off.

The game developer stayed low and darted from cubicle to cubicle, peeking out briefly to get a feel for each mercenary's facing and rhythm. When the time was right, he leapt behind his next piece of cover.

In the center of the room, he experienced a close call when his crutch scraped the foot of an Aeron chair. One operative doubled back. Tad's hiding place under the desk was especially dark. The soldier's boots stepped within inches of him and continued past.

Tad waited a beat before pushing onward. He turned a corner and almost ran into a mercenary's back. He froze, knowing he couldn't backtrack as another operative filed into the perpendicular row.

Step by step, Tad matched the soldier's march, sticking behind him. Just a little more and he'd be able to—

"We found the server room!" called Case.

A few guards, including the one Tad was drafting, immediately spun around. The soldier blinked for a befuddled moment, rifle lowered to his side.

"Who the—?"

Tad clocked him in the temple with the butt of his pistol. The soldier dropped to the floor like a rock.

"Holy shit," Tad whispered.

The other soldiers hadn't noticed and were converging on the distant server room. Tad rushed ahead now, breaking out into the open as the floored guard groaned. Unlike a video game, downed opponents wouldn't wait for him to clear the area before waking. Tad hopped ahead on the crutch and reached the door to the stairwell. He slipped inside and shut the door as someone called out.

Down the steps then. Two at a time. Three. Tad slid with his stomach on the handrail, turning at the midway point where the stairs doubled back just as a soldier opened the door above.

"Who's in here?"

Tad clenched his jaw and slid the rest of the way down. It was tough juggling a crutch and a gun, and he almost lost grip on one and then the other. As he caught them, he sped toward the floor too fast. The steel frame rang out as he crashed to the floor. Boot steps pounded down the stairs above him. The soldier rounded the corner and raised his rifle. Tad, lying on his back, braced the pistol with both arms and emptied it. His fingers kept squeezing the trigger after expending the two bullets. One had punched right into the soldier's forehead. He collapsed backward.

Tad's ears were still ringing as he climbed to his feet and barged into the thirty-ninth floor. This new stairwell wasn't as far as the other was, but he could only move so fast with a broken leg. Tad dropped the empty pistol and barreled forward, using both arms to propel off the crutch. As he reached the end of the corridor, the door behind him banged open.

"There he is!"

2120 Dungeon Siege

By the time Oakengard was in sight, the midday sun was beginning to sag. I'd been watching my notification window along the way. With the largest battle Haven had ever seen still ongoing, the text flew by so fast it was like trying to read a Matrix screensaver. I learned to spot what was important: the XP, of course.

Talon		Level	10
Class	Explorer	XP	111672
Kit	Scout	Next	113400

I groaned. I'd been hoping to level up before the big showdown, but the war was winding down. It wasn't gonna happen in time to make a difference. Oh well, ever onward.

> **Kyle:** *Talon, we're just about ready. Do you have a fix on Hadrian's location?*

I pinged the god emperor in the dev menu.

```
DEVELOPER CONSOLE
>> ERROR
>> OAKENGARD OFFLINE
```

I cursed.

> **Talon:** *Bad news. Hadrian disconnected Oakengard from the hub. It really limits my access.*
> **Kyle:** *Frickin' wonderful.*

Bandit hugged the mountains as she steered close. Based on intel from Kyle and Bravo Team, we knew Hadrian had pretty much dedicated all his troops to the battlefield, but I was still surprised to see the fortress from the air. The towers, battlements, courtyards—it was a ghost town. It didn't look like Oakengard, it looked like a theme park of Oakengard that was shut down for the day. It was eerie. Something was up.

I took a pass around the grounds to make sure we weren't flying into a trap.

"And that's all she wrote," boasted Kyle as they stepped from the mines into the shuttered lower level of Oakengard.

Dune and Stigg quietly slipped into the halls, impressed. Cleric Vagram and Bishop Tannen were more stoic about skirting the castle's gates. Kyle guessed they'd had no knowledge of the security vulnerability before now.

"Guards?" asked Dune.

Lash shook her head. "No one comes down here. But even weirder is there's no one upstairs, either."

"We bypassed the army on the way here," pointed out Tannen.

"Yeah," said Kyle, "but I'd have expected some respawns to make their way back. It's empty up there, bros."

The bishop jutted his chin upward. "It matters little if we encounter personnel. The people will respect their rightful leader."

Lash snickered. "This guy."

Dune pulled out his longbow. "What does it matter? It can't be far to where we're going, right?"

"The Speculum," said the bishop. "Follow me."

The group headed down the dark hallway.

Stigg studied Bravo Team as they silently walked.

"What is it?" asked Conan.

"Oh, nothing." He nodded to Glinda. "It's just nice having a healer around. We left ours on the battlefield."

Cleric Vagram sighed. "You're traveling with two of the most gifted healers in Haven."

Stigg chortled. "No offense but I usually rely on healers who aren't total knobs."

Vagram bit down and pushed forward. Kyle smiled.

"Okay, guys," he announced, "I just got off captain chat with Talon. He says—"

"I know what he says," interrupted Lash. "I'm on captain

chat too."

"Ditto," said Dune, eyes forward.

Kyle scratched his scruff. "Oh yeah. I keep forgetting you're a Black Hat now." He considered Stigg and Bravo Team and the catechists. "But for everyone else *who's not a faction captain*, check it out. This is like a heist, right? You seen Ocean's 11? We're gonna sneak up on Hadrian, most likely in the Speculum, and steal the Eye of Orik and the trijewel."

Tannen's eyes flared. "The usurper holds the trijewel." He said it as a statement, pale skin reddening.

"Sure. And he controls the Crystal Core. We think. It's not like we can steal that from him, but Talon has a plan."

Vagram sternly cut in. "Our mission is to revive the Trinity. Once Hero Gent, Philosopher Mara, and Bishop Tannen are together again, they'll know how to defeat the usurper."

Tannen nodded. "We'll do what we can, but the Black Hats must be instrumental in this. We couldn't have gotten this far without them."

Vagram clenched his teeth and nodded.

The group paused at the stairway leading up to the light. Despite the fresh air above, the silence was deafening.

"It's like I said," bragged Kyle, "completely empty."

He boldly headed up the stairs and, amazingly, nothing at all happened. It frankly even surprised him.

Scurrying through the hallways was much easier in the light, despite the constant flickering. Instead of whispered concerns, the proximity of their destination stymied conversation. They were finally doing what needed doing. Kyle was satisfied with that.

The amethyst banister of the Speculum staircase came into view. Two keepers rotated to face them. Kyle tensed for a moment before he spotted the twins. Hex with a fresh coat of black fingernails and lipstick, the thief in black leather. The two animated Violet Order automatons were under the necromancer's control.

"I heard you guys a mile away," complained Crux.

Lights flickered haphazardly as the brewmaster hiked a shoulder. "Like it even matters. Oakengard is a dying city."

"Don't give up on her yet," pronounced Tannen, marching forward. "I must believe she can be saved." He angled his brows toward Hex's zombies.

"Anything's possible," conceded Lash, "but Kyle's right. Have you guys noticed all the XP coming in from the war? This fortress should be full of respawns. Instead Hadrian's been relying on a recruiting factory."

"I've been thinking about this," said Glinda. The witch, usually timid, spoke more forcefully now. "Speaker Harroway respawned, but his words unsettled me. He said that many of his brothers and sisters were gone because they fell to the plague. Maybe something about the pestilence's corrupting influence, the same thing that steals the will of a person, also steals their opportunity of eternal life."

Lash pursed her lips and mulled it over. Tannen scowled as he still studied Hex's zombies. "These... monstrosities are still around after death."

"They're just corpses," explained the necromancer. "They're empty shells. My magic doesn't affect the conscious people at all."

The bishop didn't find the explanation reassuring.

"So his army's disposable," concluded Lash. "With the factory taken care of, the supply of enemies is cut off."

"Not quite," hedged Glinda. "The nature of the plague means any one of us is a potential subject."

"It gets worse," said the usually silent Vagram. "If your conclusions are accurate, and I'm beginning to suspect they are, then every single one of us is in very real danger of being annihilated forever. No more afterlife."

The unlikely companions shared a moment of sullen silence.

The brewmaster cracked his neck. "Well then, what are we waiting for? Crux, lead the way."

"You got it," said the thief.

Light boots paved the way down the staircase to the Speculum. After a quick peek, Crux signaled and the party cautiously descended. The lighting in the Speculum was harsher than before. Cold and white, it reflected off the frozen lake like a sheet of haze over a snowy tundra. The brightness washed out the colors and nearly blinded them until their eyes adjusted. Occasionally, spikes in intensity, like lightning, jump-started their nerves, elevating the room to a shining sun before dimming like a dream.

Kyle stepped down as a low hum filled his ears. The sound wasn't unlike wind, but he could swear he felt it in his teeth. The ice itself was whirring, like it was alive, or perhaps like it wanted to be.

"It's empty," he said, disappointed but not surprised.

"I haven't been able to locate Hadrian," said Crux.

"All the better," said the bishop as he pressed ahead. "The

Trinity is my priority."

Tannen wasn't especially spry, but Kyle marveled at how easily he walked across the smooth ice surface. He chalked it up to past experience. Lash, Stigg, and Conan used their large weapons to brace themselves, while the twins and Dune were agile enough on their own. For his part, since he lacked a polearm to assist his balance, Kyle stepped slow and steady toward the column of smoky quartz.

"What if he left the castle?" suggested Dune. "He's safest with his army."

"Not by the way Talon tells it," chortled Lash.

"I'd agree," said Glinda. "Hadrian's a manipulator at heart. He sent the pawns ahead while he attended to his true goal."

"Which is?"

Kyle's metal boot lost purchase for a split second. He slid forward and caught himself in an awkwardly wide stance, arms splayed outward and facing down. Colors of a crystalline rainbow blinked below the surface but were muted by the harsh white light above. The brewmaster took a breath and steadied his footing, relieved that, since he was the slowest and last in line, everyone had missed his embarrassing misstep.

"It's impossible to guess what he's up to," muttered Crux. "For all we know, he's waiting on the outcome of the battle."

Hex emphatically shook her head. "Hadrian's a puppet master. He's been at this longer than we've been in the sim. He has intimate knowledge of processes we've never heard about. Trust me, he's up to something."

Ahead, Tannen and Vagram stopped at the foot of the throne. Hero Gent was dead, as Talon had reported. A shiver, a slight tremor, ran down Kyle's spine and uprooted his foot. His balance suddenly shifted. The brewmaster lurched to the side, momentarily staving off a fall by initiating a jerky hula dance.

The performance was short-lived.

Kyle rocked forward as his legs swept behind him. Plate armor, and his face, clattered loudly to the ice. His companions spun around, every one to a man rolling their eyes when they saw him.

"Uh..." he said, "sorry, I—" Kyle's eyes went sharp. He cocked his head and stared at the floor inches from his face. Using the heel of his hand, he wiped away the sheen of white and gazed into the depths below. "I, uh, think I just found our god emperor."

The others crowded around to see Hadrian the Whisperer buried a good six feet below the surface. He was hunched forward and facing the lake floor. Trails of red, purple, blue, and green dotted in and out of him like ants.

"What the... ?" Lash blinked in horror, trying to make sense of the sight.

Hex squinted. "Is he... ?"

"Dead?" asked Tannen. "I think not. But he *is* occupied. We must hurry." The bishop returned to the throne.

Vagram frowned at its occupant. "His body is mostly stone," reported the cleric.

"It appears that way." Tannen ran healing hands over the head of the knightly caste. "Not the purple infection, but perhaps a precursor. A corruption of the keeper's ability to petrify." The bishop grunted. "This is worse than I thought. I question our ability to revive him."

Kyle made it to the throne just as they concluded with the glum news.

"What about Mara?" ventured Crux. "She managed to resist the sickness all the way to the end. Hadrian killed her because he couldn't turn her."

The bishop arched an eyebrow. "Interesting. It's worth a try."

With some force of will, Tannen activated the column of quartz and Gent's throne rotated away.

"Careful," said Kyle. "We don't wanna wake Hadrian."

The rotating column reverberated through the ice and the companions watched on pins and needles. Hadrian made no reaction. Philosopher Mara came into view, a length of crystal plunged through her chest. Vagram gritted his teeth, pulled the weapon free, and placed it gently on the floor.

"Yes," whispered Tannen after a moment of study. "The White King can work with this. I lay these hands in his name, the name of the father, the daughter, and the spirit of man. Philosopher Mara, I bid thee a triumphant welcome!"

When both catechists removed their hands, the hole in Mara's chest was gone. The old woman's head jerked sideways and her breath croaked. A shiver, and she was alive. The respected elder cracked open her eyes, taking a moment to process her predicament.

"A most unwelcome return," she said coarsely. "And hardly a triumph in sight." She pressed her lips together tightly, appearing uncomfortable. "Bishop Tannen. I should have guessed."

"He's working with us," said Kyle, "on our quest to restore Oakengard's glory."

She smiled weakly. "I'm afraid the time for glory has passed. What of Gent?"

Tannen bolstered his voice with confidence. "He is beyond even my power, but with us two we may begin to right what is wrong. We shall require a new knight. And the trijewel to bind us into one."

Mara's cheek twitched.

"Dear Mara," interjected Vagram, "let me ease your pain."

She pushed his hand aside. "The pain is welcome. It keeps me alert. Helps me combat his growing dominion over our home."

A few eyes nervously checked Hadrian below. Not only was he alive, but he was actively continuing his efforts to control Oakengard with a terrible force of will.

"He holds the trijewel," stated Tannen with a scowl.

"And the Eye of Orik," pointed out Crux. "We need that too."

Mara's gaze remained fixed on Tannen. "How can you be trusted?"

The bishop leaned forward. "Because Oakengard must survive."

Kyle grunted. "Listen, lady, I get where you're coming from, but we're talking about Hadrian the Whisperer down there. Literally every single person in Haven is a better candidate to hold those artifacts than him. Ask Speaker Harroway if you need to, if he's even still alive."

The philosopher's eyes were severe up to that point, but the mention of her colleague softened her resolve. Mara rested her eyes for a moment's reflection before sighing and nodding. "I do not know if we are powerful enough to stop him, but we can certainly try."

The old woman ground her teeth and trembled, expending great effort. The lights in the Speculum went dim and the ground shook. The rainbow lights blinked frantically as the beams of power disconnected from their host. Slowly, the spymaster's body rumbled upward. Chunks of ice crumbled away and Hadrian's body broke the surface, still encased in crystal. If Kyle was a dagger looking for a soft spot, he was sorely disappointed. The Whisperer was blanketed by gravelly pieces of sand, the crushed smoky quartz of the keepers. Not that it mattered. Simply killing Hadrian wouldn't fulfill their goals.

Tannen yanked the trijewel from Hadrian's neck. The Whisperer shuddered and coughed, ripped from his dream state.

"It is done!" cried Tannen. Whereas the trijewel was meant to be three separate crystals that aligned into one, it had been modified into a necklace, bound together by a cord of leather. The bishop hurriedly placed it around his neck.

"And the Eye?" prodded Lash.

"On it," said Crux, "but it's a delicate process." The thief hunched over Hadrian and attempted to rifle through his inventory.

"Bishop!" called Vagram. "Assist me with the philosopher." The cleric was attempting to extricate Mara from the throne but she was partially glued.

Hadrian collected himself before Tannen could respond. The spymaster shoved Crux away and stumbled forward, still disoriented. "Who did this?" he demanded.

A bronze gauntlet materialized over Tannen's right hand, the half of the set he still possessed. "You need look no further than a very subject of your design!" sneered the bishop. As Hadrian turned, Tannen pounded him with a body blow. The gauntlet flared with gold light and Hadrian flew into the far wall and bounced to the floor.

"Bishop!" pressed Vagram.

Tannen turned and hurried to his cleric helping Mara off the throne.

Mara's eyes went cold. "Don't bother, cleric."

Vagram's brow furrowed. "Whatever do you mean?"

Tannen's mighty bronze gauntlet fixed around Mara's neck and snapped her head sideways. She was dead before Vagram recoiled. The cleric fell to his knees, wise sage cradled in his lap.

2130 Gauntlet

"What have you done?" demanded Cleric Vagram.

Tannen pointed an accusing finger at his subordinate. "You walk a very fine line, cleric."

Vagram sputtered. "I did everything in your name!"

"You didn't think I would condone your actions, did you?" growled the bishop. "Working with pagans? Allying with the Black Hats? No. I'd rather see this world reduced to oblivion."

Tannen leapt aside as a pair of crossbow bolts exploded into the column beside him. A silver arrow flew with greater precision, but the bishop's gauntlet struck it from the air. Conan charged, swinging his greataxe. The bishop met the blow with the armored glove, sweeping the weapon aside and disarming the barbarian. Conan countered with a heavy fist but the frail bishop was faster. His super-powered punch slammed the barbarian to the floor.

"Do not presume to defy me!" roared Tannen. "You're outsiders. Unwelcome here. Yet as recompense for your assistance, I'll allow you to flee with your lives. I'm the Protector of Oakengard now!"

Lash scowled and traded a glance with Kyle. They nodded together. The white knight pointed her cleaver toward the bishop, and Kyle armed himself with the other half of Tannen's equipment set, the bishop gauntlet.

"Sorry, buddy, but you just messed with the wrong hombres."

Lash set her jaw. "Hand over the trijewel."

Tannen's nostrils flared at the affront. "I should have known. You look down on me and call yourselves heroes, but you're nothing more than artifact-hungry thieves."

Glinda healed Conan as Stigg pulled him behind Kyle and Lash. Crux was hurrying to safety with Hex. Vagram smoldered on his knees, still holding Mara in his arms.

The bishop's face went rigid. "So you've made your choice. Know that your blood will herald the beginning of a mighty kingdom." Tannen took a step toward Lash and Kyle.

Hadrian cleared his throat and stood up. "That's *my* kingdom you're talking about." He wiped blood from his lip and surveyed the room. "Looks like my pest problem is a little worse than I thought."

Kyle's eyes narrowed. "You don't know the half of it, buddy."

"There's a lot of things a lot of you don't know too." Hadrian's eyes fell on Tannen. "Starting with you, dear bishop. I'm sorry to say, the White King doesn't reign supreme anymore."

"Sacrilege!" he cried. Tannen turned away from Kyle and Lash and stomped toward the Whisperer. He lifted his gauntlet.

[Bishop Tannen] cast Glorious Beam

A golden laser seared into Hadrian's side. The newly

appointed god emperor dropped to a knee and grunted in pain.

"You deserve nothing less than a slow death," chided Tannen, "but the White King is merciful."

"There will be no White King," spat Hadrian in defiance.

The bishop cocked his head. "Perhaps not in form, but in spirit. It will be up to me to force his acts upon the land."

Vagram's face darkened. Kyle and the others regrouped as Tannen confronted Hadrian. Once within range, the spymaster released a spear from his forearm and thrust it upward.

Tannen smashed it aside with his gauntlet, snapping off the crystal bone protrusion. Then he once again raised an open palm.

[Bishop Tannen] cast Continuous Glorious Beam

The charge of light held on the deposed tyrant for several seconds this time. Hadrian screamed wildly as the laser forced him lower until he collapsed on his face. When the attack ceased, his shoulders and back were black and smoking. His breath came in rasps.

"There now," said the nasally bishop, equal pity and pomp. "In the end, you lie prostrate before your superior, the new and forever Protector of Oakengard."

Hadrian sniggered coarsely. "I don't need the paltry mantle of Oakengard," he spat. "I. Am. Oakengard."

Poles of crystal emerged, not from Hadrian but from the frozen lake itself. Surface ice cracked away. Tannen barely had time to drop his head before he was speared clean through five times. Purple energy ran into him like an electrical current, and it was Tannen's turn to scream.

Amazingly, the bishop still had fight in him.

[Bishop Tannen] cast Divine Cleansing

Despite being strung up like something out of a Hellraiser movie, rays of gold washed through the bishop and stalled the purple plague. Hadrian gnashed his teeth and redoubled his effort. Vagram took to his feet and raised his hands to help.

But then, slowly, he lowered them back to his side. He bit down, exchanging eyes with Kyle.

As the two despots struggled, Crux snuck close. Purple and gold nearly blinded them for several moments as Hadrian pushed up to his knees and then feet. The battle of wills was violently intense. Finally a scowl of resignation overtook him.

"If you won't be mine, you won't be anyone's!" Hadrian's fists went white and more pointed crystals shot through the floor, spiking the holy man through the back, neck, and heart. Bishop Tannen jerked before his outstretched body settled limply, like a scarecrow, suspended on a twisted web of spikes.

[Bishop Tannen] is dead!

Quest Error: **Restore Oakengard's Glory**

Quest Type: Fepic

Reward: <empty>

<Components of the quest string point to a null reference.>

Quest Abandoned!

The Speculum went silent. The lights dimmed. Kyle and Lash turned to each other.

The respawn errors. Mara and Gent may have been dead or worse, but there was still the faint hope of revival. But Tannen? He'd been partially infected by the plague. Even now, his limp body dripped with violet. His death resulted in the permanent corruption of his being. Bishop Tannen was gone forever, and with him, the possibility of restoring the Trinity.

Hadrian's breathing settled. Bars of light ran along the icy floor, pulsing like a heartbeat. Burnt and blackened chunks of crystal fell away from the Whisperer as new rocks floated from the ground and took their place. Below, deeper than the layer of ice, colorful crystals stirred.

Hadrian may not have had the trijewel, but he still had the Crystal Core.

The Whisperer snapped his head to his flank. "Thief!"

Crux sped away with a giant ruby in his hands. The Eye of Orik. Hadrian fired a spear from his arm.

[Lash] cast Shield Wall

The crystal hit the yellow energy barrier. Wild sparks flew and the wall flickered, but the attack was stalled. Hadrian growled in anger and teased fingers in the air. Several spears floated upward and pointed to the thief. A greataxe spun like a hatchet and buried itself in the Whisperer's crystal chest. Hadrian fell to a knee. His floating crystalline weapons clattered back to the floor.

"To the stairs!" ordered Kyle. "Get that soulstone to Talon!"

Crux nodded and bolted. Hadrian stood, pulled the axe from his chest, and dropped it on the ice, looking none the worse for wear.

Lash backtracked. "We'll cover your retreat!" She raised her cleaver and set her jaw.

"Idiots!" snarled the god emperor. As Crux reached the foot of the stairs, a boulder of crystal ripped through the ground and smashed the stairway and pretty amethyst banisters to bits. The only way out was up, and the exit was now blocked. "Now hand over the Eye."

Jagged crystal spears floated into the air again. Vagram leapt into the fray, bronze swords blazing in his hands. He sliced the projectiles in half, one, two, three. Instead of pausing after the last blow, Vagram spun around and slashed at Hadrian himself.

The emperor's rocky arms widened into shields. Sparks careened from the deflected swords. The three broken crystal spears sprang to life again, now six distinct projectiles.

"Get behind me!" warned Kyle, equipping his mirror shield.

The cleric's eyes widened. He dove away from the incoming bullets as an arrow from Dune knocked one off course. Kyle charged forward, managing to catch two of them. They reversed bearing and popped apart onto Hadrian's chest. They failed to penetrate his rocky armor, but his frustration visibly grew.

Hadrian's eyes went bright purple. He spread his arms and collected energy. Kyle considered swapping out to his dual crossbow, but the moment had passed. Slivers of jagged crystal popped through the floor everywhere, opening craters in the smooth lake surface that grew pockmarked, as what must have been a hundred projectiles rose into the air and spun in unison to face them.

"Reflect this," spat Hadrian.

"On me!" cried Lash.

[Lash] cast Bastion

Everyone in the room dove toward the paladin as a dozen projectiles fired at each of them. The slivers of crystal exploded against Lash's yellow dome. The repeated blows did nothing against the might of the legendary ability, and in seconds the last of Hadrian's brutal hailstorm had crumbled to dust.

The Whisperer twisted his lips in frustration. Then he repeated the maneuver, calling on yet more weapons.

This time, as with Tannen, the spikes came from underfoot. Lash's all-protective dome failed to cover the floor. Ice erupted into jagged spears. Hadrian chortled as the companions scrambled from multiple attacks. Kyle was punched in the shoulder, spun around, and thrown onto his back. He stared up as the bastion expired and blinked out of existence, thinking their bold stand was over. Above him, he could see the opening the stairway had led to, the opening that was too far away for them to reach.

The opening that a chestnut dragon peeked a growling head into.

Kyle's eyes went wide as Bandit took a mighty breath and let loose a stream of blinding light. The attack ripped through parts of the ceiling and tracked to Hadrian, who braced himself and extended his shield armor to max protect. Boulders of ice and stone kicked up and wrecked the once-great Speculum. Then the damaged ceiling rumbled as centuries-old mortar failed. The roof collapsed around them as everyone retreated to safety.

Tad yanked himself up the stairs, almost dropping his crutch for the third time. That would be a death sentence. Back on the fortieth floor, he opened the door to Kablammy Games, wishing the damned magnetic locks would come back on, and pushed inside.

The stomping and yelling InLink operatives were not subtle about following him.

Tad weaved between administrative desks as the soldiers nearly broke the door down. One, two, three men breached the west wing.

"Stop right there!" yelled one as Tad rounded a wall.

They were faster than him but he didn't have far to go. The disabled programmer beat them to Christian's office. He shut the door and clicked the deadbolt just as the operatives converged. Tad searched around in a panic before sliding his crutch between the door and the neighboring bookcase. The heavy piece of furniture wouldn't budge.

The soldiers pounded at the door. "Let us in! We just want server access. We're not going to hurt you."

Tad locked eyes with Christian Everett. The CEO was pale, the bandage on his stomach soaked with blood.

"We'll destroy it!" Tad yelled. "If you come in, we'll delete the servers!"

"You won't do that," returned the operative. "It's too important to you."

"Not to me," swore Tad. "Christian's dead. I'm all that's left, and I swear I'll wipe everything if you try to come in."

Cursing erupted outside the door. Tad slowly hopped away without his crutch. He sank to the floor beside Christian, feeling worse than the CEO looked.

"You're not serious," asked the visionary under his breath, "are you?"

Tad panted, exhaustion taking over, but he shook his head. "After everything we've been through, I couldn't do that."

The corner of Christian's mouth crooked. He leaned forward with an animated whisper. "I finished. The code integration. The patch is queued up and ready to go. All that's left to do is transfer my consciousness to the black box. Once we launch, the patch and my digital brain will be broadcast into the sky."

"Are you sure you want to do this?"

"Why wouldn't I?" exclaimed the CEO. "We could die at any moment. Here, help me up."

Tad did his best, though it was more like them helping each other up. As Christian stood, a line of blood trailed down his leg. The two men limped through the side door, into the private space of Christian's office Tad had never been in. It was a dark room. Instead of a wall of windows there was an array of local servers, the CEO's personal EXSIL unit, and another door on the far wall. How big was this guy's office anyway?

Christian sat on the machine and leaned back. He didn't bother with the bed's safety straps or the electrodes that monitored vitals. "Okay," he said, pointing, "I need you to man that console right there. The process has already been prepped." Christian slid the CAT-scan device over his head. "Proceed with the backup."

Tad wet his mouth and swallowed. He'd never actually done this part before.

"While I'm undergoing the scan," called out Christian, "you should really think about doing this yourself, Tad. There's a very real chance we won't be alive much longer."

The programmer swallowed again. "You ready?"

Christian nodded once and closed his eyes.

2140 Dragon Warrior

Dust intermingled with ice and felt cool against my face. Izzy and I leapt off Bandit's back and landed on the rocky Speculum floor, waiting for the room to clear. We couldn't see a thing.

> **Talon:** *Everyone alive?*
> **Lash:** *Bravo Team's good.*
> **Dune:** *Stigg and I are okay.*
> **Kyle:** *About effin' time you got here, bro.*

I cracked a smile. As far as entrances went, that one was at the top of the leaderboard. Unfortunately, as ripped apart as the high ceiling was, Bandit was too large to squeeze inside. She remained on Oakengard's second floor and craned her neck low. Her subdued growl filled the room, a warning to any standing against us.

"Hey girl," I called up, "can you do something about the view?"

The dragon released a staunch snort that gusted the mist from half the Speculum. The destroyed staircase and some of the Black Hats behind were still obscured, but the forward section of the throne room was immediately revealed.

Mara lay dead on the floor. Bishop Tannen was strung up and impaled, the trijewel hanging from his neck. A blackened form of rock huddled close to the ground with a piece of collapsed ceiling on top.

Hadrian.

The smoky crystal jutted upward, throwing debris aside. The rock cracked—no—transformed. Sandy and spiky pieces shifted until they reformed into a suit of crystal armor over Hadrian the Whisperer. The god emperor.

"That... fucking... hurt," he snarled.

I shrugged. "Then why change what works?"

Bandit coughed up another beam of light. Instead of shielding against the blow, Hadrian dove aside. The dragon arched her neck around the room but the Whisperer's powered armor propelled him to safety. The breath weapon cut short as Bandit approached her limit.

"There's always the old fashioned way," called out Dune. From somewhere within the cloud of dust behind, a silver arrow emerged and punched into Hadrian's head. The enchanted arrowhead split in half without effect. Hadrian sneered at us.

"So let's make it a party," called out his Viking companion. The red robe strolled from the dust and plugged headphones into his ears before banging his wooden staff to the floor.

[Stigg] cast Berserker's Frenzy
For the next 30 seconds, your physical skills do not require cooldown.

I grinned.

The Speculum erupted into frenetic battle. I dashed to the left and immediately dashed to the right. As Hadrian tried to zero on my position, I dashed up to the ceiling.

Izzy sent a barrage of ice spikes to keep him suppressed while Stigg and Conan charged. Lash initiated a series of group buffs and Hex sent her zombie keepers forward. Even Cleric Vagram joined the action. Apparently he had chosen sides. I knew there was something redeemable about him.

Hadrian fired a burst of crystals toward my midair position. I dashed straight toward him and triggered spinshield, plowing through his spears like a cannonball. An enlarged crystal fist swatted me from the air.

42 damage

As I rolled on the floor, a sliver of crystal fired my way. Before it could connect, a silver arrow knocked it from the air. I leapt to my feet and nodded at the green ranger. With his normal attack failing to cause damage, he'd taken to assisting the defense.

A quartz spear extended from Hadrian's forearm. I sidestepped and batted it aside with the dragonspear. I reversed my thrust but Hadrian backtracked. A giant spike of ice slammed into his chest. He snarled at Izzy.

Crossbow bolts exploded into his side, dousing him with sticky yellow liquid that ignited a second later.

[Kyle] dealt 17 damage to [Hadrian]

[Kyle] dealt 18 damage to [Hadrian]
DoT: 10 dmg/10 secs

As flames danced across his torso, Hadrian spun to meet Stigg and Conan in melee. Like the keepers of Oakengard, his armor seemed impervious to normal attacks. His arms turned to clubs to block their strikes and bat them away. At the same time, the rocks on his back shifted to smother the fire.

I nodded behind us. "Izzy, the stairs."

"Right." She did an about face and pointed the winter staff. Loose chunks of the frozen lake rearranged into a makeshift staircase.

"Dune, get Crux to the high tower."

A jagged line of crystal punched through my leg.

67 damage
Leg Break!
Your leg is broken. You cannot move unassisted until it is fixed.

My dash failed as I crashed to the ground. Bandit growled and snapped at Hadrian, but he was out of reach. The usurper lifted a stony hand and twisted. A chunk of ceiling above me rocked loose and fell.

Strong hands yanked me free as the boulder crashed down. A rain of crystals shattered against Kyle's mirror shield overhead.

"I knew there was a reason I gave you that thing," I laughed.

"You really gotta watch yourself, bro."

I chugged a health potion. Not only did my leg instantly heal, but all my missing HP was restored.

"That's my soulstone," called Hadrian.

Crystal bullets plowed Crux over. The depths of the lake beneath us lit with dizzying colors, and the Eye of Orik shone bright red as it propelled into the air away from the thief.

[Glinda] cast Minor Healing on [Crux]

"You're all dead!" screamed Hadrian.

As the artifact hovered his way, his eyes spiked with purple. The entire room cooled thirty degrees and went a shade of blue. I searched my notification window as the debilitating effect forced me to my knees, but nothing was reported.

"Ugh!" snarled Dune. "What's he doing?"

Izzy whipped her head around. The extreme cold didn't seem to have an effect on the frost mage. The only other combatants standing were Hex's two zombies. They momentarily kept Hadrian busy but the god emperor was wielding the same stout crystal they were made of. The difference was he could reform. His spears eventually cleaved them apart. Izzy planted her winter staff and a large blue rune overlaid the ice beneath her feet.

[Izzy] cast Sleet Storm

A rush of Christmas cheer engulfed Hadrian, but the temperature in the room continued dropping. Cleric Vagram gritted his teeth and used a bronze sword to force himself up.

[Vagram] cast Aura of Protection
You have 50% resistance to magic for the next 30 seconds.

I felt an immediate boost to my constitution. The cold wasn't as oppressive, but it still beat down on me. I tried to stand but couldn't find the strength.

[Lash] cast Spell Armor
+25% magic resistance for the next 30 seconds.

Another wave of power returned. I took to my feet. Izzy's spell died down and Hadrian stomped forward angrily.

"You can only fight this so long."

[Glinda] cast White Circle
+20% magic resistance and +10% non-physical damage resistance for the next 60 seconds.

The white witch stood. Dune and Stigg, Lash and Hex. Conan helped Crux to his feet. Kyle held the shield by my side as Vagram carved his swords together like a butcher. My eyes narrowed. "Funny, I was about to say the same thing."

Hadrian stomped forward, raising his arms, face red. His anger blinded him to the waiting threat. Bandit struck like a snake and chomped her jaws around his body.

[Bandit] dealt 142 damage to [Hadrian]

The Whisperer screamed and twisted as teeth pressed against crystal. The armor was amazingly resilient, but some of it crumbled away. The Eye of Orik, gliding through the air, sputtered in position.

"The soulstone," called Lash.

I leapt up and triggered dash. Whatever unseen force suspended the ruby released it. It plummeted from my grasp, and I could no longer immediately redirect my dash because Stigg's buff had worn out. The soulstone slipped into a shallow crater on the surface of the frozen lake and a chord echoed deep underneath. The ruby flared. Rainbow flashes lit up the ice. The dragonstone on Bandit's forehead shimmered.

Hadrian winced in excruciating pain, but between it all, he'd found his opening. "Of course." The usurper showed his own teeth. "The last of the Crystal Core."

Still clamped by jaws, he reached for the stone resting between Bandit's horns. Violet energy coursed through his arm, invigorated him, and Bandit was hit with a knockout punch. The dragon's mouth went slack and released Hadrian. Her head lolled and crashed into the new staircase. The Whisperer landed lightly on his feet, health potion in one hand and the dragonstone in the other.

My focus shot to my mount who'd collapsed in place. She was at the top of the steps, now in mountain bongo form. The dragonstone was missing.

"Lucifer's gambit," chuckled Hadrian menacingly. I ran to

Bandit as the others regrouped. Even Hadrian healed mid-speech. "My great opponent stole the aura of the Crystal Core long before I could get to it, and after his staff shattered, this was the last of it to return."

I reached Bandit and rested a glove on her neck. She was still alive but out cold. I tried to force a health potion down her mouth but she wouldn't take it. Glinda rushed to my aid.

Hadrian took the time to pore over the dragonstone. He wasn't just looking at it, he was feeling it, *experiencing* it. "This is what I've been missing," he said softly. "The last of my power is no longer imprisoned."

He was talking about Lucifer's power trap. The mad usurper tightened his grip and the temporary housing of Oakengard's magic crumbled to dust. Colorful energy danced from his fingers and sank deep into the lake, rejoining the mass of the Crystal Core like a long-forgotten breath.

At the same time, the Eye of Orik reactivated. It slid across the ground, floated upward, and affixed itself into Hadrian's spiked crystal helmet. A tremor shook the Speculum. The god emperor studied his hands, now oozing with power, and cackled.

2150 Eternal Champions

I stepped down Izzy's makeshift stairs in a deliberate fashion, vision red. It was as good a time as ever, judging by the incoming combat notifications from the distant battle. The war was almost won, the XP almost done. It was time to cut off the head of the beast. I traded silent nods with Izzy and Kyle.

Hadrian chuckled and reveled in his growing power.

"Your magic doesn't matter," I declared, walking toward him with the dragonspear. "The soulstones, the mantles, the armor— none of it matters, Hadrian, because as long as people live they won't subject themselves to you."

"I don't need you," he spat. "I can make more people."

"I don't think so," announced Kyle, producing a green gemstone. "This is a little thing I stockrigged, something like a remote detonator. And the next sound you hear is your recruiting factory going up in smoke."

The brewmaster ran his finger across the surface of the gem and the entire room shook. A blast echoed through the halls. Dust dripped down from the broken ceiling.

"And speaking of bombs..." Kyle pulled a collection of vials bound by rope, beakers of various sizes containing volatile bubbling chemicals of yellow, black, and red. The haphazard contraption definitely wasn't a professional stockrig, a fact that made it look all the more dangerous.

Hadrian's eyes flared. Crystal slivers rose from the floor. Kyle swung his shield before him but missed the real danger. A large chunk of ceiling crashed down toward him. He attempted to heave his contraption of bombs away but the glass shattered and ignited a chain reaction. As the debris crushed down, explosions of various colors filled the area. The smoke cleared to silence.

I charged forward with a deadshot. The dragonspear struck true, rocking the Whisperer backward. I went for the Eye of Orik on his helmet next, but he twirled away, casually fending off the attack as he raised an arm. The floor of the Speculum cracked and yawned open. The parties rushing to my aid skidded and fell on the ice. Vagram was closest. He fell in the chasm bisecting the room. Everyone else besides Izzy was on the other side. We were now cut off from our companions.

I continued to engage Hadrian. Icicles slashed at his arms and face. His armor held strong. I crossblocked a counterstrike but missed Hadrian's second spear. Quartz grazed my neck.

77 damage

I dashed to his flank and reversed my spear. Bullet's peppered my unguarded side.

38 damage

43 damage
39 damage

Yellow shield walls sprouted up around me, but they could only account for so many projectiles. Hadrian swatted a silver arrow from the air and the others helped Vagram from falling into the pit. As we battled, more and more shards rose from the lake floor and harried us. Daggers hit my face.

Blind!
You cannot see until your eyes are healed.

I countered with a tornado spin, some crossblocks, and desperate swinging, but the attacks kept coming.

36 damage
Critical Hit!
84 damage
41 damage

[Glinda] cast Minor Healing Aura
You are healed and instantly relieved of minor status effects.

I blinked warily at the growing frustration in our enemy. A wave of Hadrian's arm and the rainbow below intensified. An entire wall of ice rose from the edge of the chasm, sealing us off completely from our reinforcements. They stared helplessly through translucent pockets of ice, trying to break through.

Izzy flipped forward and slashed with the sharp end of her staff. A shield arm blocked the blow. Hadrian kicked her backward. Crystal spikes broke through the floor. The frost mage retreated, bashing them as she backtracked. Then her foot got caught in a pocket of ice. Izzy pulled her leg and looked down, shocked. The frozen lake grew up, over her skin, She tried to yank free and screamed.

The ice finished her off, encasing her completely in a matter of seconds.

Now alone with Hadrian, I screamed and slashed wildly but was countered at every turn. Spears came at my back. I sidestepped more than I pressed. Finally, the god emperor charged right through my guard and delivered a world-shaking body blow.

Disarm!

89 damage

Stun!

You are stunned. You may not use skills, move, or attack for 20 seconds.

The dragonspear clattered to the ice. I tumbled and settled facedown in a jagged pile of crystals. They snapped up and spiked my ankle and wrist.

Leg Break!

Your leg is broken. You cannot move unassisted until it is fixed.

> Arm Break!
> *Your arm is broken. You cannot use it until it is fixed.*

With Haven's pain filters offline, the feeling was unbearable. Stones pounded my back. It was all I could do to protect my head from a crit. When the hits stopped, I readied my inventory, watching the top half of Lucifer's staff, even though I was currently unable to use it. Hadrian scanned our party for incoming threats, saw that his wall was holding, and turned to me with a smile.

I watched the pulsing lights beneath our feet, the purple energy coursing through his eyes, the smoky rock armor as it constantly adjusted and reformed over the usurper's skin—but mostly I watched the notification window and my character sheet with growing anticipation.

Hadrian lifted a jagged hand over my head. The room thrummed.

"Wait," I said weakly. "What are you now? Some kind of dungeon core?"

Hadrian paused and took a calming breath. He had every reason to strike me down right here and now, every reason to act instantly, but I knew he wouldn't do it. What good was power with nobody to witness it? What was godhood without worship?

"Dungeon core?" he laughed. "That's what you see? Look at everything I've done. I raised a titan to besiege Stronghold, wrested Shorehome from the saints, and commanded the kraken. I single-handedly overtook Oakengard." His voice grew coarser as he ticked his accomplishments. "I've commandeered the soulstones and molded the game mechanics in my image. No, I'm no mere dungeon core, little man. I'm a *world* core. And you've rebuffed my attempts to complete the trifecta of towns twice already."

With a few seconds left on my stun, a jolt of energy streamed through the spike in my wrist.

> Stun!
> *You are stunned. You may not use skills, move, or attack for 20 seconds.*

The god emperor chuckled lightly and dismissed me. He may have been gloating, but he knew a stalling tactic when he saw one. He stepped to Tannen's strung-up body and reacquired the trijewel. I needed that if I had any hope of creating a power trap for the Crystal Core.

"Hear this, Talon, Protector of Stronghold. The core city will be mine. You'll fall and it will fall and so will Lucifer, wherever he is. No one will stand against me because I'm not just in control of Haven. I *AM* Haven."

Hadrian slipped the leather necklace over his head. "And you," he mused with a hint of derision. "What *are* you, anyway? Did you ever stop to ask? You're nothing more than a pawn, Lucifer's left hand. And pawns are meant to be sacrificed."

Hadrian stormed over as I watched the remnants of the battle notifications scroll in. The XP had slowed to a crawl. I'd underestimated how much the battle would net me.

"I need more time," I groaned.

The spymaster lifted an arm as the rock transformed into an executioner's axe. "Sorry, you're fresh out."

A heavy Indian accent cut through the Speculum. "Hold it right there," ordered Varnu.

Hadrian spun to the side, keeping his back from either of us. "Who the— ?"

The colonial-garbed soldier put his eye to his long gun. "I believe this is what us Texans call a BFG: a big friendly giant."

So much for an impressive entrance. "Wrong BFG, Varnu."

Spears of crystal shot forward and harmlessly passed through the resident companion's body. Hadrian scoffed. "This is preposterous. You're tech support. You can no more harm me than I can you."

"Famous final words of the gnat of Barstu. How strong is your conviction in that fact, sir?"

Hadrian clenched his jaw. "Strong enough to do this." He again raised his axe hand above my neck.

Varnu's rifle barked. The Whisperer recoiled several steps away, but there was no bullet. The support companion looked down the rifle barrel and frowned. "Oh dear, I'm afraid you may be correct. Perhaps this will fare better?" He put the rifle away and tossed a small doll. It bounced on the ice and came to a stop just out of my reach.

[Kogal Chibi]

The Japanese schoolgirl grew to full size and giggled. She wore a short orange skirt and a small white top with buttons about to pop off. Blue hair curled over anime eyes and a smile.

"Idiots," snarled Hadrian. "You think I don't know a distraction when I see one?" He flicked a finger at me and I was jolted with another wave of electricity.

Stun!
You are stunned. You may not use skills, move, or attack for 20 seconds.

I grumbled on the floor. I couldn't reach the automaton and it didn't much matter if I could. What was I supposed to do with a sex doll? The answer barely mattered because I was stunned and unable to act.

The schoolgirl giggled and wagged her hips from side to side. She wasn't offering any help. But I did have to admit, as ridiculous as it was, she was pretty hot. With my head on the ground, my eyes trailed up her pale legs and caught a peek of underwear.

Varnu chuckled. "You big pervert, sir."

Crown Unlocked: **Jeepers Peepers**
Graduate to full-on creeper with a second of misjudgment.
1000 XP awarded

"Always so smart," I chuckled, bracing for the XP. "But you're wrong about me, Hadrian."

"Is that so?" he spat.

"I'm more than a pawn," I affirmed, barely pushing to my

hands and knees. "I'm more than the hand of the resistance. I'm the claw. I'm the Talon."

Teal-blue fire engulfed me.

BWOOOOOM!

You have reached Level 11!

My health surged to a new maximum. The break and stun effects evaporated and the spikes in my body shattered. I braced my boots beneath me and defiantly pushed up. The dragonspear was out of reach, but my fingers were wrapped around the assassin needle.

Hadrian started at the turn of events, including the sight of his former weapon. He focused on it, eyes narrowed. It was forged in Oakengard by the saints, an OP weapon meant for killing heroes. If anything could get through his crystal armor, it was this. Hadrian fumed.

I took a firm breath. "You..."

His face reddened and he shook.

"You..."

I burst out with laughter.

"You fucking idiot," I said.

Kyle flickered behind the usurper, the invisibility granted by his decanter failing as he slid his assassin needle into Hadrian's back.

Surprise!
[Kyle] dealt 62 damage to [Hadrian]
Stun!

The god emperor jerked his head around. Izzy flipped out from behind her ice decoy, her assassin needle leading the charge.

<pre>
Critical!
[Izzy] dealt 111 damage to [Hadrian]
Stun!
</pre>

Hadrian stiffened and collapsed between them. He lifted his head as the trijewel scraped the icy floor. I took a step closer and casually flipped the assassin needle in my grip.

"The trijewel is a symbol, three forming one. But the assassin needle is the opposite, isn't it? It's a weapon, illegally forged, exploitatively buffed. And it was duplicated—one into three."

Hadrian sputtered on the floor, having trouble even forming speech.

I kneeled before him and lifted the trijewel necklace away. Then I used the needle to pry the Eye of Orik from his helmet. Finally I stuck the dagger into the Whisperer's neck.

<pre>
Critical!
You dealt 189 damage to [Hadrian]
Stun!
</pre>

I blinked.

By all accounts Hadrian should've been dead. He should've been dead but wasn't. I went to stab him again but the needle was lodged into his body. I tightened my grip and tugged but it was stuck, just like the other two. The rock armor closed around it, growing up and over the handles. The three of us blinked in horror, backing away ever so slightly.

The Whisperer's hand shot forward and snatched the trijewel. I cradled the Eye and hopped backward.

"What's the deal?" asked Kyle. "You said this would work."

I stared. "It was supposed to."

"Dude's still alive, bro."

"It was a hell of a plan," murmured Izzy.

"It still is," I countered. "We don't need to take his life, we need to take his power." I gripped the Eye of Orik as we watched the shifting quartz.

"My power is indestructible," growled Hadrian.

I recovered the dragonspear. "Lucifer and I had a long talk about the soulstones. And you're right, destroying them's impossible. That's why Saint Peter's quest wanted them removed instead of broken. But there's something else Lucifer revealed to me. Each city has a soulstone, and each city has an item of power. These six artifacts make up the founder relics, each with an opposite. So while the Eye of Orik can never be destroyed, the dragonspear can release the soul of the titan within."

I tapped the tip of the legendary weapon to the oversize ruby. The two objects had an almost-magnetic repulsion between them. They were at odds with each other, in opposition, yet sharing a common thread. Something in me found that connection, brought it together, and it clicked.

The deep red of the Eye of Orik swirled and became blue. A silent shock wave shuddered outward.

"What have you done?" snarled Hadrian.

"But the Oakengard quest," said Kyle. "It's corrupted, which means it's blocking the soulstone quest forever."

Izzy nodded. "It's true. The string is broken."

"Forget the quests. We don't need the approval of game systems to tell us we're doing the right thing. Our actions are what matter."

Hadrian stirred. Still on the ground, but his stun wore off. His body trembled. Crystal continued to grow on him, around him, up from the ground. It was encasing him again.

"I see this precursor isn't enough," he spewed. "So I'll show you more."

The ruined Speculum lit up, whirring engines beating a mountainous heart. Hadrian was part of the floor now, his legs quickly being overtaken.

"The Crystal Core," warned Izzy.

My eyes snapped to the trijewel in his grip. Crystals grew around his fingers. I equipped Lucifer's witchwood staff and leapt. My hand closed around the leather cord but I couldn't pull it away. The founder relic was also in Hadrian's grip.

"This one's mine," he insisted.

I yanked again but it wouldn't give.

"We're running out of time," said Izzy.

Instead of trying to take it from him, I focused on the soulstone below. It wasn't just an item anymore, something that could be contained in inventory. The Crystal Core was a living mass beneath us, growing and breathing. I squeezed the trijewel into the ground and focused, trying to find that repulsion, that common link that could dispel the soulstone. Once that was done I could trap the power if needed.

I encountered resistance, but not equal and opposite. Hadrian forced his will into the relic too, asserting his dominance as the Protector of Oakengard. I pushed back, fighting his growing presence, losing focus on the Crystal Core.

Hadrian growled. "The power... is mine!"

My face snapped away as crystal popped. For a second I thought the trijewel triangles had burst. No. It was the expanding quartz. It reacted violently to my touch, lashing at my face. It crusted over my hand, peeled my fingers away, submerging Hadrian's arm and the trijewel.

"Get out of there!" snapped Izzy.

Kyle helped her tug me away. I shook grains of quartz off my hand as it came up empty. Lucifer's broken staff in my other hand limped to my side. "He has the trijewel."

The Speculum shuddered and we braced against each other for support. It wasn't just the floor that shook this time, it was the whole room. The walls. The floors above.

Kyle looked around, dumbfounded. "What the..."

Slabs fell from the ceiling. I shoved my friends out of the way. The stationary schoolgirl was crushed. Hadrian was safe, mostly buried by the lake. Absorbed by it. The heartbeat of lights pounded beneath us.

"Uh, guys," said the brewmaster, "I've got a really bad feeling about this."

A deep voice reverberated through the room, carried through ice and crystal. "The power is mine," boomed Hadrian. "Arise Gigas, a titan, a god."

More chunks of roof collapsed. The ground broke open.

"We need to get out of here," said Izzy.

Lash and Conan hacked at the ice wall with their weapons.

"Get to the high tower!" I yelled. "That's an order, Lash! You need to get clear of Oakengard!"

The paladin grunted. We locked eyes for a second and she nodded. Bravo Team and the others retreated up Izzy's makeshift steps.

"And what about us?" asked the pixie.

She was attempting to carve away the ice wall but it was too heavily glazed with crystal. It wasn't reacting to her magic like it should. Kyle was tossing corrosives at it but wasn't having luck either. I scanned for weak spots, looking for a break in a wall or another door. The floor continued to shift as Hadrian was swallowed completely. I didn't want that to happen to us. I stared at the horrible power below, blinking, pulsing, breathing.

I could feel it. Like it was part of me, or at least I had my hooks in it. Lucifer called me a soulstone worker. It was too late for a power trap—the Crystal Core was too smothering to be contained now—but I had a good feeling I could tap into a small part of it.

"Wake up, Bandit," I whispered firmly.

I teased at the Crystal Core, the bit of magic that used to be the dragonstone. It was no longer physical but it was there. I called on it to activate once more.

"Wake up, Bandit."

A resounding screech answered my call. The chestnut dragon lifted her head and shook away the malaise. She locked on us through the wall of ice and yawned her mouth wide.

"Take cover!"

A bright sphere of gold exploded through Hadrian's wall, sending chunks of ice and crystal everywhere. We took to our feet and sprinted ahead. Izzy furnished the chasm with a bridge using whatever ice still heeded her call, and we made it through the hole in the wall and up the chunked stairs to Bandit.

"Bros," said Kyle uneasily as we stood on the elaborate stone tiles of Oakengard's second floor. "This fortress is shaking like a mutha. This kinda feels like the end of those old school video games where you gotta escape before the castle collapses on itself."

I grimaced. "Right genre, wrong trope," I said sourly. "I think Hadrian's about to take his final form."

>> Minigame <<

Tad pressed a hand on his leg to stifle his nervous energy. Christian's black box upload was complete, at least as far as he could tell, but the CEO wasn't waking up. Was he supposed to do something to complete the process? The man was still breathing, but none of his vitals were being tracked so he didn't have further details.

At least the InLink operatives had halted their incursion. The threat of destroying Haven was an effective one. Which was to say that only the immediate danger was stymied. At the end of the day, the two of them were still trapped in a small office surrounded by a rogue ops team.

Once again Tad checked on Christian. If there was a pulse at his wrist, it was weak enough to be ambiguous. Tad's eyes locked on the EXSIL head interface. Maybe he needed to move it away. He reached slowly, afraid of messing something up. As the tip of his finger touched the device, the entire room shook. Tad gripped the bed for support.

That was an explosion outside.

The programmer looked around but the room had no windows. He hopped on one leg back to the main office. A huge fireball floated over Harbor Island, curling into black smoke.

"Oh my God." Tad spun around. "Christian! Christian, wake up!" He arrived back at the EXSIL just as the CEO stirred. Tad would be patient no longer. He grabbed the man's shoulders and shook violently. "Get up."

Christian blinked and sat up, grabbing his stomach and wincing as he did. "I nearly forgot," he said, examining the bandage. He slipped off the bed and trudged to the console, nodding in approval. "Nice work. The transfer was a success."

"Christian, you need to see this."

Tad hopped back to the window. Christian's face fell as he gazed on the Phoenix Y launch site.

A radio beeped and sniggers came from the opposite side of the barricaded door. They quickly hushed as a light knock came rapping. A new voice spoke.

"Good afternoon, Mr. Everett. My name is Mr. Hines." The man was clean-spoken and polite, which distinguished him from the rest of the ops team. "It appears as if your backup satellite experienced a severe catastrophic accident."

Christian swiveled his attention from the barricaded door to the smoke cloud. "They knew..."

"Who are you?" barked Tad.

"Mr. Lonnerman, I presume? I believe I've already introduced myself. If you open the door—"

"I mean who do you work for? What do you want?" Tad realized he was asking questions he already knew the answers to. He was angry and in a demanding mood, and the obvious questions were all he could think to demand.

Mr. Hines sighed. "My employer's of little consequence. Mr. Everett, the servers in your office are all that's left of Haven, and there's an unfortunate reality we need to discuss."

"What's that?" asked the CEO tepidly.

"So you are still alive." Tad could hear Mr. Hines smiling through the door. "Your simulation is never going into space. The Universal Interstellar Rights will never vest. But that doesn't mean your incredible legacy will end here. We'd like to work with you as a partner."

Christian scoffed. "You seriously expect me to believe this is a business offer?"

"I do, and I have the proof." On the other side of the door were two clicks from what must have been a briefcase unlocking and the flutter of papers. "I have documents from my employer —"

"InLink," he stated firmly.

Mr. Hines cleared his throat. "InLink contracts, yes. If you'd just open the door I promise—"

"Slide the papers under the door."

Tad turned to Christian in alarm.

"This is a waste of time," came the voice of a gruff soldier. "He's not gonna sign anything."

Mr. Hines coolly replied, "I have my instructions, as do you. Give them the contract."

The other man grunted. A few seconds later a stapled pack of papers scratched against the carpet beneath the door. Tad approached carefully, worried this was some kind of trick, but the door was locked and the crutch was jammed tight and the heavy Victorian bookcase wasn't going anywhere. Tad scooped up the paper and handed it to Christian.

"You'll see," continued Mr. Hines, "that you'll be given every opportunity to work on and direct the future vision of Haven. It goes without saying that you'll hand over ownership, but you can still be the face of your creation."

"You blew up the studio and sent in an army of gunmen," hissed Tad. "What's stopping you from killing us the second we open the door?"

"He has a point," acknowledged Christian. The CEO skimmed the legalese and flipped pages as the sales pitch continued.

"You're an asset, Mr. Everett. No one here wishes to deprive the world of your genius. But the choice is in your hands: Let us have Haven and we can continue your legacy, together, or you can destroy the servers and the lives of all the people you thought you were saving. Either way, we're coming in. What do you say?"

Tad flushed with anger. Christian neatly turned the stack of papers in two hands and ripped it in half. "I'm sorry," he said stoically, "it appears as if your employment contract experienced a severe catastrophic accident."

Mr. Hines remained quiet behind the door. After a moment, it was the gruff soldier who spoke. "Heh, was hoping you'd say that."

Christian's eyes went wide. He lunged and tackled Tad as a stream of gunfire tore through the wood door. They landed on the carpet hard under incoming bullets. Tad gritted his teeth, rolled over, and crawled to the bookcase beside the door. Another round of bullets disintegrated the door handle and deadbolt. Tad grabbed the edge of the bookcase and pushed, leaning on the hard cast to prop up the great weight. The heavy antique slid on the carpet, barricading the door completely.

Case set Big Bertha to the door and it bounced in its hinges. The handle mechanism was obliterated, but the bookcase held. Another round of gunfire erupted. Tad ducked, but the solid wood and stack of programming tomes absorbed the impacts. As the soldiers continued to slam into the door to no avail, Tad turned to Christian, pleased.

The CEO was wheezing and clutching his ribs. A new gunshot wound welled under his armpit.

"Christian!" Tad collapsed beside him and scrambled on the floor for the stack of bandages.

The CEO grabbed his wrist tightly. "It's too late for the medkit, Tad."

The programmer kept searching but slowed as the tightness clamping his wrist intensified.

"I'm serious," said Christian. "We're out of time. Both of us." Christian offered him a bronze key. "You need to get to the roof."

Tad furrowed his brow. "The roof? What good's a satellite dish without a satellite?"

Christian swallowed hard. "I haven't told you everything, Tad, but I trust you completely. I suppose it's all up to you now."

The banging on the door continued. "What's up to me?"

"Did you ever find it odd, Tad, that I named my satellites Phoenix X and Y?"

The Phoenix code name spoke for itself. A new life, stirred from the ashes of death, rising into the sky. The X designation was for SoCal and Y for Harbor Island. Tad blinked. "You have a third satellite."

The CEO smiled. "Phoenix Z is an ultra-compact microsatellite on the roof of this building. It's a complete secret. Not even Abbie knew about it. You need to manually launch it from the dish console."

"Manually launch? I thought they were automated."

"The primary and secondary sites were, yes. This mini-rocket was a personal guarantee of sorts. A desperate fail-safe. It's not even cleared for launch by the FAA, and seeing as how it's illegal to put it into space at all, it won't quite matter if we launch it a bit early, will it?"

Tad nodded as he digested the information. The grim reality was that Christian might not be around to answer for the crime. "What about Talon? We told him he'd have more time."

Christian grimaced. "We've run out of time. We can only hope he's accomplished his mission."

Tad swallowed. "And what about you?"

"I've assured my future. As soon as Haven's in the sky, data will beam from the satellite dish and perform a full sync. My patch, my digital life, is waiting in the queue."

The pounding on the door intensified. Big Bertha was having a hell of a time with the bookcase.

"Go through the back door," urged Christian, placing the key in Tad's palm. "Take my private elevator to the roof. Everything's been prepped. You'll know what to do."

The wounded man pushed Tad to his feet. Tad hopped to the edge of the room and leaned against the doorway, looking back at his boss. He worked his jaw uneasily. "You saved my life."

Christian smiled. "You've been real dependable, kid. You remind me of myself, when I still had a future."

"You do still have a future."

He nodded. "I know, and it's up there. Now get out of here."

Tad backed away through the server room, pain welling in his leg as he exited the back door. More unfamiliar ground. This was just a small vestibule with a private service elevator. He limped in the open door and held the bronze key to his face. The job was simple enough, but it felt more momentous than anything else he'd done over the last few days. It could very well be his final act.

Tad glanced in the direction of the server room, a moment of indecision crossing his thoughts. Had it been a mistake not to back up his consciousness as well? As the gunfire against the barricaded door intensified, Tad saw his opportunity dwindling away. It was a hell of a gamble. If he spent valuable time at the EXSIL, it might enable InLink to prevent the launch. It would risk countless lives in the sim.

Tad slid the key into the bronze fixture and twisted. The elevator was unresponsive. The fire alarm protocols rendered it offline. Another doorway in the vestibule led to a stairwell that only went up. Tad bitterly abandoned the key and advanced, gritting his teeth. He leaned on the handrail and heaved up the first step. The effort made him wince, and when he checked his broken leg, he noticed a tiny hole in the cast below his knee.

He'd been shot as well.

2160 Mass Effect

Hail-sized chunks of ceiling crumbled to the floor.

"The faster we get outside, the better," said Izzy. She hurried to a courtyard exit and struggled with the locked door.

Bandit snorted agreement. I cocked my head at her curiously. She was a mountain bongo again. Which was strange, but no more strange than her transforming into a dragon for the second time in the same day. Without a dragonstone no less. I was just gonna roll with it.

"Not that way," I said. "The high tower. That's our evac."

Kyle nodded. "Already scouted out, my man."

The pixie stopped putting her shoulder to the door and equipped her wand. "Don't worry, I can get this open."

"That's not the point."

Izzy rested her hands on her hips. "Why do I get the feeling there's more to the plan than I know?"

I shrugged. "Did I not tell you? It's hard to keep track. Kyle?"

"Right," he said. "This way."

We charged down the perpendicular hallways of Oakengard as the fortress shook and groaned. Cracks opened in the stonework. Doorways sealed themselves off with brick.

"Something's giving me the distinct feeling we're not

welcome here," said Izzy.

"Just getting that now, huh?" I quipped. "Thing is, I also get the feeling we're no longer allowed to leave."

We leapt aside as the floor splintered apart.

"Come on!" called Kyle, holding a heavy door open with his shield. It was attempting to crush him. We slipped through and he heaved with all his might, barely recovering the mirror shield as the door slammed. "Up the stairs."

Luckily, as we climbed to Oakengard's third floor, the incidents of structural damage diminished.

"The castle's not toppling," noted Kyle with an engineer's eye. "I think it's just the foundations that are cracking."

Izzy fired off a pointed glare. "Wouldn't that have the same end result?"

Kyle's lower lip stuck out. "Good point."

We hurried into the tower. Given our home was Dragonperch, we were old hats at navigating the spiral staircase, even under earthquake conditions. It reminded me of stumbling down the steps when Orik awoke. As Bandit raced ahead, I realized the comparison was closer than I thought.

This was another titan rising from the ground. This was Gigas.

We burst into the sunlight of the high tower's roof. Stunning midnight-blue sails on the *Void* dominated the sky. The black flagship was docked alongside the battlements, hovering on magical ether. Dune, Lash, and the others were loading up.

"I knew what to expect," I said breathlessly, "and still it's amazing."

"That she is!" chimed Admiral Oates. "Now get yer arses on

me frigate 'fore we all crash an' burn."

I helped Kyle as the others hopped over. I was the last to jump aboard, greeted by Lash and Bravo Team, Dune and Stigg, Errol and Avisa, and Cleric Vagram and Papa Brugo.

"Hell of a crew," I said.

The *Void* veered away as the tower bucked sideways. Dust kicked up in the foothills surrounding Oakengard.

"What's our headin'?" asked Errol.

"What are we doing?" added Avisa as she gripped the handrail.

"The Lake of Dreams," I said.

Errol nodded and took the helm. Sergeant Avisa stomped to me and pointed down. "I mean what are we doing about that?"

A giant sonic boom knocked us to the deck. The ship bowed sideways. I crawled to our starboard and peered over at the impossible.

The fortress of Oakengard and the mountain cap it rested on rose from the ground on massive pillars, each wider than the *Void* but spindly in comparison to the mountain itself. Large swaths of land tore away and crumbled as the titan awoke.

I blinked back disbelief. Gigas, the All Mother, wasn't buried under the ground, she *was* the ground.

Trafford sighed as he took a seat on a large rock. It wasn't a particularly comfortable rock, but it was the first chance he'd had to sit in hours. The battle of the Godsbog was over. The final remnants of the plague were purged. Every last member of the Violet Order had fought till the last and fallen to the mud. The old general shifted in place to ease his back and massaged a bum knee.

He'd said it to the point his words were losing meaning, but this time it was really true. He was getting too old for this.

"Want me to give you something for the pain?" asked Caduceus. Besides being quite impressive on the battlefield, the physicker had all sorts of concoctions.

"Got a beer?"

She smirked. "I'm not that kind of doctor. Besides, older men are kinda the opposite of what I'm into."

He chortled. The girl had sass in her. "No thanks," he finally said. "I earned this pain. I'm gonna sit with it for a while."

Trafford watched as Colonel Grimwart collected the Black Army, wondering how the young man still had so much energy. He was born for this, he knew. The other leaders, too, had all done their parts. The wild king had dived headfirst into battle, fighting alongside his subjects in the field. General Azzyrk was a mighty chieftain, ruling by example, while Serpico was ruthlessly efficient with his bow. The witches kept true to their word. Even Nooner refrained from his usual hijinks.

Then there were the common folk. Ordinary men and women, NPCs and mobs. The pagans and wildkins found a cause worth championing. The legionnaires stretched their support of Stronghold to encompass Haven. And the aid of the catechists was undeniable. The Black Hats proved that it was possible for everyone to work together, if even for one shining moment.

Yup, it had been a sound victory. The kind he'd be boasting about in taverns for the rest of his years, now that it was over.

"Watch out!"

Goblins and wildkins soothing Orik shifted in panic.

Yup, Trafford stubbornly asserted to himself, IT WAS ALL OVER.

Ropes snapped. Vines uprooted from the ground.

"Away!" commanded Hood. Blackwood prisoners fled as links of magical chain popped apart.

"Fie!" cried the witches in fear. "Fie!"

The cyclops propped himself off the ground and shook like a wet dog. The army scattered. When Orik turned and gazed to the horizon, empty eye socket and all, there was a prescience to him that Trafford hadn't seen before.

He was wild again.

The Mighty One's throat rumbled awake in a deafening pronouncement of being. Orik rose to full height and lumbered hungrily toward Oakengard.

2170 Titan Quest

Avalanches of dust tumbled down the sheer rock cleft left behind as Gigas lifted higher in the sky. From the safety of the airship, we stared at the shifting mountainside in awe.

"What is that?" asked Kyle. "Some kind of rock lord?"

I snickered. "Rocks that come alive?"

Izzy sighed. "Whatever you guys are doing right now, it's not the time."

"You're probably right," I reluctantly agreed as we completed a circle around the massive landmass that was the third titan. "First thing's first before it's too late. We need to free the kraken. Papa Brugo?"

I presented him with the Squid's Tooth. Vagram's eyes widened at the artifact he'd once coveted and hated.

The Papa of Papas nodded. "It is a shame," he said in a deep baritone, "but it is also what must be done."

He grabbed the kraken's soulstone and placed his other hand over the powerchain around his neck. The links of metal rattled as he pitted his jaw. After a few moments of heavy concentration, his face eased. The Squid's Tooth went from ivory to black. Brugo opened his eyes.

"The kraken has been released," he announced solemnly.

"Two down, one to go," I said.

"Mmm hmm," added Izzy with a heavy dose of skepticism. "That's easier said than done when the third soulstone's in the middle of that thing." She pointed but it wasn't necessary. Everyone within miles knew what thing she was talking about.

Gigas was the final objective, the final boss, and it was impossible for anyone to take their eyes off her. Oakengard's steep mountain cap, famous for repelling attack, had completely broken away from its rock bed. Six spiderlike legs extended to the sides and bent at a single joint to the ground. Gigas was a walking island, sloping upward into a castle. The ground trembled, each step an earthquake, as the titan navigated down the steep mountains.

Kyle whistled. "Some legs on the old girl, huh?"

It was a major understatement. Each leg was a tower of rock spanning two-hundred feet. That was twice as high as Stronghold's walls—equal in height to Orik himself. Counting the combination of mountain cap and fortress, the spider's body accounted for another two-hundred feet at least. Gigas was aptly named. She was the single largest dynamic object in Haven.

Oakengard shivered as its four equidistant towers activated. Violet energy crackled up their walls and collected above the battlements.

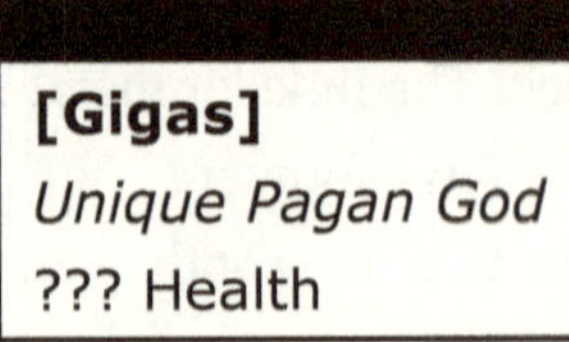

"You seeing this, Errol?" I called out.

The pirate was waiting at the helm. "Arr, an' ready fer evasive action."

The four purple energy collections shot to the center and combined before firing outward. The *Void* pulled away and the laser rushed past us.

"If that hits the sails, we're dead!" warned Brugo.

"I'm aware," said Errol. "I'll do me best, but me girl has a fat arse."

Avisa pointedly crossed her arms. "You best be talking about the ship."

Errol laughed wildly as the *Void* dove low and slalomed into the partial cover of lower peaks. As we weaved, explosions of dust encompassed us.

"What now?" hissed the sergeant.

Several chunks of rocky terrain broke away from the ground, hovered in the sky, and cracked into jumbles of legs.

Izzy's face went flat. "Tell me those aren't spider babies."

The brewmaster sang in climax: "Powerful living rocks!"

The balled-up boulder legs rocketed toward the ship. The *Void's* famed speed had been outdoing the titan, but the flyers were closing fast.

I stomped to the handrail.

"Come on, Bandit."

I didn't bother to stop and consider whether it could be done, I simply knew it could. I climbed atop her back and we hopped off the side of the airship together. As the wind whipped against our faces, the mountain bongo grew into her dragon form. We swooped away from the ground and bore vertically at the pursuing rock spiders. Bandit breathed a stream of light that hit one dead center. Pebbles exploded over us.

A couple of the flyers broke away and veered toward us. The other four continued toward the *Void*.

"Man the cannons!" ordered Avisa. "We're in for a dogfight!"

Cannon fire rumbled as Bandit swerved away from a slash. The spiders didn't appear to have ranged weapons and were attacking with pointed claws. It would've been a bigger disadvantage had they been less maneuverable. Dragon breath fired once more but the spiders were ready for it and easily dodged.

Bandit's head followed one spider while I tracked the other. They were splitting up and staying on opposite flanks, and using the same strategy on the airship. The dragon beat her wings to gain an altitude advantage, but the flyers nimbly kept pace.

I gritted my teeth. In a situation like this, it was easy to cede the upper hand. If we attacked one, we exposed our back to the other, but if we remained in the center we invited them both to close at once. No, it was better to be decisive and dictate the action.

Bandit coughed up a short energy beam at one of the flyers, prioritizing speed and surprise over damage. The rock spider swooped away. I tugged the reins toward the opposite enemy, knowing we'd just bought a few extra seconds. The dragon rocketed to the singled-out spider minion with every intent to engage.

It screeched and charged us. As we drew closer, I leaned into the pointed dragonspear.

It was a feint. The weaver pulled away at the last second so it could swoop by. My spear point missed but Bandit's neck craned backward and clamped a rocky leg. The sudden clash of momentum spun us around, forcing me to hug her close. The caught spider screeched as five free legs frenetically slashed.

Bandit's legs were larger and more powerful. Armored mitts held the smaller creature at arm's length, nails scraping, teeth chomping. The stone creature was well armored, but its health quickly dipped under fifty percent as the dragon ripped a couple of legs off. As Bandit twirled in the air to keep her dominance, the second rock weaver slammed into her side.

She cried out as a stone leg punched through dragon scales. I was dislodged from my seat and nearly fell off. The dragonspear batted at an incoming appendage. Although the damaged spider was nearly dead, Bandit couldn't hold on anymore. She released it and spun to face the greater threat.

I crouched on dragonback, steadied with my free hand while defending myself with the spear. Bandit's jaws clamped one of the spider's legs, but two more redirected to scratch her face. Instead of locking into a hold, she had to settle for repeated nips. Meanwhile, the minion was doing more damage digging into her side.

I stared in alarm as the original wounded spider was turning in the air to re-engage. My eyes shifted to the *Void*. Errol wasn't in a position to help. They attempted to suppress the flyers but their cannons were overwhelmed. Two weavers had clamped to the side of the ship. Izzy, Vagram, and Brugo were leading the charge against them while Bravo Team supported. I turned back to my predicament, knowing we only had seconds left until the second spider landed on us.

Two could play at that game.

"Get off..." I growled as I put the spear away, "my dragon." I equipped the tiger claws and vaulted between swiping legs and onto the back of the grappling spider. It stiffened as I hugged its thin body, legs frantically scratching upward. But I was on its back, outside the reach of its appendages. And just as Bandit had been forced to after being caught from behind, the spider panicked and released its prey.

For a long two seconds, we plummeted. I gripped the free-falling boulder tightly and wondered if I'd made a miscalculation. Was this rock self-aware? Did it know if it cratered into the ground I'd be dead?

But self preservation must've applied to rock lords too, because the weaver swooped around and increased altitude. It was just in time to see the wounded spider engage Bandit. Luckily, the girl was ready. She met it with a fierce bite.

Things back under control, I scratched at the spider's back as it flew higher and higher. The tiger claws had proven decent weapons in the past, though they were better used as a distraction. I wasn't gonna kill the thing but I was scraping away health and keeping it busy. It was the best I could do at this range after losing the assassin needles.

Cannon fire exploded nearby. I ducked as one of the *Void's* enemies crumbled. On deck, two spider minions were dead. The last retreated, no match for the collective might of the Black Hat leadership. With four port cannons focused on a single enemy, they tagged it out of the sky. Some ways off, Bandit ripped hers to shreds. Despite the impending victory, the pirates on deck panicked.

"Evasive action!" ordered Errol.

I didn't see the danger until I spun to Oakengard. The violet energy was building up again. It was seconds away from firing. "Bandit, watch out—"

I tensed. All the minions were dead except for the one I was mounted on. It didn't want to kill itself to get to me, but apparently Gigas had different priorities. I leapt off the flyer and dashed straight up to the clouds as the giant violet laser rumbled through my previous position. The rock weaver instantly disintegrated.

Phew. One problem out of the way. My satisfaction floundered as my upward momentum slowed in the air. Years of programming game physics flooded my head as my vertical speed hit perfect zero for a snapshot in time before the acceleration of gravity took over. I was now in free fall.

Pop quiz: A free-falling object in space has a Y value of 1,000 feet. Given standard gravity of 9.8 meters per second squared and assuming negligible air resistance, how many seconds does it take until Y equals 0?

"Hooooly Shiiiiiiiiiiittttttttt!!!!"

I plunged toward ground, thankfully nice and low due to us clearing the mountain range. The countryside was beginning to soften and green, which while beautiful offered little practical comfort. At my speed I'd be a bullet.

Bandit cried out and swooped into action. She was already well below me so she just needed to close horizontally. But as my speed increased, I was beginning to fear it wouldn't matter.

The dragon neared and veered downward. Her wings beat with furious strength, propelling her great body toward the ground. As I rapidly closed the distance from above, she folded her wings to her side and entered a free dive. I was still too fast.

Then again, textbook physics problems were often deeply flawed. They dealt with perfectly round masses in the void of space, bereft of friction and air resistance and all the tiny complications found in the real world and groundbreaking afterlife simulations.

This here wasn't an academic exercise.

"Negligible air resistance my ass," I said.

I grabbed the corners of my stranger's cowl and spread them wide like a parachute. It didn't work as smoothly as planned, but the flapping streamer minimized my speed. As Bandit's sleek form increased descent velocity, I closed with her more gently.

"Oof!"

I hit her side and the air left my lungs. The tiger claws spiked into her scales. Bandit spread her wings and steered around, swooping so low over the ground that she kicked up a stream of grass as we passed.

"Wooo!" I screamed as I climbed into the saddle. I'd never been skydiving before and it was a hell of a rush. Bandit turned her head around and I reached forward and patted her snout. "Thanks, girl. You're one in a million."

She chirped in appreciation and snapped leathery wings as the last of the sun dipped below the ravaged mountain peaks to the west.

>> Minigame <<

For some reason, Tad had expected a short flight of stairs that plopped him directly on the roof. Instead he was growing increasingly exhausted as the steps kept coming. Even though Kablammy Games was on the top floor, he must have covered three flights at least.

Or maybe it just felt like it. His strength was fading fast.

The pain was excruciating, but only small amounts of blood seeped from the hole in the cast. It gave him hope that the wound was only a graze, but soon his sock sloshed inside his shoe.

Tad reached the summit and rested on the concrete floor beside the service elevator. He turned and saw a short set of concrete stairs leading to a metal exterior door.

"It never ends."

But it did. When Tad crawled up and pushed the door open, he was greeted by a burst of fresh air. It had been daytime when Harbor Island exploded; now it was night. Christian and Tad had managed to bunker down for two and a half days and it was all coming to a head in the final hours.

The programmer stepped outside and surveyed the roof. Instead of a spacious open area, there were walled platforms of various sizes and elevations. As he hopped around a roof outcropping, leaning on it for support, a helicopter blared nearer. It rounded the building and pulled overhead.

"Don't move!" cried the pilot through a speaker.

The side hatch slid open and revealed the rogue operatives within. This was getting ridiculous. InLink commanded a small army and was pulling out all the stops. Meanwhile Tad and Christian were just two bleeding engineers.

Tad raised his hands in surrender. The chopper hovered above his head, rifles trained his way.

Christian Everett breathed.

It was no longer something he could take for granted, and it was becoming increasingly difficult, so he closed his eyes and breathed. Again and again, taking as much oxygen into his lungs as his pained chest would allow. He wasn't a doctor and didn't know if the bullet had punctured his lungs. He just knew he wasn't gurgling on his own blood. That had to count for something.

Outside the door, the operatives had completely abandoned any semblance of negotiation. Mr. Hines was silent. The others alternated between bouts of firing at the obstruction and using the battering ram. The antique bookcase trembled as splinters filled the air. As much of an old tank as it was, the furniture could only take so much abuse. Christian wouldn't be safe forever.

He ignored the impending doom and returned to his workstation. First he made sure the launch protocols were ready. His black box was processed, his patch was queued, everything was waiting on the Phoenix Z satellite launch. If they could get it airborne before the soldiers reached the servers, they'd be gold. Literally, Haven would launch and go gold.

All that was left to do was stymie InLink's tampering, which meant shutting down his hub access and other non-essential machines. It would take the operatives time to figure out what was happening. It would take them even longer if their machines were locked out.

Christian twisted the workstation on the carpet to access the power switch on the back. He breathed. The CEO clenched his jaw...

And spotted the poop emoji thumb drive inserted into one of the computer's rear USB slots.

One of Abbie's thumb drives.

He frantically spun to the monitor and checked his machine. It had been there the whole time. Throughout his code integration. For all he knew, his entire patch was compromised.

Christian Everett stared at the workstation in shock, unmoving as the door rumbled, unresponsive to the security feeds of Armored Personnel Carriers advancing across the building plaza and SWAT officers flooding the main lobby en force. InLink operatives on the ground fell victim to the sudden superior firepower. They abandoned the hostages and retreated to the stairwell.

Few of the events registered with Christian because the full implications of the thumb drive were much more dire. He was unable to accurately calculate the risk to his dream. To his paradise.

He clicked open Haven's central hub and opened the Everchat interface, pinging anyone who would listen. No one answered his call. He'd failed to give Talon the time he promised, failed to warn them of the launch. He'd repeatedly failed to protect his legacy from threats inside and out, and now, during the final hurrah, it was too late.

The brilliant CEO took an extended breath through strained features, squared himself with the monitor, and pulled the keyboard close.

Tad rested against a sidewall, hands in the air. He'd long abandoned his crutch and his leg had gone numb. It was just as well. What he didn't feel couldn't distract him. The buffeting wind from the helicopter blades stung the skin on his face. The rifles held by professional soldiers would do much worse.

As the helicopter circled overhead to find a place to land, the sky echoed the sound of its spinning rotors, growing louder and deepening. Another helicopter twirled into view, black and white with the words "King's County Sheriff" emblazoned on the fuselage.

A megaphone blared but the InLink soldiers swiveled their rifles and opened fire. The SWAT helicopter veered. Tad ducked and skipped across the rooftop, around the corner, and right up to the computer console at the base of a small satellite dish.

He'd found it.

While the SWAT helicopter pulled away, snipers on the opposite rooftop opened fire. A small explosion racked the side of the InLink chopper. They twisted out of control. The tail nicked one of three powered antennas on the roof. Seemingly in slow motion, Tad watched as the helicopter broke apart like a plastic toy. He dove to the floor to avoid the flying guillotine of the tail rotors spinning overhead. Debris hit the roof seconds before the entire chopper crashed into the north side of the building. An explosion overtook the sounds of screaming soldiers.

Tad gritted his teeth, pushed to his feet, and limped back to the console. He rapped the keyboard and the monitor blinked on. The dish was online, but where was the satellite?

The SWAT helicopter returned to the building, doing a lap to assess the damage. Just like the other guys, it looked like they wanted to land and couldn't find a spot. Instead, they hovered near the stairway entrance. Two ropes tumbled from the chopper doors and police officers rappelled down.

Tad didn't have time for this. The police would never allow a launch. He moved ahead into the manual override. When the menu opened, a large storage crate on another section of roof opened up. Motorized walls collapsed and revealed a small launch pad and rocket. The microsatellite was a metal box hooked into the contraption.

"Sir," called the first police officer to touch down, storming over, "come with us."

Tad selected Launch and pounded the Enter key. Four large drones straddling the rocket whirred to life, their rotors a high-pitched whine compared to the chopper.

The SWAT team rushed over and shoved Tad not-so-gently to the floor. Other officers with rifles arrived, everyone turning as the rocket lifted from the rooftop by drone power. Sixteen sets of miniature rotors propelled the rocket skyward. They watched the LEDs fade in the distance with equal parts confusion and awe. And then, without a hint of warning, the rocket engaged in midair. Every jaw on the roof dropped as the drones disengaged from their cargo and the rocket arced toward the stars on independent power.

"What did you do?" demanded a cop.

Tad shook his head. "It's a *really* long story. You're not gonna shoot me, are you?"

A muscled officer with a biker mustache kneeled beside him. "Shoot you? You kidding? We're here to save you." He called into his radio and said, "Go ahead."

Ramon the paramedic's voice broke through the static. "I told you I'd get you a helicopter!"

Tad was so relieved he almost laughed. Then he realized they were far from done. "Christian Everett's been shot. He's downstairs." Tad tried to get up, but the officer held him down.

"Hold on. Looks like you're hurt too."

Tad fought against the military grip. "We need to save him!"

A commander standing nearby nodded. "Don't you worry, we will." He turned to the biker. "Keep an eye on him. Make sure—"

Shouting broke out. Despite the InLink soldiers crashing the helicopter and scrambling from the lobby, there were still plenty in the building. Two of them planted beside the stairwell door and opened fire on the SWAT team.

Everyone dove for cover. A gun battle erupted. The lead InLink operative fell to return fire and the follow man disappeared back inside.

"Advance!" yelled the SWAT commander.

They rushed into the stairwell using squad tactics and short bursts of suppressive fire.

Tad turned to the sound of harsh grunting. The mustached officer was clutching his leg. He'd been shot. Well-disciplined when under fire, he slipped off his belt and tied it around his leg above the wound.

"You okay?" asked Tad.

The man nodded. "It'll take more than that to do me in."

The programmer pushed to his feet. He needed to check on Christian. The fact that InLink had gotten past him wasn't a good sign. Tad locked eyes with the officer who was supposed to keep him on the rooftop. The man winced and gave him a nod. Tad nodded back and limped to the now-empty stairwell. As he struggled downstairs, he passed the bodies of dead soldiers.

2180 NiGHTS Into Dreams...

◆━━━━━━━━◆●◆━━━━━━━━◆

It was surprisingly easy to forget but, the entire time we were battling flying rock spiders, we'd covered a lot of ground pursued by Gigas. The land under us was moistening as we neared the Godsbog and the neighboring Lake of Dreams. Night was falling.

There was something else nearing too. A giant cyclops lumbered on the horizon, and he turned toward us with supernatural instinct.

Izzy: *Talon, you seeing this?*

Talon: *Orik must be after the Eye. He's free now and it's the only thing that can change that.*

As I considered our collision course with the water, Gigas seemed to lumber more urgently. The towers crackled with energy again.

"We're gonna need to do something about that," I told Bandit.

We momentarily hovered to see which way the titan went.

This time it was Errol who needed to flee the laser's path. As soon as the attack cleared us, Bandit twisted toward the walking island.

The entire mountain canted our way. It was aware of us, watching us. Bandit dove and purple energy once again collected along the towers.

"Go for it," I said.

Dragon breath lasered into the nearest high tower. Stone buckled and broke apart, but it was the whirring violet energy that proved more explosive. As the structure of the tower failed, the electrified magic erupted. Debris tumbled away and the collecting purple charge that was the titan's ammunition winked out.

The voice of Gigas rumbled deep and low in anger. Violet magic still clinging to the other three towers fired my way. The individual bolts were much smaller and noncontinuous, but there were multiple trajectories to consider now. Bandit dove under two of them but the third caught her leg. She screamed and twisted away.

Another beam of light released from the dragon's mouth. It hit the far tower and caused some damage, but the violet energy had already dissipated. We weren't rewarded with the chain reaction of last time.

Thump.

From elsewhere within the fortress, a projectile launched straight at us. We veered aside and it rushed past, rising higher and higher in the sky until colors burst overhead like the Fourth of July. Thirty purple pulses sparkled around us. We weaved in and out, getting singed by a couple. Behind us, another tower managed to charge up. We spun away from its laser.

Thump. Thump. Thump.

Dragon breath raked a third tower, but the projectiles were coming from everywhere now. Gigas didn't have weapons so much as contain powerful energy. Hitting the towers disabled her mega attack but I wasn't so sure we could neutralize them entirely.

"Get out of here!" I yelled.

Explosions racked the sky overhead as we swooped to safety. In the distance, the *Void* approached the Lake of Dreams. The waterbed was elevated high in the mountains, a natural extension of the Oakengard terrain and the distinct opposite of the Godsbog, yet it was still a pagan holy site. The Black Army was too far out to make it in time, but anything flying or standing two-hundred feet plus had an invitation to the party.

Bandit flapped furiously to catch up. She transformed to a bongo as we reached the airship, hooves pattering against the wooden deck. I dismounted and moved to the side rail. The normally still water of the lake was a broken mass of competing ripples as Gigas lumbered nearer.

"Brugo, the Squid's Tooth."

The big man's brows raised. "You're determined on this?"

I nodded. "Is the kraken down there?"

Brugo traded study between the water surface and the blackened, empty soulstone. "There is no longer a way to know." He frowned for a moment. "Have you no reservations, Talon of Stronghold?"

I brought open the quest menu.

Remove Soulstones from Play

Quest Type: Fepic

Reward: <empty>

The Eye of Orik, the Squid's Tooth, and the Crystal Core have the unwieldy power to dominate Haven. Collect and remove them from play.

Kyle strolled to my side, jaw hanging as he viewed the quest for the first time. He actually read the text too.

"Fepic!" he chimed excitedly. "Told you it was a real word."

"Ugh," groaned Izzy. "I'll never hear the end of this."

Kyle frowned. "I thought our quest string was invalidated after Bishop Tannen betrayed us and got himself killed."

"I wondered about that," I said. "But that subquest was blocking the main one. With it out of the way, one way or another..."

Izzy grinned. "Nothing else can stop us."

"Fucking epic," he pronounced.

Everyone stiffened and turned to the brewmaster in surprise. "What's that?" asked Vagram.

"What?" he asked defensively. "Can't a bro say fucking without people fucking freaking out?"

Kyle had ditched his clean-and-sober challenge at the worst possible moment, right in front of the ornery cleric. "What did you say?" asked Vagram, approaching with an indignant eye.

"*Fepic*," I whispered to Kyle. "Say *fepic*."

"Whatever," said the brewmaster with a shrug.

"Say it."

"Fucking fepic, all right?"

I slapped my hand to my face.

The blond-haired Vagram suddenly stopped, connecting the dots with an open jaw. "Do you mean to tell me that, all this time, I've been acting in the service of a quest that used... profanity?"

I involuntarily chuckled and immediately stifled it as Vagram grew red. "We're Black Hats," I told him. "It's how we roll."

Errol elbowed the cleric in the ribs. "Hate t' break it t' ye, matey, but yer on a vessel crewed by pirates an' perverts... an' worse."

"I'm fornicatin' right now!" called Grom from below deck.

Brugo snorted indignantly. "I'm the Papa of all Papas. Never has the land witnessed a more-feared crime boss."

Stigg thrashed his head to metal and growled in song, "Crucifixion magician! Crucifixion magician!"

Vagram blinked. "Well fuck me."

Kyle grinned. "Now you're getting it!"

"It's okay," comforted Glinda as she gave the devout cleric a hug. "They're not exactly esteemed company, but I've learned to shrug it off and roll with it." She pulled him tight and his face lowered to her bosom. Glinda's eyes went wide and she whispered over his shoulder to Lash as she led him away. "He's cute!"

Fireworks erupted above the *Void's* sails. Avisa spun the wheel to avoid damage as Errol hurried back. "What would I do without ye, love?"

She eyed him sharply. "Die ten times before lunch."

"Aye, but it'd be a glorious breakfast."

The crew took to the rails and drew weapons. Ropes pulled taut. Cannons reloaded. Somewhere, the sound of Grom climaxing drawled to an awkward finish. As the airship circled over the water, Gigas set a single spindly leg into the Lake of Dreams.

"Brugo," I urged. "Drop the Squid's Tooth."

"But the kraken," he protested.

"It doesn't matter. Hadrian will exploit the soulstones to the limits of their awful power. We're casting them into the negative world where they'll be stripped of their strength."

"I hate to cut in," said Izzy, "but don't you think Orik might have a thing or two to say about that?"

I stubbornly shook my head. "All I know is I made a promise to the pagans. I'd free the titans and let Orik fend for himself. I can only hope removing the Eye from play will satisfy him. If he gets it, we might need to fight him to steal it back. Otherwise someone in the future will, and they might succeed, and everything we've done will be for nothing." I turned to the Protector of Shorehome. "Cast the Squid's Tooth into the water."

The crime boss produced the founder relic, set his jaw, and pitched it overboard. All eyes watched the tooth plummet and splash down into the water.

The *Void* lurched sideways as a violet bolt ripped through her side sail.

"Tie the sails!" screamed Errol. "Tie the sails or ye might as well tie a noose 'round yer lanky necks!"

Pirates scurried across the deck to repair the damage. The airship careened awkwardly toward the lake surface. Waves crashed together as Gigas took another step into the depths.

"Fire!" called Avisa. The *Void's* cannons barked.

BABOOM, BOOM. BABOOM, BOOM.

Stone chunks tore away from the heavy Oakengard walls, but the damage was minimal. Firing at the massive brownstones was next to useless.

"Deeper!" I yelled. "Fly deeper over the lake!"

"Fly?" growled Errol. "I'm doin' me best not t' crash!"

"Controlled fall!" I corrected. "Controlled fall!"

The *Void* steadied with minor turbulence and blazed toward the far coast. We'd beaten the titans to the Lake of Dreams, but this was still a race for second place. The walking fortress slowed drastically once three legs were in the water, no doubt wary of our tactics. Too much hesitation would allow Orik to catch up, and the cyclops was a wildcard I didn't want to deal with again.

I yanked the Eye from my inventory and brandished it above my head. "You want this?" I screamed to the mountainous titan. "Come and get it!"

The soulstone was currently without a soul, but it still possessed the power to harness one. Between the Squid's Tooth in the depths, the Eye of Orik on the airship, and my brazen challenge, Gigas took a heavy step deeper into the lake.

Carrot, meet stick.

The plan was working, but as we sped toward the center of the lake, my heart tugged. My whole being, even. I clenched my teeth together and fought off sudden nausea. This wasn't air sickness, it was the influence of the shadow essence. It was a harbinger of what was coming.

"No," I groaned. "It's too soon."

A black mass welled in the Lake of Dreams.

Another round of fireworks popped overhead. The *Void* madly weaved between dozens of projectiles as if part of a 16-bit shooter on hard mode. At the same time, Gigas fired several more energy bolts. Between those and the raining pulses, we had nowhere to go. A violet missile ripped across the deck, flattening Avisa and two pirates, and snapping the rear mast. The flagship rocked violently as burning fire rained from the sky. Glinda and Vagram returned to action to assist the wounded. Errol cursed and fought the wheel. Papa Brugo caught the mast in his bare hands.

"I need all hands on deck!" boomed the crime boss.

Bandit rushed over before Brugo's mighty strength slipped. The mountain bongo planted broad horns into the base of the broken mast, steadying it. Kyle, Conan, Stigg, Grug, and Grom in his skivvies all piled together to support the mast before it completely buckled.

The temporary measures weren't a sure thing. The *Void* retained some semblance of control but was still in a dive. Against flapping wind, I trudged to the helm. "What are you doing, Errol?"

"We need t' set down in the water," he urged through gritted teeth.

"No. We need to go up."

"By the Maelstrom, Talon! We either be landin' or crashin'. The lake be the only safe—" The captain stopped as he realized his words. The airship dipped to the side and he peeked timidly at the water as a gaping maw opened across the surface. I had once likened the smell of the Godsbog to a toilet. That might be true, but the Lake of Dreams was the drain pipe, and that toilet was going flush.

"Repair the sails ye lazy scallywags!" cried the captain. "We need altitude I tells ya!"

One of the pirates hit with the bolt was dead, but the other and Avisa were revived. The sergeant nodded at her captain and rushed to help Brugo keep the dying vessel afloat.

I collapsed to one knee. With the Maelstrom open, the pull of the shadow was supreme. What I'd once feared to be an evil presence I now knew to simply be Lucifer. He was using his power, the power of the negative world, to call the shadow essence back to him. The draw was so strong it physically hurt. I could only hope that gaining some distance from the whirlpool would deaden the pain.

Izzy leaned close and yelled over the whipping wind. "You okay, Talon?"

I growled, "Never better."

"How do you plan on getting the Crystal Core away from Gigas?"

I winced. "I don't. Not anymore. You saw the Speculum. The Crystal Core was growing, reproducing. It's not something we can pocket in our inventory. The only way to cast it into the abyss is to take the whole damn city with it."

"And the pagans? You'd be banishing their All Mother. Are you sure you want to do that?"

I set my jaw. "I don't think that's really Gigas anymore."

2190 No Man's Sky

The airship lurched through the sky, nearly capsizing but somehow keeping level. The diligent pirate crew worked with impressive unity when they needed to, and the life expectancy of the *Void* increased from seconds to minutes. The braced rear mast was upgraded to serviceable, though we were now less maneuverable for the trouble. We wouldn't be able to sustain another direct hit.

The Maelstrom was fully raging now, and Gigas grew wise to our strategy. The titan paused its gargantuan mass, six legs in the water but still adjacent to the coast.

I blinked at the Eye of Orik in my hand and the vortex below. I could get rid of the second soulstone right now, but that wouldn't net me the grand slam. I cursed and leaned against Errol Oates, aiming a determined finger backward. "Fly for the titan. It's our only chance."

His eyes widened but he saw it too. The Maelstrom had attempted to claim its sacrifice too early. Gigas was too entrenched in the shallows to be sucked in. It was up to us to execute a kick in the pants.

I pushed forward to the head of the ship and held the soulstone high as we flew straight for the spiderlike fortress. It was enough of an incentive to momentarily stall the titan's retreat. As we bore toward it, purple magic tittered at the ready.

Hadrian wasn't firing because we were approaching with his prize.

"Dune, Kyle," I called, "gonna need your bows."

The archers came to my side. "How can we be of service?" asked the ranger.

I handed Kyle the Eye of Orik. "Can you stockrig this to a bolt and fire it to Gigas? Not all the way—I want him to work for it."

"No can do, bro. I used up my one for the day."

"Can't you tie it together or something?"

"Not unless you want it to drop straight into the water."

"Let me help," interjected Izzy. She took one of Kyle's heavy bolts and tickled her fingers to generate ice, binding it with the soulstone. "Will that do?"

The brewmaster frowned at the makeshift arrow. "Okay, how about this?" He produced another bolt and lined it up with the other. "Glue this one too." After Izzy complied, he tested the double projectile's weight.

"What do you think?" I asked urgently.

Kyle canted his head. "She'll be an ugly bird, but she'll fly."

"Good. Dune, once she's in the air, you'll give it the final nudge."

I grabbed the projectile and removed the shadow essence from my inventory. Concentrating on the power innate in the soulstone, I forced the darkness inside. The Eye swirled with an angry black pupil. My own little power trap.

Dune did a double-take. "Dude, that's your teleportation power."

"It is what it is," I said, handing the projectile back to Kyle. He loaded them both, attached together by the Eye of Orik, onto his dual eagle crossbow. "Okay, Hadrian," I muttered. "You want it, you can have it. Ready on my mark."

The airship barreled ahead with a heavy tail that dragged sideways. It was a rough ride. It would get a lot rougher if we were hit again.

Gigas took a step toward us.

"Thar she blows!" screamed Errol at the top of his lungs.

The ground rumbled and waves splashed below.

"Now!" I called.

Kyle had already settled his aim so he flicked the double trigger and the dual bolts fired in unison. She *was* an ugly bird, but her initial velocity sailed her through the wind with ease. Dune nocked a silver arrow and waited. The Eye of Orik cut across the sky and the living mountain shivered in anticipation. Just when I thought Kyle had overshot the range, the projectile arced downward, caught the wind, and tumbled apart in a tailspin.

Gigas leapt toward the plummeting soulstone in a panic to prevent it from falling short, moving deeper into the lake.

"Get it the rest of the way, Dune."

The ranger released a silver-tipped arrow. It cut downward, covering a great distance while the Eye of Orik floundered in the sky. Gigas lurched again, lifting a giant spire from the water and reaching forward to catch the founder's relic.

Dune's arrow chipped it in the side, knocking it anew. The Eye suddenly jolted forward, past the reaching spider leg. Gigas stuttered and the ruby tumbled into a debris pile that used to be a high tower, into the depths of the fortress.

"Nailed it!" I exclaimed.

The tug of the shadow essence had fled me completely. Hadrian, or Gigas, or whatever this abomination was now, paused warily. It had what it wanted. Or did it? The walking island twisted its mass around as it was suddenly influenced by a foreign gravity.

The shadow essence was pulling the island toward the Maelstrom.

The foot that had grasped for the soulstone stumbled down and slipped. Stretching legs lost purchase with the lake floor. The edge of the walking island dipped to the surface as Oakengard lurched sideways. The entire body of water shifted, a bathtub being rocked, forcing a tidal wave toward the Maelstrom. The pull of the shadow essence intensified and dragged the titan nearer the black hole.

My knuckles went white on the handrail. "Come on... come on..."

A low rumble reverberated through the water, sending a sphere of ripples outward. Stone spider legs spiked downward, embedding in the rock through the shallow water away from the lake's center. The land mass stopped dead as it secured itself.

"It's no good," cried Avisa. "We need to uproot her legs!"

Errol looked to me and I nodded. Desperate times and all. "How's me rear sail?" he asked.

"The *Void* will need a proper repair when we're in port, but she's airworthy," answered the sergeant.

"An' me tricorn?"

Avisa smiled in collected surprise. "It fits you like the perfect woman."

"Then hold on t' ye puffy shirts, 'cause we're goin' in!"

The airship entered an aggressive dive toward the stalled titan. Violet energy sparked up the nearest tower. Instead of firing a laser, the magic spread and overlaid a giant hologram of Hadrian's face on the brownstone wall. The visage was unholy: part man, part rock, and full crazy.

"Talon," bellowed the would-be god, voice pounding my eardrums. "You release Orik's soul, yet hand me the Eye. Attempt to entrap me with the shadow essence, yet deliver me its power. Can you not see that with every blow, I grow more and more powerful?"

Izzy leaned in. "Didn't he already do the evil-villain speech?"

I snickered as the *Void* flew closer. "I won't tell him if you don't."

"Ready the guns!" ordered Avisa. Errol spun the wheel as another purple bolt missed us by a hair. "Fire!"

BABOOM, BOOM. BABOOM, BOOM.

It was a direct hit. All four starboard cannons struck a tight grouping around the titan's knee. Or appendage joint. Or whatever spiders had. Dust exploded outward and Hadrian visibly grimaced.

The leg itself, however, barely shook. And considering Gigas had five more, the island remained perfectly stable.

Another tower filled with dangerous energy. Errol steered the ship down, between stony legs and right under the massive titan's belly, nary a laser turret in sight.

"You're a genius!" said Kyle, grabbing the captain by the shoulders and giving him a congratulatory shake.

"Arr, as self evident as that may be, these cannons aren't cut out fer a titan."

I joined them at the helm. "How about a special?"

"Alas, the *Void* has no special weapons."

"But it has an Atlantean anchor."

"And what of it? Gigas ain't stupid enough t' chase us into the Maelstrom."

"We're not going," I assured him. "Your crew's adept at field repairs. What if we retrofit the anchor onto Gigas?"

His brow stretched in alarm. "You want t' WHAT? The anchor'll guarantee Hadrian safe passage through—" He froze.

"Exactly," I said with a smile. "Passage is passage. We just need to make it happen."

The admiral nodded his head, encouraged. "In that case, we'll need a spot o' land we can hook the anchor to."

Avisa approached. "Somewhere *not* in sight of the lasers."

Kyle's eyes lit up. "The mines." He scanned the titan's underbelly. "Tunnels run deep through the mountains." He pointed. "Look, there! An open passage."

The titan's underside was mostly barren rock, but one of the bisected mine tunnels provided an easy way in. As Gigas struggled to hold onto solid ground and waited for us to emerge and make a move, Grug and Grom unloaded the item into the tunnel. They hastily retrofitted Gigas with the Atlantean anchor, deployed it, and hopped back onto the airship.

"Right in 'er asshole!" laughed Grug.

"That's what she said!" guffawed Grom.

Avisa shrugged in dismissal. "I'll allow it."

The pirates cackled as the *Void* dipped away. The mystical

anchor fired straight toward the Maelstrom, dragging a magical black line in its wake.

"What did you do?" snapped Hadrian.

The mystical anchor caught hold. The line went taut. Stone legs ripped chunks of wet ground away as Gigas jerked violently toward the center of the lake.

The sudden shift of position removed our umbrella of cover. No longer under Gigas, Hadrian's face rematerialized on the backside of the fortress to face us. He sneered.

Thump. Thump. Thump. Thump. Thump. Thump.

Explosives launched upward and multiple bolts fired. Bursts resounded everywhere. The hull took a glancing hit. A trio of cannons were taken out as a destructive beam ripped a gash in the side of the *Void*.

The crew tumbled to the deck as the airship spun out of control. The Oakengard high towers flared violet again, ready to do us in.

Gigas lurched sideways as the pull of the negative world increased. The lasers activated but dragged over our heads and we spun away.

"How hard are we gonna hit the water?" yelled Izzy.

Errol struggled with the wheel and shook his head. "The water'll do us no good, lass. With the size o' the hole in the hull, we'd sink faster than a cannonball. Our only hope is t' go fer the coast."

"Watch out!" screamed Kyle.

The *Void* tumbled in wild circles. Orik's angry countenance spun into view. He bore down on us, already in the water. The ship twisted around and Gigas was back on the horizon, struggling with the anchor's hold. We twirled again to see the cyclops lifting a giant paw to bat us out of the sky. Fingers spread and the hand came down.

Hull Phase Activated

The airship went black and the titan's blow whooshed through us. He was too big to phase through entirely, though. We solidified and clipped the side of his giant body. The collision scraped us with more damage, but it also miraculously steadied our bearing. The *Void* was no longer in a tailspin. Setting his targets on the coast, Errol sailed through the sky on an accelerating downward trajectory.

We weren't gonna make land.

Everybody grabbed ropes, masts, and handrails as the airship crash-landed into the shallows. The belly flop in the water greatly dispersed the collision forces. While the keel violently snapped, the rest of the *Void* held together. The flagship skidded through the muddy bank and came to a grinding stop, leaving the crew with a slew of fall damage notifications but no fatal wounds.

"That wasn't so bad," I said.

"Thpeak for yourthelf," muttered Kyle. "Ah bit ma tongue."

The two titans were some distance into the lake now, gargantuan forms filling the sky. Orik was two-hundred-feet tall and still only half the size of Gigas. His head just reached the spider's underbelly.

Hadrian's face projection hardened to a scowl. He focused on the downed airship. Tugging against the anchor's pull, the black line seemed stretched to the limit. Still, Gigas heaved. Violet energy crackled up the titan's legs. The mountainside glowed with the magical plague, and the fortress shone brightly. The collapsed stones of the high tower began to stack, climbing up and up.

"Gigas is repairing itself," said Izzy.

"Thon of a bith," said Kyle.

I arched an eyebrow at him. "I thought you were cursing for real again." Izzy chuckled.

"Thcrew you guyth right up the ath."

We laughed as the Maelstrom exerted its pull on the titan. Our mirth disappeared when Gigas began to push out of the water. Even way back in the cheap seats we couldn't deny it. It was impressive. It was impossible.

But then, that was the god emperor's MO all the way. Hadrian, through the use of his Trojan, his plague, was attempting to control the impossible. NPCs and mobs, saints and angels, cities and titans—it was his will against theirs, and he was dominating at every step of the way.

The toppled high tower completed its repair. Four beams of energy converged in the space between them, collecting an impossible amount of destructive power for one focused super beam. The *Void* was literally dead in the water, but Hadrian still wasn't satisfied.

"Abandon ship!" cried Errol.

Avisa scrambled the crew. Pirates tossed ropes overboard. Oakengard's towers burned bright.

As the All Mother fired the mother of all lasers, Orik roared mightily. Dwarfed by the other titan, all the cyclops could do was pound a spider leg that stood as tall as he did.

But they didn't call him the Mighty One for nothing.

The spindly knee buckled. Gigas stumbled and the beam projecting at us skewed down, blasting a crater in the Lake of Dreams. Water exploded skyward into a crashing typhoon that filled the air with waves and mist. When it cleared, Orik was grappling the walking island, yanking another of the stone legs free.

The usually surefooted Gigas toppled sideways.

"The Leveler of Cities," I whispered in awe.

With the spider island now in a lowered stance, Orik grabbed the mountainside and heaved himself up. Gigas shifted, attempting to stabilize, lifting Orik above the waterline. The giant affixed a meaty paw around a glowing high tower. Orik was going for a ride.

Hadrian's face on the fortress shifted, looking up as Orik towered above. "You're a wild one," he spat. "But I'll take you too."

Gigas welled with magic again. The building purple energy flowed into Orik this time. The giant's hands, arms, and body took the brunt of the plague. He spewed a mighty cry, hanging onto Oakengard with one hand as the other beat his chest in a fit of rage.

Still wracked with magic, the cyclops brought the fist down into the center of the castle. Stones caved in. Orik screamed and punched again. Over and over, one titan laid into the other, bashing the rocky ground open wide. Finally, Orik plunged his arm deep into Oakengard's bowels and yanked outward, ripping away a mass of pulsing crystal.

"What are you—" Hadrian's face flickered and spun around. "You can't—"

All strength fled the tall spires supporting the island. The mountainside, fortress, and raging cyclops splashed down like a meteor.

"Ugh!" cried Hadrian.

Gigas began to lose its violet glow. Oakengard started to collapse. Hadrian struggled to hold his face together as it flickered and distorted.

But Orik didn't rest. The angry god was a vengeful one. He roared triumphantly as the island shook and slid in the water. Gigas turned with the current and the Atlantean anchor reasserted its hold. Slowly, the violet energy was overtaken by a growing mass of the blackest shadow. The darkness picked at Hadrian's face.

"No!" he boomed. "I will not be—"

The floating island spun in the water and began to submerge, its impossible size being sucked into the Maelstrom.

In a last gasp, Hadrian's eyes went wide. Orik blustered above him, howling wildly for freedom, for the will to live and die as he chose. The cyclops would rather see Gigas banished than live as an abomination. The soulstones had been taken back, the natural state restored. The titans would endure no further abuse.

The voice came weaker now. "I will not be..."

But Hadrian's control was an illusion that had run its course. Gigas, Orik, and the soulstones were swallowed into the negative world.

> Quest Complete: **Remove Soulstones**
> **from Play**
> *Quest Type: Fepic*
> *Reward: <empty>*
> The soulstones have been removed from play.
> Haven is safe.
> <empty> XP awarded

The mighty vortex collapsed under crashing waves. A violent current rocked the Lake of Dreams and splashed water a mile into the sky. When it broke, a refreshing mist bathed the Midlands. Sparkling moonlight welcomed the fallen night with an aftermath so serene, it was dreamlike.

It was over. We had won.

Tad finally reached the bottom of the stairwell. Going down had been easier than going up, and the fact that his leg was numb actually helped. Adrenaline coursed through his veins as he pushed ahead into the server room.

The machines still hummed. The console's monitor displayed a notification announcing the start of the Haven sync. The satellite had reached low earth orbit and the data transfer was steadily progressing. Christian would be over the moon.

Something rushed over Tad. Relief? Exhaustion? The feeling was too confusing to parse, and he was still in a fair amount of pain. He wondered if Talon and the others inside the sim would notice any difference after being space bound. He wondered if he would see them again.

But that wasn't Tad's concern.

He limped toward the voices in the other room. Past the body of Mr. Hines. SWAT officers were still clearing the studio, but a couple attended a man on the floor. As Tad reached the doorway, the kneeling commander frowned at him. A large pool of blood soaked the carpet, but the man lying on it wore an expression far past remorse or suffering.

Christian Everett was dead.

2200 Wii Party

My cowl snapped in the wind like a tattered flag, soaring high above the magnificent and unforgiving terrain of the Sunscrapers. Amid the craggy peaks was a huge crater where an entire zip code of land had been relocated. Oakengard was no more. The top city was completely upheaved. Left behind was a shuttered network of mine tunnels and who knows what else.

The last of the Violet Order was scraped from the land. Flying northward, vivid purple banners littered the ground. Tunics were torn from armor. What remained of those living, those never infected, no longer had a home. They were nomads.

Bandit continued patrolling the landscape. We needed to be sure the hardship was truly over, that all loose ends were tied off for good. The dragon dipped low and glided over the Lake of Dreams, sending ripples through the now-calm water. The mountain reservoir was dormant again. No Maelstrom, no soulstones. Orik and Gigas were no longer on this plane of existence.

The wreckage of the *Void* didn't look so bad from a distance, but she'd need extensive repairs. Her body was intact but her spine had buckled. For now, the flagship was abandoned. The retrofit would come soon enough. Tonight there was a world-spanning celebration, and as a rule pirates never missed a good party.

Bandit veered toward the Godsbog. The wetlands were heavily populated with Black Army activity. Torches dotted the horizon like fireflies. Instead of gearing up for war, the soldiers were steeped in drinking and revelry. Goblins danced with humans, catechists broke bread with wildkins.

Faced with the end of the world, our little differences seemed smaller still. This night, at least, saw a suspension of all hostilities. It wasn't everlasting peace, but it was a good first step. Change was in the air and we were its agents. That was cause to smile.

Lacing the laughter, however, was another emotion. Something closer to fear or uncertainty or maybe the desperation inherent in hope. Haven was going public in a few short hours, and everything would change all over again.

Bandit's heavy paws touched down, tamping the wet soil as she changed back to her true form. I rubbed her neck as it went from scales to fur. It was nice being able to fly for the sheer joy of it as opposed to dodging boss mobs and watching a timer. I dismounted and hugged the mountain bongo.

"We've been through a lot together, you and I, back since we first met in the small forest outside Stronghold." I chuckled inwardly. "Can you believe we were running from a few goblins?" I sighed. Times changed fast, especially for a couple of power levelers like us.

I dug through my inventory and gave Bandit the best treats I could find, handcrafted dark chocolate peanut butter cups. She unceremoniously gobbled the handful up.

Nearby, horses nickered. We'd landed on the sure ground of the stables, since swamps weren't especially conducive to hoofed feet. The crusader mounts shuffled nervously at Bandit's presence, but Artax cantered up and stomped the ground playfully. After they smelled each other's noses, the black stallion neighed and hoofed away. Bandit watched after him.

"Go play with your friends," I said. "You deserve it."

Bandit simultaneously farted and winked before galloping off. I swear she was getting a sense of humor.

I shook my head and marched toward the crowd. With hundreds of soldiers, rather than a big party it was more like fifty little ones, all bouncing and intermingling, feeding into the greater energy of the whole. Nervous excitement tickled the air. The beta test was officially ending. In some ways, it felt like the whole world was.

I passed through the camp of Black Hats. Phil was here, to my surprise, still wearing nothing but a loin cloth and pink socks. Between incoherent grumbles, he waved a sign that read, "The ~~End~~ Beginning is Nigh!"

"Oi!" called Nooner, standing behind a table. "All-you-can-drink wristbands! Get yer wristbands here!"

I arched an eyebrow dond approached the petty criminal. Beside him, another gangster manned a money bucket and a pile of fluorescent-yellow bracelets.

"What's this?" I asked sharply before they noticed me.

Nooner jumped. "Talon! I thought you were off on a scouting trip. I just figured—"

"That you'd make money selling useless wristbands?" I guessed.

The gangster swallowed. "It don't concern you, of course. You bein' faction leader an' all. You get the pick of the booze, on the house!"

My snide smile didn't wane. "*Everybody in camp* gets free booze, Nooner. We all fought together. We all won." I snatched the money bucket. "How much are you selling the wristbands for, anyway?"

Nooner gulped. "Er, five silver."

Five silver coins clinked at the bottom of the bucket. I turned a pointed eye to Nooner's assistant in crime. He was the only person in sight with a bright-yellow wrist. "Only one sucker, eh?"

"He made me buy one," confessed the assistant. "As a show of support."

My eye turned to Nooner.

"It's a damn savvy lot you got here," he complained. "What was I thinkin', trying to get one over on a guild of Black Hats? Now them goblins, *there's* a good mark!"

"No scamming," I said firmly. "Especially against the goblins. They've had it hard enough. Unless..." I turned away and paused for effect as they hung on my words. "Unless you're looking to pick up a blood feud or three. I hear goblins are quite partial to those."

Nooner's eyes went wide as I strolled away.

Speaking of trouble, the next group I found myself in was the catechists. They'd held up their end of the alliance, most of them anyway, but I still wouldn't group them into any category remotely adjacent to good company. No drinking, no gambling, no cursing—I wondered what it was exactly they were getting up to.

"Protector."

I turned as Cleric Vagram approached for a word. *Great.*

The blond-haired cleric was an enigma. We'd just won a war but his expression telegraphed the opposite. He was as devout as they came but had gone against his old leader. I still didn't know what to make of him.

I waited on him and nodded as he approached. "*Bishop* Vagram, I take it?"

He shook his head solemnly. "No. I may be the most powerful cleric in Haven, but a cleric is what I am. There's no more Oakengard, no more Trinity, no more bishop."

I nodded respectfully. "Yeah, I'm sorry about that. No one foresaw Gigas. And I'd say I'm sorry about Tannen too but..."

"The man was a power-hungry prophet. I could no longer look past his sins. I'm afraid we have to admit he was another Hadrian in the making."

"What will you do?"

He shrugged. "Wait for a sign from the White King, I suppose. It's clear we need to rethink a great many things. But I'll take up the leadership mantle for my priests. It seems fitting, in a way, for Oakengard to fall. We catechists have already broken away and the knights are riding with the Black Hats. Maybe this is as things were always meant to be."

My immediate thought was to offer them a place in the

faction, but it didn't feel right. The catechists were powerful but not a good culture fit. Besides, I was pretty sure Vagram would reject the offer. They had to find their path and travel it, even if it did eventually lead to Stronghold.

"I wish you well," I said, offering my arm.

"And I you," returned the cleric as we clasped wrists.

We walked off and I pondered his reference to the White King. What would it mean to Christian Everett if Oakengard was gone? We'd succeeded at ousting the Whisperer, but the Trinity was dead, the trijewel destroyed. Where did that leave his seat of power?

The flow of catechists naturally led to some reuniting crusaders. Many knights still wore their armor and black tunics. When I spotted a friendly face, I didn't hesitate to hurry over.

"Buildmaster general!" I called out, laughing and rapping his shoulder. "You did it! The Black Army kicked ass."

"Aye," agreed Trafford. "I've done it and now I'm done."

The chuckles silenced. I studied the present knights, who included Grimwart. "What do you mean done?"

"I've been tellin' ya for ages—I'm too old for this. You're officially looking at my retirement party, didn't you know?" He spread his arms wide and shouted to the sky. "Everyone's here for me!"

Spectators held tankards high and hurrahed. I scratched my head uncertainly while the noise died down. Before I could ask a follow-up question, the old man helped me out.

"Don't look so stunned, son. I'll still be around. I'm a Black Hat for life. But I'm giving up the welcome shop and army duties. Gonna streamline my life. I'll still watch over

Dragonperch and Oldtown. I'll keep the quest book too. Jixa will make a good buildmaster, but that's your call."

"And what about general?"

Trafford smiled. "I'm sure you'll approve of my replacement." He shoved the black knight forward. "Let me officially present General Grimwart of the Black Army."

The stout though slightly inebriated crusader cleared his throat. "It would be my honor if you would have me," he said. "All the crusaders, in fact. We need a permanent home, and it would do us no greater pleasure than to serve Oldtown."

I blinked at the collected group of knights. The turn of events had nullified their need to follow their oaths and serve Oakengard. "Hell yeah!" I exclaimed.

"And look," said Trafford, holding up the crusader's full helm, lacquered black. "He already has guild-appropriate headgear. It's a perfect fit!"

A round of laughs erupted. Someone handed me a beer and we did a round of toasts as well. We chatted about the immediate implications of the promotions, but we kept that discussion light. This was a party, not a work meeting. Nothing was gonna stop our fun.

After a bit I pulled the old man aside. "I guess it's time to say goodbye to Buildmaster General Questkeeper Shopkeeper Trafford. Maybe cutting out a few job titles will make room for a new one..."

"Over my dead body!" snarled the crank.

I winked. "Got ya."

"Why you smug little..." His face reddened. "Aw, who am I kidding?" The old man grabbed me in a bear hug. He released me and clinked his glass to mine. "We love you, son. Keep doing your thing."

"You too, Trafford. I couldn't imagine running the Black Hats without you around." I realized the old man had always been there whenever and wherever we needed him. Whether it was manning the sanctum master panel in Dragonperch, cleaning up Oldtown, or just smacking me with some old-fashioned good advice, he'd always sort of worked in the capacity of a general manager. "You know, I'm serious about that job title. While Izzy and Kyle and I are off battling world-ending threats, you do a great job running the day-to-day at home. You spin a lot of plates and keep them spinning. How'd you like to be the official faction GM?"

His eyes lit up. "Guild Master?"

"Well, actually GM stands for—"

"Guild Master," he said assertively. "I love it." He clapped me on the shoulder and rejoined the group.

After a moment's deliberation, I decided to let Trafford have it his way. I waved them off, wondered where Kyle and Izzy were, and wandered in search of a refill.

The wetlands shivered under heavy stomps. I circled a column of large tents to investigate. Various friends were face-to-face with ogres violently bouncing off each other. I rushed over before realizing it was Baz and the rest of Jixa's team.

Stigg prodded a few goblins with lutes. "Harder and faster," he said. "Like this." The Viking thrashed an air guitar and mimicked screeching riffs with curled lips. "Can you do that?" The goblins eagerly nodded.

I snorted. "You're teaching ogres to mosh?"

"That's the easy part," said Stigg. "They're naturals."

Baz wore black eyeliner and made devil horns with his fingers. "Hail puny yooman moosik!"

Stigg put his hands on his hips with a frown. "I'm still trying to figure out a way to electrify the lutes."

"Let the big guy have his fun," cut in Caduceus. She was sitting with the white knight.

"Hey," said a drunken Lash, "sheck out my new helmet!"

She placed the new gear on her head. It looked just as menacing as before, but now her pony tail protruded from the back of the helmet and flared around her head like a peacock. It was a bold look for a bold fighter.

"I like it," I said, deciding not to comment on her drinking. It was the opinion of quite a few of us that Lash needed to find more ways to blow off steam.

"I don't know," warned Dune, sidling up to me. "It's trouble letting those two conspire together."

"You're just jealous." I shook the ranger's hand. "Getting friendly with other Black Hats is a rule of membership. Nothing to be done." We watched as Glinda and Conan drank sparkling champagne, the chessboard between them worn from heavy use.

"Check," said the barbarian.

"I didn't know he was into chess."

"Apparently a star member of the chess club, back in real life," reported Dune. I turned to him in astonishment. "You said being friendly was a faction rule, right?"

I shook my head. "I guess it finally makes sense why Glinda likes him."

"Oh, don't sell the old woman short, either. I saw her

sneaking out of Trafford's tent earlier."

I burst into laughter. "Too much information!" I filled my beer from a nearby tap and said, "It looks like you're settling in nicely then."

"That I am. Finally made level 10. But I'm giving the loadout a rest for now and enjoying the company of friends. You down for a game of hopcoin?"

I scoffed. "With you? Might as well give my money away. But Serpico should be around here somewhere. He might give you a good run."

"Not on his best day."

Another round of lute metal kicked up. Hex stormed into the fray and began dancing, a nameless zombie headbanging at her side.

"Talon?" came a young voice. Dune and I jumped.

"Crux!" snapped the ranger. "Stop sneaking up on us like that!"

I rolled my eyes. "He's a bit of a show off. Imagine that."

Dune's eyes narrowed.

The thief cleared his throat. "I just wanted to say thank you for believing in me. And for supporting us getting Hex back."

I shook my head. "Hey, kid, it was all you. You kept your promise to your sister. You did what you had to do with a clear conscience. She wouldn't be here if it wasn't for you stubbornly searching her out."

"But everyone helped. You scouting Oakengard with me, Bravo Team charging in."

Lash stumbled over just in time to catch the end. She latched a heavy arm around the thief. "That'sh family for you," she slurred.

Crux beamed and raised his eyebrows. "Even Kyle was incredibly resourceful."

"Kyle," coughed Dune. "That's a surprise."

"Not really," I said. "He has a lot of grit and persistence when there are people to fight for. I could say the same thing about you two."

Crux and Dune shared a glance before turning to me. The thief was receptive to the lesson and nodded. Dune? Well, let's call him a cynic. "Izzy's right about you," he laughed. "You get a little sappy when things work out."

"Totally," Lash snickered, ironically unaware she was still hugging Crux.

The laugh at my expense was shared by a few. The mirth died down but the smile on the ranger's face persisted. "We needed someone like you," he finally said. "Someone who saw the good in everyone. Someone to give us hope." He paused and went serious. "Jeez, did I just say that?"

"I'm infectious," I said.

"Nah," said Lash. "You're jusht a good leader."

Dune nodded. "She's right." He pointed a finger behind me. "*That's* infectious."

I turned to the nearby pirate camp. Grom and a lady of ill repute lay in a cattle trow half filled with drool water and floating pieces of hay that clung to their wet bodies. Grug, so blitzed that he didn't even notice their presence, was puking his lungs out into the same trow.

Our faces scrunched in disgust.

After that train wreck killed the mood, our little party broke away. I wandered into the pirate camp, giving a wide berth to the cattle trow. Seamen crowded close, boisterously shoving each other and slamming down tankards of mead. I suddenly found myself partaking in some kind of drinking game while spectating a slapping contest.

"Ain't it a grand sight?" boasted Errol, sidling up with an arm around Avisa's waist.

I looked knowingly at the two before turning my attention back to the sport. "It's something all right, but I don't know if grand describes it. Then again, that's kind of how you roll, Admiral Oates."

"Captain my captain!" shouted Avisa.

The Scar of the Six Seas grinned a silver tooth. "Ar. Now that the exhaustin' work be done an' we be lookin' at peace time, I wanted t' properly introduce you t' me lady love."

"Reunited at last," beamed the sergeant.

"Aye, a rough history we've had, but this latest adventure proves we can do anythin' so long as we're together."

Avisa smirked. "We went to hell and back, literally and metaphorically."

"An' I wouldn't have it any other way." Errol gave her a long sloppy smooch before disengaging and tenderly holding her hands. "With that in mind, methinks it's time t' pop the question."

Her eyes widened.

"Me sergeant, me love," he started. Avisa covered her mouth and spectators gathered round. "Me first mate, *emphasis on mate*." Sly snickers followed. "Would ye, Avisa o' Shorehome, do me the honor o' joinin' the Black Hats?"

Everyone held their breath in anticipation. I scratched my head awkwardly, not sure what I expected of the rascal. Avisa blinked for a few stupefied moments before grinning wide. She pulled her hands away and socked him in the jaw. Errol hit the dirt.

"*That's* all you have to ask me?" she snapped.

The captain pushed to his feet and groggily shook his head. "What did I say?"

Papa Brugo regally strode up wearing a garish smile. "I believe it is what you *didn't* say."

Sideshow over, the pirates returned to the festivities, cheering loudly for a new contestant. I stared in disbelief as Grug returned from the cattle trow, wiped a bit of vomit from his chin, downed a cup of ale, and stepped up to the slapping table.

"You guys really do party harder than anybody else."

Errol laughed and grabbed a mug. "To long nights an' short memories!"

As we watched the festivities, Papa Brugo leaned into me. "It occurs to me, Protector, that without the saints, you are the only one with the means of managing factions."

I took a sip of drink and realized he was right. I opened the dev menu and studied the faction controls. "Do the Brothers in Black need help from an ally?"

Brugo clasped his hands behind his back as a particularly hard slap knocked Grug to the ground. The pirate clutched his head to keep it from spinning and struggled to his feet.

The Papa sighed. "In retrospect, I've had enough of black. The division in Shorehome has been repaired, but the brotherhood must adapt rather than wallow in its former shadow. We need a new color, a new start. Besides, your faction made its own claim to black."

"Yeah," I acknowledged, rubbing my neck, "sorry about that. There should've been a color-coded chart or something." We watched Grug warm up his palms with a fan-riling rub before using an open hand to knock his opponent out. "What will you do?" I asked.

"Choose a color that suits me more," answered the crime boss. "A nice gaudy scarlet."

I grunted. Then I used the dev menu to unlock faction controls. Papa Brugo went through his menus.

Global Haven Alert:
Papa Brugo has named a new faction: the Scarlet Knives.

I smirked at him. "Not the most subtle of names."

"Has it been your experience that I am a subtle man?" His tone was deadly serious.

"Good point."

Avisa hooted as she returned with a pile of coins. "Look at the silver your man won me!" She gave Errol a kiss.

Short memories was right.

Errol proudly canted his head. "Grug be me most reliable man, fer sure." He rubbed a sore jaw. "Wonder why I forgot t' bet on him."

"Don't fret it," she said. "I've got enough loot for both of us."

Despite her statement, she stuffed the coins away. "It's time to make me your most reliable woman." She produced the two rings Lucifer had gifted her—gaudy, jewel-encrusted, and worthy of a pirate's spoils.

Avisa bent to one knee. "Captain, Admiral, oaf, and one hell of a lover, will you do me the honor of taking my hand in marriage?"

"I—" Errol took a backward step and looked for an escape route.

I mouthed the words, "Say yes."

Captain Oates shrugged and turned his eyes to his lady love. "Ye caught me fair an' square. Let's do this."

The crowd cheered and everyone pressed close. Brugo moved before the couple as Avisa gussied up Errol's face. Once satisfied, they turned to the crime boss, and I was pushed closer before realizing this was going down right here and now. Pirates didn't waste time.

Errol grabbed the rings and stuffed them in my hand. "Hold onto these, will ya?"

I blinked in shock. "Errol, I didn't know I meant that much to you."

"Don't overly dwell on it. Grug may be me most reliable man, but he'd pawn these in a heartbeat fer a bit o' goblin hooch."

I chuckled and Brugo authoritatively cleared his throat. "Do you both swear to lie, steal, and cheat from this day forth?"

"I do," they both said.

"And when possible, to lie, steal, and cheat together?"

"I do."

My brow furrowed as he recited the vows. I wasn't sure if

everyone was joking or not.

"And do you swear," continued Brugo, "to limit your betrayals to no more than once per week?"

"Once per week?!?" exclaimed Errol in disbelief. Avisa flashed a stern glare and the captain quickly swallowed down further objection. "Well, I suppose it ain't too much t' ask, bein' as how we're married an' all."

I massaged my temples. I was beginning to think these wedding rings would be better off pawned.

"You need to swear," urged Brugo.

They both said, "I do."

"And do you also swear to pay me a twenty-percent tax on all your pillaging?"

"Where'd that come from?" asked Avisa. "You're crazy!"

Brugo frowned. "Ten percent?"

"Not gonna happen," barked Errol. "Now get on with it."

"Worth a try," said the crime boss. "Rings?"

I handed them over. The bejeweled rings were perfect fits. Lucifer's game was on point.

"Then by the power vested in me, the Protector of Shorehome, the Papa of all Papas, the head of the Scarlet Knives, and the most fearsome man in all of Haven, I name thee man and wife. Have at each other."

The newlyweds locked lips in a surprisingly tame show for pirates. After the vows I was simultaneously relieved and disappointed.

"I don't suppose," said Brugo, "that you will be returning to Shorehome, Sergeant Avisa?"

She bowed her head. "If it's all right with you, Papa of all

Papas. If only for someone to look after the *Void* until you win it back in a game of bones."

Brugo erupted in laughter. Errol rolled his eyes.

"Is that really your boat?" I asked.

"Damn right it be," said the admiral. "We pirates be a mischievous lot, but we ain't nothin' if we don't abide by our compacts."

"And vows," prodded Avisa.

"Honor among thieves," said Brugo. "We have little else."

"Well," hedged Errol, "there is the drinkin', gamblin', cavortin', and pillagin'."

"But little else," laughed Avisa.

Brugo nodded. "Just remember, the couple that revels together levels together."

It was a happy affair and I was proud of them, Errol especially. He had a boat, a crew, a first mate—he was finally living his legend. As the pirates began iterating the benefits of being a scoundrel, I slipped away to get a break from drinking. It's not that I was a lightweight, but pirates were impossible to keep up with. Besides, it was a best man's job to know when you were no longer needed.

I trudged deeper into the Godsbog where the occasional fires were fewer and farther between. The drink and the merriment left me momentarily oblivious to the souring mood. Yellow eyes tracked me, and I was disheartened to see many of the expressions harsh.

I wiped the sentimental smile off my face when I realized, like the crusaders and catechists, the goblin horde had lost something dear to them. They'd witnessed the death of not one but two of their gods. I scanned the swamps for the boggart witches to find out what it meant. I encountered their cauldron abandoned, the fire cold.

Heading toward the chieftain tent, the wild king lay on the ground gripping a jug of wine. Three sprightly women wearing nothing but purple helmets bounced around him in song. I watched the celebratory mockery for a quick moment, mesmerized. Theoderic's skull crown turned to me and nodded once before returning to his revelry. Off in the distance, Hood's eyes glowed a cool white as he stood vigil. At least the wildkins were happy with me. I decided it best not to interrupt either and entered the chieftain tent.

Azzyrk scowled at my entrance. "The boys are ornery."

"I noticed."

"I don't blame you for putting Gigas down after the usurper merged with him, but you had no right to send Orik away."

"It was his choice, Azzyrk. I dispelled the soulstone. That was Orik's will."

"Maybe, but it wasn't a happy ending. For the humans, sure, but not for the horde."

I gave him a conciliatory sigh. "Why does it need to be about humans and goblins? Why can't we all just look after each other?"

"Heh." The general crossed his arms and shook his head. "You ever notice what happens when players and NPCs fall in battle? The combat log says, 'Talon is dead!' But when simple mobs go down? 'Azzyrk is defeated,' like I'm some blight on the world. Our deaths don't even justify an exclamation mark."

I frowned. I guess I hadn't really noticed.

"*That's* why," said the general.

"*Cha!*" snapped Jixa, pushing into the tent. "*Cha!* You be nices to Mister Talon. Heses do much for goblinkind. Heses friend of pagans."

"He's friends when he wants us to fight for him."

"Heses made Jixa buildmaster."

The bitter father's countenance softened a tad. The girl was such a refreshing dose of sunshine it was hard to sustain a foul mood around her. But Azzyrk persisted.

"All right," he muttered. "What happened, happened. We've made an alliance and we'll live by that tonight. Haven will enter a new age and we'll part ways, and then who knows? Maybe we'll work together in the future. Or maybe our blood feud will resume."

"*Apa!*" snapped Jixa.

"What? I'm a goblin general. I have appearances to keep up."

I stifled a chuckle and gave the girl a high five. "Thanks for the vote of confidence, Buildmaster Jixa. But I understand where your father is coming from. You'll be a bridge between our worlds. A line of communication. An olive branch."

The general pouted uncertainly. "I *do* like olives. As long as they're stinky rotten."

I grimaced. "We'll work something out." Jixa embraced her dad and he hugged back hard. I took the opportunity to head out, but Azzyrk stopped me at the exit.

"Protector," he called. "I know they call us the errant folk, but with Orik going down the Maelstrom, I feel a little more... lost than usual. Our future's uncertain."

"Welcome to an undetermined world of free will. Maybe that

was Orik's parting gift to his people."

The general nodded glumly. "That still doesn't tell us what to do next."

I thought of Theoderic and his easygoing band. "Do like the wildkins do. Revel in today."

"And afterward?"

I bit down. "Tomorrow will turn into today, and you can do it all over again."

2210 Project Reality

I wandered some more, looking for my friends. It wasn't like Kyle to disappear like this. The dude never missed a good party. Izzy, on the other hand, definitely preferred her solitude. I traced the outskirts to see if she was around but ran into a different familiar face entirely when a man in a British red coat with gold buttons popped into existence.

I stopped in my tracks. Familiar face wasn't quite the correct phrasing. Instead of the usual blond hair and blue eyes, this resident companion was a jovial Indian fellow with a mustache and tufts of loose dark hair over his ears. It was his smile that was familiar.

"Varnu?"

The man dipped into a low, formal bow. "At your service, Talon of Stronghold."

"I *knew* you weren't from Texas."

"Yes, as the edgy teens of your American culture would say in their cutting-edge slang parlance, the jig is up."

I blinked, glad Izzy wasn't around to hear that. "Er, yeah, but only the cool kids."

"I regret to inform you that, along with the shuttering of my company, various assets are being systematically wiped from the servers. It's just like the ancient city of Travatal, am I correct?" His chuckles cut short when he saw my confusion. "What I mean to say is I no longer have access to the Varnu Son of John avatar."

"I see. So am I correct in assuming this is what you really look like?"

"I know this will come as a shock, but I am one hundred percent Indian. I deeply regret the charade that was forced upon us by management and our parent company." He bowed again and I waved it off.

"No, really, it's fine, Varnu— Is your name really Varnu?"

"It is, but again the Crocodile of Arcos rears its triple heads. I am no Son of John. My name is Varnu Patel."

I stepped forward and offered my hand. "Pleased to properly meet you."

He proudly clasped my hand.

"Why's your real body image scanned into the system anyway?"

"Ah," he said emphatically while our hands shook. "I scanned myself during off hours for my more discrete proclivities." He leaned forward and whispered. "One fellow pervert to another, I sneak into Stronghold's media rooms and conjure only the finest sari-wearing women."

My hand, still clasped to his, abruptly stopped shaking. "You use this body for virtual porn."

His eyes lit up. "Oh yes! You should see the armpits on these ladies."

My face soured. I pulled my hand from his grip and wiped it on my coat. "Armpits, huh?"

"Dastardly, are they not? That forbidden fruit of the sugar palm, that last frontier of the appendage, ripe for licks and tickles and..."

My head was shaking back and forth a mile a minute. He finally got the hint and stopped. "TMI," I explained under my breath.

"Ah," he said, "Too Much Indian. I understand. My friend Amit advised me to tell residents I enjoyed women's breasts overstuffed with bags of poisonous silicone."

I cracked a smile. He *was* screwing with me. "That's fair. Listen, I can't thank you enough for being around. You really didn't need to help out."

"I suppose I have broken quite a few rules in the handbook. It is no matter. It pains me to say it, but I will soon be unable to log into Haven at all."

"Say it isn't so."

He nodded. "Even though my company is shuttered, we have received a bulletin from headquarters. Apparently the automated message was sent to every Kablammy employee and contractor, no matter how low on the wrestling pole. Your simulation is now being hosted on a satellite in orbit, limited to minimal interactions with Earth over a secure, unhackable connection. Some mumbo jumbo about blockchain. There will be no more interactions with saints and developers. Everchat will continue in some form, but the status of tech support remains questionable." His smile disappeared for a solemn moment. "I am afraid resident companions didn't have the best user feedback record."

"Don't say that, Varnu. You were a huge help in your own

way. A full five-star rating from me, would recommend to a friend."

"How very kind of you. I believe you still have time to submit an official review via the help menu."

I tensed. "Oh, have I not done that yet? I'll get right on it. I could've sworn I'd..." I stepped away and trailed off as the reality of space and time hit me. My being, the electrons and ones and zeroes, was hurling around the planet at seventeen-thousand miles per hour in the void of space. That was a mindfuck. "Will there be patch updates? New players?"

Varnu pondered a moment. "I imagine there were plans for periodic uploads, but the incident at Kablammy headquarters in See-Ah-Tell has left everything in doubt."

"The explosion."

"Explosions, plural. And the following hostage crisis. I don't have the latest information, but the master uplink is said to be destroyed. With the data transfer complete, it is only a matter of minutes before my connection is terminated."

I tensed at the suddenness of it. This is what General Azzyrk felt like. The future really was uncertain.

"Well," I sighed, "if you really only have a few minutes left, you shouldn't waste them on me. I imagine you'd like to spend it in a media room for some forbidden armpit tickling."

Varnu grinned. "Oh, we are way past tickling, sir. I am forging into uncharted territory. Let us just say, it will be a tight squeeze."

I'm not sure if I chuckled or choked. "They really do make things bigger in Texas."

He winked at me. "You do not know the half of it, sir." With that, my favorite resident companion disappeared.

I rubbed my eyes and took a few listless steps. Haven was being cut off from the world, but how completely was an open question. Were we at risk of being truly alone?

I basked in the night air, thankful for a quiet moment. The journey from real life to simulation had been a difficult one, rife with life lessons and coming to grips with my new status quo. When I thought about it—really thought about it—I was okay with the unexpected ride. Sure, semi-dying sucked a bag of dicks, but in hindsight I wouldn't change a thing. This was who I was.

Life's a bitch, then you die and respawn in a virtual reality MMO. I could live with that.

As far as my place in Haven and the fate of the dev menu? It seemed to have less purpose without a Pantheon, without a hub, and without saints and angels. I decided to give up some of my controls. With no more saintly blessings, it seemed appropriate to return power to the people. Power to create factions, to Everchat with loved ones, to stake a claim to whatever kind of life whoever wanted, wherever. It would take time to find out what that meant, but the afterlife was abundant with that particular resource.

I was in the midst of such grand plans when the air beside me ebbed with energy. A black portal opened, which should've concerned the average gamer but only reassured me. Its magic was familiar. I didn't miss it, but I knew who it came from.

I beamed at the night sky full of stars and stepped inside.

2220 Oblivion

The negative world was a place of stuffy damp air. It didn't reside in positional correlation with landmarks in Haven, but the Maelstrom was a good placeholder; it felt like I was under the weight of an ocean.

I peered into the dark, which was not exactly clarifying but settling, at least. I was beside a mound of mud and bones. Lucy Black sat atop her throne of dirt, face bearing an unfamiliar expression: desperation.

"I caused this," she lamented.

"What do you mean? We won."

"Far from it."

"What is it?" I asked softly. Gently.

"Oakengard has fallen."

"That had nothing to do with you."

"Not directly, but in a very roundabout way, this was my legacy. I gave the people free will, and with it came the power to deny the White King. That was my doing. Now the Trinity is buried, the trijewel is lost. What place is there for my father?"

"None of that matters," I said, encouragement in my voice. "Everything you've taught us led to this. Game systems and their constructs don't mean anything. This world is what we make of it. Look at everything you and I have done—you think the CEO of Kablammy can't manage?"

She picked at the dirt, hood drooped toward the ground. "You have a hail."

I bit my lip, taking a moment to understand her meaning. I opened my menu and checked my notifications. They'd been muted. "Your dad on Everchat." She suddenly stood and stepped off her mound. My brow furrowed. "It looks accessible?"

Lucy's voice wavered. "The negative world counts as a secured level instance. Open the hail."

With the girl at my side eagerly awaiting an update, I swiped into Everchat and was greeted with a spinning icon and a prompt.

> Call canceled.
> **View prerecorded message?**

Lucy's nervous excitement waned. "It's not live."

Which made perfect sense. I hadn't been in a position to answer the hail when it occurred. It was good to know we could send video messages on a delay. I opened the recording.

"Talon!" said Christian Everett in a great state of urgency. He was hunched over a workstation on the floor, in the same awkward angle as before but looking much worse off. The days had frayed him. There was shouting and banging in the background. Lucy tensed.

"It doesn't look like I'll reach you in time," hurried the CEO. "Just know that the assistance of your real-life counterpart has been invaluable. The two satellite sites were destroyed but Tad's launching my personal backup. Haven will survive. By the time you watch this you'll be free." Christian put pressure on his rib cage and winced. He was hurt bad and breathing in rapid spurts.

"Pete... Pete... I'm sorry to say, I couldn't finalize Pete's last goal. I worked so hard and it was finalized and queued but..." His eyes squeezed shut for a few seconds. "But Abbie... InLink... they managed to corrupt my machine. They slipped a virus into the patch." He leaned toward the camera and spoke with more authority than he should've been able to muster in his condition. "Get this video to my daughter. Tell her... *show* her that everything you both did for me, for Haven... You were right, dear. I was wrong and you were right."

Lucy's eyes watered. "I don't care, Dad," she whispered.

Christian cleared some phlegm from his throat. "Tad is a bright young man. I trust him, and he told me something I know to be true. Haven doesn't need those patch corrections. *You* don't need them. I have every confidence in you to succeed on your own. I believe in the world I created. I believe in all of you."

A loud crash jerked Christian's attention to the distance. People were trying to get to him. He was in immediate danger. He faced the screen.

"Lucy, I have something else to tell you." The girl leaned forward, her fingers cutting into the circulation of my arm. "There's a greater problem. The EXSIL machine, the last surviving unit in the building... It was corrupted as well. I transferred my mind to a black box but... I had to remove it from the sync queue."

Lucy's face broke apart. "No!" she said weakly.

"The only way I could save the world," he lamented, "was to send it off without me."

Lucy released my arm and screamed. "NO!"

As much as Christian fought it, he couldn't hide his full sorrow, either on his face or in his voice. "I'm sorry, honey, but I can't go into the future with you. Don't think of it as a death, think of it as me reuniting with your mother and sister. This is a good thing." He nodded and sniffled. "This is good. Because I saved you. Parents never truly die, they live on through the legacy of their children, of their world, of their actions. That is where I'll be."

Lucy was sobbing, screaming and silent all at once, attention plastered to the last vestige of her father and only family.

Christian Everett breathed deeply to rein in his emotions. He picked up an object from the floor and hugged it to his heart, an old external hard drive covered with dust. He spoke softly, even as the banging in the background intensified. "You are my light, Lucy. More than anything, I wanted you to live forever. That's the greatest gift I had to give." He assessed the situation at his office door and swallowed hard. "Have an honest shot at life," he said quickly. "Live by your heart. Never forget the sacrifices that got you here. It breaks my heart that I can't be there to watch you live, but it fills my soul to know that you will. I love you." After a quick moment of indecision, he flicked the video message off.

"Daddy," squeaked Lucy hoarsely. It was an instinctual call, a plea with fate for one last moment with him no matter how illogical. The girl shuddered through a stream of tears. She was a tattered wreck.

I remained quiet for a while. The darkness that encompassed us was colder and heavier than before. I licked my lips and searched for the perfect words. Such sentiments didn't exist. Instead, I laced an arm around her in the silence. In that desolate place, time had no meaning—we could've been leaning on each other for a minute or a year. But even the abyss couldn't stand still. All things, no matter how stout, were subject to change. That was the one constant in the universe.

"What was it all for?" she breathed quietly. "My glorious rebellion. The death of my family. I saw the hardships and compromises my father had to endure. You think I couldn't tell because I was eight? Little girls are supposed to be loved. They're supposed to be safe and surrounded by family." Lucy sniffled. "All I ever wanted was family."

I kneeled beside her and squared her face to mine. "That's what he built for you."

"And in the meantime, we lost any semblance of love. Him, buried in his work; me, my rebellion. Couldn't we have just lay in the grass somewhere and watched the clouds?"

I offered a solemn smile. "You can still do that. You have family here." But I knew the words felt hollow, more insubstantial than the air of this place. I relaxed and thought of my own struggles. "It's about moving forward, carrying the time you spent together within you. That's something you can't ever lose."

The girl frowned. "But what was it all for?"

"Do you even need to ask? You believed in this world. The afterlife. You said you were willing to die for it. Don't you think your father felt the same way? This was his creation. His legacy.

Both of you did this all for Haven."

She sniffled and looked away. "The one thing of worth my father created."

I shook my head and turned hers to face me. "Besides his children."

For the faintest of moments, I could swear she almost smiled. It wasn't in her lips, but a tightening of her cheeks, a twitch of her eye. It was gone even before it could form. Lucy Black turned away and snickered. "You could say this entire reality exists solely for me. It was supposed to be a heaven but, well, you know..." The girl started slowly up the dirty mound of sticks and bones.

I inhaled sharply. "Come up with us," I said. "Everyone's celebrating."

"I'm not much in the mood for parties."

"Do it to see the joy you've caused."

She spun and plopped down at the height of her throne. "I'm not ready for joy either."

My excitement deflated. It started to feel like we were just going through the motions. I shook my head softly, disheartened and nearly defeated. "You put a lot of thought into protecting this world from Hadrian, into guiding me and others who wanted to stand for something—stand for *ourselves*. You should be a part of the future. Maybe not now, but sometime."

"What would I be but another dictator?" she bemoaned. "No, that's not what I fought for. There's no role for a devil in the absence of a god. My dream is dead. Yours still lives. Fight for it, won't you? I'll hold the fort down here."

"In the negative world?"

"This is Hades now. A place for lost things."

I shook my head. "I'm not leaving you here."

She did smile now, a half lip crooked up. "Talon," she said with a hint of admiration, "that's exactly why I chose you. But you have no choice in this one. I have the Atlantean anchor and the shadow essence. I am master of this world. This is my hell now. And it's time for you to rejoin the living."

I clenched my jaw and repeated. "Lucy, I am NOT—"

She snapped her fingers and I appeared back in the Godsbog, amid the music and revelers and the electricity of life. Time passed all around me as I stood frozen in a daze.

2230 The Last of Us

A short while later I was back in friendly territory. Fun and good humor abounded, but I wasn't sure I was in the mood anymore. I finally found Izzy a little ways off, sitting on a log by a fire. She had a book in her hand. This time she was scratching away with quill and ink.

"I've been looking for you."

"Sorry," she said with a sigh and a stretch. "I needed to recharge."

"They have potions for that." She wordlessly jotted down another sentence. "I'm surprised you're not reading."

She looked up and smiled. "Kinda surprised myself, actually. I was hit with an exciting feeling but couldn't find something I was in the mood for, so I just started writing my own story."

"Your own story? Like a journal of our adventures?"

"It's about a starship captain who transforms into a sexy space vampire, so not really."

"Is she beautiful and misunderstood?" I asked.

"Sure, if you replace those words with brilliant and ruthless."

"Okay, but I bet there's some interplanetary space sex involved, am I right?"

She shrugged. "What's a novel without a little smut?" She put the feather pen down, closed the book, and tapped the log next to her. "Wanna sit down? I could use a break."

"Was hoping you'd ask." I joined her and she leaned into me. "Using a feather pen instead of a keyboard, too. You're such a hipster."

The pixie's eyes narrowed. "I'll let you live if you never call me that again."

"You're just saying that 'cause you wanna be a sexy space vampire." I challenged her with my eyes but surrendered when she started pinching. "Okay, okay! It was a bad joke. I think it's kinda cool you're writing a book. Just make sure the hunky love interest is a strapping man, full of charm." I modeled my head into a heroic distant gaze.

She smirked. "Oh, he's full of something, all right."

We kissed, the warmth of the fire tickling our skin. When she pulled away, I took a long breath. "Thanks, I needed that."

"Wanna talk about it?"

"Let's not ruin the night."

Her eyebrow arched mischievously. "I think I'm fully recharged now..." She pushed me on my back and leaned in, but we were interrupted by pattering footsteps.

"Look at us," blathered Kyle as he hurried to the fire. "You two enjoying each other's companionship, me with my harem." A small gaggle of women in silken wraps closely hugged him.

"Where did you... ?" I blinked a few times to make sure this wasn't an illusion. "How in the... ?"

Izzy sized up the small crowd and sucked her lips. "Ooh, maybe I'll write a reverse harem."

Kyle scoffed. "Yeah, like *that's* realistic. Okay, ladies," he said, peeling their grips away. "I need a breather. Why don't you go see if Glinda's stew is done? That'll get our stamina recharged."

Their eyes lit up. "Ooh, stamina stew!" They giggled and raced away, occasionally dropping pieces of clothing.

"Bro, who would've thought harem keeping was such hard work?" Kyle waited for us to say something. When we didn't take the bait, he hiked a shoulder and added, "Yup. No biggie. Just my personal harem of devoted ladies—"

"We both hate you," said Izzy, which was great because I didn't need to say it myself.

He conceded a good-natured chuckle. "I know, right? I've never been the talk of the town before. Even Grom's envious." Kyle sat down across from us, depleting the last of the sexy mood. Izzy and I sat up and the three of us quickly got to chattering about anything and everything, falling into friendly comfort like any other day back home.

I caught them up on the news of Lucifer. That got us chatting about the big picture, which led to us recounting all our adventures from the beginning. Me, the new guy, avoiding beer pong with a frat-boy roommate while trying to get the attention of the standoffish hot chick. It was only a couple of months back but it seemed so long ago. The levels we experienced were real. We'd come a long way. Who knew where we'd end up?

"We did it, bros," said Kyle. He jabbed himself with a thumb. "An outcast." He nodded to Izzy. "A loner." A finger pointed my way. "And a mistake." The brewmaster produced three crystal mugs and a special-edition bottle.

"Too bad about failing your clean-and-sober challenge in the final hours," I said.

"No worries. That was before I was chased across the wilderness by a walking city. Plus, harems necessitate booze. Trust me."

I laughed. "You're the expert, I guess."

"I'm glad someone finally acknowledges that."

"Guess I'm off the hook for being your wingwoman," said Izzy in relief.

Kyle snorted. "No offense, but I decided I don't need romantic advice from someone who reads alpha shifter porn."

Izzy's eyes narrowed. "Don't make me murder your harem."

"I'll be good," he peeped. He took an introspective moment to think. "Besides, I'm not original enough not to curse. WTF, F bomb this, F'n A that. I mean, what's the A in F'n A even stand for?"

I chewed my lip. "Hmm, I never thought about that before."

Kyle turned his attention to three perfect pours of beer, handed them out, and raised his glass. "We put our heads together, and somehow it all worked out."

I joined his toast. "Just don't ask me how. It'd be impossible to pull off again."

Izzy lifted her drink. "It was mostly luck," she admitted.

The brewmaster proudly cocked his head. "Here's to throwing shit on a wall."

The glasses clinked and the bottle ran dry.

Somewhere, in the middle of the night, a countdown appeared.

> Haven 1.0
> 59 minutes and 59 seconds...

Everything stopped. The drumming, the jokes, the pours. Well, we kept drinking, mind you, but for the moment we stopped the actual pouring of more spirits.

Black Hats and pagans, priests and wildkins, all stopped to study the timer.

> Haven 1.0
> 59 minutes and 43 seconds...

Every soul in the Godsbog rose to their feet. This was momentous. It shut everything down. People congregated in groups for safety. At their tents, around their fires. It was the Moon landing, or 9/11. It was the only thing on TV.

An extended burp, bubbling with gravelly juice, loudly escaped Kyle's lips. "Sorry!" he called out.

Slowly, the masses came out of hibernation. Feet shuffled, music resumed, and inevitably, the alcohol poured anew. It was halfhearted at first, but as the minutes ticked the celebration became a release.

This was it. It was actually happening.

Some days later, Tad Lonnerman parked his car at the curb of his new house. It was Christian Everett's house, the one he'd grown up in.

The CEO had made a last-second addendum to his will, gifting the remnants of his fortune to those he deemed worthy. Pete's family was a notable beneficiary. Other Kablammy employees were taken care of too. Tad's biggest surprise was to discover some of the company rights being conferred to him.

He'd gone over it multiple times with the lawyers. Kablammy, as a corporation, immediately entered the process of forced dissolution. The vast umbrella of corporations was sharing the same fate. In a bid to cut all previous business commitments, every tech initiative Christian had owned was being scuttled. Kablammy was, essentially, going kablammy. All except for a small upstart, Afterlife Online Incorporated, gifted to one Tad Lonnerman.

Other events rocked the news cycle. The sabotaged launch sites. The near destruction of Kablammy headquarters. The death of a business titan. Of course, the raid on InLink headquarters and the string of arrests that followed proved an immediate sensation.

Tad's time getting up to speed on his new company was intense. Most of it amounted to assets and arbitration and releases, which translated to a bunch of paperwork. Still, the details of an actual business plan were sparse. Kablammy's computers had been destroyed, corrupted, or seized. There was no need for them anymore, but the loss of the EXSIL units seemed to spell doom for Haven. How much technology had been lost, and how much could continue without it?

No one had details on happenings within Haven, either. With the simulation cut off from the world and safely in orbit, it was an independent universe now. Tad found himself the owner of little more than a license.

He slammed the door of his car and approached Christian's family home. It felt a breach of privacy to intrude. Then again, the CEO had left him the property for a reason. An odd amenity, seeing as how the house was in Christian's name. A private entity unconnected from Kablammy and its ventures. Tad took a heavy breath and hit the button on his brand new remote clicker. The garage door opened and his breath left him.

An outdated computer rested on a foldout table, along with several iterations of prototype equipment. A helmet with brain scanners prominently rested on a shelf. It was the first working EXSIL unit, probably the one Christian had used to capture his daughter on that hard drive so many years ago.

Right here, in this garage, was where it had all started. It was a fitting place to continue his work.

-Finn

Character Sheets

Talon		Level	11
Class	Explorer	*XP*	116150
Kit	Scout	*Next*	171075

Strength	19	*Strike*	445
Agility	24	*Dodge*	500
Craft	6	*Health*	341 / 341
Essence	10	*Spirit*	283 / 283

Coin	
Silver	1269
Plates	5
Bars	4

Skills	1
Spear	3
Crossblock	3
Deadshot	3
Tornado Spin	1
Spinshield	1
Knife	1
Claw	1
- - Dragonrun - -	

Awareness
Exploration
Tracking
Darkvision
Intuition
Survival
Navigation
Cartography
Traversal
Dash
Vault
Wall Run
Scale
Stealth
Sneak
Subdue

Reputation	
Pagan	-500
Catechist	50
Wildkin	200
Scarlet Knives	100

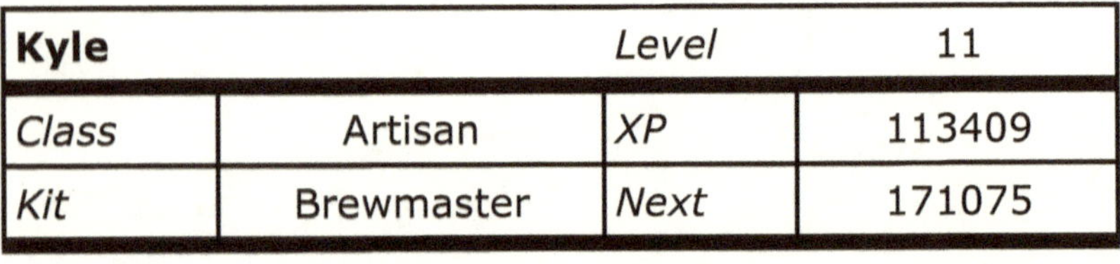

Kyle		*Level*	11
Class	Artisan	*XP*	113409
Kit	Brewmaster	*Next*	171075

Strength	23	*Strike*	407
Agility	5	*Dodge*	209
Craft	20	*Health*	280 / 280
Essence	10	*Spirit*	242 / 242

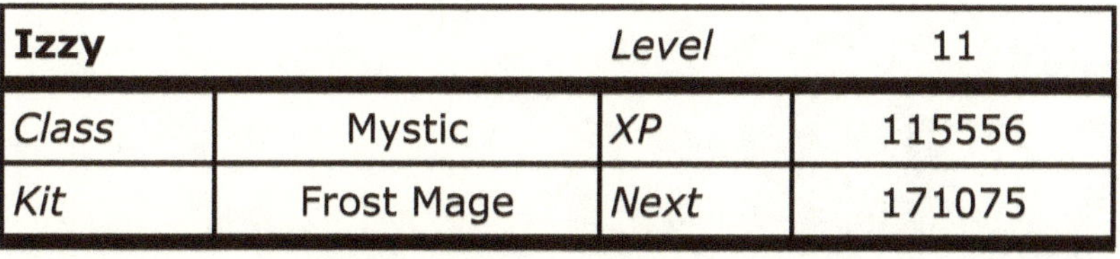

Izzy		*Level*	11
Class	Mystic	*XP*	115556
Kit	Frost Mage	*Next*	171075

Strength	9	*Strike*	247
Agility	18	*Dodge*	346
Craft	6	*Health*	198 / 198
Essence	25	*Spirit*	486 / 486

Game Over

> **Story, Design, and Development**
> Domino Finn
>
> **Edits**
>
> Philip Newey
>
> **Programming**
>
> Kablammy Games
>
> Shot on location in Portland, Oregon; Seattle, Washington; and Outer Space.

Azzyrk has sent **Talon** a Blood Feud request.

Talon has denied Blood Feud request.

Lash
Do *you* want fabulous lashes too? Ask me how with my new makeup line!

Conan
Wait, is this one of those MLM schemes?

Crux
Don't tell me they got you too.

Glinda
It really works, you guys! I made $1,000 of passive income just last week!

Hex
Do you sell nail polish darker than Vantablack? 'Cause that would be rad.

Nooner

What's your dragon name? First name is your mother's maiden name. Last name is your social security number.

Stigg

Joke's on you. I'm not from the States so I don't have a social.

Caduceus

Plus I'm pretty sure your mother was a brown bear.

Stigg

And definitely no maiden!

Talon
Man, this ad targeting is getting eerily specific.

Izzy
Spam seems to be getting worse lately. Did someone change the algorithm?

Focus testing courtesy of Boost Systems. Focus testing indicates that focus testing is a surefire way to make your game as bland as possible. Someone doesn't like those rough edges? Polish them down to a fine turd. Boost Systems, boosting your turds since 2010.

InLink, provider of project management, deployment, corporate moles, and bloody office raids. Guaranteed slow-motion helicopter explosions or your money back.

Kablammy would like to thank its QA partners in Thiruvananthapuram, Texas.

Azzyrk

Mob Lives Matter! Come to the swamp march!

Serpico

Hey, what about NPC Lives?

Azzyrk

NPCs are okay I guess.

Skoal

What about pets? Or summons? Wait a minute... what am I?

Azzyrk

You're a monster. Obviously.

Jixa

No uses that word, *apa*!

Azzyrk

Oh, give me a break.

Crux

Guys, guys, can't everyone get along and stop the infighting? Everybody counts or nobody counts. (At least if we take lessons from Harry Bosch.)

Azzyrk

Shut up, PLAYER!

Azzyrk has sent **Talon** a Blood Feud request.

Talon has denied Blood Feud request.

Grom
<This post has been reported for indecent content.>

Kyle, Izzy, and I stood in a circle.

Haven 1.0

1 minute and 17 seconds...

The launch was imminent and there was nothing left to say. Whatever was coming, I was ready for it. Side by side, we'd forge our path, fight on, and level up.

We watched the timer and waited.

Haven 1.0

11 seconds...

"This is it," I said. I offered a hand to each of my friends.

Izzy smirked. "Our eternal destiny."

"Here we go," said Kyle.

We held hands and watched the timer count down.

Haven 1.0

3...

2...

1...

Global Haven Alert:

Haven has crashed! Please uninstall and reinstall.

REBOOTING...

We blinked at each other, still holding hands.

"This is it," I said.

Izzy looked around uncertainly. "Our eternal... destiny?"

Kyle's lips flapped in boredom. "Here goes nothing."

```
Haven 1.0
3...


2...


1...


Installing Day 0 Patch
Estimated Wait Time: 3 days, 12 hours, 27 minutes
```

"Eternal is right," snarked Izzy.

Kyle hissed. "Screw this. I'm gonna go home and play Call of Duty. Call me when something happens."

I watched them walk away, waited a beat, and grinned. This was far from game over.

The likenesses of Chris Cornell and Anthony Bourdain were used with the utmost respect and appreciation. No actual dead people were harmed in the upload process. Except for Karen. We don't talk about Karen.

The Entrails of Our Souls courtesy of Brain Fart Records. Engines of Dissection courtesy of Butt Fart Records. Apocalypse Bagpipes courtesy of... well... let's not go there.

This game is dedicated to the memory of Christian Everett and Pete— Pete... Hmm, I don't have a last name. It must be written down somewhere around here.

Azzyrk has sent **Talon** a Blood Feud request.

Talon has denied Blood Feud request.

Talon marked himself **Invisible** to Blood Feud requests.

Talon

Ugh. Is it just me or does social media totally suck these days?

Dune

More trouble than it's worth, my friend.

Izzy

Is it possible mankind's most narcissistic tendencies boil down to a desperate cry for help? That those of us who live fuller, richer lives prefer experiences over constantly seeking the validation of strangers? What if, instead of dividing our attention on this zombie slot machine hamster wheel, we pour our whole selves into meaningful targets of our own choosing? Strive for a world of closeness and intimacy? Not perfect presentations, but perfect friendships? Then, in the end, ...

... maybe we'll find a bit more of what we're all really looking for: a life that is its own reward.

Kyle
But then how will everybody know what winners we are?

Errol
Ar, man has a point.

Trafford
EVERYONE has a point on social media. That's the whole problem!

Talon
Whoa, Izzy, I think you're onto something.

Izzy
Although, come to think of it, I do like to share pics of my food.

Talon
That's it. I'm done.

Izzy
And I do look killer in a bikini. Would be a waste not to show off a little.

Talon
Aaaand I'm back.

Install Complete!

Haven version 1.0

Online

New content initializing...

New residents activated...

World map updated (Timberlands (+))

New cities initialized (Winterhearth (+))

New relics added (Tusk of the Ancients (+))

New titans awoken (Krkyor, Bringer of Terror (+))

New quest strings integrated (The Eternal Cold (+))

Universal Interstellar Rights have been declared.

Welcome to the new world.

Welcome to Haven!

About the Author

I'm Domino Finn: game-developer-turned-fantasy-author, media rebel, and product of my generation. (You have died of dysentery.)

If you enjoyed this book and the *Afterlife Online* series, please spread the word. Reader recommendations in Facebook groups, reddit, and other sites are the absolute best promotion for my books, hands down.

> Each online review = a *Deadline* level up.
> Please help!

Wanna keep in touch?

Reader Group (http://dominofinn.com/newsletter/) - the official word on new releases, flash sales, and giveaways.

Facebook Group (https://www.facebook.com/groups/dominofinnfans/) - cover reveals, art, and extras, including chat with me and fellow readers.

DominoFinn.com - my complete book catalog and social media links.